Cease to Blush

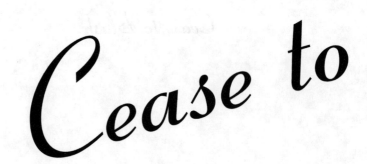

Cease to

BY THE SAME AUTHOR

The chick at the back of the church
Going Down Swinging

Blush

A NOVEL BY

BILLIE LIVINGSTON

Random House Canada

Copyright © 2006 Billie Livingston

www.randomhouse.ca

Library and Archives Canada Cataloguing in Publication

Livingston, Billie, 1965–
Cease to blush / Billie Livingston.

ISBN-13: 978-0-679-31322-9
ISBN-10: 0-679-31322-2

I. Title.

PS8573.I916C42 2006   C813'.54   C2005-905357-7

Printed and bound in the United States of America

10 9 8 7 6 5 4 3 2 1

Cease to Blush

One

~

AS WE PULLED UP TO THE CURB I COULD SEE THEM A LITTLE
ways off, gathered around the grave like long black shadows. The
sky was the blue of a cheap paint-by-number. Leonard tugged his
door handle to get out. Sitting in the passenger side, I squinted
behind sunglasses and sipped my vodka tonic from a travel mug.

"Viv?"

"Let me be for a minute." I reached up and shoved the sun
visor, pulled it so it blocked the ripping afternoon glare. "Wish
to hell it had rained today." Contrary to its ceiling now, the city's
floor was one big sog after an onslaught of rain falling in sheets
and drizzles and sheets again. Today was the first sunny one in
three weeks. Timing is everything. Len sighed, closed his door.

I had shown up at his apartment an hour ago so we could
head out together. His building is less than a block from mine.
Len liked my mother. She liked him too, as much as she was
capable of liking a guy. Frank, on the other hand, didn't care for
my mother, which was appropriate because she loathed him. She
had loathed my choices in lovers pretty much across the board.

"Wow. Bright," Len had said at first sight of the stoplight-
red skirt and jacket I chose for the occasion. He was wearing his
navy suit, a little beat up, shiny in spots, the only one he owned.
I always thought if I won the lottery, the first thing I'd do is take
Len shopping. Len deserves the things he can't afford.

"I need a drink. Have you got anything?" I stood in his living room, clenching and unclenching, gulping breaths and heaving them out like garbage.

"Ah—" he touched at his suit as if patting himself down for cigarettes "—sure. I think we're running a little late though."

My hands jumped to shore off demands and questions, flicked him off toward the kitchen. "We're already too late. It's a funeral."

Unscrewing a bottle from the cupboard over his stove, he stopped on the verge of pouring. "Scotch or vodka?"

"Vodka."

He rescrewed the cap and grabbed another bottle, poured. "What the hell," he muttered and poured a shot in a second glass. Dumped tonic in both. I sat on the couch and gawked straight ahead at the blank wall. He'd painted over the mural that had been there before.

"Hair of a mongrel, madam?" He handed me the drink and I looked some more at the nothing in front of me. Yesterday there was floor-to-ceiling rendition of Leonardo da Vinci's *Vitruvian Man*. Now it was blank with eggshell white. He must've done it after I left last night.

"What's with the blank wall?"

His brows hopped. Off my blank stare he said, "Come on, you've been drunker. Last night. You kept bitching about it." He swapped his tone for a whiny shrewish imitation of mine. "*I hate that ugly Spider-Man with his dink hanging out.*" He shrugged. "I want to do something else there anyway—You sat right *there* while I painted over it."

I nodded. Last night I had wanted to drink myself to tears as though the tangibility of drunken rivulets might shove me past the gauzy void, up against some nice flinty edge. But it was more like anaesthetizing a corpse. Part of me had an urge to turn the stove on high and slap my hand on the burner and part of me thought, Christ, millions are doping themselves up with antidepressants every day to get this sensation, maybe I got a good thing going.

"Frank never showed up this morning," I said.

He looked at his watch. "Where is he?"

"I don't know. Probably still in bed, jerking off to porn."

"Ach . . ." Leonard raised his hand against the image. "Please."

Len's a bit precious when it comes to things too raw in the sex department. When we were eighteen, out of curiosity we rented *Deep Throat*. I was no virgin but still sat with my face screwed up in skepticism: "Gross, he can't stick it in *there*." "Girls don't have clits in their throats either." Len, meanwhile, clutched his head like a Vietnam vet experiencing flashback, shock searing its way though his frontal lobe. I suggested we fast-forward to the story part. There was no story part. We pressed eject. Len rolled a joint and sketched my feet the rest of the afternoon.

"Don't you think it's just this side of obscene not to accompany your girlfriend to her mother's fucking funeral?" I asked.

"You told him you didn't want him there. At least that's what you said last night. They didn't like each other, you said, so why put on a big phony show."

I stared into my glass and sloshed the fizz around. "He should want to be there for me."

"What?"

Taking a gulp, I looked past him to the blank wall again. "So, what are you going to paint there. Did we decide?"

"How 'bout I paint you?"

"You're done then. It's a masterpiece of photo-realism."

Leonard slid the pads of his fingertips up and down the steering wheel. When he finally spoke again it was to remind me, "She never liked this car." I'd tossed my keys to Len feeling too shaky to drive. He tapped at the push-button transmission.

"She thought it looked like some old Valiant she sold when she first moved here," I said. "And she didn't like the colour."

My car is black. Like the guy I bought it off. Though he had a kind of pimped-out affectation he was actually a student/actor

I'd met on set. He was about to drive back home to New Orleans, when he decided to sell the car and fly instead. I hadn't made up my mind whether the car was my style or not and met up with him on campus to have lunch and another look. He was flirtatious but I wasn't much interested. Then, outside the Student Union Building, we ran into my mother. Between the guy and the car—the look on her face!

I wrote the cheque immediately and the moment I touched him it was like being shot out of a cannon.

I reached forward now and yanked the chrome lock in the middle of the glove box. As the little door dropped open with a clank, I felt around inside.

Leonard watched me. "What're you looking for?"

"I left a joint in here somewhere."

"Come on, I don't want to get stoned here. It'll freak me out."

"So, don't."

"Vivian," he said plaintively. "I don't want to end up babysitting you."

"*Don't.* I'm fine." I slapped the glove box shut.

"We've missed half the service as it is."

"We're here, aren't we? Look, if you want to go, go." I took another deep swallow from my mug. I could feel him taking a deep breath, a different tack.

"I want to say goodbye to your mum. Come with me." His eyes had gone moist and mournful and I wanted to pound him for it. My own were stingy and dry. I thumped the mug down on the dash and yanked open the passenger door.

Standing there on the green close-cropped lawn of the cemetery I stared toward the gravesite, my feet tarred in place. I could sense Leonard coming round the back end of the car toward me as the heels of my pumps slowly sank in the soggy grass. He held out a hand as if ready to catch me in the event that I might fall trying to unsuck my shoes. Squeezing at my purse straps, I dug fingernails into my palm and pulled myself tall. I couldn't feel them though, my nails or my purse straps.

"I can't breathe," I whispered, wishing so bad that Leonard would take my hand. But he's not good at that sort of thing. He's not a toucher, generally speaking.

Most of them glanced furtively as we got closer. All except Sally. She glared long past the moment I met her eyes, and, after giving me the once-over, shook her head just enough to show me, and anyone looking closely, her disgust. I stared down through dark legs to the coffin. A couple of crows squawked as they settled on telephone wire in the distance and a new luxury car shushed past, its old-money motor whispering away from us.

I had never been to a funeral. I'd never really known anyone who died. There was Mrs. Eisman about six years ago but she was Leonard's friend. For lack of a better descriptor. No one close to me has ever died.

Len was right, we'd missed the meat of the thing; they'd finished with the committal, the talking was all done. We were now observing a minute of silent prayer or something. The sun's heat sank into the back of my head and shoulders. I unbuttoned my jacket. Those who could see without turning or making a spectacle of themselves let their eyes flick to me once more. *Go screw yourselves*, I thought. *She would have liked this suit.*

My heels sank again as someone said amen. I tried to push my weight forward onto my toes. The effort under the insistence of that high sun wilted me and I gave up, let my heels relax into the ground. A moment later, my mother's coffin was lowered.

Sally made her way out of the crowd, travelled around the outer edges and came to where the minister had stood a second ago. She had a shovel in her hand now and, clutching the wooden handle with both hands, she addressed us.

"Josie and I used to talk about how different cultures have different ways of celebrating life or, in times of loss, giving themselves closure. And so, ah . . . well, it probably, ah, might come as a bit of a surprise for most of you, but I come from a Jewish background. I was never—my family was never observant, but I do know that one custom at a Jewish funeral—and maybe others too—is that, as mourners, we each partake in the burial of the person we've lost, and this way we help ourselves to understand that our loved one's body has passed and we can say g—" she swallowed and smiled, brushed a hand under her brimming eye, cleared her throat "—goodbye now." Tears popped and dropped down Sally's cheeks. Clear cosmetic-free tears. I don't think I've ever seen makeup on Sally. The eternal earth-child hippie goddess.

Bending toward the earth, Sally stuffed the shovel in, turned, mumbled something that sounded like Hebrew and tossed the dirt down into the grave; followed by the thud of clumps hitting the coffin. Silence. The crows started up once more in the distance. Sally's jaws worked and her eyes welled again as she handed the shovel to the woman next to her and walked a few unsteady paces away from the grave.

I'd last seen Samantha Barnes, one of my mother's colleagues at the university, on the news discussing the academic's perspective on sex trade workers. She was a sleek dyke of the urban designer-wear, Annie Lennox variety, in the midst of writing a big fat book on the history of strippers in Vancouver for which she'd received a hefty government grant, making her a target for neo-conservatives across the country. She'd looked as though she'd grown more robust on controversy. Or perhaps it was the resulting adoration that fed her.

But now, a shovel in her hand, a friend in the ground below her, she looked muddled, as if she didn't quite know how shovels worked anymore. Letting go of her girlfriend's hand, she pushed the square emerald frames of her glasses closer to her charcoal-lined eyes, moved in and took a half bladeful, then let it hover above the grave before slowly turning it over. More dull thumps as dirt dropped onto lacquered wood. Some small terror pulled at Samantha's face as if she couldn't believe she'd just done such a thing. She handed the shovel to her girlfriend and staggered off toward Sally.

I watched, unfolding and folding my hands, clutching my purse, feeling eyes on me, inching along as a line formed to the head of the grave. Len's face was suddenly at my ear. "You okay?" I reached back for his hand, but they were rammed in his pockets. I hated the hell out of Frank at that moment. And Leonard too. Everyone's so fucking neurotic. My hands drooped empty and pathetic. And then the shovel was pushed into them.

I stared at the wooden handle a moment and then into the face of the young man whose grip it was still in. I didn't know him. He looked about twenty-four, twenty-five. Probably one of her students. Another one of these fake feminist ponytail-wearing bullshit artists who take gender studies and feminist literature classes for the sole purpose of getting laid. He peered into my face as though he knew me from somewhere then let the handle go. I glanced into the squared-off hole that held my mother's coffin. I tried to get some sense of her. As usual, I wasn't careful what I wished for and the disintegrating cancerous image of her hit, from six days before she died—the last time I saw her. The looming sense of that dark toothy thing—down there with her still, in that box, eating her from the inside out—slammed me in the solar plexus and sent my stomach flying throatward. "No," spurted from my mouth and I dropped the shovel. Sure that I was about to throw up, I backed from the hole into the thick of the headstones around us.

Behind me, the thump of the shovel was followed by gasps. I slowed and looked back, seeing the confusion and fright on their faces, the minister stepping forward with reassurances. Len leaned far into the hole and pulled out the shovel.

I reached a blue marble headstone sculpted into a bench and sat down, my back to the grave.

"Nice of you to show up."

I turned. Sally.

"That was quite the performance. Terrific getup too."

As if I were fourteen again, I blurted, "What is it to you what I wear? I like this suit. And she liked it on me."

Sally's hair was a furious mass of copper and grey snakes. "It's always about you, isn't it? *Everybody look at Vivian.* Why be respectful or appropriate when—"

"Oh fuck, here we go." Suddenly I was bellowing. "She didn't *like* black."

"Because it was dark, like a *funeral*." Sally's voice was flat but loud, like that of a teacher trying to quell a classroom. "Well, guess where we happen—"

"Hi," Len interjected, calm and easy.

I looked to him and then away, the overblown holler of my words still clanging. Len unjammed his hands from his pockets and reached for one of Sally's, awkwardly shaking it while stiffly holding her shoulder. Practically a hug. He repocketed them and moved back a couple steps. "You did a really nice . . . um, it was a beautiful ceremony . . . all those pussy willows and freesias. Is that what those are called? I remember Josie really liked those, yeah."

Sally forced up the corners of her mouth. "Yes. She did. Thanks. I never arranged anything like this, I didn't know . . ."

And asshole Vivian, I thought, Vivian wasn't there. Vivian didn't contribute, didn't help, didn't offer, didn't didn't didn't. Bad, crummy, shitty old Vivian. Stupid, uncouth, slaggy Vivian in her red red red bloody suit.

"She would've liked it . . . she, yeah . . . would've loved it." Len's chin bobbed to confirm his assessment. "You even had sunshine brought in."

Sally's face gentled. Suddenly her squiggles of hair looked less menacing, and I caught a flash of how they seemed the first time we met. As a six-year-old, I was crazy about her. "You'll be coming over to the house, then?" she said, addressing Len.

My "Ah, sorry" trampled his "Of course." He looked to me and blinked. Sally rolled her eyes.

"All right." she said, "Well, thank you so much for coming, whatever you decide." And off she went to a small group of my mother's colleagues a few metres away.

Len wouldn't look at me.

"What?" I muttered.

He shook his head, folded his arms in that way he has, as if cloistering himself.

"Fine, yes. *Of course* I'm going." We started back to the car.

I asked Len to drive us around for a little while, downtown through Stanley Park so we wouldn't have to be early. He obliged me. We drove in silence. By the time we got to my mother's house, every spot on the block was filled with a car. I tipped the travel mug back and swallowed any last drops. "All right then, here goes nothin'."

Len went ahead up the gravel path and I dawdled, staring up at the pale yellow wood of it, the white trim. The garden looked weedy. Once I moved out and Sally moved in, Sally had created a wild rocky English garden. She'd always kept it lush but immaculate in the weed department. I supposed there hadn't been time for that lately.

The door was open. I filled my lungs: *Showtime!*

Inside, the black shadows from the cemetery milled about. Sarah McLachlan crooned plaintively on the stereo. I walked at Leonard's heel through the house. From kitchen to family room, pockets of my mother's friends and colleagues, from UBC mostly, gobbled hors d'oeuvres and jabbered softly—geek-chic women like Samantha Barnes and her flapper-style girl-friend, as well as a handful of ineffectual tweedy men and Sally's crowd from the community college where she taught sculpture and pottery with a side of textiles. You could spot Sally's world-beat friends a mile away with their untucked heavy cotton shirts covered in embroidery or appliqué, getting in touch with their inner Indian and Afrocentrics whether their skins were brown or summer-cloud white.

Vegetable platters, fruit platters, plates with crackers, pseudo-cheese and ersatz meat sat stationed around the room. The CD changer hushed over to Tracy Chapman. "I need a drink," I said, sighing toward the liquor bottles on the counter.

"You need a sandwich," Len stated.

I made a gagging catface at him.

"You'll barf for real if you keep drinking on empty." He stuck a paper plate in my hand. "Or worse."

I obliged, spooning on a hunk of vegetarian lasagna. Len stuck a bottled water in my free hand and its chill seared my skin like an inverted burn. I gave a little yelp. "Can you get me some coffee instead?"

He turned to the samovar, filled a cup and replaced the bottle in my hand. "Okay?"

"Yeah. Sorry. Thanks."

"Comes naturally." Len's money job was waiting tables for three or four different caterers around town.

I stared at the fridge, my mother's handwriting on bits of paper under magnets. I gulped the coffee, saying, "Do you think—" No Len. I glimpsed the back of one shoulder as he drifted through strangers toward the billow of Sally's hair. Samantha moved in beside me.

My eyes pricked across the tossed white salad on her head, a carefully constructed tussle of pomade-stiffened eggshell hair, set off by the shriek of red across her wide mouth. The consummate lipstick lesbian. I set down my coffee cup and shoved a forkful of lasagna into my mouth to stave off speaking.

When my mother first submerged herself in the women's studies world, it seemed most of the women who came around the house eschewed makeup and bras, their breasts jiggling freely under loose tops. She had a hard time with it at first, it seemed to me. Like most women who'd grown up in the fifties, she was raised with a sense of propriety and vanity—you didn't go out into the world without your face on. When she started leaving our house with no makeup, it didn't strike me that she held her head quite as high.

I recall a couple women she had over for drinks one afternoon in the backyard. I was about eight. Sally had come back to town and she was over to see our new place. She and my mother were just reconnecting, and here my mother had made these new friends. It was all a little stiff. The four of them sat in lawn chairs, my mother in a daisy-covered sundress sipping white wine rather chastely in comparison to the straight-from-the-bottle beer-gulpers around her. Sally had on one of her ankle-length Indian cotton skirts. The other two, with their Billie Jean King mullets, wore Bermuda shorts and tank tops.

Bunching her skirt up between her thighs, Sally hauled an ankle up across her knee and dusted a hand over the pale down that covered them. As a redhead she never had much body hair to speak of and as an all-natural hippie chick, she couldn't be bothered shaving anything. I lay on the grass, off to the side, eating a Popsicle, eyes closed, thinking about whether or not I was glad that Sally was back in the picture. I definitely didn't like these new ones with the hockey hair. I didn't like their construction-worker hands and mocking laughter or that my mother's speech became clunky around them, stumbling and fidgety. Suddenly, one of them bent forward and grabbed hold of my mother's foot.

"Oh *ladies*—" The foot-grabber feigned shock. "Look at this: *silky-smooth plastic leg.* You're like a little rubber dolly, Josie."

My mother pulled back with a nervous laugh. She didn't much care for strangers touching her. The more anxious she looked, the more those spiky broads har-harred. The second one actually got out of her chair and made a show of rushing to get a feel. My mother pulled her knees up to her chest under the tent of her skirt.

"That's enough." Sally's voice was calm but with the kind of tone a kid wasn't about to argue with. That teachery sort of voice she had started to use on me just before she left town. "You're like a couple of damn longshoremen. Hands off."

The women reacted about the same way I had in the past: backing off with a swagger, grinning to prove they'd moved of their own volition not because they'd been told to. "Just tryin' to let her know it's okay to be a real woman, that's all," the foot grabber said.

I think I would've shaved it all, after that, starting with my toes and ending with my bald head, to get even with them. But my mother let her leg hair grow in starting the next day. In the mornings at breakfast, she would touch her calves and the sight of all that coarse dark hair made her grimace but she refused to shave.

As the weeks went by, her leg hair seemed to grow lighter somehow. Or I didn't notice it as much. Then one night before dinner, her door stood slightly ajar and I came into her room. She jumped a little then smiled nervously, sitting there on her bed with a layer of white cream over both legs from the knees down. "I'll be down in a minute, sweets." She winced and waved her hands around the creamed shins as though they stung. I walked closer and picked up the package lying beside her. *Extra-strength bleach for problem hair.* She plucked the box from my hand. "I'll be down in a minute, okay," she repeated. It was a tone I didn't recognize.

Suddenly there was Sally, pink-cheeked and breathless from the night air. "I picked up some dessert," she announced, holding up a bag, then frowning at my mother's legs, which had dropped to the floor as though she were about to bolt.

A bemused look crept over Sally's face. "What is *that*? Nair? Have you given in to your feminine urges and *Naired* your legs?" she giggled.

"N–o," my mother said, with two-syllabled agitation.

"Extra-strength bleach for problem hairs," I said.

Sally cocked her head.

"Well—" my mother tried to explain, grabbing the box and the directions, the little plastic spatula she'd used to mix and smear. "They didn't match. That's all. The hair on my thighs is light but the shins were so . . . I just—"

A howling cackle burst from Sally. "You're bleaching your leg fur?"

"Fuck!" my mother spat.

Sally and I looked at each other, with the old amused conspiratorial bond we used to have back when she was the new neighbour, before she and my mother became friends. Mum stood up and yanked the towel she'd been sitting on off the bed. "I'm just a slave and a pawn and I have no will of my—"

"Oh, don't get all wigged out—what's the big *deal*? Just because a couple of bull—" Sally flashed a look to me. "Hey, kiddo, why don't you take this dessert downstairs and put it on a plate." She pushed the bag to me.

"I don't—"

"Go downstairs, okay?" The tone. My mother sat on her bed again looking forlorn. I snatched the bag out of Sally's hand and she closed the door behind me.

I hadn't thought of that in years. My mother was probably thirty-three, thirty-four. About the age I am now.

"Vivian," Samantha Barnes was saying, "I don't think we've ever formally met: I'm Sam. Sam Barnes. I'd like to offer you my condolences. We all loved Josie. She was really a terrific woman . . . just so smart and generous and funny and, of course, beautiful. I can see a lot of her in you." She smiled and paused, took the green arm of her eyeglasses and pulled them closer to her face. "I wanted to give you my card as well." She planted one in my palm. "If there's anything I could possibly assist with, if you need help getting things organized or even selling the house—I'm not sure what you plan to do but I have some close friends in real estate who would be pleased to advise you. You and Sally will be sorting that out yourselves soon enough, I'm sure, but I just want to make sure you know you've got friends and support around you. It can be terribly traumatic losing one's mother. Such a core relationship, it can feel as though your whole world is coming down."

Across the room I could see Len's head bobbing as he smiled and chatted—being generally liked. He struck me as heinously selfish at the moment. I glanced back at Sam Barnes. Her girlfriend joined us. They looked so all-fired-up *downtown*, the two of them.

"Hi, I'm Glynis," the girlfriend said. She stuck out her hand. That hair of hers must've cost a mint, precision-cut edges, gleaming 1920s perfection. "I only met your mother a few times but she made such an impression on me—so strong and smart and really lovely."

"Thank you." What is a person supposed to say to that, to any of this? There was a long silence. "I really like your hair." *Shallow.* I shifted, wanting to lose myself down a crack in the floor. *Josie's trashy, insubstantial offspring strikes again.*

"Oh thank you," Glynis said with one of those self-help-section smiles. I tucked my own hair behind an ear, my fingers catching in tangles. Catching a glimpse of myself in a nearby mirror I winced: like something washed up on the beach, my hair hanging in long chunky snarls, a skunk stripe of dark down the brassy crown of my head. A crack-addict mermaid.

"That's neat, that you wore red today," Glynis said. "I remember when these guys—" she waved toward Samantha "—were organizing an event for the department and Josie was really pushing for red in the decor. It's a victory colour, she said . . ." She swallowed and, pleasantly enough, I thought, appeared momentarily unsure of herself. "So," she brightened, "Sam told me you're a journalist?"

"No, no," Sam patted her arm. "Josie said once that Vivian has a sharp, curious mind and that she *might've made* a good journalist. Vivian's in the entertainment business. Actually, Vivian, I've been meaning to talk to you: I'm in the middle of a project and I've been conducting a lot of interviews lately with women who—"

Jesus Christ. "I'm not a *stripper.*"

"Oh." Sam looked slightly nonplussed.

"I just played one on TV a couple times. I'm an actor."

"Oh."

Now she had a face on as though she was insulted that I was insulted. That divinely middle-class expression of haughty indignance that social workers and feminist anthropologist types get on them when someone questions whether Mary Magdalene was really a prostitute. The one that precedes, "Of course she was a *prostitute.* There's no *shame* in that. What other occupational choices did a woman in her position have?" As if busloads of them were about to head to the downtown east side and whore for solidarity.

"Not that there's anything wrong with strippers," I shrugged. "I'm just *not* one. I modelled for a few years. Arguably, the same thing." I caught the gaze of two of those effete tweedy men smiling sheepishly in my direction. A fat agitated sigh escaped me.

Ol' Sam Barnes misses nothing. She leaned into my shoulder. "Hey, they can't help themselves. Men loved your mother too. No matter *how* she tried to hide her light under a bushel."

"Will you excuse me? It was nice meeting you," I said and headed for the front hall.

I stopped as the young man from the funeral, the one who had handed me the shovel, touched my sleeve. "Were you, I mean, are you Josie's daughter?"

I nodded, my chest caving in on itself.

"You look like her, the same mouth." I looked at his mouth as it explained that he had been a student of my mother's. "There were only a couple of guys in the class I had with her but we were totally knocked out by what she had to say. Like, about women in literature, the way they can be portrayed when someone appropriates—"

"Vivian, hello." Another hand on my shoulder. A woman I didn't recognize, someone drapey and purple, likely one of Sally's. "I don't know if you recall, I'm—" Ellen, I think she said. Eva? I couldn't hear anything anymore. There were probably only forty people in the house but it felt like throngs, like chomping needy maws, pecking birds.

"Excuse me." I rushed up the stairs into the quiet.

I pressed my back against the wall outside my mother's bedroom and realized the paper plate was still in my hand. The door beside me was closed. I inched closer, reached over and set the flat of my palm against it. Feeling for a pulse.

I could hear the murmur through the floor, under my feet. All those people.

I turned the doorknob and let myself in.

The drapes were drawn. Light from the hallway filtered in, illuminating her king-size bed: a rumple of sheets and blankets in the dusky yellow. Their bed, I guess I should say, though Sally had been sleeping in the guest room the last couple weeks. I had the impression they'd argued about it. Sally wanted to be there if my mother had needed anything, water, the bathroom, anything. But my mother wanted stillness. Toward the end, the grinding thump of her own heartbeat was getting too much to bear. She asked Sally to keep visitors away. It was too much work being grateful for their presence. Keep them all away.

Except you, my mother said, the last time I saw her.

I pulled the drapes and leaned my forehead against the cool glass.

The knowledge of what was in her felt like having bugs inside me. Hopping and biting and stinging. Flapping. A murder of crows, I thought. It seemed to me that a dying person would sense the black flapping of another soul, that internal squawking and shredding of loose debris.

Nine days ago I sat in this room in that chair by her bed. The jostle of someone actually sitting on the mattress would have been too much. Everything hurt. An intravenous bag hung near her, morphine dripping steadily down the line into the back of her hand. The eyes that had once glittered blue were dark pits. Before she'd been diagnosed, I'd noticed that her near-iridescent skin had dimmed, that her eyes didn't have their usual frightening purity. But I'd chalked it up to age, maybe a little depression, maybe the wear of the philosophical differences she had with the new *grrl* power regime coming into her department.

By the time they named it cancer, its teeth were into every part of her—her liver, her lymph glands and ovaries. A course of treatment wasn't even discussed. They sent her home with painkillers; it would be a matter of weeks.

I have read that people—women—often come to some understanding with their mothers, in their thirties. Things always take me longer: I had anticipated this scorpion dance of ours might fade away in my forties. But she hadn't given me the luxury of time. I was furious with her for it. I was always furious with her but this was the capper.

She had never wanted me to find things out for myself—she was always pushing and prodding me to become some kind of starkly sensible brain-on-legs. *A mind is a terrible thing to waste.* When I graduated high school and started modelling, she patiently enunciated, "You're a smart young woman. Why waste something so precious prancing around for the camera, looking like a drag queen." My clever comeback: "Well, there's 'sposed to be a *Playboy* scout coming to town. Then I could wear less and make more." I tapped my temple. "Always thinking, see."

"Don't be an *idiot*—that's what you'd like to be?—one of Hefner's heifers? Hugh *Hefner*," she snorted. "Inventor of brothels where the whores are observed but not fucked."

"Which feminist text did we extract that from, Mother? Dworkin? Steinem?"

She grabbed dramatically at the air between us. "Vivian. You have a terrific lateral mind—the kind that creates, that *invents*. Why not *use* it? Why not get *behind* the camera at least? Why be the model when you could be the photographer? Why parrot the words when you could write the text? That's where the real power is, the respected and *sustainable* income."

Who knows what I said to that. Len had been taking pictures of me for his photography class, much to Josie's chagrin—she accused him of exploiting my sexuality as a way to impress his male teacher. As a result he'd shown the shots to a visiting free-lance professional who in turn showed them to a modelling scout. A few weeks later I was offered a two-month contract in Tokyo. My mother refused to give her parental consent. I turned eighteen a month later and hopped a plane without her blessing.

And now here she was fucking off on me for good. Before either of us was ready to say uncle. That cawing and tarry raven self was still demanding answers: *Why do you always have to . . . Why didn't you ever once . . . Who do you think you . . .*

I'd kept as still as I could on that last visit. There were no clocks in the room, the drapes were shut. I didn't know what to say to her that wouldn't involve my life, my work, my boyfriend. I wanted to say something neutral. Something quiet that would not cause flapping in either of us. My father? Seemed inappropriate to ask about a dead man right now. I'd never met him, he died before my time; what could I ask that I hadn't already asked as a child? Never saw so much as a picture.

John Smith. Really. Once when I was very small, I tried to look him up in the phone book and discovered pages and pages, a phone book inside a phone book of John Smiths.

I opened my mouth, modulating my voice, keeping it smooth and low. "Are you glad you went to New York when you were young?"

She moved her head to get a better look at me. "It's always better to know," she said.

Before I was born, before she'd seen the light, she had gone to New York in hopes of a career singing and dancing. She waited tables as she held out for a big break. The only thing that got broke, she said, was her back. She learned hard and fast that even when she sang, even when she danced up one stage and down the other, she was still somebody's waitress, a dolly whose only purpose was to serve everybody's appetite but her own. Men owned the bars and clubs, the stages. She was just the menial labour, the thing looked at rather than the person looking back.

And then she got pregnant. The Vietnam war was raging. Hundreds of thousands of boys and men died. John Smith too.

It's all so vague. No family, no pictures, nothing of him. I don't think they'd been together long when he got shipped out. I think it embarrasses her.

What I wanted to know about New York was where she'd gone wrong, how it could've been if she were more on the ball. My ego: I could have swung it if I'd been her. If it had been *me* singing and dancing, I would have gutted that town. I would've gotten to know whoever it is you had to know and gone for it. None of that wallflower shit.

Why didn't you just . . . If I were you, I would've . . .

Her hand slipped out toward me, palm up. I laid my own palm over hers. Wasn't sure how to touch her. She was so sensitive, her skin, her eyes, as if she were one big inflammation. I let my fingertips touch hers. Then backed off, too scared. All that grinding inside me, those gargling black furies.

"I wish," she said, "you didn't react. So much."

I clenched hands into my lap. Even now. She couldn't help herself. Why can't Vivian be settled? Why must Vivian be so reactionary?

She should talk.

"To me," she added. "I didn't know—" Her words were cut off by a deep cough, almost a gag. I reached for the waterglass, aimed the top of the accordion-bent straw toward her. She waved it away. A long high cry came out of her and she seemed to levitate with a sudden racking pain.

I panicked and got to my feet. "Sally? Sally!"

The door flew open. Sally had a kit with her. On her knees in a flash, she took out a hypodermic needle. I backed off from the bed.

"No, no, no . . ." Mum whimpered as she turned her head to Sally who had hold of a rubber stopper along the IV tubing. "Don't let her see it. Where's little Vivvy? Don't let her see." Sally injected the extra dose of morphine into the tube. "Don't," my mother said again more slowly as her body relaxed. Sally's jaws worked. She kept her eyes on my mother.

"Okay," I whispered back against the wall now. "I'll let you sleep." I wanted to go close again. I thought I should kiss her. I thought I should be the sort of daughter who puts her lips to her mother's forehead, infuses her with love and light. But I was a dark troll, terrible from every pore. I stood there crumpling my hands, scared to touch her, scared to leave and hating myself.

The door creaked open a few inches. Sally. I was stationed beside the bed in the chair I'd been in that day. I'd brought it over from the corner and I didn't realize until another person was in the room that my lips had been moving, I'd been whispering, mumbling to my dead mother.

I held Sally's gaze a moment and then I looked away, back into my hands. She pushed the door a little wider. "I want to apologize for my outburst at the cemetery," she said. "I know this must be hard for you. I'm not in your skin. I shouldn't have, uh . . ." I didn't answer, couldn't think what to say. "Maybe you could phone me when you're ready and we could talk about the estate. The house. I think I'd like to put it on the market, but half of it is your . . . you might not, ah—we don't have to talk now. Maybe in a few days. The car, she wanted you to have her car so—I already told you that in my message. Or she did. I'm sorry, Vivian, I'm not handling this very well." She sounded so tiny and lost, it threw me.

"No, it's—me neither. I don't know how," I said. It was hard to tell the difference between our voices now. "I'm sorry."

"Okay." The word scratched off her throat. "We'll be okay. You call me." She drifted back down the hall. I heard more footsteps and Len's voice, then the rustle of their clothes as they negotiated their way around one another. Perhaps they embraced. Perhaps Len made an exception.

Two

~

Standing outside the door after Len dropped me off, I could hear groaning inside my apartment. I put the key in the lock and opened it to a man's low-voiced encouragement: "That's right, good girl, don't stop." Then the moan of a woman with a stuffed mouth. As I closed the door, the VCR clunked off and switched over to television—the Discovery Channel.

In the living room, Frank did up the fly of his jeans as he lay on my couch, tumbler of beer beside him on the coffee table. The air smelled skunky. Next to his glass was a Baggie, quarter-filled with pot, and half a joint tamped out on one of my red and yellow paisley-printed saucers. Crumbs of ash spilled over onto the coffee table. A likeable thing about Frank: he does not watch televised sports. He does, however, watch a lot of science and sci-fi, from Klingons to clones. "Hey, baby," he said.

"Hi." I frowned at the TV screen, filled now with the balding pate of a forty-something man. "When did you get here?"

"About an hour ago. I figured you'd be back soon. Check this out—stem cell research. One day, man, one day they'll reverse the aging process altogether." Onscreen now was a pink hairless rat on whose ass a small patch of new fur had been grown through the miracle of science. Frank has a thinning spot on the anterior crown of his head, and now, apparently, stem cell research held hope for bald men everywhere.

"Did you work late last night?"

"Yeah. Way the hell out in Langley with about three hundred extras. Took an hour just to wrap everyone out." The rat was replaced by a man doing backflips down the sidewalk—a commercial for Viagra—and Frank sat up and set the remote down. "You okay? How'd it go?"

I shrugged and flopped down beside him, stared at my knees poking out from my skirt, the sheen of my hose vaguely rouged from the skirt's red reflection. "How are funerals 'sposed to go? I've never been to one before."

"Yeah." He stroked my arm and glanced back at the television. "The agency called. They want you back on *Three Hot Days*. There's a message on your voice mail."

Three Hot Days. Pouring rain five days straight last week, and they kept us outside in a tent, the makeshift floor sopping up more and more water, thirty extras in white Lycra dresses, stiletto heels, fourteen hours at a stretch. On the third day, the flatboards underfoot were so thick with mud Production gave in and moved the tent to higher ground for fear our whites wouldn't stay white.

An involuntary shiver took me. "I'm not going back there. The wrangler was an asshole."

Frank's an extras wrangler too. That's how I got to know him.

He sat up now and put his arms around me. "Did he hit on you?" I shrugged again. He kissed my temple. "I'll kick his ass. Want me to kick his ass, baby?"

Dropping my head on his shoulder, I delivered a pained whine into his neck.

"You're shivering." He reached for the lap blanket he'd been using as a pillow, flipped it open and cloaked me in it. "Is it cold outside? You're not getting sick, are you?"

I slipped my arms round him. "Stay here," I said.

"I'm not going anywhere."

Another tremor shook me straight through and I was taken

with the notion that I just might fall off the couch any second. I let my weight drop sideways and pulled Frank overtop of me. I craved the gravity of him, his heat, like the insistence of that day's sun after weeks of rain.

"Whoa." Frank gave my hair a nuzzling growl. The crimson of my lapels rose up at his face and suddenly I felt starved and empty. He started to pull my jacket off.

"Leave it."

"You are such a horny girl," he whispered and opened his mouth wide on my skin. I would've crawled inside him that moment if I could have. It was the pressure I needed, inside and out; to be enveloped in another layer of flesh. His hips shoved in hard against me.

I lay on my back with Frank's arm under my head. My neck was starting to cramp. I stared at the ceiling. "You all warmed up now?" he asked.

"Uh-huh." My eye caught the blinking eye of the phone's message indicator. "Did you talk to them?"

"Who?"

"The agency?"

"Nope. I let the voice mail get it."

The phone's high-pitched jangle jolted me, the red light pulsing with each ring. Frank and I looked at it. "Not gonna get it?" he asked.

I shook my head. It looked sinister, that red pulsing.

"Might be them again. I think they want you back for continuity."

The phone gave a last truncated yip before the caller was switched over to voice mail.

"Tough. I don't want to. Sally wants me to come over in the next couple days and sort out the estate stuff. Junk in the basement, furniture—and the *house*. I guess we're selling. She doesn't want to live there and I sure as hell don't."

"Think you'll buy an apartment?"

I grunted.

"What? I mean, we've got keys to each other's places. You got commitment issues."

"Living together isn't a commitment."

"What is it then? If we're going to go into business together, it would make sense. Why not cut our overhead and put the money into good equipment?"

"I can't talk about this right now. And I'm not going back to that shit-show tomorrow."

Frank reached for the television remote and poked the on button. "Why do you need to be doing anything tomorrow? I was surprised you were working *last* week."

I snatched the remote out of his hand and hit the off button. "What do you care? Did you even phone me this morning?"

"Yeah, I phoned. You weren't here."

"When? When did you phone?"

"I don't know."

Up off the couch, I grabbed the phone off the wall, pressed the call-display button back past the agency's number to Frank's: "12:27 p.m. That's not morning. What were you doing? I had to go to my mother's fucking *funeral* and where were you?"

"Christ!" Frank chewed skin off his lip a second. "You said you didn't want me there. You're just pissed off at yourself because you didn't see her last week. You hid out on set."

"Oh, bullshit. You hated her guts."

"Speak for yourself." On his feet, he pulled on jeans and reached for his T-shirt.

I chucked the receiver on the couch and sat, naked from the waist down, and yanked my jacket closed. Frank did up his belt and snatched his coat off the floor. He grabbed his lighter and Baggie off the coffee table and stuffed them in his pocket, headed out of the room.

Chest thumping, an ache hit hard from the backside of my eyes. "Frank?"

Nerves in my thigh jumped when a drop of salt water hit. "Don't go. I'm sorry." I wiped at my face. Tears dripped down to my jaw and it was such a relief.

~

We met for the second time on the set of a cop show, Frank and I. There were about twenty extras that day, all of us background in a scene at the precinct. I was the obligatory streetwalker. Frank was the wrangler. When I signed in that morning, Frank looked up from the list and peered at me a moment. He said, "Hey, didn't I rape you about ten years ago?" A couple heads turned. "On *What Evil Lurks*," he continued. "Your hair's lighter now. I'm Frank. I was the second guy that chased you into the woods, remember?"

"Right." I couldn't really recall him. But I was flattered that he remembered me. "I played Angel." Angel was in the movie just long enough to serve a few beers to some guys in a bar before two of them waited outside, raped and killed her.

"Yeah." He suddenly looked self-conscious. "It was a weird gig. I couldn't look my mother in the eye for a few days after that."

"Mine saw it on TV. She asked me if that was the extent of the contribution I wanted to make to the world."

He winced. "Well, you were amazing. And I remember seeing you in a beer commercial right after that. You were in a blue dress, right?"

I nodded. Good god, the guy had a freakish memory. I'd done that ad nearly fourteen years ago. I was all of nineteen at the time. The scene featured me on a bar stool wearing a tight blue spandex dress. Back arched, I was supposed to wrap my arms around one man's neck, then look sideways to a second man and roll my hips toward him. When the second guy spied my hotly lit rear end moving his way, the cigarette fell out of his mouth. We shot it over and over to get that cigarette to fall on cue. "Arch a little more, a little more, sweetheart . . ." My back ached for days after.

"You must've been out of town when you saw that. It was banned in B.C." The B.C. censor hadn't liked the concept.

Frank laughed. Then he remembered a few more things I'd done: a poster for a power-tool company, a billboard for Bootlegger Jeans, and more recently a small stripper role on

DaVinci's Inquest. I asked him if he was still acting. Not really, he said; he got the odd audition but wrangling brought in steadier money, and with all the hours of boredom on set he could get paid to work on his business plan. He wanted to become a manager. "And when I do, I want to manage you—you should be a star," he said, adding in a whisper, "not one of these mooks." He waved behind at the rest of the extras.

We went for drinks after work that night then back to his place where he invited me to get even for our first encounter. I threw him up against the wall and he loved it. And that's what I loved about Frank. He didn't have candy-assed fears of a woman with a sexual appetite. A girl didn't have to play up all the false-virgin crap with Frank, saying no, no, no until at least two-thirds through the story.

A month before I ran into Frank again, I'd been dumped over breakfast in Sophie's Cosmic Café by a guy who informed me that I had been too sexually eager, that I hadn't played hard enough to get. "I guess I want a relationship like in an old forties movie, you know, with banter. It should be more like playing a game."

"You want to play *games,*" I said, flabbergasted. "I don't do games. I'm a grown-up."

"All relationships are a game. With your parents, with your friends. You should have made me work for it. A guy likes to play cat and mouse." He fidgeted over his ketchup-covered eggs. I pushed my plate away, got up and left him to pick up the cheque. I didn't return his e-mail the next morning. He sent a couple more, expressing concern that we couldn't at least be friends. Eventually I answered. "The problem with cat and mouse," I typed, "is the mouse always dies." That shut him up.

Frank, on the other hand, worshipped my sexual appetite. There was nothing I could say that would throw him, nothing was obscene, nothing was forbidden. After a month together he told me that he loved me so much that even if I were to sleep with another man he wouldn't leave me. We were in bed at the time. He tilted my chin up and peered into my eyes. He wanted me to respond in kind, it seemed. "I would do anything for you, absolutely anything," he said. I couldn't hold his gaze; no one had ever said that to me.

It was Frank who encouraged me to go whole hog with my hair. My mother hadn't liked the highlights, which she said looked cheap. Frank thought with all the American cop shows shooting in town, I'd probably make more money going all-the-way blonde. Americans love their blondes, he proclaimed.

"What about you?" I asked him. "What do you love?"

"You, baby. But, yeah, guys are kinda programmed to like blondes. I'll take you to a hair salon for your birthday and you can check it out for yourself."

It was supposed to be Champagne—a compromise between the Million-dollar Platinum Frank liked and the Sunny Honey I thought would compliment my skin. I grinned into the mirror at Frank and the stylist, giddy with the pleasure of bleaching Josie completely out of my head.

My finger twisted a rope of hair now, dry and broken and old. Frank came to stand beside me. "I would've gone with you if you wanted me to."

I blinked up at him and nodded. "I know."

"I don't know how to be through this."

"Me neither."

Frank woke me at six the next morning, his erection running on overdrive. Briefly, I was contented by it: I usually liked his intense need for me at all hours of the day. Normally he would fall back asleep, but this morning, he leapt up and ran for the shower. He was back in what seemed like seconds.

"Where you going?" I mumbled. Morning light slipped through the curtains in shafts of amber.

"Work."

"Wrangling?"

He grunted an affirmation and did up his jeans. He was looking lean this morning; the stubble on his jaw gave him a sexy carnivorous look. He wasn't classically handsome but he had a full, lusty mouth and near-black irises. Those things, coupled with his slight swagger, caused female extras on set to toss their hair at the sight of him, giggle more than necessary.

The sadness that had slammed me so hard the day before began snuffling its way back under and into me. It mingled with the fog of sleep and for a millisecond I wondered if I'd had a bad dream.

"You didn't say you were working today."

He shrugged. "Well, I am."

"I wish you didn't have to go."

"You and me both," he said, yanking on his T-shirt. "But I gots to, baby doll, I gots to." Grabbing his coat off the door-knob, he leaned and kissed me. "I'll try and call you."

I listened to the door open and close, to the key in the lock. I stared up at the ceiling and wondered if Len was working today. Probably. I hardly saw Len lately. If it weren't for Frank, I thought, I would be an orphan right now. Completely alone. Then I imagined that Frank wasn't going to work at all, that he was going to another lover's house, a woman who wouldn't just lie there when he slipped inside her at six in the morning, a woman who would spoil him, invite her friends to join in. Frank had made noises about threesomes in the past and the idea had irked me. I have never shared well with others. He insisted that having another woman was more for my benefit than his, that he and this other woman would lavish attention on me. "I'm not a dyke," I answered flatly.

"Well, what about for my birthday sometime," he cajoled, "Wouldn't you do that for me?"

"How 'bout we invite another guy. Now *that's* a threesome. Or you boys could just go at it together. I wouldn't even have to be involved."

He tucked his chin in revulsion, then his inner used-car salesman got the better of him. "Well, what if I made love to you with another guy and then next time, you made love to me with another girl?"

"That's stupid. It's just trading discomforts. Shouldn't we

get old and bored with each other before we start swinging?"

He laughed. But maybe he was bored with me already. Maybe he wasn't coming back. Maybe no one was coming back. I got up and grabbed the phone off my dresser, punched out Frank's cell. He answered on the second ring. "Hey, babe, what's up?"

"Nothing. I miss you."

"I just left."

I couldn't think what to say. "I wish you could just stay in my bed and make love to me all day."

"Mmm," he said. "Vixen."

"What are you working on today?"

"Umm," he said, struggling to recall the name. My chest thumped. "Oh—*Near Miss.*" Off my silence, he added, "Whaddya think, I'm going to see my mistress?"

"No." I wished I'd kept the petulance out of my voice.

"I'll call you when we wrap."

I hung up and felt shivery and insubstantial. I skittered to the foot of my bed, to the trunk where I kept extra blankets. Goosebumps took me over from foot to scalp and I bypassed the down comforter and dragged out the heavy wool blankets. There were three. I threw them on the bed and grabbed the housecoat off the hook on the door, wrapping it fast around my flesh before I spread the blankets one at a time.

I turned up the thermostat a few notches, then detoured to the bathroom and looked in the medicine cabinet. There was an old Ativan prescription in there somewhere. I just needed to calm down and get some more sleep. Sleep heals all wounds, I said out loud and swallowed one before I turned off the ringer on my phone. Climbing back in bed I wished I knew how to meditate. Meditators sleep like fiends.

It was noon before I woke. Just as it had this morning, the bleakness lagged a moment or two before seeping back into my consciousness. I rolled over and fell back asleep.

I opened my eyes to Frank standing in my bedroom door. "I called and there was no answer."

"You're *here.*" I held out my arms.

He came and sat on the bed. "You okay?"

"You're home." I wound my arms round his neck and gripped him in a stranglehold.

"Woof," he said. "I think we better introduce you to a toothbrush."

After Frank and I got home from dinner, I kept him up as long as I could, but he'd been awake since six in the morning. Whereas I'd only really been up since about six that night.

I moped from room to room. I wished I could talk to Erin, my last good girlfriend. She and I used to really tear it up, but she'd met an American director on the set of a commercial she was catering and moved down to California with him. What was his name? George something. I left her a message once, a year or so ago, but she never called back. I wondered later if it had come across in my voice, the resentment I felt that she'd taken off, married some George and abandoned me.

I called Leonard. "Jee-zuz," he grogged. "It's three in the morning."

"Well, sometimes you work nights and you can't get right to sleep . . ."

"Shit, Vivian." He took a sharp breath as if trying to get enough oxygen to make sense of things. "What's the matter? You upset?"

"About what?"

"Your mum."

The words sounded utterly foreign, a peculiar non sequitur. "No."

"You fighting with Frank?"

"*No.* I thought you might feel like grabbing a coffee. Or talking."

He sighed. "I'm sorry you're awake. I'm going back to sleep." He hung up.

I slunk around the apartment some more, poured a vodka tonic and turned on the TV. Glass in hand, I clicked around from channel to channel, happened across the opening funeral scene of *Family Plot*, Hitchcock's last kick at the can. The graveside gathering, the 1970s clothes and hair—it all reminded me of Sally, the fact that I still had to get over there and clear out my crap. I should do it tomorrow, I thought, get it over with—sign whatever I had to sign, and never see her miserable face again. She wouldn't even have to be there. I flicked the remote and glowered at a parade of bikini-clad 1–900 girls. I wished I were tired enough to sleep again. I turned off the TV and moments later clicked it back on. The quiet was too much.

In the bathroom, I stood in the mirror as the infomercial girls in the living room beckoned for callers in dulcet tones. Most had hair like mine—without the skunk stripe of dark. I stared at my scraggles of pale yellow.

I rummaged under the sink to see if I had any dye left and found a box of Summer Buttercup, one of half a dozen drugstore shades I'd tried over the past couple years, trying to match the salon's Champagne. I heaved myself up with the box, dreading the ordeal of peeling off my housecoat so it wouldn't get stained, mixing and slopping the cold goop onto my head. I sighed and slumped. It'll make you feel better, I assured myself and left the housecoat on.

By five in the morning I was beginning to fade. I grabbed a blanket and another Ativan, closed the blinds and made my bed on the couch—where I could stay in my night-skin, wake when I wanted to wake. I didn't hear Frank leave.

Three

~

IT WAS NOON WHEN I WOKE. WHY HADN'T I MADE IT TO three or four in the afternoon? I counted back the hours, wondering why I had gone to sleep at five. I should've kept myself up till at least nine. I called the house and Sally answered. She seemed taken aback at the sound of my voice. I asked if I could come over.

"Uhh . . ." There was a substantial pause. "I guess so. Yeah, sure. I just imagined you'd want to wait a few days. But, no, if you're up for it, maybe I should get up for it too. At least make a start."

When I got there, I knocked rather than using my key. When there was no immediate response, I tried the door.

Sally sat hunched over paperwork at the chestnut table in the kitchen. "I'm just looking at the . . . house shit. I've never had a great head for this. Josie said she was going to transfer ownership to the two of us so we wouldn't have to pay the estate whatsits, the uh . . ." She sighed and pushed the papers aside. "The lawyer's coming tomorrow. She'll figure it out." Sally set her glasses down and rubbed her eyes, dug her fingers into her feral curls and scrubbed them into a frenzy before dropping her hands and looking at me with a small almost-defeated smile. "I made an executive decision to list the house." I didn't respond. She continued. "We could each get ourselves an apartment." I nodded. "And there's some stock that she wanted us to divide. Might not be the best time to sell but you can decide that for yourself. And the car is yours . . ."

I looked toward the garage. "It is?"

"You already know that."

"Oh." Sitting down across from her, I ran my eyes over the scattered papers and absorbed nothing. "I couldn't talk about that stuff when I was with her, it just felt so morbid."

Sally glanced away from me as she sipped from a cup in front of her. "Well, arrangements have to be made." There was a long silence. "Want some coffee?"

I went to the counter and poured a mug, keeping my back to her a moment or two. "So, you said there was a box of stuff she wanted me to have?"

She had been watching me while my back was turned and she was watching me still. The last time I'd worn the striped low-risers I had on, she'd asked me if I had to shave to be seen in public in them. My gum-pink T-shirt didn't come close to reaching the waistband of the jeans.

I wasn't about to react. Just kept my face pleasant and took a swallow of coffee.

"I think she would have. You should have it."

Sally could be a little cryptic. As a child I thought it was fascinating. As an adult, I found it pretentious; an artist's pose. I had vowed to remain detached today, immune to such provocation though she was peering at me as if attempting to solve a puzzle. She opened her mouth and closed it again. "What is it?" I finally asked.

Her tongue played at her lower lip. I wasn't having much success interpreting her expression either, to be frank.

"A few of her things." She stood and started toward the basement stairs. "Come on, you can have a look at what else you—" The phone rang. "Shit," she sighed. "Go ahead, I'll be right there."

I stepped past her as she picked up the receiver.

Downstairs was relatively clean and organized. Our old bikes leaned against each other in the corner. My mother's looked as if it hadn't been ridden in about as long as mine. Sally's had bits of mud dappled here and there. She rode hers to work in the warmer months.

A shelf on the wall held clear containers with rows of compartments for various sizes of nails and screws. A tool box and power drill sat beside them. A plastic bag of plastic bags. Some of Sally's old tarps were heaped in the corner, bolts of her fabric. Most of her paints and paraphernalia were upstairs. At eighteen, when I returned from Tokyo, I got myself some fake ID, a cocktailing job in a bar and moved out. Sally moved in and my room became her studio.

Against the far wall, cardboard boxes were stacked three high, labelled with black felt marker: "Winter Clothes," "Taxes," "Vivian/School," "Christmas Decorations," et cetera. I wandered over and ran my hands across them. The two marked "Christmas" were nearest, one sublabelled "Outdoor Lights," the other "Tree." I stacked the tree box on top of the lights and pulled its lid off. Silver garland lay coiled on top. I draped it round my neck and let most of it dangle and shimmer down against the hot pink of my top. Even when I was very small, Christmas had had a melancholy feel. My mother always seemed to be missing something or someone. When Sally started coming around, the low-level tension of her being in on our Christmas was better than the void of melancholy anyway.

Beneath were Mum's boxes of ornamental balls, individually wrapped in tissue, all snugged in their own compartments. She collected them; each was unique, hand-blown glass or a painted delicacy that one of her friends had found on their travels. Others were gifts that Sally had painstakingly made. I gingerly unwrapped one of Sally's ceramic balls, holding it in my hand a moment before I held it up to the bare bulb on the ceiling, let it spin on its hook to see the peacock blue and gold ropes of colour looping in and out of each other. Sally's some kind of genius, I'll always give her that. My gaze left the ball to take in the other boxes—*Do we have to comb through all of this crap?*—and the hook slipped from my fingers. The ball shattered on the cool concrete.

"Shit!" I stepped from foot to foot.

Why couldn't it have been something foreign and meaningless, not *hers*.

Curved clay shards were scattered across the floor, some shining painted side up, others with their dull innards to the ceiling. *Christ!* I searched for a broom, a brush, anything I could use to make the mess disappear before she got off the phone. I was spinning in circles, wiping my hands on my jeans, feeling cursed, when I noticed the trunk pulled out from the wall. It was familiar and not, one of those old wooden things with the leather straps for handles. I sort of remembered it from when I'd come down here alone and small. I remember mucking around, staging a play for myself. With these garlands. And tinsel. And I was standing on a box. And then trouble: my mother coming downstairs and pulling the tinsel off me. She didn't want me playing down here by myself *ever*. I might break something. I could get hurt. She checked the trunk to make sure it wasn't broken. She jerked at the padlock. "What is wrong with you, jumping on my things like this. Go play outside." It wasn't quite a rage, though, now that I think about it—it was closer to fear. On some level, she always seemed afraid, as though the world was a room full of dynamite waiting for a match.

Sometimes my mother's fear was terrifying. I looked at the remnants of Sally's ceramic ball, smashed, like a bottle.

I was six the morning the old Italian man gave me a fifty-cent piece. My mother was in her room studying for an exam and I was bored again. I got it in my head that I should make my way around a few gardens and bring home a bouquet. At the corner was the most fabulous garden in the neighbourhood. My mother had admired it dozens of times walking me home from school, stopping to breathe in the climbing roses, gazing up at the trellis-full of twisting wine-red blossoms. Sometimes the old Italian lady was out front, digging or pruning. She'd smile and nod but she never offered us a rose. So, I was going to get some for my mother myself, I thought, like Robin Hood. Along their little fence I went, snapping roses off her bushes, red ones, yellow ones, then getting really greedy and snatching flowers I didn't even know the names of. I was just reaching for a tall fabulous stock of hollyhock when I came face to face with the old Italian man, so old he looked like a goblin to me. He was half-blind and often caned his way up and down the block. He shook his head and wagged a finger at me, but his eyes were so gentle I instantly wanted to wail with guilt. "For you momma?" he asked. I nodded. He said, "Enough, okay?" and reached into his pocket and gave me a fifty-cent piece. Smiling, he put a finger to his lips, "No more flower. My daughter," he explained, "she . . ." and he clenched his fists as though he were strangling the air and we both laughed.

I hope I said thank-you. I hope I said I was sorry. What I do know is I hightailed it to the store and charged back home with the booty—a bouquet and a feast.

I came in the door guzzling Mountain Dew with one hand, a reserve bottle of Orange Crush in the other, my pockets full of chocolate and my armpit spilling flowers just as my mother came yawning downstairs. She stopped midstep. "Where did you get all that?" she asked suspiciously. I told her. "What do you mean?" she enunciated. "*Who?*"

"The old Italian man. The one down there. *You know.*"

Suddenly she was on me, dragging me by the arm into the bathroom, flowers tumbling to the tile floor. She ripped the unopened bottle out of my hand, shrieking, "Don't you ever, *ever* take anything from a stranger again," and smashed it on the side of the tub. I don't recall if I made a sound. I remember orange pop all over the bathroom floor and splattered up the walls. Chunks and shards of glass everywhere. I looked down and saw one thin sliver sticking out from a drop of blood on my foot and that's when the tears came. From both my mother and me. She knelt and looked at my foot, tweezed out the glass, her hands and voice shaking as streams ran down her cheeks. "If anything ever happened to you . . . You can't ever do that, Vivvy. Never."

Then she picked up the wilting flowers strewn from the front door to the bathroom and put them in water, made me a hot chocolate and took me outside on the bench swing. We both tried to explain our points of view. "But you know him," I repeated. "The old blind guy with the cane." It didn't matter, she insisted, I should never take anything from anyone.

Just at that very moment, a curly head popped over our fence.

"Hey! I'm Sally Ray, your new annoying neighbour starting today. Geez, listen to that, I'm a poet!" She laughed.

My mother forced a smile, and said hello. I sat up to get a better look. And there was Sally, beautiful as the good witch of every perfect story. I'd never seen anything like her hair. If gravity hadn't weighed it down, she would've had the biggest reddest Afro of all time. I wanted to dig my hands in like it was a bucket of candy.

Sally grinned at us. "I hate to be a pain in the butt so early in the game, but I can't for the life of me figure out where my sister keeps her hammers. Don't 'spose you've got one I could borrow for the afternoon?"

"Yes! We have hammers. We have everything. We even got nails." I leapt off the swing, dumping my mug, unsettling my mother, the hand with her hot chocolate swinging out from her lap with a "Vivian! Jeez . . ."

Tearing down to the basement, I got the hammer, flew back and handed it up the fence.

"Holy catfish! This hammer's bigger than you!" Sally looked at Mum. "I'd love an assistant today, if she feels like hanging around and it's cool with you."

"Oh, I don't think so. We've got some—"

"Oh, please! Mum? Please!"

"Well, she's a little rambunctious, she's likely to get under-foot more than anything."

I glared. "I am?"

Mum ducked her head.

"Actually, I think it's company I'm after," Sally insisted. "I'm going to be house-sitting for the next six months or so and right now it just feels a bit, um . . . spooky? I'm used to something more communal than this, I suppose. So if she—what's your name anyway?" She glanced down at me and I whispered it up. "If Vivian wants to come over, I'd love to have her. I'd love to have you both, actually."

My mother said no, she had to keep studying, but when it came to me she relented. "Send her back if she's the least bit pesky."

"If I'da knowed you was gonna be pesky," Sally said, "I'da moved in here a who' lot soonah."

From then on, after school and weekends, I spent my time with Sally. My mother had a standing invitation but begged off to do her school work. Sometimes I'd paint with Sally or tie-dye out in her backyard, but most days we sat in the Pottery Palace. Sally had cleared her sister's things out of one of the bedrooms and replaced them with wall-to-wall plastic and a potter's wheel. I would watch, fascinated, as she heaped great wads of clay on the wheel then proceeded to squeeze and caress vases from them, some tall and elegant, some squat and pot-bellied, their surfaces softly ringed from top to bottom by the revolutions beneath her fingers. My job was to apply what Sally called the Vivian Touch.

It was the best part of the whole undertaking and could mean many things. Often it involved me lending a hand by carefully poking a bit of wire between her fingers as they ran over the spinning wet vase and letting it dig along the surface to create a thin furrow. We used twigs and rocks for different effects. Sometimes we used silverware: the light touch of a tablespoon could give us a smooth shallow valley around the belly of a vase. A fork's cat-clawed effect never failed to make us both whisper "ohhhhh" as I set the tines in. We experimented with leaves, flowers and cookie cutters, anything that would leave its mark.

My personal favourite of all was the Punch. When a vase had dried just enough to hold its own, Sally would set it up on the table, hold it steady and ask me to punch it, producing a gaping hole that sometimes she would leave ragged, or other times she would smooth. Destruction and creation at once; it was intoxicating.

Once the pieces were fired, Sally would introduce stiff fabric—organdy or a thick raw silk—wrap it into the spoon-grooves, stuff it through finger and fist holes and let it spritz out the top. And all the while, she would ask me about myself. Where was my father? He died before I was born. What was my mother taking at school? English stuff, I thought. Where did she work? She didn't. How did she support us? That one stumped me at first. Then I recalled: we had an inheritance. Her parents were dead too. Sally's forehead would furrow. "Is she sad?" she would often ask. "Is she feeling sad today?" "Was she blue yesterday?" "I never see anyone come over. Does she have friends?" "Josie's so beautiful, she must have lots of boyfriends." If my mother had a boyfriend, I'd never seen him. It didn't occur to me my mother would ever want one. "She's scared of men," I said once, and Sally dropped what she was doing. Often when we'd talk about my mother, her eyes would scan my face and she would touch my hair, as though she were soothing Josie through me. The thought of Josie hurting was a new sad movie every day.

After one of those conversations, Sally spun a round, deep bowl, smoothing it and working it for hours and hours, squinting and examining for flaws until she had something she believed was good enough to glaze. Once it had dried she brushed it all over with a heavy sunset yellow. A solid red circle went on one side. When the bowl was fired and glossy and shockingly bright, she put it in my arms and sent me home with it. "Tell her whenever she feels sad, she should put her hands on this bowl and it'll be just like holding the sun."

My mother held that bowl for what seemed like forever before she spoke, just staring inside it. "She *made* this? For *me*?" She ran her fingertips round the rim. "Did you see her make it?" At first I was pleased that she was so awed. That's what my Sally made, I thought. See? But her face went soft the way it did when I'd drawn pictures for her or wrote poems.

"It's just a bowl," I said.

I called home from Sally's the next night to ask if it was okay if I stayed for dinner. "You're invited too. Sally said."

"Ah. Okay."

I had grown to like having Sally to myself. She was my secret. And at home was my other secret. Neither of them seemed to know anyone in the world but me. I wasn't sure about these two worlds coming together.

"When should I come? Did you remember to thank her for that beautiful bowl?"

She showed up holding Sally's bowl filled with unshucked cobs of corn, a bottle of wine under her arm. "Is this where the hooligans live?" she asked.

Sally, who had showered forever and put on clean jeans and a crinkly hippie-blouse, took the yellow bowl and said, "Josie. I'm so glad you're here." Sally told her how lovely she looked, how sharp she always looked in the mornings going to school. My mother turned pink. I'd never seen her blush. I was embarrassed by her all of a sudden.

Sally put the corn and wine in the kitchen before offering my mother a tour of the house.

In the studio, as the three of us stood looking over the finished sculptures, I pointed out my "blueprints" for past and upcoming pieces. My mother held up one of my drawings beside the fabric and clay vase it had become. "Well, aren't you girls the clever ones. What made you think to do this, bring these two elements together?"

"I don't know," Sally said. "I guess it's the obviousness of what a vase should look like, then punching holes in that expectation and running something soft and teasing through it."

My mother gave a nervous giggle. "Yes, that's what makes it interesting." Her fingertips drifted over edges of silk and ceramic. "Do you sell your work?"

"Here and there. These vases are all for a show in New York."

"Really?" Mum's head tilted in fascination.

"Yeah, my sister always gets on me about not treating my art like a business. So I finally got off my butt and took some slides. I sent them to a few places in New York and a gallery in

the Village actually said yes!" Sally laughed and readjusted the
scarf that held back her masses of copper hair.

"I can see why." My mother poked her finger through a
loop of silk spurting out the top of one.

"Anyway, I signed a contract saying that I would have fifteen
pieces by the fall. Meanwhile, my sister had planned to go on sab-
batical with her husband—which is where they are now—in
Zurich researching a book on the psychological effects of birth
order." She rolled her eyes and laughed. "So here I am."

That evening we lit every candle in the house and put all ten
on the dining-room table where we ate chicken, potato salad
and my mother's corn for dinner. Sally made French toast with
maple syrup and ice cream for dessert. I fell asleep on the couch
and the two of them stayed up talking. When I woke the next
morning I was in my own bed.

Sally was the first real friend I knew my mother to have, by
which I mean not just a neighbour lady with whom she traded
plant slips or platitudes about the weather. Sally got my mother
wearing blue jeans and T-shirts on the weekend; she had her
eating ice cream straight from the tub, drinking Orange Crush
from the bottle. More amazing to me, she even got her swap-
ping memories I'd never heard.

I knew she'd once had a roommate named Annie West who
used to say, "Ain't life grand when you got the guts for it." But
this was the first I learned that she had actually roomed with
Annie in New York City. Or that she'd worked as a cocktail waitress in a bar. There was something about being with Sally. Her
irreverence made my mother's eyes dance.

Late that summer, the two of them drinking the homemade wine that she and Sally had cooked up, my mother con-
fessed that she had once wanted to be a singer. Before I was
born, she said, she had dreamed of Broadway and Carnegie
Hall, roses and ovations—that was what had driven her to go to
New York. But it hadn't worked out.

I sat on the floor on the other side of the coffee table, just a
few feet away, but I could barely hear their intimate murmurs.

I picked up an X-Acto knife Sally had left lying out and began sawing off tiny slivers of coffee-table leg. Nobody noticed.

The last morning of Labour Day weekend, Sally announced she would be making us a special Goodbye Summer dinner in the evening and that she needed the house empty from one o'clock on. "And don't be spyin' on me neither!" she told us. We were to be at her door at seven.

When we rang the bell, Sally swept open the door wearing one of her sister's evening gowns. "Ah, la bébé!" she swooned in a French accent. "La beautiful robe!" She plucked at the sleeve of my new red school dress. Then she turned to my mother. "Ah, la Diva, la Belle Diva has finally arrived." She sized my mother up. "Mmmm, ah . . . no. No-no, madame, though you look lovely, it's all wrong," she said, putting her hand on the waistband of Mum's white pants, their legs so wide you could mistake them for a skirt. "I must beg of you: *Be* the Diva!"

I looked at my mother. "I told you you should've worn a dress like me."

"Come, come." Sally hustled us upstairs.

We came into her bedroom and eyeballed what she'd laid out on the bed: a royal-blue velvet evening dress and a red feather boa. My mother grinned and picked up the boa.

"Of course, we must be careful, madame," Sally continued in her thick accent. "C'est la robe de la cranky sister. So, try not to get le crud on it."

That night, after dinner and wine—a quarter-glass topped up with 7-Up for me—the three of us piled ourselves into my mother's car and giggled our way slowly down the dark side streets to Kitsilano Beach.

It was later than I'd ever been allowed to stay up. Sally, Mum and I stood on the Kitsilano Showboat, meant for showcasing small-time acts on summer evenings and weekend afternoons. Sally danced her flashlight beam over the brass-rimmed portals painted onto the stage wall. The long wooden bleachers before us were deserted and I could only make out one or two figures walking along the sand in the distance.

Sally turned to my mother and told her to please join the audience. "We're about to lend this theatre a little class, and frankly, I'd appreciate a smattering of applause."

Josie took our three flashlights and found a seat in the front row. Sally and I fussed with the ratty boas she'd picked up from god knows where.

"Lights," Sally hollered. My mother turned the beams of two flashlights on the stage.

Sally and I muttered about what to sing and opted for "You Are My Sunshine" flapping our feather boas lavishly.

My mother giggled from her bench. Holding our spotlights with her thighs she clapped and screamed for more.

So, next, we sang "My Darling Clementine" and hardly got the last note out before Sally announced it was time for the Diva.

"Can't we do one more?" I asked.

"Don't be a hog, we're about to hear a real chanteuse."

I rolled my eyes and we took my mother's place in the front row, me with one flashlight and Sally, a couple feet away, with two. Sally hooted for the show to start. My mother stood halfway up the stage, chewing the inside of her bottom lip, staring at us for what seemed like an age before saying, "I don't know if I *can* sing anymore."

"Awwww, go-w-a-a-an, go on and sing!" Sally heckled. "Show us whatcher made of!"

I looked around us. There was no breeze on the warm night air. Up past the bleachers, leaves hung quietly, enormous evergreens stood stock-still. On the other side of the Showboat, Kitsilano Swimming Pool was a broad sheet of glass shimmered by the near-full moon with English Bay glittering beyond it.

She cleared her throat and playfully sent her voice up and down the scales. The notes resounded and it was quiet again. Finally she took a big breath, walked down centre stage and threw a hip sideways. Her eyes took on a harder cat's glare. She looked straight down the beams of light coming at her as though she were attempting to stare down a locomotive. Her pale skin was luminescent. Like a magazine girl, I thought, a movie star. And then, she opened her mouth and, slow and smoky, she sang:

You had plenty money 1922.
You let other women make a fool of you.
Why don't you do right, like some other men do.
Get outta here and bring me some money too.

Sally let out a low wolf whistle. My mother's eyes followed the sound and stayed there as she moved into verse two, her voice taking on a sleepy rasp. By the third verse, her inhibition was all but gone, her hands stroked slowly down the boa, her hips had begun a slow roll. Beside me, Sally gaped. I had thought she'd see what a fool my mother was making of herself, but she didn't. Sally liked it and now I was embarrassed by both of them. I wanted to go home.

My mother's head cocked and her eyelids sank dreamily as she stared into the two lights Sally held and oozed her last *Get outta here and bring me some money too.*

Then quiet.

My mother continued to gaze with a small smile, waiting. Sally tucked the flashlights under her arms, dropping one as she leapt to her feet and applauded. "Encore!" I slapped one thigh in ovation. Their eyes were locked on each other.

I fell asleep on the drive home and woke up in my bed to the sounds and smells of the two of them cooking bacon and eggs for breakfast.

It wasn't long after that Josie and Sally talked me into going to see a matinee with a couple neighbourhood kids and their mother. I didn't even know these kids. My mother had set it up somehow and both she and Sally made a big deal out of the fact that I should make an effort to have more friends in my life, kids my own age.

I don't recall much about the show other than that it was a kids' western and that I had a knot in my stomach the whole time I was in the theatre. I couldn't stop wondering about what my mother and Sally were doing, the idea they didn't want me around, and the more I thought about it the more agitated I got. I'd never wanted to go home so bad in my life.

In front of my house, I climbed out of the neighbours' car as if I were escaping rabid dogs and raced up our front walkway. I didn't know what it was I wanted so bad, I just *wanted*. The door was locked. I opened it up with the key I kept round my neck only to have the door stop inches from the jamb. Someone had set the chain. In the middle of the day. I shoved hard against the steel links and heard laughter coming from upstairs. Suddenly the rage emanating from that knot in my stomach took over and I began slamming the door over and over, hollering for my mother at the top of my lungs. I rang the bell and banged the door until I heard her over my own voice, yelling, "I'm coming, hold on. Hang on, for godsake! . . . Vivian, let go, so I can undo the chain." The door closed in my face and I listened to metal slide against metal before my mother was there before me in her bathrobe.

"Why was the door locked?" I fumed.

"I don't know." She tucked her robe farther closed. "I must've done it without thinking."

"Why?" I demanded. "Why are you in your bathrobe?"

Suddenly Sally was there at the top of the stairs in her sweatshirt and jeans, looking as if she just woke up. "Vivian, knock it off," she said in that flat stern tone I would come to know well.

"You knock it off!" I roared. "This is my house."

"That's enough," my mother snapped. "What is wrong with you?"

"Nothing. I just want to go home." I pushed past, up the stairs and into my room, slamming the door behind.

By October, Sally was just about finished her vases for New York and she lined them up in two curved rows at the foot of the bed. She set two in front, entitled *Josie* and *Vivian*.

Josie looked the way my mother did that night at the Showboat: slim and long, indigo glaze with pale blue silk looking slyly out the holes and spilling over the top. *Vivian* was red. An unglazed strip of terra cotta ran diagonally as a path for stick-figure chameleons wearing ant-faced frowns. The stiff organdy she used was cream with slate-blue dollops.

"Well?" she said.

"Magnificent. You are going to knock their socks off!" My mother looked wistful.

"What?" Sally asked, "What's wrong?"

"I'll miss you, that's all."

Sally looked as though she'd been slapped. "I'll only be gone a couple months. But I'm coming back! My sister will be home by then but—" She stuttered for words. I was suddenly struck with a fear that she might move in with us. "I'm not moving to New York!" Sally insisted. My mother's expression suggested she knew something we didn't.

Soon, we were into November and Sally's flight wasn't far off. Her pieces had been shipped ahead. The time she planned to stay in New York had shrunk. "I'd just have to spend a lot of time with my parents. Two weeks is enough," she said. It was late Sunday afternoon. Sally's stove had blown a fuse and we were in the midst of transferring dinner from her place to ours, walking across the front lawns in winter coats and slippers. "When I get back, maybe I'll have some commissions and maybe we could open a store together and sell vases and paintings and—"

My mother's glance switched across the road to the woman peering at us from behind her curtains. We often saw her trimming her roses in the summer but we'd never spoken.

Sally prattled away. "That could be the name of it! All Things Pretty. What d'ya think?"

Mum's face twitched as she waited for me to open the front door.

"What?" Sally looked at her. My mother wouldn't answer. Inside, Sally kept at her. "What's wrong?"

Mum peeked out the door window. "That woman across the way. Why does she keep *staring?*"

Sally giggled. "She's about a hundred and she's all alone. Wanna invite her over?"

My mother screwed up her mouth. "She watches us like she's FBI or something."

We walked to the kitchen.

"Maybe she's KGB. You know what they say: keep your friends close and your enemies closer." Sally glanced at me. "Viv, go invite Spy Biddy for dinner."

"Haw-haw," my mother replied. "We're all out of prune juice and binoculars. She can stay home and and—"

"Give herself an enema," Sally blurted.

Mum swatted her. But she was strange that night. Twitchy.

It must have been soon after. My mother and I were in the supermarket. She was staring at the price of Granny Smith apples, when she looked up to see another one of our neighbours watching her. This one lived next door, on the other side. She'd given my mother tips on pruning roses in the past, told her what terrific fertilizer fish guts made.

The woman's smile managed to be smug and self-conscious at once as she steered her shopping cart in our direction.

"Hello, Sharon, how are you?" My mother's expression was pleasant in that false way I had thought was natural for her until I saw the way she was around Sally.

"I'm just fine, Josephine. Vivian, how is school?"

"Fine." I stared at my feet. I let myself drift a few feet and tried to look absorbed in the apple display but I could feel the neighbour watching, willing me farther out of earshot, which merely prompted me to tuck my hair behind my ear the way the Bionic Woman did, homing in on their conversation with all the high-tech focus my no-tech ear could muster.

"You're looking well," the neighbour said.

"You are too," my mother lied.

"Well, I try. Hard to compete with the likes of you over my hedge looking like a million dollars every day!" They laughed.

Phonies, I thought. The neighbour leaned closer. "Did you see in the paper yesterday about the woman in Utah who had her child taken away? Good gracious!" Her voice lowered. "Though, I don't know how she ended up with a child in the first place."

"Why is that?"

"Oh, well . . ." Her voice dropped lower still. I inched closer. "She was a *you-know-what*."

"A drug addict?"

The neighbour glanced away and back to my mother. "You know."

Mum began to fidget as though she didn't have all day. "A prostitute?" she offered with a barely concealed sigh.

The neighbour leaned forward again and whispered.

"Pardon?"

She whispered a little louder, "A *lesbian*."

I looked at the apples. I'd heard older kids at school call each other that. It was a synonym for *dipstick* or *gomer*. Seemed to me that if people could have their kids taken away for that, no one would have parents anymore.

"Oh . . ." My mother turned up her plastic grin with a thousand-watt flash of teeth. "Well, Sharon, your kids are all grown, I shouldn't think you'd have much to worry about."

"Oh! You!" Sharon swatted a hand at the air between them. "I just found it very interesting. A few neighbours on our block found it interesting too. I just wondered if *you* did. Or if you'd heard."

Mum shook her head in bewilderment. "No. I hadn't. It's sad, actually. You don't think about, ah, about those people ending up with children, I suppose. Do you?"

Several apples dropped on the floor around me and caused both women to swivel. My mother scrambled to pick them up as the neighbour stood with her hands on her cart. "Oh dear, have you got them all?" then, "I suppose I should do the rest of my shopping. It was nice to chat with you."

Mum looked up from where she crouched. "See you,

Sharon. Your chrysanthemums are looking gorgeous this year, by the way."

The neighbour grinned and tootled off into the next aisle.

My mother carefully set the apples back with the others, muttering, "Idiot—why would she tell me that miserable story? Why is she *telling* me that!"

"What's a lesbian?"

She put the last apple on the pile. "It's a—the *nerve* of her." She yanked me by the hand and wheeled us down the aisle, glaring ahead, putting nothing in our shopping cart.

"Don't we need pickles? You said we needed pickles."

"Stop dawdling."

"I'm not! You're running like we're doing Sports Day or something."

"I'm not *running*! Pick up your feet."

That night, over dinner, Mum told Sally she thought that it was silly to spoil her trip to New York by cutting it short. "This is a real opportunity for you. Why rush back here when you've got an opportunity to, to—there are a million artists who would give their eye teeth for an opportunity like this."

Sally cocked her head. "I don't really like New York. It's loud. And dirty."

"You're just nervous. It would break my heart to see you fritter away your, your—"

"Opportunity?" Sally suggested flatly.

"Talent, I was going to say."

Sally's eyes narrowed and she seemed to grind each mouthful three times longer than necessary. My mother had her supermarket voice on. I watched her hands as they searched for a relaxed pose.

After dinner, they had brandy and I had hot chocolate, but it struck me as though my mother had wanted to leave since we'd arrived. "I think maybe we should get going," she finally said. "I have a ton of homework and I haven't been sleeping well, so I think we'll just make an early night of it."

Sally nodded. "As you wish, Josephine."

As we crossed the front lawns back to our own house I looked across to Spy Biddy's. She was watching. Her lights were out but I could see her white nightie and spectral face. My mother threw her hand up, waving with an grin more terrifying than neighbourly. The woman jumped back, letting the curtains swing together.

"That's right, you old bat, go tell the others."

In the morning, the doorbell rang. As I finished breakfast, my mother, who'd been reading across the table from me, looked up, frowning. She glanced at her watch, rose and strode toward the front hall.

I heard the door open, then Sally's voice: "Can I talk to you for a minute?"

"I'm trying to get Vivian off to school and get this reading done before—"

Sally's voice was soft, indistinguishable. Then my mother's "Nothing!"

"How can it be nothing? Obviously it's something."

I got up so I wouldn't miss any more. Sally looked past my mother's arm in the door frame and gave a nervous half wave. "Hey, Viv."

Mum's head snapped around. "If you're finished eating, go get dressed."

I couldn't quite figure my mother's sudden cold shoulder but I thought maybe she wanted some time for just the two of us again. I did, too. I started slowly upstairs. My mother glanced after me. "Go! I don't want you late again." Her voice lowered. "All right. My class ends at two. We can talk when I get home. Okay? I'm sorry, I just, I've got a child to think about."

Yeah, I thought, *she's got a child to think about, Sally. What kind of fish are you, Sally? A sel-fish, that's what.*

At two I stared at the classroom clock, imagining my mother on her way home from the university. By two-thirty, I envisioned her in our living room. With Sally. Just them and their secret conversation. A minute later, I couldn't stand it any longer and asked my teacher if I could go to the bathroom. When I detoured through the cloakroom, she followed and caught me as I grabbed my coat. "I'm cold," I blurted. "I'll put it back."

"Cold?" she repeated and came forward to feel my forehead.

"It's okay. It's just because of fall-time and stuff and the halls get cold," I explained. "I have to go pee," I added and winced. She let me pass but watched from the door as I walked down the hall. I glanced over my shoulder and made a show of heading into the girls' room. Waiting a couple minutes, I peered around the corner so see if she was still watching. Coast clear, I scuttled out a side door and headed for home.

The car was there but she wasn't in our house. I marched next door to Sally's and eased open the front door in time for my mother's exasperated "Are you *deaf*?"

I crept down the hall as Sally shot back, "I just don't see what it has to do with you."

"For godsake, it was an accusation!"

"It was a story about what a bunch of idiot Mormons in Utah did. I read the article."

"You *read* it!?"

"This isn't about that story. This is about you running away from me. You just don't want anyone getting close to you. You liked your closed unemotional world just the way it was."

I moved right into the kitchen where I could see their faces. Idiot Sally. I felt like punching her in the throat for talking to my mother like that—that, and for being so greedy.

My mother snorted. "*Please!* You have no idea how the real world operates, what it means to take on responsibility. I am trying to raise a child and I do not need a bunch of nosy bitches destroying what I have worked very hard to build."

"Must blend in with the other Stepford Wives." Sally glared away and looked me straight in the eye.

"Don't give me that shit—" my mother blurted.

"Vivian," Sally said flatly.

Mum's face whipped round to me. "Oh for godsake. What are you doing here?" She looked at her watch. "It's not even three."

"She's eavesdropping is what she's doing. Viv, this is private, okay. We're having a—"

"I'm sick," I snapped with all the venom I could muster.

"You're sick? Oh Jesus." My mother jumped up.

Sally gave me a look that said she knew damn well what I was up to. We stared each other down as Mum rushed to feel my forehead.

"I can't talk about this anymore," my mother told her and we went home.

If they had another conversation before Sally left town I didn't catch it.

My mother decided it was time to move. Maybe the Kitsilano area would be nicer, she said. Shaughnessy was too expensive anyway. Kitsilano was full of freethinkers and artists. She called a Realtor. I had thought she didn't care for artists anymore.

"You found it," Sally said now, coming down the basement steps.

I looked up, a little dazed. "Huh?" I was sitting on the trunk. "Oh. Yeah. Oh shit," I added when I realized I hadn't done anything about the smashed Christmas ball. "I'm really sorry. I didn't mean to break it—"

She crouched and picked up the chunk with the metal crown and hook attached.

"I was admiring it and it slipped. I'm such an idiot." I rubbed my hands on my thighs.

"We broke a few over the years. It's okay." She handed a little key to me. "She's all yours." She glanced to the trunk.

"Oh." I got up. "Should I open it right now?"

"If you want to."

Christ. I twirled the key on its string and knelt, picking up the old padlock. Self-conscious and clumsy, I wiggled the key in and popped the lock, slipped it out of the hasp. I couldn't rid myself of the feeling it was a trap: a Jack would pop out of the box.

Slowly, I lifted the lid and came face to face with fur. A thick layer of it ran from corner to corner as if the chest were pregnant with mink. I stroked it a moment and looked over at Sally. She took a deep breath and went back to sit on the steps.

Easing the coat out, I shook it as I stood, held it by the collar and let it hang heavy off my hand. "Mink?" I asked over my shoulder, just to be sure. She didn't speak. Sure as hell felt like it. The label at the collar read, *Maximilian*. It must have been beautiful once but the skins were dry now and permanently kinked where it had been folded. Why would she leave a mink coat down here in a trunk like this, let it fade and turn brittle? "This was Mum's?" Sally nodded, folded her arms across her knees and dropped her chin against her arm.

I shook out the sleeves and slipped it on. Surely, the touch of this fur would have been burned into my memory if I had ever seen it on her. Brittle or not, I could hardly take my hands off it, or keep my cheek from dipping sideways against the lush soft collar. I traced the tawny black stripes in the rich brown until my hands found the pockets and slipped inside. In one was a rock-hard package of Dentyne. I sniffed it. God knows how many years had passed and it still had that sugary pepper smell of fake cinnamon.

Back into the trunk: a pair of black pumps sat on top of gold-and-blue fabric. I picked up the shoes. The heels were high and slim. The gold-tipped toes were long and pointed. Holding one in each hand, I let the basement light dazzle them like something stolen and brought to the Wizard of Oz. "These are amazing. I can't picture *her* wearing them though." Sally was mute.

Setting the shoes on the floor, I pulled out the fabric they'd been resting on. Big brilliant flowers mingled over the dress's slim gold hourglass shape. A bra was built into its low-cut bust. Standing up, I took it by the thin shoulder straps and let it fall to its full length, holding it against my body. Cut to about midcalf, where it flared, it looked like a number Sophia Loren would have worn for a night on the town. The mother I knew tended toward quiet conservative classics, things that made her look like a politician's wife. "This dress is so *cool*! Jesus, what's it doing down *here?*" My mind flashed again to that night at the beach: my mother's hips sliding beneath a borrowed evening dress, the way it had infuriated me to see her transform like that, roll out some secret self like a red carpet. And all for Sally.

Pulling the fur coat across my legs, I came down on the floor again, and draped the dress across my lap. A large manila envelope was the next layer.

I opened it up and pulled out the contents: black-and-white eight-by-tens, publicity photos. The first of them was a full-length shot of a busty woman, standing in a three-quarter pose, wearing nothing but fishnets and a gun belt turned so that the holster covered up what her fishnets didn't. A cowboy hat was on her head and a loosely coiled rope dangled from around her neck, just covering her nipples. *Annie West* was printed across the bottom. And there in black scrawl the incantation I'd heard my mother quote whenever she became resigned to something: *Ain't life grand when you got the guts for it! xox, Lifers, Annie.* "Hey, this is that chick she met in New York!" I said. "The one she wait-ressed with or whatever. Jeez. Mother must've been a little more open-minded in the old days, because this babe looks like a *stripper*." I glanced back. "I take it they never kept in touch."

"Apparently not," Sally said.

Next was a headshot of a thin man in a suit jacket, his fore-head crinkled as he glanced into the lens. His face was a little craggy, his hairline receding. My mouth formed his name and I said it out loud: "Frank Sinatra? Holy shit. Is this really his hand-writing? She said she'd seen him sing, but she didn't say she got his autograph." Out loud I read, "'*Celia, You're cruel, baby! But when you're right, you're right. Frank.'* Who's Celia?"

Sally shrugged and shook her head. I sighed and shuffled the pictures to look at the shot underneath. I was paralyzed a moment by the next face: the long lashes, big limpid eyes, the mouth smiling coquettishly. Her hair was white blonde and her nose a little on the Roman side. I let my eyes fall past the nose to her mouth again. I stared at her mouth for close to a minute, a voice squawking at me from the recesses of my mind. Printed at the bottom was *Celia Dare*. "This looks like my mother," I finally said. No sound from behind me. "This is her, isn't it?" I finally pulled my eyes away to get an answer. "Her hair's all Marilyn Monroe-y. Is this, like, a stage name? Was this when she was singing?"

"Yup." Sally's voice was small and distant.

I shuffled to the next picture: My mother—again with platinum hair and a nose more like mine than the one I knew her to have—lying across a piano, languid and feline in a full-length satin gown, long matching gloves. She gazed up toward a hot light that brought her cheekbones into such relief she didn't look real.

An ache started up behind my eyeballs. "Why didn't she tell me she had a nose job? She went ape on me when I was talking about getting one. And let's not even talk about the shit she gave me over my *hair*."

Sally's voice scratched into motion. "Her nose got broken somehow. They had to reset it."

I set the envelope aside, tucked the mink under my butt and sat down on the floor. Reaching into the trunk, I snatched up a miniature photo album. On the cover, in pink glitter, were the words *You Oughtta Be in Pictures!* I flipped it open to a black and white of my mother, still with that bleach-blonde hair, and two other women sitting in a plush velvet banquette, each lit up with jewelry and a cocktail. Looked like it was taken sometime in the early sixties. On the next page she stood with a sleazy-looking silver-haired man in a sharkskin suit. Both of them leaning against the side of a white convertible. She clutched her purse, waving a hand and laughing as though the man had just said something ridiculous but endearing.

Then came a shot of Annie West sitting on a countertop. She was spilling out of a skin-tight low-cut shiny dress, with her head back and what looked like cake and icing stuck in her open mouth, and falling off her chin onto her boobs. Two sharply dressed men mugged for the camera on either side of her, licking cake off her face, each with a smooshed-up piece in his hand. One man was short and black with his hair in slicked finger-waves. The other was tall and white and elegantly handsome.

Across the album was my mother standing stageside in a nightclub, reaching up to let a skinny guy in a suit kiss her hand, the blur of other patrons clapping and laughing in the foreground.

Next was a shot of my mother, Annie West and a slender swarthy woman with wooden-looking breasts and a boyish body, standing under a theatre marquee that read *Celia Dare and Friends*. All wore fur, with a hand on one hip and the other hand up presenting the marquee. On the opposite page they were standing in front of the theatre doors. I turned the page: a sandwich board reading, *For the Love of Carmen*, over a caricature of Carmen Miranda, bananas and strawberries spilling over her head. *Starring Rosa Ramos.*

Next: a colour photograph of my mother and Annie lounging by the pool in bathing suits. They wore sunglasses and held martinis. Book in her lap, my mother glanced over her shades with a Mona Lisa smile. West blew a kiss.

Last shot: my mother sitting on the edge of a stage, her legs dangling in capri pants, her feet in black low-heeled slip-ons. Another woman danced and clapped down on the floor, mouth open as though she was about to make a smart-ass remark.

Tucked into the last page of the album was a folded piece of paper. Inside was written: "I'll move. Write me at my mother's," along with an address in San Anselmo, California, and a phone number.

Inside the trunk, I reached for a bulging silk handkerchief and almost dropped the heavy weight it held: a heart-shaped chunk of red crystal, veined with gold, about the size of a young girl's palm. On the back it said Tiffany. On the front an inlaid gold heart with the inscription *My heart is wax moulded as she pleases, but enduring as marble to retain. B.* A book of matches blared *The Silver Slipper's Gaiety Theatre!* on the front and on the flip side: *The Beating Heart of Vegas!* I remembered telling her, when Frank and I were first dating, that he wanted to take me to Vegas for the weekend. She got a look on her like she'd bitten something rotten. A gold lighter was the last thing left inside, two blue stones glinting on its lid like eyes, the back engraved with *The Flames of Celia Dare*. I flipped the album pages, fanning them off my fingers when the stairs creaked and I remembered Sally. "Who's B.?" I said out loud.

"A boyfriend."

"Well, are you going to elucidate any of this?"

"Elucidate?" she repeated. Then a sigh. "You remember that night we did our talent show at Kits Showboat? Before I went to New York."

My chin bobbed.

"By the time we got home, you were sleeping. Josie was really exhilarated after singing—well, *exhilarated's* maybe not the right word. She said she wanted to show me something but I had to swear on my life that I would never tell anyone." Sally paused as if reconsidering. "Next thing you know, she's got the silverware drawer out and she's underneath pulling off a key taped to the bottom and we tiptoe to the basement like we're about to steal the crown jewels. She yanked out this trunk and kept looking up at the door like she was scared you might catch us. And at first she was excited, you know, like these were her glory days, showing me this and that. But then she suddenly slapped the lid down, said she never should've shown me, that now she'd put me in a bad position because she needed me to swear I wouldn't tell anyone."

I closed my eyes, searching for words. "What did she even keep this shit for if it was such a life-or-death secret?"

"To remind herself, she said—*There but for the grace of god* sort of thing."

"So what's the big fucking deal anyway?"

"What do you think, Vivian?"

I hated it when Sally used my name. From her mouth it was always synonymous with moron. "She bleached her hair and partied a little. Oh dear! Not the feminist for all seasons. God forbid she used to be fun." Sally's face read the way her voice did when she said, *Vivian*. "What?" I stared at her then looked down at my lap, the eight-by-tens, Annie in her gear, my mother lazing across the piano. "Are you saying she was a *stripper?*"

"She was a lot of things."

Again with the cryptic reply.

Sally stood up on the step. "You got told what to think your whole upbringing. Never did you any good far as I can see. Probably time you figured it out yourself." And she turned and went back upstairs.

I slumped a few moments before I jammed the pictures back in the envelope, stuck the heart in the coat pocket and stuffed it all back in the trunk, which I lugged up the stairs.

Sally stood in the kitchen pouring herself another coffee.

"You really hate my guts, don't you?" I said to her back.

"Oh god." She rubbed at her forehead, turning around. "I don't hate you, Viv. I love you. I've always loved you."

I stared at her, up to my chin with trunk.

"That stuff—" she nodded at my arms "—it's a betrayal. I've betrayed her, but . . . I, I think that trunk could save your life and I think she'd want you to have it."

"Save my *life*? What am I, the walking dead? Just because I'm not some fucked-up knee-jerk feminist dyke?"

She wrapped both hands around her coffee cup and didn't answer.

"Fuck you both." I grabbed a tighter hold on the trunk and stormed down the hall to the front door. Fighting with the knob, I refused to put the trunk down. Sally followed, moved around me trying to get the door. "Don't help me," I yelled at her. I kicked my way outside.

$\mathcal{F}our$

~

THE PHONE RANG AS I OPENED THE DOOR OF MY APARTMENT. I thumped the trunk down and dashed to answer it.

It was my agent. My film-extras agent, who, as usual, sounded as though the office were burning down around her. "Oh hi, Vivian, it's Maude calling. Could book you for a photo session tomorrow on *Kiss of Death*. These would just be crime scene photographs of a dead body. Pays principal-actor rate with no buyout and a minimum four-hour call. So that would be about two-fifty and then sixty-five an hour after that. Can you do it?"

I sat down and blinked. "A dead body?" How apropos. "Okay. How do they cast for something like this anyway?"

"It's a show about serial killers. And you'd be photographed as one of his victims. You know how there's usually an MO with their victims, like they all have red hair or something. This guy is killing prostitutes. You played a prostitute on something recently, didn't you?"

"Yeah." I picked at the seam of my jeans. Usually I wouldn't hear my start time and location till later in the evening but she had all the details on hand and I scribbled them down.

Hanging up, I flashed to my mother in the gloom of her bedroom that last time. They asked me to work all the next week, I told her. Go, she said. Work. No point sitting here in the dark. So I did. I sat in that goddamn tent in a tight white dress with the rest of the spandexed blondes for a week, reading magazines and adding another twenty bucks to my tally as each hour passed, rainwater gathering underfoot, refusing to think about her.

The corner of her trunk poked out at me now from the hall. The red light on my phone flashed and I dialed in for messages. Just one from Frank: "Hey, baby, I got a call from Brian, the guy with the Internet hookup. We're gonna head out tonight and bang out the details over a couple beers. I'm working early again tomorrow, so I'll probably just crash at my place."

"Figures," I muttered and poured myself some wine.

Staring the trunk down, I clutched my glass as if something might jump out and take me by the throat.

The next morning, I straggled into the studio building late, rain pelting the streets behind me. An assistant director sent me upstairs to a small room jammed with a boardroom-style table and a dozen chairs.

Three others booked to die this morning glanced up as I came through the door, collectively giving me the once-over. Together they looked like a small pocket of high-rent suburbia: salon highlights of chestnut and gold layered their dark sensible bobs in three variations on pixie-cut goodness. Their lips were coloured with muted-rose tones, their eyes lined in understated earths. Their torsos could have fit easily on any Banana Republic display of new spring arrivals.

An AD followed on my heels. "Hi, girls," he said, touching at the headset he wore. "Hang on." He raised a finger, turned slightly as he listened to the voice in his ear and barked, "Copy that" into his mouthpiece. "Okay, ladies, I'm Tom, the second AD. I'll be keeping you posted on what's going on. We haven't got the details worked out but it's almost ten-thirty and we gotta shoot by noon. The director's figuring out what he wants as it comes to mind—everyone's gotta be photographed by water somehow—so we're just winging it. One of you might be by the river or by a big puddle or maybe a bathtub . . . but we don't actually have a bathtub." His eyes snapped ceilingward. "Go for Tom," he suddenly said in answer to an incoming voice from his headset and wandered out of the room.

The girl with the six o'clock–news version of the pixie cut glanced at me. "You must be for a different episode. They're probably doing pickups for more than one."

"How do you figure?" I asked.

She straightened her cardigan over its matching shell. "You're a different look than us."

I could feel my eyes narrowing to lizard slits. "I guess it's all the same when you're dead." I took a swipe at the mascara likely sliding off under my eyes.

The pixies smirked. "True enough," the talkative one said. They all seemed to know each other. I wondered if they'd worked together on other sets, shows that featured slain gamines. As I filled out my pay voucher they went back to their conversation. "You guys going to go up for the weather-girl thing at BCTV?" Cardigan asked and suddenly her news hair made sense.

The one with deep-set brown eyes and wisps of hair that layered forward into her face hugged herself through her fitted dark denim jacket. "My agent never said anything. I don't think I'd be much good at that." She paused with a couple rapid blinks. Her eyes set deep in the wisps of hair gave her a fawn-in-the-ferns quality. "I mean, you have to exude a kind of confidence to be a weather girl. But still seem friendly? And approachable. And I just get so nervous at auditions."

"Totally," said the third pixie, whose bob was a little tousled and devil-may-care. "They like blondes for weather girls anyway. They look more fuckable, I guess." She laughed and cast a glance at me. "No offence."

I glanced up from the magazine I'd hauled from my bag and paused to carefully tuck a lock behind my ear. "Quite all right. I am a *very* fuckable girl," I said.

They all chuckled as though the real joke was beyond my grasp.

"Hair colour's not the issue," announced the newsy one, running her thumbs over the French-manicured acrylics that tipped each of her fingers. "Ultimately yes, to do the weather, you have to look approachable and still confident, but that's something that comes with practise. If I seem confident it's because I practise in the mirror. No, seriously—I totally do. It might sound silly but, ultimately, I want to become an anchor-woman, not just a weather girl. And you really have to look the part, like you know what you're talking about. But still approachable. You should try it: deliver into the mirror, get to know the angles of your face. If you can't look yourself in the eye, who's eye can you look into?"

Tom the AD came back, and called for Kelly to come with him. The nervous pixie in the denim jacket rose and followed him down to the makeup trailer.

Devil-may-care Hair chewed at the stumpy nail on her baby finger as she continued to mull over the newsy one's last point, then nodded reluctantly.

"That's the beauty of being an anchor, you're set for life," Newsy One stated, patting the back of her mushroomed bob. "I mean, there isn't an age limit. Look at Barbara Walters. Or Jane Pauley."

A snort from Devil-may-care Hair. "*Pauley?* She got fired off *The Today Show* for being too old. They toss you for crow's feet just the same. Marrying rich is still the only secure game in town."

"Rich guys can leave you," Newsy pointed out.

"Can't leave their alimony payments."

Fifteen or twenty minutes of vaguely tense silence passed before nervous Kelly returned in a pantsuit and trench coat from the wardrobe department. Newsy left to take her place in the makeup chair. Kelly's hair was no longer the soft fernlike wisps, but stringy and soiled. Her face was bleak with a grisly white foundation and deliberately running mascara. Her rosewood lips had been paled to lifelessness and blood smattered the corner of her mouth. A handprint of purple bruising encircled her throat. "God, I'll be twenty-eight next month," she said, slumping in her chair. "Keep thinking about what Margaret said about getting in the ring before you're too old."

"Let me see your neck," Devil said. Kelly tilted her head and flicked her tongue over her paled lips. "Wow. Creepy. Anyway, big deal, Margaret wants to be a weather girl. Maybe she'll read a TelePrompter on the six o'clock–news chair." She glanced in my direction. "Either way—" she lowered her voice "—I just said to her, *If you wanna be a spokesmodel—*"

"You did not!" Kelly's eyes flew wide. I dropped mine back into my magazine. "Oh my god, you're so mean."

"It's not mean. It's true. The news is all pretty little girls sitting beside ugly old men."

Tom scooted back in, talking into his headset and waving at me to follow him.

As I stepped into the trailer, the wardrobe woman looked up from the rubber pants and T-shirt she was readying for me to wear so the rainwater wouldn't soak through to my skin. I stood behind the clothes rack and wiggled out of my jeans, gratefully replacing them with the fleece-lined rubber.

I had fully expected that I would end up shuddering in wet sludge, soothing myself with the knowledge that I was making sixty-five dollars an hour. I slipped their secretary clothes on over top and headed to the next trailer.

The makeup artist threw a used sponge in the garbage. "Have a seat." She looked at me in the mirror and jammed her fists onto her hips, exasperated. "Is this what you're wearing? How are we killing you?"

"I don't know nothin', I just work here," I answered, attempting levity.

She threw a smock across the front of me, took my chin in her fingers, grabbed a fresh sponge and set to work briskly dabbing and blending the grey-white into my face and down my throat, into the neckline of the olive-drab shirt. As I watched her mix the bruise colours onto her palette, I tried some idle conversation. "So, which do you prefer: the pretty stuff or this special-effects makeup?"

"I prefer—tilt your head, please—" she patted purple grease into fingerprints on my neck "—having enough time to do the job right. Not this slapdash . . ." Her words trailed and she pursed her lips as she squinted into the mirror at the four-finger imprint she'd created. She added a thumbprint under my jaw, on the other side, about where a doctor would take a pulse. Pulling my sleeves up, she deadened my hands then dismissed me.

The four of us who were about to die were led out back of the studio. Another AD, a tall strapping babe in the mould of a horse-wrangling farm girl, brought us to the photographer, who stood under a double-size umbrella and blinked through his rain-dappled spectacles at the camera in his hands. The farm-girl AD held an oversized umbrella in each of her hands, trying to keep us dry, at least until we had to get down in the muck. A hairstylist joined the group along with the makeup artist. The photographer muttered down at his digital camera and reluctantly said hello.

"There's a stream," he mumbled. "Should work for one of you. Has he said anything else?" The AD hadn't heard anything and queried the hair and makeup women.

"Fat chance we'd hear anything first," said Makeup. "Director couldn't hold a thought if it was chained to him."

We tromped around rain-filled potholes.

"So," the farm-girl AD asked, making conversation, "are you girls all aspiring actresses?"

"Yes," said Nervous Kelly. "But I teach yoga as well. I think I might start doing it full-time. Maybe open my own Bikram centre. Or Pilates."

Margaret the impending weather girl was stonefaced, her anchorwoman facade replaced with a wet-cat one. She looked as if something were pinching under her fleece-lined rubber pants.

Soon, we stood by the edge of gurgling water. The photographer muttered inaudibly at the sky and down at the muddy streamside.

"Whoever goes first," the AD offered, "gets to go back and warm up first."

I stepped up. Steeled by rubber pants, I was impervious.

A foam pad was set down on the muck and I lay on it. I closed my eyes as Hair and Makeup swooped in. "I'm just dabbing some mud in your hair and some leaves and twiggy stuff," Hair said. I could feel her fingers working it a little too vigorously into my scalp. "We'll wash it out for you when you're done . . . now some on your face." Cold fingers smeared and dabbed my jaw, my neck. Another voice announced a bit of blood. Wet grass slithered up through my fingers as someone daubed grit into one slack palm.

Rain splatted my clothes and skin and the line of scalp they had bared. The stream trickled a few inches from my head. I could smell the rotting leaves, feel the frigid mud through my layers. I sensed them stepping back from me.

The photographer's mutter came close again. "That's nice. That's perfect."

I stopped hearing. I was drifting off someplace just outside my corpse.

A dollop of rain hit my ear.

I was sinking into the earth. The sense of my heels sinking in as my mother's coffin lowered.

Rain on my ear trickled inside like a cool worm.

In a couple of months, strangers would laze in front of the television and stare at photographs of my dead self while they ate dinner. Me and the pixies. One of these things just doesn't belong here, they'd think. I wondered if those proper-looking girls would strike them as more or less deserving of murder.

The photographer tapped my elbow. "Thank you. Nice job. Really good." I opened my eyes. He reached out a hand.

The AD helped pull me up. "You okay?" she asked suspiciously as I got to my feet. I smiled the way Lazarus must have and accepted one of her umbrellas. She stared into space. "That's the blonde one?" she asked the air. She was listening to her headset. Then, turning to me, said, "You're Vivian, right? You can head back but don't go anywhere, 'kay?"

Back in the trailer, warm soapy water felt like soothing affection. A new stylist cradled my head with one hand while her other kneaded mud from my scalp. My eyes watered. Normally I was only treated this well when I was on set as an actor and I hadn't gotten a real part in close to a year. As an extra, generally speaking, one was hardly regarded as human.

Towel around my head, I heard a microwave oven ding in the corner. An assistant makeup artist pulled out a hot wet towel and came grinning toward me with it. She shook out the steam.

"Oh god," I groaned happily "Do I get sushi with this?" I plastered the towel to my face. She handed me shaving cream to help get the greasepaint off my neck.

In the bathroom off extras holding, I changed out of the mucky wardrobe then settled down to wait with *People* magazine. In front of me was a feature on an eighteen-year-old pop star. Her hair was bleached the colour of mine. She wore an ass-high, schoolgirl's plaid skirt and a white blouse unbuttoned to her black push-up bra. Heavy blue lined her eyes; a blackened mole sat above her glossy red lips. "WHY SHE'S STILL A VIRGIN," the headline bellowed in block letters.

Tom came back. "Vivian, we gotta rekill you for a different episode." He stuck a finger in his free ear as he listened to his headset and backed out of the room. "Copy that," he barked and poked his head back in. "I don't know what's going on. I'll be back."

An hour later the wardrobe woman strolled in with Farm-Girl AD. "So, here's the scoop so far," Farm Girl said. "The director wants to have you lying on the floor with a shower curtain wrapped around you. But the problem is, we don't really have a tiled floor that would work as a shower. So we're workin' on that."

"And the other problem," Wardrobe said, "perhaps more importantly, as far as you're concerned, is he wants the shower curtain to be transparent."

I cocked my head. *"Transparent*-transparent?"

"Yeah," Farm Girl said. "How do you feel about this shower-curtain stuff anyway?"

"I think I'd like to wear a body stocking underneath. I mean, they can't show me naked anyway, it's network TV."

"Exactly," Wardrobe said. "I don't know what's he's thinking."

Another young woman of unknown job description came flying up the stairs and said, "So, yeah, he just wants the transparent one. I think he means opaque but he keeps saying transparent. How's that by you?" She looked to me.

A shudder made its way through my belly and down. "I want a body stocking."

The interloper sighed. "Then we gotta go to the store and buy a bunch more shower curtains so he can approve one." She turned to Wardrobe and muttered something I didn't catch. Laughing, she glanced back to me and offered, "No offence. It just gets so complicated."

"That's that," said Farm Girl to the interloper. "Guess we'll see you when you get back." She turned to me again. "Are you *sure* you're okay with this? Just say if you're uncomfortable and it's off."

My chest ached a little that this stranger was worried about me. I counted my hours. Another three would pay my rent for the month. "I'm fine. She'll get the other curtain. I'll wear the body stocking. It'll be okay."

It was four in the afternoon when we broke for lunch. I went to the catering truck and stood in line, the rain still pelting down around me. The catering is often the high point of any day on set. Where else can you get a free steak when you're short on cash, where else do they serve you crab, blackened Cajun shark, curried tofu, five kinds of salad, deep-fried avocado, grilled peppers, and chocolate cheesecake for dessert. I loaded up a tray and headed back to holding.

After I ate, I checked my watch and tossed *People* aside, rummaged in my bag for the book I'd brought: *Selected Short Stories of the Marquis de Sade*. It had been a offering from my mother, yet another book taken from her shelves upon shelves of feminist theory and literature, one of the many books and articles with which she began pummelling me as soon as I hit puberty. Sally stayed in New York and Mum came to crave female company in her place: big-legged, loud-mouthed warrior women. My mother had always seemed pissed off to me, but when she found these women and their books, she found the words to express just how much.

Germaine Greer, Andrea Dworkin, Catharine McKinnon— I'd actually read a fair bit of it. Well, *read* might not be the right word. It's difficult to read with your eyes rolled so far back in your head. But I'd scanned enough to arm myself against her in debates over second-wave feminist theory. She also kept copies of Simone de Beauvoir, the Marquis de Sade . . . She hated de Beauvoir for defending the Marquis. And she would never have read any de Sade if Andrea Dworkin hadn't written so many diatribes against him.

The first time I ever saw my mother give a formal lecture at the university, I was fourteen. For two weeks she had had a Marquis de Sade quote tacked to the bulletin board above her writing desk. "Women without principles," it said, "are never more dangerous than at the age when they have ceased to blush."

I adored it. I thought it was a riot: a big fuck-you to whoever might stand in my way. I thought that perhaps my mother had finally lucked into a sense of humour, using a quotation of the sadist who begot all sadists as a maxim of feminine fortitude.

She worked on that lecture frenetically, pacing around her office, uttering that quote as though it were a mantra, a salute to fearlessness.

Going to the lecture hall for her debut out of duty as opposed to inclination, I invited Len, who was a big fan of my mother's. He loved her beauty, her grace and her honey-voice. Had she known, she would have sat him down for a three-hour screed on the diminishment of women.

Len and I sat second row centre, marooned among the feminists. Big shoulder pads were then in vogue and the room was filled with what looked like a football team of radicalized Joan Crawfords.

Len whispered as Mum walked to the podium—"Lookit her, lookit her, she's like a kick-ass Jackie O."

"'Women without principles are never more dangerous,'" she opened, tasting that last word as she spoke it, "'than at the age when they have ceased to blush . . .' So wrote the king of pornographers, his heinous, the Marquis de Sade." A chuckle rippled among the Crawfords. "Two hundred years later, a widespread belief still prevails that those of us who make our opinions known, those of us who do not bat our eyes and blush in the face of patriarchal demands are unruly, unacceptable and un*principled* women. With the heart of a rapist, this man is just one of many, who in various media, made and still make a vocation of depicting the eroticized deaths . . ." I stopped listening after that. I'd heard the play-at-home version of this lecture and others like it dozens of times.

My mother gave me a copy of *Pornography: Men Possessing Women*, the chapter on de Sade bookmarked, of course, and a copy of de Sade stories, which I didn't need to bother with after reading Andrea Penetration-Is-Rape Dworkin wallow in de Sade's fantasies, retelling his stories in page after page of what seemed to me like her own pornographic obsession.

Now, in extras holding, it struck me as ridiculous that de Sade had ever gotten famous in the first place. He couched each dark deed in an insistent piousness . . . *And then dear reader, this dastardly beast did the unspeakable* . . . That sort of thing. Why that quote about blushing had stuck in my mother's craw seemed especially baffling since it was one of de Sade's hyper-sanctimonious female characters who spoke it. At best, it read like laughable melodrama.

After seven hours on set I checked my messages. Just one from Frank. "Hey, baby. I'm at work, where are you?" The sound of squealing children sailed through the background. "Can you come out with me for a drink tomorrow night and meet

Brian?—hold on, these little buggers are killin' me— Hey, you guys, everybody be careful. No bleeding!—sorry, I got a flock of five-year-olds to wrangle. Um, yeah, you wanna meet Brian? Maybe Saturday night? Call me."

After eight hours, Wardrobe came to holding with three different styles of beige underwear that I could wear with my shower curtain: a G-string, cycling short–style underpants, a strapless bra and a body stocking. The body stocking had straps. I would need my shoulders bare. I chose the cycling shorts and the bra. She gave me a thick terry robe, socks and fleece-lined booties to keep warm in.

At hour nine I was counting what time-and-half translated into in dollars as I was brought down to the makeup trailer to have my face, arms and calves sponged with the ashen greasepaint I'd had on earlier.

In the tenth hour they led me to a stark high-ceilinged room that was tiled in black marble. Farm Girl was with me all the way, reassuring me some more. It would be just me, Farm Girl, Hair and Makeup, Wardrobe and the photographer. Maybe the producer. The rest of the crew was off filming actors elsewhere in the studio.

The new shower curtains waited in a box when we arrived. The photographer stood beside a long folding table in the centre of the cool room, shifting from foot to foot, checking the digital images as they came up on his laptop computer. The corners of his mouth jumped as though we were about to do something indecent. A ladder nearly three times his height had been set up a few feet from where he stood.

Hair asked me to tilt my head upside down so she could wet my mop with her spray bottle.

The producer ambled in. Forty-something with a boyish face and ball cap on, he looked like he was on his way to coach Little League. The photographer straightened and suggested to me and the splinter crew where I should be situated.

The women stiffened and suddenly surrounded me with towels, forming a tiny cave that would prevent the men from getting a glimpse of anything above my ankles. Wardrobe eased off my terry robe and Hair shook out a folded peach-coloured shower curtain, slipping it around my torso and bringing it up over one shoulder. Confident I was covered, they parted to present me.

"Nice toga," the producer laughed. "Is this gonna sell like a shower curtain? Looks like a bedsheet."

Hair, Makeup and Wardrobe all shrugged.

I lay down on the tile and Hair began spraying down the shower curtain and my arms.

"Hold off on the water," the producer requested, stuffing his hands in the back pockets of his jeans. "'Sposed to look like she's been dead all night. She would've dried off by now."

The photographer climbed his ladder for a bird's-eye shot. "How are they 'sposed to have gotten this high to shoot her anyway?" he chortled to the room. Nobody responded. He squinted through his viewfinder.

The cool tile bit into my flesh. I closed my eyes and the photographer snapped off a few frames.

"Do we have any shower-curtain hooks?" the producer asked. "Might sell better if we had some hooks."

No answer. The photographer climbed down. My eyes slit open to see him move the ladder over three feet. He climbed back up, quietly whirred off a few more frames. "Maybe one or two with your eyes open. Sort of a blank dead stare?" I opened my eyes.

"What about the bruises on her neck?" Farm Girl said. "They had bruises on her neck before."

Suddenly fingers were at my throat. "Everybody's got to put their two cents' in," Makeup grumbled and I opened my eyes to her patting drabs of purple and fuchsia on my neck again.

Hair and Wardrobe tossed thick towels down the length of me. "You must be cold," Wardrobe said.

"It's good with the towels," I murmured.

"What about," the producer began. His voice seemed like

big dog barks compared to the soothing voices of the women. "—she's so *covered*. Couldn't we pull the curtain up a bit to show her legs?"

All female eyes turned on him. Wardrobe folded her arms. Makeup released an irritated breath, squinted at her handiwork and stood up. "Her legs aren't done," she said.

The producer blinked a moment. "Can't you make them up now?"

She huffed a sigh, lips pursing as she knelt beside me.

Their sighs were like hers. My mother's.

The curtain was raised to my knees. "Just to there," she said. "That's it." Sponges dabbed over my calves. I closed my eyes. *Maybe this time you should figure it out yourself.*

The camera whirred into motion. The photographer asked me to open my eyes again.

By the time I signed out it was nine at night and the rain had not subsided. I sidestepped a brimming pothole and stopped, turned back to the trailers. Gold light came from the windows. I could make out flashes of Hair and Makeup as they crossed from one end of a trailer to the other. They had massaged shaving cream over my face and arms—any portion of my skin covered with death—and wiped it clean away with hot towels. My eyes stung now.

Five

~

FLIPPING ON THE BATHROOM LIGHT, I TURNED ON THE HOT water in the tub before I even got my coat off. In the living room the phone was blinking. Another message from Frank. I listened to him wonder over my whereabouts as I stared at my mother's trunk sitting in the middle of the rug. The other line beeped.

"Shit, there you are! Where've you been?"

"Working. Photo session. I had to be a corpse."

"Photo sessions pay awesome. Did you get a Polaroid?"

"It was digital. The photographer's going to e-mail me one."

"Cool. Why didn't you call me back?"

"I just got home."

"You wanna meet Brian with me tomorrow night?"

"No."

"What's with you? You're like, *no* . . ." He mimicked my flatline. *"I just got home."*

"I'm cold. I have some stuff to do."

"I'm here late but—"

"Shit, my tub's overflowing, I gotta go. Talk to you tomorrow." I put the phone down.

I poured some wine and, stepping around the trunk, drifted back into the bathroom. I dreaded shedding my layers. I lit a candle and turned the light out. Dropping my clothes on the toilet seat, I stepped into the tub and winced against the heat, then submerged all but my eyes and nose.

In the flickering candlelight I saw my mother's face crowned in that white-blonde hair. Her long slim body. Even in black and white, her eyes glowed like a husky's. *Figure it out yourself.*

An hour later, in sweatpants, a flannel pyjama top and a bathrobe, I crawled into bed.

Sometime later in the dark, I shot up, gasped for breath and stared round the room. It was four in the morning. I was sweating under damp slabs of clothing and quilt. I had dreamt I was curled up in the trunk and there were boxes heaped on top. Getting out of the box was easy if you knew the code. I couldn't figure it out and I was suffocating. I have always hated the obvious symbolism of my dreams.

I wiggled out of my layers and closed my eyes. The lid closed over my head again and I bolted upright with a screech.

Light seeped into the room now. It was just after six. I pulled my housecoat on and trudged down the hall, shoving my palms against my eyelids as if it might help ease the panic in my chest. My shin cracked against a solid edge and I cussed and yowled. "Fuck you!" I barked at the trunk and kicked it, predictably smashing my big toe. I was against the wall now, and everything hurt. I bent at the waist, hands on my thighs, and took a few breaths. A skid mark of blood was ripped across my shin bone. Thick red started down, sliding muddily, as if my blood had turned to sludge. I limped to the bathroom for a bandage. My bed called to me as I passed but I was scared of its gremlins and headed for the coffee maker instead.

With a tablespoon of sugar and Irish Cream for comfort, I sat down on the edge of the coffee table and looked at the trunk some more. I reached the foot that didn't hurt toward it. Pushing at the lid, I shoved it open.

I pulled the mink coat to me and sniffed it. It smelled like basement. Laying it out on the rug, I smoothed it flat, set the sleeves akimbo. I shook out the gold dress and tucked it inside the mink as if I were dressing a paper doll. It assumed an hourglass shape. I closed one side of the coat, leaving half the dress exposed, and set the coat sleeve against the dress as though a hand were on the hip. I placed the black-and-gold pumps just beneath the hem. Sipping my coffee I walked around the ensemble and tried to imagine my mother's figure filling the fabric. I couldn't though, I just couldn't see it.

I took out the envelope of pictures and kneeled, scattering them in front of me: my mother, Annie and Sinatra. I opened the photo album again, hoping to see her in the dress. Wasn't in there. Nothing but someone else's memories and no guided tour. Glancing up at my desk I stared at the computer.

I Googled "Celia Dare." Twenty-two results. I hadn't expected anything to come up. My heart shuddered. Maybe there was more than one Celia Dare. I clicked on the first site: Glenda LaRaine's Home for Wayward Freak and Girl-Show Fans. The home page read: *It seems that every gorgeous gal of days gone by has an Internet shrine: Marilyn Monroe, and Bettie Page, and all of the other dream girls. But where does one go to fuel an obsession with the boys, girls and boy-girls of carnival burlesque? Right here, my lovelies, right here. The average person tends to look askance at strippers anyway, but the canvas big top has often met with sneers of derision. Don't they realize that the likes of Peggy Lee got her start as a carnival barker?*

Let me introduce myself. I'm Glenda LaRaine. Born Richard Donaldson, I became Glenda at the ripe age of sixteen, the year I first ran off with the carnival. There is nothing like a family of carnies to give a girl an instant education. A photograph of Glenda followed with the caption "1955 at the *Gilda Liberty Show.*" He/she wore a garter belt and stockings and his/her substantial breasts were covered in pasties only. The boobs looked authentic and there didn't appear to be a basket of goodies in her G-string.

She introduced the men and women with whom she'd worked. *In the* Chaser McGill Show: *Big Box Brenda, Tina TaTas, Sasha the Smoker (later known as Sasha Kane in Montreal where she made a mint importing Cuban cigars), Kasha, the African Devilgirl (who became intrepid civil rights reporter Lola Slash). In Sherman's*

*She-Show and World-Famous Freaks and Geeks: Freda, the Furry
Figure (later Hairy Hannah, the Bearded Babe), SheRa, the Wildgirl
of Borneo (who went on to sing and dance in Vegas and New York as
the extraordinary Celia Dare) . . .*

I stopped, dumbfounded. SheRa? I clicked into the photo
gallery, hunting for pictures. Kasha and TaTas and Glenda herself dominated. There was one black and white of the tent
with a banner declaring SheRa, the Wildgirl of Borneo. A pot-
bellied MC wearing a top hat and tails stood out front smoking
a cigar. I flipped my cursor across the page, trying to find
something more. Back on the home page was a notation soli-
citing donations of any memorabilia or photographs. I clicked
on *Contact Glenda*. A box popped up with her address in the
sender line.

It felt as though a dog were chasing its tail in the pit of my
stomach. I pressed the knuckles of one hand against my chest
and glugged back some more coffee.

"Dear Glenda," I typed. "My name is Vivian Callwood. My
mother recently passed away and a family friend informed me
that she once performed in New York under the name Celia
Dare. I wondered if you might have any information you could
share with me." I signed off with, "I do have a couple pictures
of her as Celia. Thanking you in advance, Vivian."

Scanning down the search results again I clicked on Don's
Diggable Girls of the 50s and 60s. *Welcome to the Don's Bachelor
Pad. Let me introduce to you the most diggable hotties ever put on
earth for your viewing pleasure. From the swinging celeb babes of all
your wet dreams to the vixens you never heard of, I'll tell you how they
stacked up, with whom they shacked up . . .* etc., etc. "Piss off,"
I muttered and clicked my way to his *Complete List of Diggables.*
After "Craig, Yvonne: TV Star from *Batman*" but before "Dio,
Amanda: Cuban stripper and Gangster's Moll" came "Dare,
Celia: Stripper, Impressionist and Gangster's Moll."

On my mother's page was a picture of her in a tight black
jacket, fishnets and stiletto heels. She bent forward slightly at
the waist, her palms balanced on a walking cane. Her hair was

platinum, tossed and sexy, and the expression on her face said she'd just gotten out of bed.

Date of Birth: July 7, 1943
Place of Birth: Pittsburgh, Pennsylvania
Measurements: 36–24–36
Special Talent: Dare started out in the early 60s as the property of New York mobster and Gambino Family associate Teddy "the Ghost" Gossitino, who got her working as a showgirl in Vegas before he was thrown in the slammer on charges of murder, racketeering and tax evasion. (As with gangsters before him, tax evasion was the only charge to stick.) Dare quickly saw the writing on the wall—the real dough was dropping her duds for the dudes of America. One of the few strippers who possessed talent beyond the obvious, Dare, like a female Rich Little, donned wigs and costumes and sang in the voice of everyone from Nancy Sinatra to Tiny Tim. For those with a little jungle fever she could even do a mean Billie Holiday.

Lovers: The list of men who bedded Dare reads like a veritable who's who of the underworld: Sam Giancana, Johnny Rosselli, Ben (Bugsy) Segal, Teodoro (Teddy the Ghost) Gossitino. Like hottie Judy Campbell of the same era, John Kennedy slept there as did Frank Sinatra. Other lucky bastards included Bob Hope, Bobby Darin, Gene Kelly and the best of them all . . . drum roll please . . . the luscious Marilyn Monroe. Think about these two together if you got some time to kill in a jail cell.

I blinked at the screen. My mother was born in Toronto and her birth date was June 21, 1945. Bugsy Segal was dead by the time she was five. I went to get more coffee.

The next Web site was of the same ilk, but this one put her date of birth in May 1944. Born in Pennsylvania, measurements 36–22–36. This site said she was a singer and dancer who had been labelled a stripper but in truth bared little more than contemporary performers like Britney Spears or Christina Aguilera. She slept with both John and Robert Kennedy, Sam Giancana and all of the Rat Pack but Joey Bishop. Marilyn Monroe was not mentioned but the rumour of a "girl-girl" romance with "the leggy Cyd Charisse" was. Charisse's name linked to a cover of *Photoplay* magazine featuring her with Fred Astaire. The caption read:

Fred and Cyd:
"She's Beautiful Dynamite!"
"He's the most perfect Gentleman I've ever met."

I remembered Mum had turned on *Singin' in the Rain* when I was a kid, home one afternoon with the flu. She pointed out Cyd Charisse in one of the dream sequences. She said she'd seen Charisse first when her parents took her on a trip to New York right around her fourteenth birthday. She had been taking ballet for years, so, as a special treat, they brought her to Radio City Music Hall to see the film premiere of *Silk Stockings* starring Charisse and Fred Astaire. In those days, before a film, the Rockettes would start off the night with a high-kicking stomp across the stage. Seeing their long legs flying, their costumes flashing, Mum said she was beside herself and told her parents: "I have to be a Rockette or I'll die."

"Over my dead body," her mother had said.

Her stepfather had whispered, "Don't waste yourself on the warm-up act, honey. You're going to be the star."

"After that," my mother told me as I lay on the couch watching Charisse in her shredded green skirt, "I tacked every picture I could find of her to my bedroom wall."

I rolled my eyes at the computer screen now. Most of the Rat Pack and two Kennedys—Christ, why not Jacqueline too? Why not the Pope? People and their boring little lives; all they want to do is sit around and extrapolate about who's screwing who.

The next URL put me into a mob Web page. *Johnny Rosselli, aka Filippo Sacco, right-hand man of Chicago's Sam Giancana, overseer of L.A. and Las Vegas crime scenes, and mob liaison to the CIA in the government's attempt to assassinate Fidel Castro . . . An illegal Italian immigrant . . . Though stripper-turned-FBI informant Celia Dare disappeared before she could testify against Rosselli, he was nevertheless convicted and went on to serve . . . In 1976, Rosselli's decomposed body was found in a 55-gallon steel drum floating in Dumfounding Bay, Florida.*

"Jesus Christ," I whispered to the room. "That can't be right." Suddenly her rants about my dating habits took on new meaning. She told me she thought Frank looked like a hood when she met him. "You think it's sexy, glamorous, this bad-boy bullshit? You think it's attractive to go down in the muck and shit with low-lifes? Because that's where you're going."

I gulped more coffee. A bio link took me to a copy of the mobster's business card. *John Rosselli, Strategist*, and an address in Los Angeles. The story that followed detailed his work with Sam Giancana, the Kennedys and the CIA. No mention of Celia Dare. Only Judith Campbell Exner, a socialite who dated him as well as Sinatra, Giancana and JFK. Campbell was later forced to testify in court about her simultaneous relationships with Giancana and Kennedy. In the seventies, she'd hauled off and written a book to set the record straight. "Hell hath no fury like a hustler with a literary agent," Sinatra was quoted as responding.

Then I was into an interview with an old B-movie and pin-up babe who said she was Marilyn Monroe's roommate as well as a lover of John Rosselli's. Of course Bobby and Monroe were lovers, she says, he was crazy about her. She often joined the two of them on trips to a nude beach out past Pepperdine. When Monroe died, she claims Rosselli called her and told her she'd better get out of town, that Marilyn had been murdered by the mob as another warning to Bobby Kennedy, who was Attorney General at the time.

I cocked my head. Everybody's got another version.

Another site detailed *Kennedy Sexcapades*. Lists of women streamed down the page: *Kennedy Conquests in Film: Kim Novak, Marilyn Monroe, Lee Remick . . . Kennedy Conquests in Striptease: Blaze Starr, Tempest Storm, Eden East, June Day, Celia Dare . . .*

Only one site in the Googled results yielded anything more: the neo-burlesque DevilDoll Dance Troupe. The site gave their past and upcoming performances. A sidebar with the words *Heroines of Burlesque* featured a small hive of snappy dancers' names buzzing in and around the caption. Celia Dare was one of them. I clicked on it to find a publicity photo of my mother in black tights, kicking so high she was doing the vertical splits. Her tights ended at the hips with a jewelled thong, while a matching blouse flounced around her waist and wrists. *Born Cecilia D'arelli in Pennsylvania, 1943, Celia Dare studied voice and ballet from the age of six and first hit the entertainment world as a chorus girl and fill-in chanteuse for girl shows in Las Vegas. Some say her big break came when she took an ill Keely Smith's place onstage with Louis Prima. Others say it was a one-night comedic performance with her pal Sammy Davis Jr., during the infamous Rat Pack shows at the Sands Hotel in 1960. Either way it was the day our girl showed up in a San Francisco coffee house and made local headlines with her hilarious performance as a drunken Rosemary Clooney that Ms. Dare performed her first-known striptease. Arrested for indecent exposure, Ms. Dare was quickly released and went on to play packed houses at the Coconut Grove and the 500 Club in Atlantic City, where she burlesqued such luminaries as Peggy Lee and Julie London, took chances with blackface renditions of Billie Holiday and Dinah Washington, and knocked 'em dead by boy-dragging Neil Sedaka and Wayne Newton. Even Marlene Dietrich wasn't safe. Dare kept the era alive into the late sixties and we'll always love her for it!*

The phone blasted me out of my trance.

"Hey, baby, what's up?" Frank yelled into his cell. It sounded as if he was surrounded by screaming kids again. "You sleep last night?"

"Yeah."

He laughed. "Sounds like you're still sleeping. We on for tonight?"

I looked at my watch. "Shit. It's two o'clock?"

"I'll be out of here by seven-thirty at the latest. They're only shooting daylight. You want to meet me at Nevermind? I told Brian we'd see him at eight-thirty."

My teeth clenched. My hands were shaky. Probably just hungry. I tilted my coffee cup and slurped back the dregs. "All right."

"What's wrong? You want me to pick you up?"

"No."

There was a sigh at the other end. "Okay, I'll pick you up at quarter after."

"I have some things to do. I'll meet you there."

Phone down, I went into the kitchen and opened the fridge, closed it and turned to the cupboard. Dragging out crackers and peanut butter, I slathered a few of one with the other, paced the living room and crunched and paced some more. I looked into the trunk, the red glass heart. *My heart is wax moulded as she pleases, but enduring as marble to retain. B.*

"B. Bee Bee Bee," I said, sputtering crumbs. Snippets of Internet gossip mosquitoed through my head. "Buhhh . . . Bobby Darin. Bobby Kennedy? You did not sleep with Bob Hope," I said, scowling at her picture. "Or Bobby Kennedy either, the bucktoothed bastard." I stuffed the last cracker in my mouth, and wandered back to my computer. Five new e-mails: Three offers for Viagra and one for penis enlargement. And something from Richard. *Richard?* The subject line was empty. I clicked. The body of the e-mail read: "Celia Dare? How wonderful! If you're interested in chatting, please call anytime. (360) 441–2720. Drop by the shop!"

That's it? I paced up and down the living room past the coat and trunk. I couldn't tell anymore what was nerves and what was coffee. Picking up the phone, I tried to think where area code 360 would be and finally dialed.

A raspy voice answered, "Glenda's."

"Hello, ah this is Celia—I mean, this is Vivian Callwood."

"Yes?"

"I'm Celia Dare's daughter."

"Oh, goodness! *Hello!* Isn't this exciting. I love to hear from old friends."

"This is Celia Dare's *daughter.* You remember my mo—"

"Where are you calling from, sweetheart? New York? That's fun."

"Vancouver. Canada."

"*Really!*" the gravelly singsong at the other end said. A deep cough followed. "Excuse me—filthy habit—I'm not far from you, Celia, or ah . . . ah, I retired in Point Roberts."

"Washington?"

"We're neighbours! I have a little shop here. We have everything—all the pasties and feather panties and that type of thing.
Are you a dancer? You must come down to my shop. Girls come
from Seattle and Vancouver . . . they all come see me. Burlesque
is very big again."

"Where did you meet my—where did you meet Celia Dare?"

"Meet her? Well, Sherman's. Sherman's She-show. I practically *was* the She-show, you know. I have a Web site that tells all
about that, sweetheart. Why don't you come down to my shop
and have a look around. I'm here till six, all year-round but
January and February."

I looked out the window. "All right, I w—" The phone
clunked down at the other end and I heard Richard/Glenda
rasp, "Can I help—" before the line went dead.

Point Roberts is only a forty-minute drive from Vancouver.
I went back onto the computer and clicked on Glenda's carnival
site again. The banner at the top of the home page read:
Come Visit Glenda's Gilded Lily in Beautiful Point Roberts,
Washington. All things Burlesque and Boudoir. Pasties, G-strings,
Fans and Feathers!

I got dressed and put some makeup on. I took a little time
to curl my lashes and line my lips. The idea of paling by comparison to Celia Dare didn't sit right.

Point Roberts is B.C.'s tiny American tip, so small that hospital
emergencies are brought over the border and kids are bussed back
and forth through B.C. for school. The border crossing is usually
quiet and lax, though they say reports of kids smuggling through
knapsacks of pot on the school bus have tightened things up.

"Hi there, where you headed this afternoon?" the guard
inquired.

"Glenda's Gilded Lily."

He smiled and winked. "All right. Have fun. Spend lotsa
money."

Thick trees line the road into town for the first quarter mile
or so. The Point Roberts population couldn't be much more

than a thousand but the main road is infested with gas stations, luring Canadians in with cheap fuel. Not far in the distance is Boundary Bay, its pleasure boats sitting in the marina. I spotted the shop on the left just up from TJ's Restaurant.

Glenda's was actually a small house that been painted hot pink. The sign over the veranda sparkled with gold lettering against a rainbow backdrop. Two 1940s-style pin-ups hugged either end of the rainbow. Next to the other establishments, the shop looked a bit like a streetwalker in a convent.

The bell jangled as I came through the door. A small man dressed in Katharine Hepburn chic—wide-legged trousers and a silky white blouse—stood up from the stool where he'd been perched. "Can I help you?" The same raspy voice I'd heard on the phone earlier. His shoulders were slightly stooped and his hair was white and short with boyishly long bangs swished to one side. He wore no makeup and everything on his face was upturned and pleased with itself.

"I'm Vivian Callwood," I said, hand extended.

We shook. His grip was firmer than I expected.

"Vivian, how nice to meet you. Are you a dancer?"

"No, no. We spoke on the phone earlier today about Celia Dare?"

"Celia Dare. Uh-huh, see!" He pointed to the black-and-white publicity photos of carnival acts and burlesque dancers that covered the upper walls. The photo of my mother on the piano was next to a picture of Tiffany Torch. Fabric flames shot up across Tiffany's butt as she glanced over her shoulder into the lens. "Celia Dare once worked with me on the other side of the tent as SheRa, the Wildgirl of Borneo." Richard/Glenda grinned. "Not many people know that."

"Celia was my mother. I wrote to ask about her, remember?" I paused and glanced around at all the shelves of shining kitsch. "Do you recall much about her?"

"Your mother? Oh, for goodness' sake. Isn't that *something*." He set his bottom back on the stool and pinched at his chin. "Yes, yes."

I took the envelope with the eight-by-tens out, showed him both the photos of Celia first.

"Look at that," he said. "I've never seen this one . . . she had very dark hair when I met her. It was almost black." The word *black* pounced out of his mouth as though he were telling a ghost story. "Black hair and those violent eyes. *Violet*, I should say. But that's showbiz: they like a girl blonde. Always been that way. I was a dancer once, you know. I was Glenda." His eyes twinkled now. "See, there's me, up there." I looked up at a small poster of Glenda.

"I saw that picture of you on your Web site." He looked pleased so I leaned in conspiratorially. "Did you get silicone?"

"No, that was before implants. We used to get what we called *water tits.*" He laughed. "I went to the doctor once a month or so and he'd inject water into my chest and that would make my breasts. It hurt like the dickens the first couple times, but after a while your skin stretches out and it's all right. They looked good. Not now. Looks terrible now, all loose and wrinkly. But who sees them now. Back then they looked very nice. Very real. Nobody talked about the boy-girls much then, so when fellas came in to see you dance, they just thought you were all ladies. At the Herman shows, they used to bring me right out on the bally—you know what a bally is? That's the little stage out front that the barker uses to call up a crowd. Anyway, that's how good I looked. I was the bait! The barker would stand there beside me and he'd say, *You gotta be between eighteen and eighty years of age to go in this tent cuz this is red-hot hoochie-coochie. If you're under eighteen you won't understand it and if you're over eighty you couldn't stand it. All you fellas with your hands in your pockets, take a gander here at Gorgeous Glenda.*"

I laughed and leaned against the glass counter beside him. My eyes drifted down. "I guess you just kept your G-string on so there wouldn't be a riot, eh?"

He giggled. "Not always. Sometimes I flashed." He spoke more softly. "I used to take a rubber band and loop it around my business and tuck it all back. The elastic was attached to a rubber ball and you just take the ball and stick it right up there."

"Up where?"

He smiled.

"Oh!" I laughed again. "Well, who knew!"

"Hardly anybody," he said with his sly grin.

"Do you remember when you first met Celia Dare?"

"Sure," he said with the pride of a name-dropper. "Cecilia we called her. Cecilia D'arelli. She started up in the spring with us down in West Virginia."

"Do you remember what year that was?"

"Oh golly. I was probably about twenty-nine by then. No, I was thirty. I remember because, well, never mind, but that would put it in '59 I think. Anyway, she showed up one day. Lot of carnies got picked up along the way and she had ID but she was as twenty-one as I was. She looked about fifteen. Very fresh-faced kind of girl. The kind that probably came from money, probably had her own horse. We figured her for a run-away. For some girls it's better to be in the carnival than where they came from. And she did have ID. Anyway she was there to be a tap dancer or some crazy thing. Torch singer, something like that." He coughed deeply, reached for his cigarettes and offered me one. We both lit up. "I guess she thought it was a variety show. And some shows were. But this one—" he leaned into me again and whispered "—was a cooch show."

"A what?"

"She got pretty upset when she realized the only job was stripping. We always said, what's the big deal, you practically show that much at the beach, and if you want to be a star, this is a springboard. Look at Peggy Lee. 'Course, she was a barker not a stripper." Balancing the elbow of his smoking hand on the opposite wrist, he took a pensive drag and looked past my shoulder to the street.

I glanced behind me. A couple cars passed but no one was stopping. "So, did you get her to dance?"

"Mmm. She had to or she'd have been out on her derrière. I could be very persuasive. I gave her a couple stiff drinks and a little massage with baby oil. Lots of baby oil makes a girl all shiny and special. And it looks good under the lights. With the new ones I'd say, *Just dance the one song down to your panties and run off the stage.* I remember this night she started, though, because it was a nasty one. We were just outside Quantico where the marine base is. Henry put the fix in with the cops like usual but a couple of them came into the tent that night and stood at the back."

"Why? Didn't you have a licence?"

He stared at me a second. "This was a *cooch* show. You couldn't do that back then—always pasties and G-string. So, we would strip down to our skivvies and go off and then I'd come onstage and ding the boys for another dollar if they wanted to stay and see the girls in their altogether."

"So my moth—Cecilia agreed to that?"

"No, she was just going to go down to her undies. But, it got rough that night." He tamped out his cigarette and folded his arms.

"How do you mean rough?"

"The crowd, those marines were hairy and we were thinking maybe we should skip the penlights."

"Penlights?"

"Oh yeah. At the end, I used to come out there and announce Sasha. I'd say, boys we got a lady back there who can do something with a cigar that'll give you a nicotine fit from the waist down. And I'd sell them penlights for a buck apiece— two bucks if it was busy—and she'd come out with nothing on below and spread her legs and smoke her cigar. Just regular, puffing on her cigar. But the guys, every one of them, would line up to look at her business with their light. One of the other girls would ring a little bell when his time was up and then I'd get my penlight back." He blinked toward the front door and I couldn't tell if he was bored or wistful or what.

"So, what happened Cecilia's first night?"

"Well, at first it was like usual. One at a time, we came out and took it off. She was very nervous though, so we called her, uh, something virgin . . . Virginia. Sweet Virginia. Something like that. 'Course, the guys *loved* that. I think it was true too, she was pretty virginal. Then it got time for the first ding."

He lit another cigarette and stood up, strolled over to the front door. "It's slow today. It's very slow."

My cigarette had burned down to the filter and I tossed it in the ashtray. I watched Richard's back a few moments, then, pushing the ashtray to one side, I looked down at the pasties under the glass. "I love these gold ones with the blue feathers. How much are they?"

He glanced back, the smoke of his cigarette curling up across his folded arms. "Those are thirty."

"My boyfriend would love them. The red ones are great too."

He walked back toward me. Stepping behind the counter, he slid the tray of pasties out and set them on the counter.

Lifting one off the black velvet, I asked, "So how did you get Cecilia to take it all off?"

"I didn't really," he said wearily. "I started talking her up onstage, telling the boys to show her some appreciation and maybe they'd get a treat or something like that. Eventually she gave in and took one bra strap down but—oh god." He sighed. "It's not a very nice memory. Usually we had a terrific time."

I kept my eyes on him. He sighed again. "Well, next thing you know, some marine runs onstage, grabs hold of her bra, says he wants to see those titties. I jumped in—I really did, but he shoved me so hard I landed on my caboose. And then, well, I just upped and clocked him one and the whole place exploded. They got hold of Cecilia and pulled her over their heads into the crowd." He sipped from his smoke again and stared at the wall of photos. "The cops just stood there at the back. And someone, our drummer, I think, grabbed the baseball bat. I plowed through those sons-a-bitches like my life depended on it. I really did. They were grabbing up my skirt and I was thinking, if they find my little surprise, we're all fucked, pardon my

French. But I did it anyway. I could almost touch her, and then all of a sudden a screech came out of her like nothing you ever heard. She was all teeth and nails and spitting and kicking. None of them could get a grip on her—I think because of the oil. Then *bang!*—the cops fired a shot in the air and everything stopped. One of them says, *S'time you boys all get yourself a soda now.* I'll never forget that. And out they went, fellas with their heads cracked open being dragged by the able-bodied ones. I don't think there was any of them not bleeding."

I peered into his face. "Did they, I mean did they—was she—"

"No. The oil saved her—they couldn't get a good grip on her. No." He puffed and shook his head vehemently. "Just a little beat up. I got beat up too. Maybe worse. She scuttled over to the side and sort of huddled there. Cops said for another two hundred they wouldn't charge us with indecency. We broke down the midway that night and got the heck out." He gave a vague smile. "Henry put her in the other show. The Wildgirl of Borneo cage around back."

"And she didn't mind?"

"She liked it better, I think. She was sort of animalistic after that marine mess anyway, you know, liked to keep to herself, didn't bathe much. Actually, I remember a girl came in there looking for her one day, making a big fuss. A stripteaser, big bosoms . . . what was her name. Guns . . . ?"

"West? Annie West?"

"Maybe. I remember she was sort of famous at one time. And she was very upset about Cecilia."

I turned over the pasty in my hand and let the tassel drop down toward the counter, slowly twirling it.

He watched my fingers. "But there was Cecilia out back in a cage biting heads off chickens and all dirty and it wasn't very glamorous."

"She bit heads off chickens?"

"Well, not for real," he said, still staring at the pasty I held.

I looked at it too and back at him. "Thirty bucks?" I asked.

He brightened a little. "Oh, these are very nice." He took

the one from my hand and its match off the velvet. "I make these myself, you know."

"Really? . . . So she didn't really bite chickens."

"They'd tie the chicken's real head down and put a fake one on with a blood pellet inside and she'd bite it off and everyone would scream. She stayed in a doghouse and an MC would come out and he'd say—"

"That guy on your Web site picture with the cigar and the top hat?"

"Yes. He'd say she was raised by wild apes and there should be no harsh noises because it was feeding time and then he'd dump the sack in the cage. And the chicken would run all over the place banging into everything because he couldn't see, you see. It was a good gimmick."

He placed my pasties in a small box on a bed of tissue and carefully folded the paper.

"How long did she work there?"

"Oh, I don't know, couple months. Mostly I remember her because of that big upset and because she switched to geeking. And she was very pretty. High-class type of pretty. But girls came and went. And I did too." He set the lid on the box and pulled a length of slim ribbon from a roll on the wall.

"Did she just get sick of it and quit? Do you know where she went?" I watched him clip a second length and pull scissor blades along it to form coils of shimmering blue.

"That was another mess." He looked at the ceiling. "She stole a fella's car. Okie Joe, the candy butcher, he had it bad for her, and I think they shacked up in a hotel room once or twice. She used to get insomnia and I'd give her pills sometimes. I can't remember how it all went but I think she gave him those pills and stole his car while he was sleeping. He was a real crumb that guy. Probably had it coming. That gal who came looking, she really grilled him. Made a big fuss. What was her name? . . ."

"Annie West?"

"Mmm . . ." He set the box in front of me and I gave him my credit card. "Funny days," he said and swiped the card. A poster of a grinning magician framed his head as he set the card back in front of me. We waited in silence for the receipt to roll up.

Back at home, I sat on the couch a few minutes before snatching the photo album and pulling out Annie West's number. I grabbed the phone and poked the digits before I lost my nerve. *We're sorry. The number you have reached is not in service* . . . I dialed again. What did I expect? She was going to stay in the same house for thirty, forty years? I tried directory assistance for San Anselmo. Nothing. San Francisco. Nothing.

I lay on my sofa the rest of the afternoon until the growling of my stomach hauled me out of the carnival. The sun was down, and the windows were black. I flipped my wrist: 8:35. Shit. Frank. I sat up and pressed fingertips to my eyelids, tried to get the circulation going.

In the bathroom, I threw my head forward and finger brushed my hair, hairsprayed the underside and flipped it back up. I rushed some extra concealer under my eyes, and relined them, touched up my mascara and threw on some lipstick. Rushing down the hall, I pulled a scooped-neck top off a hanger and checked myself in the hall mirror. Normally, I was happy when I was down a couple pounds but my reflection was lank and bedraggled.

I didn't want Frank to be embarrassed by me in front of this Brian guy. I reached down my top and pulled my boobs into some reasonable facsimile of cleavage, went to the bathroom mirror and dusted brown shadow between them for contour.

Seeing vodka on my horizon, I called a cab.

Down at Nevermind, the music pumped and waitresses in black Lycra pants slithered through the crowd of university boys in loose jeans and leather jackets standing around the bar. I ran my eyes over the room, across the pseudo–log cabin walls and the dingy lacquered wood tables until I caught sight of Frank sitting at one of the black light–lit booths in the back with another guy. I approached their table as the waitress strolled past. Frank's friend leaned to watch her go.

"You're late!" Frank called. I paused beside the booth on Frank's side. "Brian, this is my girl, Vivian. Viv, this is Brian, Webmaster extraordinaire. He's gonna hook us up."

Brian ran his eyes unabashedly up and down the length of me. "Girl's got potential!" he hollered as if we were at a rodeo.

"Damn right," Frank bellowed back, apparently at the same event. He reached out and looped his arm round my hips, tugged me into the seat beside him.

"Ever operated any sort of Internet business from home, Vivian?" Brian asked. He was a cartoon version of handsome, all his face bones overgrown and determined. I opened my mouth to answer but he continued. "Not that it matters, because this game is unlike any other. And the *money*—you will cream your jeans when the cash starts coming in."

Frank yucked it up beside me. I'd never heard that particular laugh out of him and tried to think what it reminded me of, when suddenly his hand reached across the table to high-five Brian's. A girl in an ass-high pink cheerleader skirt, a white blouse tied at the waist and knee-high black boots stood beside our booth now. Attached to the back of her sleek brunette hair was a sixties-style hairpiece. She swung her butt in beside Brian with a singsong "I'm ba-a-ack."

She had large brown eyes that gave her the look of some sort of woodland creature. False eyelashes sprang off her lids and liquid eyeliner sloped upward as though she were trying to give her doe eyes a little feline scratch. She reminded me of one of the girls in the *I Dream of Jeannie* reruns, the ones Major Nelson would date in the episodes when Jeannie still addressed him as Master. "Are you Vivica?" she shouted over the music.

"Vivian." I reached across to shake her hand.

"Oh!" she giggled, shaking my fingers as though they were a novelty item. "I'm Sienna? Vivica's a cool name."

Frank waved down the waitress and ordered me a vodka cranberry.

"So, you're getting into the business too, hey? Are you gonna do the Jerkflirt stuff from home or are you gonna do

movies in Brian's studio?" she asked. The shrill of her voice
carried well over the bar's sound system.

"Home."

"Cool," she grinned and bobbed her head several times.
"Are you just gonna do one-on-one shows? Or videos too? Lots
of girls when they do videos just do girl-girl at first or only do
it with their boyfriends or whatever?"

"Just the model shows. Maybe videos with Frank."

"Hank?"

"Frank," I said and pointed beside me.

She bobbed her head some more. The waitress put a green
martini in front of me. I tried to catch her but she slipped into
the crowd. Sienna's head followed her and snapped back. "She's
totally got a great ass, hey?" she giggled. "You could bounce a
quarter off it." Her eyes glazed on the black faux-logs on the
wall beside us. A moment later she added, "I work out a lot? Do
you work out?"

"When I can," I said, adding my own nod for good measure
since the likelihood of being heard over the music and our men,
who'd taken to hollering most of their conversation, wasn't great.

"Because you totally have to in this business. To look good
from all the angles? Especially when you're a girl? With guys,
it's not so . . ."

My gaze drifted around her face but I'd stopped listening.
I took mouthfuls of sweet green appley vodka. Beside me,
Frank leaned into the table, hanging on Brian's every word.
"This chick, man," Brian was saying, "she's got me in her ass,
my buddy Paul in her snatch, Sienna's workin' the camera and
this broad wants Sienna to put the camera down so she can lick
her tits at the same time—she couldn't get enough!"

Frank let out a hoot of exultation. His eyes were saucers.

Sienna had realized I wasn't listening to her and tuned in to
the men. "Yeah," she shrieked. "Wasn't that girl *funny?*"

The waitress slid past the table again, setting a vodka cranberry down just as I reached the bottom of the martini glass.
Brian doodled a finger-circle over the table as he barked, "'Nother

round." His eyes left the ass of the retreating waitress and shifted to my chest. "So, Vivian . . ."

"Vivica," Sienna corrected.

Frank laughed; Brian turned a blank look on Sienna and then continued. "Vivian, you thinking about getting your tits done?"

I knew I should have worn my push-up.

"Implants are so *over*?" Sienna looked at me, shaking her head with a boys-will-be-boys eye roll. "Don't you think they're out of style?"

"Big tits are never out of style," Brian announced. "Sienna's got little titties but that's her specialization while she's young like this. She's doing the sweet baby virgin thing, but that's not your look."

I glanced to Frank, whose face had become pensive verging on concerned.

"You're like . . ." Brian paused for words. "Well, you're the insatiable slut, you know?"

"Got that right." Frank leaned over and spread his lips over my ear.

"There's a big-big market for that. Guys like the idea that there's this bitch who's just a fuck machine and she can't get enough." Brian pointed at me. "That's your mien," he added, pronouncing it *me-enne*, as though it were a kind of French raunch. Like ménage à trois.

I must have had a frown. He explained. "Mien is like, ah, your *thing*, your externality that tells everyone who you are."

"Mien," I said, "It's *meen*."

"I'm not sayin' you should be mean," Brian clarified patiently. "You gotta be approachable too. Accommodating." The waitress set four more drinks on the table and walked away as I tried to order something to eat.

The black light over our heads lit up Brian's teeth. I said, "It's pronounced—" and Frank kicked the side of my shoe.

"What'sat?" Brian asked. As he tilted his head, the light hit pockmarks along the sharp edge of his jaw.

Frank shrugged. "It's an investment to consider—whoa, makin' up for lost time?" He nodded at the last of the cocktail sputtering up my straw. "My little alky," he said playfully and put his arm around my shoulders, giving me a squeeze.

"I'm hungry," I told his neck.

"So, Frank, which way do you think you wanna go with this?" Brian hollered over the techno remake of "Push Push in the Bush" pumping through the bar now.

"Why don't you order some food," Frank said into my hair and waved to the waitress with his free hand. I liked the reverberation of his voice against my head and wished he'd take me home.

Frank must be a far better waver, I thought, when the waitress appeared suddenly at my side. I ordered chicken fingers.

"Frank, *Frank*," Brian bellowed, leaning back into his corner of the booth. Frank's hand dawdled off my shoulders and he leaned in to hear.

"Hey, where you going?" Frank called after me. I'd slipped out into the alley between booths. I'd forgotten. Looking at him a moment, I said, "Cigarette."

"Bad girl—when'd you start smoking again?" he asked, grinning.

I shrugged and headed through the crowd.

Outside, a few other pariahs were puffing on the terrace. I moved away from them out on to the sidewalk and lit up, taking a long drag as I stared out across the expanse of Fourth Avenue to the deserted park. Car lights rushed toward me like a locomotive, exploding in my brain as they passed. I closed my eyes and opened them to the pool of street light I stood in. I stared at the edges of my chewed nails as I blew smoke. When I broke my tobacco fast the other day, I'd gotten such a rush off the nicotine. Now the rush was down to nothing, just simple relief from craving. I should get my nails done, I thought. Sienna has long acrylics like that weather-girl wannabe. Men love those. If I'm going to do this, I should at least get my nails done. A semi-truck rolled by and I shut my eyes to the roar, threw down my cigarette and walked back down the steps. Staggering a little, I grabbed the railing. Had to get something in my stomach.

The music slammed as I came through. Everything felt so sensitive all of a sudden. Two girls in glowing white spandex tops and bare midriffs above their low-risers shoved giddily past me into the crowd and I paused, swaying. I have to keep swimming, I thought, or I'll drown.

Chicken fingers sat waiting in a basket when I reached our table and I plucked one up and pushed it past my teeth before the seat of my pants hit the bench.

Sienna's fingers wiggled at me in greeting. I stirred my next drink and Brian glanced at my chest once more but didn't acknowledge my return. "Speaking of investments," he yawped, "I'm thinking of starting up a Bambi Hunt out in Kelowna like that guy did in Vegas?"

Frank's face lit up. "A hunting lodge? I used to go deer hunting with my dad."

"Well, this is not your father's deer hunt." Brian winked. "This guy in Vegas has a ranch where you can pay ten grand to chase naked girls around and shoot them with paintball guns, and they videotape the whole thing for you."

"No way," Frank said.

"Totally," Brian confirmed.

"That's so gross?" Sienna said.

"Ah, you'd love it." Brian nudged her. "These chicks, each of 'em makes a grand for the hunt and twenty-five hundred if they get away without being shot. All they wear is running shoes. I'm looking into some property out in Kelowna. Maybe something near Hope."

I sipped. "It was a hoax," I said.

"What?" Brian's eyes grew suspicious as they turned to me.

"There's no Bambi Hunt," I snapped. "Some asshole staged it for the media so he could sell videos. It was in all the papers."

"I never heard that." He paused as a thought occurred to him and he sniggered into his glass. "Probably got shut down by a herd of pissed-off feminists."

Frank gacked with laughter. "Yeah, the 'Wimmyns Studies'—"
he crooked the first two fingers of either hand into quotation
marks "—department at the University of Nevada came and ran
the poor guy's ass out of town."

I sucked greedily on my straw. Their teeth all glowed
demonically now under the black light. You're just drunk, I
thought, eat. I picked up another chicken finger and chewed
and imagined being in McBride Park across the street, walking
in the quiet. Bar lights against the shellacked tabletop became
flashlights in the park: hunters with guns slung over their shoulders wearing fatigues, and me naked and cold, blinded by
beams of white light. *I prefer to play cat and mouse.*

Leaning my cheek against the knuckles of one hand, I
glanced at Frank. I wished he'd take his eyes off Brian's glowing incisors and say something gentle and comforting. I put
my lips on my straw again and watched a drop of something
land in my drink. I leaned over to examine the blood-pink
liquid and poked it with my straw. Looking up at the ceiling,
I wondered if the pipes were sweating. "Holy fuck!" Sienna
shrieked. "Your eyes look like lasers right now. They're, like,
glowing, like they can see through walls? Can you see my
bones, Vivica?" She laughed, holding up her palms. Her face
dropped and she leaned in. I couldn't make out her words. She
traced two fingers from her eyes down her cheeks. I touched
my face.

Christ. I was crying. Like a nosebleed, I couldn't even feel it.
I slipped out, off the bench seat and headed down the hall to
the bathroom.

Running into a cubicle, I slammed the door and yanked a
yard of toilet paper.

Into the bathroom, a small voice called, "Vivica? Are you
okay?"

My heart kicked against the wall of my chest. I lifted my
heels up onto the seat.

"Vivica?" she repeated quizzically. She knocked on my door.
Suddenly she was down on all fours. Peering underneath, her

dark eyes were dopey and cruel at once, like a hunting dog's. "I saw your shoes go up."

I stared down over my knees at her.

"Are you okay? Is it cramps? Are you on your period?" She couldn't have been more than twenty-two. "I have a um—" and she rummaged in her purse "—Tampax?" She shook the paper-wrapped tube at me as if it might lure me into the open.

"No, thanks." She didn't move. "I'll be out in a minute," I said a bit more sharply.

She blinked, her nose and forehead crinkling up at me.

"I just have cramps, that's all," I offered.

"Ohhh . . . yeah?" Wagging her way out by her back end, she clambered up on her high heels and scampered into the other stall. "My sister gets *bad* ones." Suddenly her soft pale hand was under the stall with a sample package of Midol. "Will these help?" The flesh of her hand was so dewy, it verged on pudge.

"Thanks, sure. Thanks." I plucked the pills and stuck them in my pocket as I quietly dropped my feet back to the floor, stealthily unlocking my stall.

"You're not going home, are you?" she whined as I stepped across the bathroom.

Slipping out the door, I dashed for the bar's back exit.

I ran down the alley and came up a side street back to the main drag. Fourth was quiet and I trotted across toward the park, looking for cover, a bush to hide in, something to disguise me until a taxi came. I thought I heard my name called and, instead of stopping, made for the nearest big tree and ducked behind as an old Volkswagen's sewing machine engine churned past. I was rummaging in my purse for my cell phone when I saw another car coming; its roof displayed a light lit for business. My eyes welled in gratitude.

Peering out from behind the tree, I caught sight of Frank across the road just as he sprang up onto the sidewalk in front of the bar. He looked up and down the road.

The taxi bore down on me. I couldn't just leap out from the trees and flag it. He would see, call my name and paralyze me.

He turned toward the steps that led back down into Nevermind and I rushed out to the sidewalk, waving frantically at the cabdriver who slammed on his brakes as he passed. Anything for a fare on a slow night. Frank turned at the sound of squealing brake pads. The cab reversed the few yards back.

"Vivian!" Frank hollered. "What're you doing?"

I threw myself into the back seat before his words could take hold and I shut the door.

I didn't know where to go. It was only ten-thirty. I couldn't go home though. Suddenly the trunk came to mind. My mother's trunk. Frank would go to my apartment and I had to get that trunk out before he did. I didn't want him touching it. I didn't want anyone inside my mother's trunk. Staring out the back window, I wondered if I'd know Frank's car from this angle. I went back in my purse and turned my cell off for fear it would ring.

Leonard. I could hide with Leonard.

As we pulled up in front of my house, I turned my head a hundred and eighty degrees in either direction, hunting for headlights or men of concern. I needed to get into my apartment. Maybe Frank was already inside. No, he never could've made it here yet, I reasoned, and paid the driver.

Rushing to the side entrance, I rocketed down the short chunk of hall and let myself into the apartment, careful not to turn on any lights. I felt my way along the wall and turned on the penlight attached to my key chain. The image of soldiers, marines crowding along my windows, assaulted my senses. I grabbed the large manila envelope from the couch and tossed it into the trunk along with the small photo album for which I had to hunt along the coffee table, knocking over god knows what in the process. A sparking current coursed through my limbs as I tripped over her shoes and crouched to roll up the dress and mink. My penlight was in my teeth now and I half expected a bell to signal my time was up, that doom had come to suck me into the bowels of the earth.

I jammed the fur and shoes in and turned in circles trying

to think if I'd left anything out. "Your heart?" I whispered. "It's there." I slammed the lid closed, and then, pulling my purse over my shoulder, lugged the trunk down the hall. I reached around under the load for the door handle, wrangled the box onto my hip, balancing it against the wall to free up my hand.

In the outer hall, I listened for footsteps or the rattle of the building's entrance before I slipped out, locked the door and snuck back out the side exit.

I scurried through the parking lot, behind the fence and down the alley, eyes darting, stomach somersaulting until I came to the back of Leonard's building. Along the fence I went, checking over my shoulder, feet hesitating with the sound of each of the three or four cars that passed out front of the building. Finally I nipped into the entranceway and nosed Len's intercom button, whispering hoarsely. As the entrance buzzed, I fought my way in.

Len stared at me from his apartment as I came toward him. Neither of us spoke. I stopped in front of him and whispered, "Are you alone?"

"Yeah," he said, full-voiced.

"Can I sleep over?" The moment it came out of my mouth, I felt as though I were waking up from a foolish dream.

He shrugged, "Sure," and looked at my trunk. "Is that Josie's stuff?"

"Well, *yeah*," I said, suddenly irritated. I pushed past him.

"Why are you whispering?" He trailed down the hall after me. "Are you drunk?"

"No," I snapped, standing in the middle of his living room holding my box.

"You smell drunk." He wore his white tuxedo shirt and cummerbund over his black pleated trousers. His bow tie sat on the table.

"Did you just get home from work?"

"Mrs. Chelsey called last minute and asked me to do a cocktail party at her house." He gnawed at his thumbnail.

The phone rang. My head spun. "If it's Frank, I'm not here. I'm not here if it's *anybody*."

His eyebrows raised. "Whatever you say, lady." I watched him carefully as he spoke into the receiver. "Oh hi. Yeah, sure. No problem . . . ha ha . . . that's right . . . Tomorrow? Ah, no, I'm free, sure . . . Okay then . . . You too, Eunice." He put the phone down. "Mrs. Chelsey. Bridge party tomorrow. Are you just going to stand there holding that thing all night?"

Glowering at the trunk, I said, "*Eunice?* Befriended another old crone, have you?" and grudgingly set the box down.

An hour later, my mother's things were spread out on Len's rug and a pot of tea was between us. Len had changed into loose jeans and an old flannel painting shirt. I wore one of his tees and his sweatpants. He had been slowly shaking his head in awe since I opened the box. "This is so cool. I always knew there was something. 'Member she said she saw Sinatra sing in New York? I mean, didn't you just know it was *something*. But you can't just ask that type of thing." His lisp sounded especially pronounced to my ear at that moment.

"You're starting to sound like those old ladies you wait on," I said. "You sound like Liza Minnelli's ex."

"Stop being a cunt," he said serenely as he examined the glass heart's inscription. "Who do you think B was? Think it was Bobby Kennedy?"

I had told him about the Web sites. "No."

"Yes, you do." He turned the heart over. "It was someone pretty flippin' rich; this is from Tiffany's. You think you'll keep in touch with that Glenda?"

"His name's Richard. No."

Leonard picked Sinatra's picture off the floor. "I bet he was nuts about her. She could've had her pick of anyone she wanted. Remember when she came to our grad ceremony and every male teacher and every father in the gym was staring at her, offering her gum and cigarettes and rides home and . . ."

I felt sulky now. With something verging on a hangover—and Frank was going to be furious with me. "Do you think I need a shrink?"

Len shrugged. "You were pissed off before she died. Did you think you were suddenly going to get unpissed after?"

"Whatever that means," I sighed and reached for the phone, dialed into my voice mail. *You have three messages,* the computer announced. A phone company operator once told me that the computer voice is known as Marsha. Her directions to the listener are called Marsha prompts. Marsha gets under my skin in a way I can't describe. *First message,* she said. "Hi, Vivian. Listen, I'm ah . . ." and then a sigh, "I just wondered when you think you'll come get the car. Or *if* you'll come get the car. You can always sell it if you don't want it. Or sign it back over to me. Let me know when you're coming and I'll leave the keys on the kitchen table or in the mailbox or something. Okay . . ." another sigh. "I hope you're doing okay. I'm . . ." Her voice broke a moment. "Okay. Lemme know." *To erase this message,* Marsha's puckered voice explained—I deleted before she had a chance to natter on.

"Sally," I told Len. "I think she was drinking."

"Takes one to know one," he said, reevaluating Annie West's gun belt now.

Next message: "Vivian, it's Corinne. I've got a last-minute audition for you tomorrow at noon for a new series called *San Diego Sugar.* You would be reading for the part of the Blonde. There's just two lines but the scene would be with Jim Belushi. It's a fantasy sequence with a blonde and a brunette maid but only the blonde has lines. I'll e-mail the sides to you." *To save this message* . . . I hovered over the keys. It was so rare to hear from my acting agent. Marsha asked, *Are you still there?* I deleted.

Next message: "Vivian! What the hell is wrong with you? What the . . ." Frank gasped, "What the fuck are you on? You . . . *humiliated* me in front of my friends. I don't know where you are. I went by your place. I'm tired of your shit. You need your head read." Click. *End of messages.* I pressed the number-one key. *You have NO new messages,* Marsha said emphatically.

I put the phone down and watched Len watch my mother. He squinted as he held the picture at arm's length.

"Do you think I look like a slut?" I asked. Len glanced. "I mean, do you think when guys look at me they think I look like a fuck machine who can't get enough?"

He tucked his chin in a moment before replying. "Well, that's kinda what you were always going for, wasn't it?" Seeing the look on my face, his voice sped up as he tried to clarify. "You know, like a Courtney Love, kind of, fashion-slut, urban . . . Madonna the Whore–type thing. You used to *like* the word *slut*. You used to wield it like a machete or something."

I did. I do. "This is fucked up." I hugged my knees and rested my eye sockets against them. "My whole life is fucked up."

"Poor Vivian," he said with the near-genuine soothe he used when he was without sympathy. I raised my head and gazed at the scar under his left brow. With a mind reader's repartee, he added, "My father's birthday is this weekend. I gotta go out to a big family brunch in Coquitlam on Saturday."

He never flinched when he mentioned his father.

"You gonna get him something?"

He shrugged. "I might get a boxed collection of John Wayne movies. This one time when they took me with them to dinner, the chef came out from the kitchen to meet my father. Apparently he used to cook for John Wayne when Wayne came up here on fishing expeditions. He couldn't get over how much Dad looked like him."

I spun the heart in place on the rug. "Does he like John Wayne?"

"Loves him."

"Figures."

He took the heart out from under my fingers as though I was being disrespectful. I reached into the trunk for the Vegas matchbook.

"There was a piece of paper," I said, "with Annie West's address and phone number in here too."

"You told me. You left it at the apartment."

"But the number's out of service."

"Yeah." He wrapped his fingers round the heart and held it there. "It's a nice weight. And it's cool. If you were sick—" he held it to his temple "—it would be soothing."

By one in the morning, pillows, sheets and blankets were laid out on the two couches that hugged his walls and met in the corner. Our sleepovers had been this way since we were seventeen, the year Len got his first apartment. He would come home from his shift as a janitor at Ron Zalko sport club and I'd meet him there, and we'd smoke weed and watch movies, fall asleep exactly where we were.

"You think Annie West would still be alive?" I asked from my couch.

I heard his shoulders shrug against the covers.

"At the bar tonight," I said, eyes to the ceiling, "we were talking about that Bambi Hunt shit that was supposed to be going on in Vegas? That stuff never happened, you know. It was all bullshit. He made it up."

Len didn't answer.

"Do you want my mother's car?"

"Mrs. Chelsey gave me a hundred-dollar tip tonight."

I rolled onto my stomach and stared over at him. He was on his back, looking up. "Oh yeah?" I said. "You make her some special *dessert* or something?"

"She said I was dear to her. She's nice, I mean she's really beautiful and interesting. You should keep your mum's car."

I dropped my face into the pillow, breathed cotton and foam and turned my gaze to the columns of light still dancing on Len's silent stereo. "You want *my* car? I don't need two."

"A psychic told me once that I shouldn't drive, that I was a speeder and speed would be the thing that killed me."

"You're not a speeder. You're a neurotic. I want you to have my car. You want my car or not? It's old and slow."

"I guess. If she's not at that old address, the new people might know where she is."

"Would you drive down with me?"

"To California? No."

"Erin lives down there now. Right near San Anselmo, I think. Marin County. We could stay with her."

"No. Who's Erin?"

"Erin. Remember? She married that director and moved to California?"

"Oh her." He sighed.

"What?"

"She's a compulsive liar."

"She just exaggerates a little to make a good story. You take things too seriously." I rolled back to face the ceiling. "Who's Louis Prima?"

"The guy who sang 'Just a Gigolo.'"

"That was David Lee Roth."

A snort through the darkness. "Before him."

Len's phone rang and he said, "Frank, I bet."

"Don't *answer* it. I'm not here."

Pulling the blanket over my head, I listened to Len's end of the conversation. "Oh hi, Frank . . . Yeah, she's here, but she's going to sleep . . . No, I don't think I better. She's pretty emotionally, you know, ah, overrode right now . . . yeah, yeah, me too . . . Okey-doke, I'll let her know. Bye." He put the phone down.

I pulled the blanket off my face. "Thank you."

"Uh-huh." He settled back.

"*Overwrought.*"

"Whatever."

Six

~

Light eked its way through Len's batik curtains. He was still asleep on the other couch and I lay on my side, watching the frown on his face as he dreamt. He looked so young in the dim light, I wanted to reach over and smooth out the creases between his brows. He almost looked like he did the first time we ever spoke. We were in high school, grade nine.

Spare had just ended, the bell had rung and I was late as a result of sitting across the street at Tim Hortons, drinking coffee, having a smoke, picking at my nail polish. I was just sauntering back onto the school grounds, thinking about dying my hair Goth-black, when I saw Len. He was crumpled up in the courtyard near the side door of the school. I thought he'd fainted or maybe he was an epileptic like a chick in my gym glass who used to drop and wriggle fairly regularly. I became an expert at sticking a sock in her mouth so she wouldn't bite her tongue.

There was blood around his nose and lips. I crouched and touched his collar, asked him if he was okay. He sat up, holding his stomach. I remembered him now. He was part of the year-book photography-class crowd: tall, cute, a slight lisp and rumour had it, gay. I imagined that's what had happened to his face, some sort of fag punishment. I pulled a Tim Hortons napkin from my purse and kneeled beside him.

"Don't bother," he said in a rather snide tone, considering.

"Don't get pissed off with me, I'm not the one who hit ya."

"No, but one of your loser boyfriends did."

"Ah, go bugger yourself, you don't even know me. Do you want a hand or not?"

He let me haul him to his feet. "What boyfriend?" I demanded.

"Gordy Bewly," he mumbled.

My next class was gym, which I could skip. He looked pretty bad and I suppose I felt some convoluted guilt about Gordy Bewly, so I brought him back to my place to get cleaned up.

Mum was at school. Len stood at our bathroom mirror, staring at himself inches from the glass. His lip had fattened and a bruise was starting on his cheekbone. He checked his front teeth for loose connections. Gordy Bewly wasn't what I would've called a boyfriend. I'd gone out with him only once in a dating sort of scenario. Got drunk in the back of his dad's Buick on a half bottle of gin, didn't want to have sex with him so I gave him a hand job instead. We weren't buddies anymore after that, old Gordy and me. I would say I didn't have much in the way of friends at all after that evening. Turned out Gordy Bewly and Angie Alexander were going around together. As of the night before.

That about did it for my social life, which is why I had taken to taking my spares in the doughnut shop. My lunch hours were spent there too, except over lunch I had more company. Across the tables I would watch the girls flick their feathered hair, listen to them smack gum and mutter "slut" as they passed my chair.

Leonard didn't normally skip classes. His beauty and his uncertain sexual orientation had prompted my ex-friend Angie Alexander to join him in the darkroom yesterday. Before long she had her tongue in his mouth, her fingers on his belt. Len shoved her off. He knew enough to be scared of Gordy. Apparently, the bell rang and Angie stormed out, snarling, "You'll get yours, asshole."

He received a few peculiar looks around school the next morning, kids nudging each other, whispering. As he walked out for spare, he looked up from rummaging in his knapsack and Gordy Bewly sucker-punched him in the face. Twice.

"I think he was aiming for my teeth," Len said into my bathroom mirror. "My teeth are the only decent thing about my face, and I think he was trying to wreck them. Then he says, 'That's for Angie, you faggot rapist,' and knees me in the stomach."

Sitting on the side of the bathtub, I fingered the facecloth he'd bloodied. "I wouldn't've pegged you for a rapist."

"Thanks," he said and stood back a bit from his reflection.

"She probably said you groped her or something."

He glanced down at my hands as I peeled a bit of blue polish off my thumbnail. "Why do girls wear that chipped nail polish? Why don't you put it on nice if you're gonna wear it?"

I flicked my thumb's nail against my fingers. "Fag maybe but not a rapist," I said.

Len rolled over on his couch now and faced the other way. It was six in the morning and I felt more lonesome than I could ever recall. Just before I woke I dreamt that Frank was beside me on the lookout up at Cypress Mountain. Morning sun lit the water below us. It was shriekingly bright and Frank wouldn't open his eyes. I kept caressing his face, trying to get him to look at me, but his mouth and eyes were sealed. Everything jammed tight.

I wanted to feel him against my back now. Slipping out from the covers, I went into the bathroom and changed back into my clothes then tiptoed out and quietly laid my mother's things back in the trunk.

"You leaving?"

I turned to see Len watching me.

"Yeah. Thank you for not sending me packing last night."

"You going over to Frank's?"

"No." I closed the trunk. "I'll leave the keys for my car. It's in front of my building. I'll get some papers and we'll transfer it over later." He watched as I pulled on my coat and lifted the trunk. "Watch your ass around that Eunice Chelsey."

He looked away, a slight frown on his face.

"Are you pissed off at me?"

He shook his head.

"Okay," I said, "go back to sleep. I'll call you later."

The sky lightened steadily as I walked the half block home, my shoes foreign and clumsy against the soles of my feet. Unable to bear underwire so early, I'd crammed my bra in my coat pocket. Birds twittered overhead and I felt as if neighbours were peering out their drapes, assuming I had just crawled from the bottom of an orgy.

Doors, I discovered, were much easier to manage when I set the trunk down and used both hands. Inside my apartment, I called out Frank's name. No answer. I put the trunk in my hall closet and went into the bedroom. The long lump of him was sprawled centre-mattress where he generally tried to sleep whether I was there or not.

I sat down on what would have been Frank's side. His eyes were closed but he was awake all right. "I dreamt this," I said.

"What?" he grunted.

"I dreamt you wouldn't open your eyes and see me."

"Stop the world." He rolled to face the other wall. "Vivian's here."

"I'm sorry about last night. I guess I'm more stressed out than I realized and I probably shouldn't have been drinking on an empty stomach." Silence. "And then that Brian guy started talking about his Bambi shit, and that idiot girlfriend of his—I don't like that guy. He's—"

"You don't like *him*?" Frank turned over and glared at me. "Not only were you bitchy and rude but you *ditched* me without so much as a *kiss my ass!* And then you head straight for that faggot's place. To what? Piss and moan about me?"

"Of course not. I'm sorry. I don't know what got into me. I just needed to be somewhere, I don't know, neutral. I'm all screwed up right now. I'm thinking I might take off for a few days and clear my head."

"What're you talking about?" Frank sat up. "We were supposed to start our page on Brian's site in a couple days. This was your idea!"

"It was not my idea. It was yours. You said—"

"*You* said. *Shit, we could fuck at home and make better money than all our acting jobs combined,*" he mimicked me. "*We could wear masks and shoot it in my bedroom. Who'd know?*"

"My mother just died."

He stared down at the mattress and fidgeted with the sheet.

"I want to drive down south and try to find this friend of hers."

Another silence. Then, "Down south? What does that mean?"

"I have an address in California. But the phone number doesn't work."

He looked at me. "Are you seeing someone?"

"No. For chrissake." I took a calming breath and lowered my voice. "I need to do this. Please." I touched his chest and he swatted my hand away.

He shook his head. "I don't get you. You never wanted anything to do with your mother. You acted as if you didn't even *like* her. And now suddenly you're pushing me away and you're on some kind of *quest*."

"I'm not pushing you away. I just need a couple days." I reached out again to his stubbly cheek. When he let my fingers stay, I moved in and kissed along his jaw and down his neck. As I reached his chest, his hand came up and stroked my hair. I moved down his stomach and under the covers.

Two hours later, as Frank slept behind me, his arms around my waist, the alarm sounded. I lay awake wondering if there were women somewhere in the world capable of sleeping with their bodies squeezed like this, wrung like chicken necks. I slapped the snooze button. His breath still snarling in a near snore, I could feel him fully alert at my tailbone. He put a hand to his mouth and sleepily licked his fingers. It was his usual ritual of transferring his saliva to my cunt in order to grease the wheels for his morning entrance, but for the first time in the two years we'd been together, the sound of spittle slopping against his fingers repelled me. He reached between my thighs and ran his wet fingers along the folds of me and it was everything I could do to keep from slamming my elbow back as he slipped inside. I felt raw. My fists clenched. Morning hormones surging, it was only a couple minutes before he groaned behind me.

The alarm rang out again and I smacked it silent. Frank kissed my shoulder, reached round to grope me. I crossed my thighs. "Someone needs a shave," he teased, patting my pubes. I chewed a ragged edge of my fingernail. He reached for my wrist and pulled my hand away from my mouth. "And what's with the nail-biting? You used to have such nice long ones and they felt so good," he growled. "Now look at 'em. Like you've been busting rocks at the quarry." He grinned and turned to get out of bed. "Have to get you some like Sienna's."

I rolled onto my back and watched him pull his underwear on, tried to figure out why I suddenly wanted to kick his balls. "Are you wrangling today?"

"Yes ma'am. Gotta be out at Vancouver Film Studios again."

"With the kids?"

"No, same as yesterday. That fashion-show thing—forty lingerie models." Frank did up his belt. "And they're all, like, seventeen, eighteen years old," he added incredulously. I recalled the squealing I'd heard in the background when he called the day before. "One of them was fifteen—she still has braces on her teeth! The grips had their hands in their pockets all day."

"Very nice," I muttered.

He pulled his wrinkled shirt on over his tee, swatted my ass through the quilt and said, "What're you gonna do today?"

I shrugged. "Might get my mother's car."

"You should sell it and we'll get a really good camera." He grabbed his jacket. "We'll probably do at least fourteen hours today. I'll call you later."

When Frank locked the door behind him, I felt as though a boulder had been rolled in front of my cave. I reached for the phone and dialed directly into the voice mail at my mother's so as to avoid actual contact, and left a message asking Sally to go ahead and leave the keys out for me.

Closing my eyes, I tried to sleep some more. An hour of tossing later, I got up, had a shower and got dressed. I went to my closet, hauled out a canvas bag and stuffed in a few things. In the bathroom I threw in makeup and toiletries and wondered how long it would take to drive to Marin County. Probably two days. It would be good to see Erin.

I rooted around the bedroom for my address book and dialed her number. The answering machine picked up. Her husband's voice suggested I leave a message. I was coming their way, I told them, and left my cell number in hopes she would call back and invite me to stay. They probably had a pretty swell spread down there: lots of bedrooms and maids, long stairwells, a pool. Erin could smell money like a shark could scent blood.

I cabbed over to my mother's. A For Sale sign stuck out of the front lawn. Sally's Jeep was gone so I slipped inside, grabbed the registration papers and keys.

The interior still had new-car scent. Mum had only bought it about a year and a half ago, decided to treat herself to something sporty: a red Toyota convertible. I think I'd ridden in it twice.

Back at my place I loaded up the car with the trunk and my bag, then sat at my kitchen table and composed a note to Frank explaining that I'd decided to leave sooner so that I could be back sooner. I apologized. I said I would call him from the motel that night.

Plates of guilt shifted inside. Not because I was leaving but because this note felt fake. I added that I loved him and scribbled X's and O's and felt worse for it.

On the way out of town, I stopped at the agency to pick up a cheque for some extra work I'd done on an American cell phone commercial. The beauty of commercial extra work is that now and then a production company will film more than one ad on a given day. In this particular case they shot four spots and I was paid a separate day for each. All in U.S. funds.

Going by the bank, I took out five hundred in cash and deposited the rest. I wouldn't tell Frank about the windfall. I just needed to get the hell out of town and not think about him or Brian or Sienna or camera equipment. Walking back to the car, I passed a bookstore and stopped dead. Smack in the middle of the window was *Extravagance: Too Many Rats in the Pack*. I bent closer to the pane. A blurb along the bottom said, "A compelling biography of the excesses and intrigues that bound Las Vegas, New York and the White House." I went inside and snatched a copy off the shelf. Fanning the pages, those names fluttered back at me: Giancana, Rosselli, Kennedy, Lawford, Sinatra. I flipped to the back and searched the index. No Celia Dare. I put the book down on the sales counter anyway, along with a guide to California.

On the other side of the Peace Arch border, I went into a gas station, filled up and bought sandwiches, apples, protein bars, water and lighter fluid. I wanted to get as far as possible as fast as possible and I damn well wasn't about to stop at some highway Denny's. I picked up salt-and-vinegar chips and saw Sienna's skinny little body, heard her squeaky caution regarding a fit form from all angles and dropped the bag back on the shelf.

It looked like rain so I put the top up.

Driving her car, after my rickety old beast, was like riding a plush cloud. New shocks absorbed every bump and road ridge and, with the roof up now, it was as though I were in a cocoon. I turned on the radio. Her classical-music station filled the space and I searched for something a little more palatable. Everything irritated me though and I snapped the radio off.

As I rolled along past dense evergreens, the sun shone silver behind dark clouds and brought a luminous green to the trees in the distance. The bay water glowed like the front of a Christian greeting card.

I snapped the radio back on, hunting for the classical. Maybe I should listen to it, maybe it would soothe me the way it did her. I pressed the search button and when the static cleared, Dean Martin sang "Return to Me" in both English and Italian.

Normally the sound of that tired old man would send me screaming, but now, all of a sudden, I saw him at a table with my mother. Like those paintings with James Dean, Marilyn, Bogey and Elvis, only I'd imagined Sammy, Dino and Frank in a diner with Celia Dare. The four of them sat at a table. Peter Lawford leaned back at the counter.

I bit into a sandwich as Rosemary Clooney got into my back seat and crooned "Come On-A My House." Eventually she moved over for Dinah Washington and that old carny, Peggy Lee.

The farther I got from bigger towns the less music I could find. Often I was stuck with nothing but a preacher braying on about Judgment Day. Somewhere between Portland and Eugene, Oregon, the Reverend Arnie Somebody-or-other started in with a quotation from Saint Paul—*You who are wives, be submissive to your husbands*—and shot me right back to a pew in the Lifeline Christian Assembly with my mother.

We weren't churchgoers for long and, as with most of our early experiments, this one took place sometime in the interim that Sally was gone. We had sold the old house and moved to Kitsilano. School was out for summer and I suppose Josie was bored or lonesome. Church, she said, over dinner one night, would bring us into the community.

"But you don't like communities," I reminded her.

"Well, I'm trying, okay?"

I was too old for Lifeline's nursery school but not old enough to have any interest in an hour of one man's drone. I squirmed. I doodled on the church bulletin and tried, now and then, to pass Mum notes.

The first Sunday after school was back in session, I brought my homework. The minister took the form of Muzak as I scratched away in my notebook. Until I glanced over at Mum.

Her lips were a pursed rip across her face. I looked to the minister.

" . . . Now when Paul said, *Wives be submissive to your husbands*," he explained, "this was the most caring and wonderful thing he could have told you ladies." He went on to explain that, as women of the seventies, wives were in more danger than ever before. Feminists, abortionists and homosexuals wanted nothing better than to unravel the fabric of the family but we should all guard against this. "Have we not all seen these strident feminists become remarkably submissive when the right—or even the wrong—man comes into their life? Women long for—"

"Bullshit!" my mother burst like a cork. Electricity zigzagged across my ribs. Nobody turned. In my mind, the word had exploded, had echoed through the halls of the universe but nobody so much as glanced and I realized it had actually been a whisper. I watched her cross and uncross her legs until it seemed she might hyperventilate. Finally she grabbed her purse and pulled me up the aisle with her.

"My Duo-Tang," I yipped as it hit the floor. *Somebody* had to say something out loud.

"Male chauvinist pig," she breathed as she pulled me along. Billie Jean King had just been on the cover of *Time*, a photograph of her presenting Bobby Riggs with a piglet prior to their much-hyped Battle of the Sexes tennis match. The symbolism had been clearly explained to me.

We always sat fairly close to the back but I hoped we were at least a bit spectacular in our exit. All was quiet. The minister droned on as though nothing had happened. Still, I felt it was a minor display. I was glad I'd worn my canary-yellow dress.

Once we got out the front doors, she broke into a trot, her head down and I bellowed *Bullshit!* into the air. She shushed me but her frown eased into a careful smile.

It was coming up on ten o'clock by the time I drove into Redding, California. After eleven hours of driving, it was about ten degrees warmer than home. I had wanted to find myself a place to sleep before dark, but flying down the I-5 had eased something in me and I couldn't bring myself to stop.

Cruising along Redding's main drag, motels and lighted signs with burnt-out bulbs screamed out deals. A place made to pass through. I stopped for gas and as I attempted to get back on the main street, I went the wrong way and found myself back on the highway. I swung off and tried a couple different exits but that dingy strip of insistently cheap motels had disappeared. I finally came upon an Econo-Lodge and pulled in there instead.

There were a few empty spots in the parking lot, which I took to mean there might be space in the motel. In the tiny glassed-in reception area, a middle-aged wiry guy gave me a peculiar smile as I came in, one that made me feel as though a stranger had just asked if I'd like a Pap test. *He's giving me the fish eye,* I thought as some Internet mobster site came to mind. *Teddy the Ghost had hooded fish eyes. Or was it Sam Giancana? Who cares,* I thought. *This guy's no mobster. Girls like me make old men like him scared; they like to look, but tight jeans and big-heeled boots send them scurrying for cover.*

I told him I'd like a room and he asked if I was alone. I wouldn't normally have made much of that question, but now something in me clenched and receded. Maybe crossing the border had softened my spine a little. I stuttered slightly when asking the rate of his least expensive room.

"$49.95," he said, "unless you got Triple A."

I paused. "Oh yeah, let me just see where I put my card." Mum was a member. I wondered if she could have left her card in the glove box.

"That's okay." His eyes ran down the length of my hair. "I trust you—$44.95."

Snapping my wallet shut, I dropped it back in my purse. *I trust you,* I sneered inside. Was that some kind of crack?

He slid a reservation card across the counter. "Smoking or non?"

"Smoking." I wondered if I should say non. Maybe smoking wouldn't sound tough to him, maybe it would sound slutty. Maybe he was giving me a deal because he thought he was going to get some. "Actually, did I say smoking? I meant non. I just quit."

He took the card back. "There's only a smoking left. Lotta times people don't smoke in them. Why don't I show you the room and you can decide for yourself."

He came out from behind the desk and gave me the once-over, boots to boobs, as he walked out the door, leading me past the tiny fenced-in swimming pool to the deepest darkest end of the motel.

The light above the room was burnt out. He muttered that he'd have to get that fixed as he fumbled with his key. Stepping back, I inched closer to the light from an adjacent door.

As the vacant room opened, a swampful of stale smoke wallowed over us. "Hang on, now, where's the light?" He worked at the switch but nothing happened. "What the *hell* . . ." and he moved inside. I stayed put. He poked the upper half of his body back out.

"I think that's a bit too smoky for me. Thanks, though."

"Well, hang on, ah, y'know, there's a king-size room. It's on the other side above the office. That's nonsmoking. But it's more expensive too."

"Oh. Well, no, I'd better not." I backed up another step.

"I'll show you. It's right above the office. Just gotta check a fuse, I'll meet you there."

Wandering over on my own, I wondered if I should bolt. I felt out of my element. It occurred to me that I'd never stayed in a motel without a guy before.

Oh don't be such a pussy, I thought. *Just don't go inside the room with him.* Besides, the motel was almost full and if I screamed, someone would hear me. I tried to feel my inner swagger, the kind that Frank claimed made me look like a biker chick. Frank said it was scary. He said it turned him on too. I cursed Frank as I stumbled on the first step up to the room.

The manager was outside when I reached the top. Opening the door, he stepped in and it struck me to play this all very *Erin*. My friend Erin, the money shark, would have charmed him at a cool arm's length, the way she did mechanics, stockbrokers and, apparently, commercial directors. "Always play the elegant virgin," she used to say. "Until you get them into bed, then fuck their brains out."

Walking around the room, he pointed out the king-size bed and reminded me that they all had television and air conditioning. "Costs a little more though."

I stayed in the doorway and cooked up a polite look of graciousness. "Oh yes, it feels much *safer* than the other room too." The safer bit came from an old boyfriend who once told me that the most depressing thing a girl said to him in high school was, *I feel safe with you.*

"The king-size ones are $59.99," the manager said.

That's like, eighty bucks Canadian. For this flea bag? "Oh dear," I said. "Well, thank you so much for showing it to me but I'm on a bit of a budget this trip."

"What about a coupon? They got them in those tourist magazines—I probably have one downstairs."

"Oh! I would really appreciate that." I was almost starting to enjoy myself.

"I don't do it for everyone, you know."

"Well, *thank you*. So much."

He nodded back, a bit bashfully.

As we came through the glass door, into the office, he commented, "Smells in here too."

"Does it?" I sniffed the air.

"It's *those* people," he shrugged over his shoulder. I looked past him to a door leading into an apartment. The muffled sounds of a television came through. "The people who own the place are *East Indians*."

I filled out the rest of my reservation card. He glared at the apartment door then rifled through some reservation cards and surreptitiously ripped a coupon off.

"Is that going to be okay?" I asked. "Taking their coupon?"

"S'an old one," he growled and stapled *Econo-Lodge $38.99* to my card, mentioning again what the room was supposed to cost.

I gave him the winsome grin Erin always used when a bartender slid her a free drink, and he handed me a key. I headed out to the car, grabbed my suitcase and clomped upstairs as he watched through the window. I went back down for the trunk. He watched.

In the room I locked the door. My hands shook a little. I sat down and ripped open the last protein bar and took a slug of bottled water.

What if he figured he should get something extra for a twenty-one dollar discount? "That's almost thirty Canadian," I observed out loud. I put the protein bar between my teeth, got up and shoved a table against the door. Dragging a second table over too, I arranged them for maximum weight and blockability.

I sat on the bed and turned on the TV, flicked from channel to channel until I heard a laugh track. I had a sudden longing for Frank and hauled the phone onto the bed.

No answer at my place. I called his. No answer. I called his cell and left a message telling him where I was and that I missed him, that I was sorry I'd left without saying goodbye but I just . . . and I ran out of words. I wasn't sorry really, not for leaving, more for being alone.

Standing at the window, I peered down toward the office. It was almost eleven. The fish-eyed manager was gone and a plump brown woman in a sari had taken his place. My shoulders loosened. I went back into my food bag, pulled the lighter fluid from the bottom and set it in on the nightstand. Then I rifled in my mother's trunk until I found her lighter with the sapphire stones. Pulling the lighter apart, I opened the fluid and filled it up. I jerked my thumb across the striking wheel a couple times until the flame billowed.

Checking the office again, I saw that the Indian woman was still stationed there so I pulled the tables back, went out on the step and lit a cigarette with *The Flames of Celia Dare*. Turning it over in my hand, I pictured her out on a fire escape somewhere, her blonde hair swept back, her long dancer's legs slipping out of a white chenille housecoat, her feet bare—my mother all mixed up with an old photograph I once saw of Monroe smoking on a balcony.

Back inside, I shoved the tables against the door again, pulled off my jeans and sat on the bed in my thong and T-shirt. I looked down at the crop of stubbly black hairs coming in on either side of my bikini line. *Somebody needs a shave.* I pulled the top of my underpants out and looked down: a swath of regrowth. Normally it would be clean-shaven but for a tiny landing strip down the middle. Frank liked it like that. Or for a change, a Hitler moustache. When it came to his own pubes, he didn't even bother trimming.

I would've killed for a bottle of something forty proof right then. I pulled off my T-shirt and underwear, climbed under the covers. Cracking open *Extravagance: Too Many Rats in the Pack*, I sank into a biography that read more like a true-crime novel. Deep into the night, I wandered around Vegas, saw suitcases of cash at the Sands, listened to Sinatra and his pack and their smart-ass repartee echo from Vegas to Miami, watched Marilyn swill back pills with bottles of vodka, sat with Judy Campbell on the side of a hotel bathtub in New York as John Kennedy and Giancana talked business in the main room, gossiped about their all-night parties and fixed elections, and spied on Rosselli and the CIA as they schemed to fix Fidel.

It was the sound of the door crashing open that woke me: my platinum-blonde mother and my boyfriend, drunk, entwined, falling down on the tables in a crack of laughter. Josie's hair flipped to black as her head lolled off the table's edge; her giddy eyes met mine. Her leg slipped bare from the slit of her red satin gown. From between her thighs, Frank said, "I thought you said it was a secret." My mother howled like a maniac, lifted her head to him, turning her hair platinum once more as she showed him her penis.

"Bullshit!" I hollered and bolted up to see them fade into coloured sprinkles.

The door was closed, still blocked by tables. I stared around the room. 8:33 a.m.

I held out my hands and watched them tremble in the grey light. My Frank, Frank Sinatra. Reaching for the nightstand, I turned on my cell. No calls. I tried Erin's number again and got voice mail.

"Hello, you guys. It's Vivian calling with a progress update—I'm already in Redding and I'll probably be in your neck of the woods by tonight. Call my cell when you get a chance. I'd love to get together." I left the number once more.

I turned on the shower and stared in the mirror at the brassy glare of my hair straggling down over my nipples. In the tub I pulled the curtain across and let piping water pummel my face as though it might sculpt me a new one.

It was around three in the afternoon when I reached San Anselmo, which looked like an average American small town: trees, a few hills, fast food and strip malls. The air was dry and warmer by another seven or eight degrees. With Annie West's address in hand, I stopped at a gas station for directions.

Coming into a cul-de-sac at the end of Hampton Avenue a few minutes later, I pulled up in front of number twenty-three. In the vanity mirror I took out my lipstick and slid burgundy across my mouth. A shudder took me. I could see my mother in this car checking her own face. I threw the lipstick back in my bag.

Opening the door, my hair caught in my armpit and I yanked it free. It felt scraggly. I felt scraggly. I went back into my purse and rooted for a scrunchy. As I flipped my mop into a topknot, two small blonde children tore along the side of 23 Hampton Avenue out to the front lawn. They looked four or five years old.

A woman's playful voice called after them as I walked toward the house. "You little rats should come back here!" Her arms swung like a young girl's but she was likely forty-something. She saw me then and said hello as she scooped up one tow-headed kid, and squeezed him while the other hugged her thigh.

"Hey," I said. "I'm looking for a woman who used to live here. Annie West?"

"Is she a cowgirl?" the girl on the ground inquired.

"Sort of," I told her. "Cute kids," I said to the woman. "Are they yours?"

"Nope. Not my rats, are you?" The screen door opened and another woman stepped out. "Hello?"

"That's my sister," the woman near me announced. "My sister, Dodi."

"That's my mummy-Dodi," the girl said and pogo-hopped over to the steps as Dodi paused. "We were being rats, Mummy," she said and wriggled her nose.

"Can I help you?" Dodi called, pulling off brown-greased rubber gloves and sticking them in her apron pocket as she came closer.

"Maybe," I said. I took the address out of my back pocket and held it out to her. "I'm trying to find a friend who used to live here. Annie West?"

She turned the paper over and handed it back as she glanced at my licence plate. "You from Canada? That's pretty country up there."

"Annie West's a cowgirl!" the little girl shrieked.

"Ahh, lemme think. Sorry, I've been cleaning the oven and I've got a headful of fumes. I've got a few old addresses from people who wanted their mail forwarded . . ."

The girl made rat faces into her stomach, scratching her belly until her mother blurted, "Stop!" Dodi turned to her sister. "Lucy, take them to play out back."

Lucy told the kids it was time for another rat jamboree and they all squeaked their way alongside the house.

"You wanna come inside and I'll see what I can dig up?"

We walked up the steps past a tricycle whose front wheel was lodged between the teeth of Dodi's railing, its back wheels hanging.

In the hall I tripped over toys strewn around as she nimbly missed the kids' stuff only to be caught by a pair of men's shoes.

"Jesus crap," she muttered, kicking them out of her way. "If he wasn't paying rent . . ."

In the kitchen, the oven door splayed open and there were dishes piled in the sink. The tap dripped one solemn drop at a time. "Lemme think." She closed her eyes. The kids and their aunt Lucy squawked from the yard. Dodi whispered for them to shut their traps. "I hope you use good birth control," she said then—"I know where it is." She hauled a chair over, reached above the refrigerator and pulled out a plastic bag of papers before she jumped down.

She dumped the bag, mumbling, "No . . . no . . . not that," as she flipped through scraps. "They get passed on from tenant to—here's another bugger that's got all kinds of bill collectors after him. Doesn't even live *there* anymore." She crumpled and tossed him toward the garbage. She flipped the pile and started from the bottom. "Oh, what's this, West? S'at what you said? Marianne West?"

"Yeah, that's it, I think."

"Marianne West, 222 Beresford Street, Vallejo. Not far." She handed me the yellowed scrap. "May as well take that with you. First one who's ever come looking for her."

"Thank you. I really appreciate your trouble." Same words but this time I meant it.

Kids screamed out back again. "Oh Jesus crap," Dodi said. "I'd like to chat with you some more but those idiot kids take after their father and Lucy's not much brighter."

"That's okay. I'll just see myself out."

Back in the car, I shivered, imagining my hands in greasy gloves, dishes to the ceiling, tripping over Frank's shoes while the fruit of my loins wailed their gullets raw. I threw the car in drive.

Next door to 222 Beresford Street, a woman worked a spade into the earth under her front window, weeding. I pushed the buzzer and tried to breathe away butterflies.

"They're not home." It was the gardener. About the age I imagined Annie would be, she wore what looked like a thick auburn wig under her straw hat.

I came back down the steps. "You know them?"

She stood. "The Laytons—is that who you're looking for?"

"Annie West doesn't live here anymore?"

"Oh! You're looking for Annie? You're not her daughter, are you?" She came toward me. She wore moulded rubber gardening shoes. I'd seen them displayed outside hardware stores but I'd never seen them on actual feet before.

"No. Just a family friend."

"What am I saying? You would know she wasn't here anymore if you were her daughter. I never did meet her daughter. I guess I was meaning a *friend* of her daughter's. Last I heard she was living in New York somewhere with a nice fancy job."

"Annie?"

"Her daughter. My name is Eva. I'm a friend of Annie's. Or Marianne. Some people call her Marianne. I've got a forwarding address for her if you'd like. She's in Danaville, half hour or so south—oh goodness, I shouldn't be offering out her address to strangers. Not with the IRS, are you?" she chortled.

"Annie was friends with my mother a few years back."

"I miss Annie. We used to have coffee now and then but we haven't done that in some time. She doesn't like to talk on the phone."

We looked at one another a moment with awkward smiles until she finally said, "Why don't I get my address book."

I didn't actually get going for another twenty minutes. Eva liked to talk. She seemed all alone out here but, after a while, I discovered her husband was inside watching golf on television.

Frank doesn't watch sports, I reminded myself. Not at home.

Eventually I pried myself off her stoop and headed south.

By the time I'd turned up Annie's road, the butterflies were back with a vengeance.

As the road wound into another cul-de-sac, there, in the round, sat an ambulance, emergency lights blazing in the sunlight.

Neighbours stood on the sidewalk and lawns, all seniors. I came toward them as paramedics eased a stretcher into the back.

The ambulance doors shut. It was her. I stared as it rolled away.

"Excuse me," I said. "Was that Annie West? In that ambulance?"

A woman shook her head then looked down at the road.

"Marianne West?" I repeated, pointing weakly in the direction of the ambulance.

"Yes?" a second woman said.

"Yes?" I looked at her.

"What?"

"That—are *you* Annie West?"

"Yes."

"Oh! I was just—" Grasshoppers jumped in my throat. "You're Annie West!"

She smiled at me as though I were simple. Or she was. Her shoulder-length curls were almost completely white, the front pulled back in a barrette. I guessed her to be in her mid-seventies, one of the youngest on the block from the looks of her neighbours.

"Were you at one time acquainted with a woman named Celia Dare?"

West's face dropped. "Nope. Sorry." She turned and walked away and had made it to the steps of a small pink house before I started after her. "Ann—Mrs. West. Wait!"

The screen door thwacked behind her. Her front door slammed, followed by the sound of locks snapping into place.

Behind me the seniors stared. *What the fuck?* I grumbled. *Did she owe you money or what?* I opened the screen and trotted my knuckles against the door, politely as possible. No response. I peered into the lace curtain, hoping to catch some movement. All was quiet. I rang the doorbell. Nothing. Christ, maybe she's senile, I thought, let the screen clack shut and made my way around back.

A rock garden with small bursts of colour coming through

here and there, a patch of grass with a set of patio furniture and a chain-link fence.

It was nearly five o'clock.

Maybe it was that ambulance that did it. Smelled like death to her or something. Maybe she just needs some time to absorb. I checked my cell for calls. Nothing. I'd have to shell out for another motel. Closing my eyes against the sun, I breathed warm dry air. This town was too hot for jeans.

Seven

~

MAYBE I SHOULD HUNT FOR A TOURIST CENTRE, I THOUGHT, GET my own coupon so I won't have to pile tables against my door.

I parked on the town's main strip. There had been nothing in my stomach since breakfast. Looking across the street at the Avalon Bistro, it struck me that I had never gone to dinner by myself. My cell phone rang.

"Hello?"

"Yeah, hi. Is that Vivian? This is George MacIntyre. You called here looking for Marcella? Excuse me: *Erin*. She goes by Marcella now. And she doesn't live here anymore."

Shit. "Oh. Is she back in Vancouver?"

"No. She's in San Francisco. You want the number? And if you do," he added in a sardonic singsong voice, "you better watch your wallet."

I chewed off some fingernail and watched people pass my car, nipping into little shops, talking to one another on the street as though the whole world were on a first-name basis. There was hardly a soul under fifty.

Into my silence, he said, "I just think people should know what she's capable of."

"Ah . . . did you say *Marcella*? I haven't talked to her in—well, hardly since you guys got married. I guess things didn't work out."

"You might say that. Perhaps if you get hold of her you

might ask her how it felt to drain my insurance policy while I was on the brink of death in the hospital. Tell her she's not going to get another *cent* out of me and if I have it my way, she'll get her ass deported."

"Oh. Ah . . . let me get a pen. Just a second." I copied down Erin's number. "Okay. George. I'm sorry things didn't . . . I hope you're feeling better."

I dialed Erin and voice mail picked up. "Hi . . ." I paused. "Kiddo. It's Vivian. Hey, I'm in California, not far from you, and I wondered if you might want to get together over a drink and catch up." I left my number and got out of the car. Looking up and down the block, I couldn't even spot a fast-food joint. I wandered down the sidewalk. Maybe I should go see if I can find a motel with a kitchenette, I thought, and stopped at the window of a second-hand bookstore.

The bell jangled overhead as I entered. The guy behind the desk had hair the colour of spent coal and wore steel-rimmed glasses. He kept his head in a book. Clearing my throat, I asked if he had anything that dealt with mobsters and politicians in the early sixties.

He settled his gaze on me three or four seconds. "Non-fiction?" he asked in a distant flat tone. His own book appeared to be on beekeeping.

"Yeah. The whole sixties . . . entertainer / political / organized-crime crossover, I guess. And anything to do with stripteasers from that era? Have you heard of Judy Campbell?"

He rose, opening like a mechanical flower, and led me down an aisle. "Judy, Judy, Judy," he said in a corpsey attempt at Cary Grant. "She married," he added and pulled a tattered blue hardcover entitled *Judith Exner: My Story.* Between her name and the title, was a quotation: "I knew them when the dream of Camelot was real—Jack Kennedy, Frank Sinatra, Sam Giancana, and John Rosselli." He pulled a memoir of Tempest Storm, *The Last Superstar of Burlesque.* For his next trick he pointed out a celebrity biography section, two shelves of mafia books, and three of Kennedys.

I put Campbell Exner under my arm and slid *The Chic Mafioso* off the shelf. A book on John Rosselli. His name was spelled differently everywhere I looked. Black-and-white shots of the man they called the Silver Fox were in the centre of the book along with his known cohorts. Flipping to the index, I scanned down the D's and found *Dare, Celia* and a single page notation. My stomach lurched. I flipped madly to page 229, scanning the words for Dare. " . . . *by the end of 1967, the FBI had begun targeting not only Rosselli's friends but any and all of his sexual conquests including Vegas showgirl Maggie Gale and stripper Celia Dare who had come under scrutiny as a result of a reputed romance with Senator Robert F. Kennedy. According to sources in New York, Dare was subpoenaed and subsequently driven underground by the fear of testifying against Rosselli, her sometime lover and benefactor.*"

I leaned back against the shelf and reread the passage twice before I added *The Chic Mafioso* to my armpit. Another book caught my eye: *Mob Wife.* I flipped it open to find it was a memoir, the woman's own story "as told to" a journalist. This one would come too.

I paid for the books and drove off to hunt for a motel.

My pad for the night had a queen-size bed and a kitchenette. All rooms opened out to a cool blue pool about the length of three cars end to end. Sixty-five bucks. I didn't dicker this time, just tossed my card down and signed.

Closing the door, I heaved my suitcase onto the bed, unzipped and pulled out a pair of shorts and a clean T-shirt. The trunk sat in the corner. I went into the bathroom and turned on the shower. My hair was still up in the topknot. Like something that got dragged out of Nashville, it mushroomed around my skull, bits slipping down from my temples and jaw and down the back of my neck.

I kicked off my boots, tossed my T-shirt and bra and tugged off my jeans. Tomorrow I will get a sundress, I vowed. My thong yanked at the crack of me, all the cracks of me, and I kicked it into the pile at my feet. Heat like this, in my opinion, dictates that nothing should be wedged between the cheeks of one's ass. I got into the shower and soaped off the day.

Back in the main room, I opened the door to let in some air and flopped on the bed. There was a message on my cell from my acting agent. "Vivian, it's Corinne. If you're not going to an audition, I'd appreciate a phone call. Also, you should know that I've decided to cut back my roster. So you'll need to find new representation. Good luck."

I took the cell from my ear and stared at it. Snapping it closed, I reached for the hotel phone and called Frank. His line went to voice mail. "Hey, it's me," I said. "I'm in California, um, about forty minutes outside San Francisco, I think. Just wondering how you are. I haven't heard from you. I . . . um . . ." I picked at a hangnail. "I found that lady I was looking for. She wasn't very friendly. But I'm going to try her again tomorrow. So, I'm just hanging out in a motel. Erin split up with her husband. Sounds like it was messy . . . Well, I miss you." A fat pause followed. I was lonesome, but in truth, I didn't know what for. "Call me."

I piled up the pillows and broke open *Mob Wife*. It was odd to read "I" and know it was a woman. Everything I'd seen so far had said *she*. "The woman formerly known as *Conquest*," I murmured. She wrote about running away from home at fifteen, heading for New York to be near the action, going on dates with cops and gangsters both, dining and dancing at the Copacabana, the Boom Boom Room and acting as a beard for mobsters at business dinners. Her side of the story.

After a couple hours, I put down the book, wandered to the door and stood in the frame, looking outside thinking of mob bars in Little Italy and Miami. The motel was quiet, a few chaise lounges around the pool but no one in them. A door opened two rooms to the right of me and I heard a woman's laughter and running water. A man called back as if over a crowd, "Why don't we have ourselves a cocktail before we start dinner." The water stopped.

"I'm on it, hon. Just adding a few more ice cubes and the strawberries."

A loud crunch and whirr followed.

Blender drinks. I mentally licked my chops.

The whirring stopped. Foot-slaps against the pavement. I looked over to see a man in his late fifties, thick rubber flip-flops on his feet, staring at the pool. He patted his broad chest then stretched his arms, fingers scratching the air, turned his head and drawled, long and Southern, "Get on out here, darlin', it's beautiful. Must be eighty degrees still."

I bet it wasn't even fifteen degrees in Vancouver. Leaning in my doorway, I rubbed a bare foot over my prickly shin-skin trying to figure what 15 Celsius would be in Fahrenheit, when Darlin' herself came out, a tall blender-container of frozen drinks in one hand and two motel drinking glasses in the other. She looked a few years younger than he was with red curly hair to her shoulders and an ankle-length sleeveless dress, slit up both calves to the knee.

"Honey, can you take this and I'll get us some towels to sit on." Her drawl was prettier than his.

"I certainly will, my darlin'." He took it all off her hands.

I wished someone would call me Darlin', and decided to head for the store, get some tequila and frozen strawberries of my own before the sun went down.

Shading my eyes, I squinted toward Honey and Darlin' on the other side of the pool as they drank and gazed through the chain-link fence across the highway to the setting sun. "Excuse me, sorry to bother you." Both heads turned. "Do you recall which way the supermarket is?"

"Honey?" Darlin' said.

"I believe it's to your right as you come out the parkin' lot."

"Are you fixin' to get yourself some dinner?" Darlin' asked.

"Yeah, I think it's about that time." I returned her smile and started off. "Thanks."

"Excuse me, you're not dinin' alone, are you?"

"Yes, I am. Don't worry, I'm fine."

"Would you like to join us? Abe and I just bought a whole *heap* of food—do you like chicken? We'd love the company, wouldn't we, Abe?"

Abe nodded. "That's the joy in travelling, all the folks you meet."

"I wouldn't want to trouble you."

"Nonsense, we'd *love* it." Her voice jumped high on love. "I'm Charlene and this is Abe." We shook hands. Charlene gave a splashy grin and blinked up a moment before she gently asked what my name was.

"Oh! Ha!" I slapped fingers to my forehead. "Vivian."

Charlene suggested I join them in a daiquiri while the sun set and I ran to get a glass and a towel from my bathroom.

As I parked my lounger on Charlene's side, she took my glass and poured. "Look at that big mess a'yellow hair, Vivian. You look like a sweet little buttercup."

Buttercup. Her southern accent made me shy. I felt as if she was going to spout down-home wisdom any second, tell me she saw through me like a possum does darkness or something.

"Here you go," she said. "Abe and I are having a little cele-bration tonight, so there's lots where this came from."

I lay back, the relief of icy berries and rum in my mouth. "What are you celebrating?"

"Oh, a little adversity."

I smiled into my glass. "I'd never be sober again . . ."

"S'all you can do sometimes," Charlene said, laying her head back. "Our motorhome broke down not far from here. But that's okay. The mechanics promised her to us by morn-ing."

"We're gonna concentrate on the right-now instead," Abe said. "A daiquiri, a sunset and we're happier than gophers in soft dirt." He raised his glass to me.

"Where are you from, Vivian?" Charlene asked.

"Vancouver."

"Canada?"

"Yeah."

"Vancouver's real beautiful, I hear."

Abe grunted, adding, "Get some real frog-stranglers up there, don'tcha? Like Seattle."

"S'cuse me?"

Charlene translated. "It rains a lot?"

"Oh! Yeah, we strangle frogs all the time."

We all three laughed and then they asked where I was heading and what I did up in Canada.

"That's a tough business any way you slice it," Charlene said. "We have a friend who's an actress in a Christian soap opera and she's getting somewhat disenchanted herself. Everything comes down to ratings and sponsors."

"Hmm." I stared into the orange sunlight. "I went to church with my mother when I was a kid and it seemed like there was a built-in market for Christian bands and books and movies. Surprised they even have to worry about ratings."

Abe looked around Charlene at me again. "Which church did you go to?"

"Lifeline Christian Assembly."

"What sort of church is that?" he asked. "Pentecostal?"

"Just basic evangelical I guess."

Abe set down his glass and reached into his shorts for his wallet. "This is what we do." He handed over a peach-coloured business card, which Charlene passed on to me.

Christian Ministry Center
Pastor: Arnold ("Abe") Abraham
Gathering of God Church
10th & Jones, Bartle, California
Services: Sunday at 6:00 p.m.

"We've been settled in Bartle a little while now, but before that we were on the road two years, taking God's word to the streets. We travelled and listened to God until He said it was time to go on home."

Bullshit! I heard my mother yell inside my head. "You guys don't speak in tongues, do you?"

"We have prayer in tongues in our church," Abe said.

Charlene chimed in. "There's two different kinds of tongues: prayer in tongues, which God just gives you the words for. God understands your problems and puts the holy words—

a sort of gibberish—right in you so it's as if your prayer comes straight from the Lord. The other type is a more holy language and sometimes there's someone there to interpret. If not, you're supposed to keep the words to yourself."

I mulled that over. "Don't they say if there's no interpreter in the room then it's the devil talking through you?" Erin had told me this years ago—she came from a long line of Bible-thumpers.

Their heads shook in dismay.

"That's not in the Bible," Abe said. "Some churches believe you're not born-again without tongues but that's not in the Bible either. Paul said there will be times for tongues and times not. Paul told a story of foreigners and God's intervention so that they could understand one another. That's where the word *babble* comes from."

"Oh, right . . ." I said, thinking still of Erin. "A friend of mine, her father was the pastor of a Pentecostal church, and when she was a teenager, she felt this intense pressure to speak in tongues. Everyone said she wasn't full of the Holy Spirit until she did so she finally just faked it. She felt better."

"She felt better or she felt like a hypocrite?" Charlene poured some more daiquiri into Abe's glass, a little in her own, the last in mine. She waited for an answer, holding her pitcher midair.

"I guess she felt better being a hypocrite if it relieved the pressure of being a pastor's daughter who couldn't speak in tongues. She's not really in touch with her family anymore."

Charlene shook her head and tsked. "Goes to show you how these silly ideas undermine not only Christ but family." She stood. "I'm going to get our dinner ready."

"Let me help you," I said, jumping up after her.

My job was to make more drinks. Dumping frozen straw-berries into the blender, I poured rum over them and tossed in a few ice cubes. Charlene, meanwhile, took out a plate of fried chicken that she'd been keeping warm in the oven.

Pressing the cover down on the blender, I flipped the chop button. The blades growled and bleated then choked.

"You gotta stop it and stir," Charlene explained.

The breaking ice whirred into motion again as Charlene pulled out containers of potato salad and a Jell-O mould from the fridge. Her tone seemed cooler and I wondered if she was pissed off with me mentioning Erin and her fake tongue-talk.

I took the blender top off and splashed a little more rum in. Maybe it would relax us.

Charlene started organizing our plates and silverware. She spooned potato salad and a wiggling hunk of gelatinous red with suspended bits of indiscernible fruit onto each and asked if I could manage all three out to the pool deck.

"Sure, I used to be a waitress. A lousy one but then again the plates aren't ours."

Abe looked up as I set the food down. His glass sat empty and his eyes were beginning to look dopey with sun and rum.

"More daiquiri? I just made another pitcher." I was gone before he could answer. I didn't want to sit alone with Abe. Though I supposed we wouldn't be alone exactly, since Jesus clearly would be there. I giggled before I could stop myself.

"What's so funny?" Charlene asked, taking the container of drinks off the blender.

"Nothing. Just my friend in school who faked the tongues. Silly."

"We're all tempted to do silly things when we look for worldly acceptance rather than God's."

"Do you and Abe speak in tongues?"

"Yes, we do!" Charlene handed me the plate of chicken and we headed for poolside. "We've been speaking in tongues a lo-o-ong time now."

Soon we were all staring at the last glow of the sun, biting off hunks of fried chicken. Charlene had said they'd been speaking in tongues about twenty-six years. I was dying for a demonstration. Erin did it once for me but we were in a bar and I couldn't hear well over the music. I asked instead if they'd ever experienced the Toronto Blessing.

"Funny you should mention that." Abe gazed at his drumstick. "We first experienced it at our old church in Houston. And recently we got it in Bartle."

"I've only seen it on the news." I'd seen a story on a church out by the airport in Toronto with an entire congregation literally rolling in the aisles, gales of laughter spewing out of each parishioner as the Holy Spirit sailed through the pews. "I heard some people felt it had no place in a church."

Abe reached for another bird limb. "I guess I've heard stories of it getting out of hand."

"Out of hand?"

"People grunting and making pig noises, things like that."

"I think, like your friend," Charlene suggested, "they're trying to copy what they see and they're not actually being blessed by God, so that's the way it comes out."

Charlene asked if I had any children then confided that they had four kids, youngest eighteen. "I was a little wild before I met Abe," she said and put her nose back into her glass.

By the time we finished dinner, the electric lanterns around the deck had flickered on. This time all three of us went inside to replenish the blender drinks.

I used their bathroom and came out in the midst of Charlene and Abe discussing Debbie. Debbie, Abe said, was a parolee who lived with them. She had done six years for armed robbery. He reached into his wallet and took a picture out: Debbie was pious, smiling, arms crossed over her chest. I felt obliged to comment and was about to say she had gentle eyes then stopped. They were more dead than anything.

Debbie was their first and now they brought in a new parolee every few months.

"Oh, we're almost out of strawberries," Charlene said. "How 'bout peach? We got a whole bag of peaches! We'll have our dessert in a blender!" She set to cutting open fruit and tossing the pits before Abe and I could say a word.

"Do you ever bring male parolees in?"

"No," Abe answered, "just the gals. We got another one

due out in a few days. This one was in for kidnapping. She kidnapped two women."

"How come?"

Charlene dropped another pit in the sink, and shook her head. "Terrible—"

Abe interrupted. "Wasn't there a baby involved?"

"A video," she mumbled.

"What kind of video?" I asked, hoping for espionage.

"It was of her. She was a—" Charlene unscrewed the rum bottle and dumped some in. An inch left, she splashed in the rest. "You know. She—" Her face reddened as she punched the blender into action. Crunching ice and the roar of the motor took up the room as I looked at Abe, who had turned to watch the darkening sky. A vague haze of pink still lay on the horizon.

She was a . . . ? My mind blinked then suddenly green apples fell on the supermarket floor and seven-year-old me yelled, "A lesbian?" just as Charlene flicked off the blender.

She started at the word. "Yes. She thought those two women had a video of her and—"

"Her lover?"

"Yes." Charlene looked as though she was about to cry but pulled herself together and poured peach daiquiris. "Oh, that whole lifestyle, it's just so—I'm hoping this girl will find her way out. No good comes of it."

She picked up two glasses, handed one to me and the other to Abe who said, "Well, there's a lot of homosexuality in prison. And a lot of hatred and anger. When y'got all that hatred, s'no longer the person talking, it's the anger. What I've found over the years is that God never lets you down if you just give it . . ."

I was agitated now, feeling the fluster of Mum's hands in the supermarket, hearing the candied threat in our neighbour's voice. I took a slug of peach daiquiri.

"So, Vivian, I have to ask you this," said Abe. "Have you had a personal relationship with Jesus Christ?"

My head swivelled. "My mother was a lesbian." Abe winced. Charlene put a hand over her eyes. "She died a week ago," I said.

Abe nodded gravely and sat down on the edge of the bed. "I'm deeply sorry for you, Vivian. It must have been difficult for you."

A tear sprang from Charlene's eye and she wiped it away. I looked back at the dirty dishes and empty rum bottle.

"Vivian," Abe said, "do you ever wonder what your world woulda been like had y'brought Jesus in, if you'd given all your troubles to Him?" Voice low and warm, he watched me with concern.

I was suddenly aware of my breathing. Abe looked deeply and steadily into my eyes and something in me slipped. Maybe they weren't being judgmental. Maybe it was the *kidnapping* lifestyle that upset her. "I guess I haven't thought about it."

"I think you're quite a girl," Abe said. "A passionate girl who probably didn't have a daddy around to look after her and help her up when she fell down."

Nerves jumped in my neck. My head shook no and I looked past him to the sky outside. No pink left. We were turning into shadows.

"Ever'body," Abe drawled, "needs a daddy 'round to hold her and listen to her when she's troubled. Or where does she end up?"

My limbs had gone heavy and the shrug I managed took everything I had.

"Lookin' for boys and men," Abe told me, "to try and fill that void and all of 'em disappoin'er in the end, don't they?"

This was that Southern voodoo shit I was worried about. I was suddenly a swallowed lamb before him. He was a storybook woodsman ready to slit the belly of the wolf and pull me free.

Glass to my mouth, I sipped to hide my face. I folded my arms and tried to balance the drink casually against my elbow. "'Jesus don't want me for a sunbeam,'" I said.

Abe cocked his head.

"I just—it's a song. Nirvana."

Abe smiled knowingly. "Jesus *does* want you, Vivian. He brought you to us. He brought *us* to *you*. He took our motorhome away so we would have no choice but to find you—t'show you His face not the face that some snake in the grass showed you. You're one'a God's *masterpieces*, Vivian." Abe clapped hard at the air and shouted, "You're his baby-girl and He ain't *never* gonna let you fall!"

The corners of my mouth rose.

"Hallelujah," Abe shouted, grinning, and I wrapped my arms a little tighter.

The cold floor reminded me that I was barefoot. *I need my boots. I really need my boots.* The clang of the words in my head was unbearably loud.

The next thing I knew, Charlene was wrapped around me, pinning my arms, her forehead buried in my shoulder. Weeping, she squeezed and trilled *Hallelujah!* into my neck and the glass dropped from my hand.

"Shi—d—darn. I'm sorry, I'm sorry." I shook her off and swooped to the floor. "Oh, it's all over everywhere. Look what I did."

"Sh-sh-sh, it doesn't matter. You're with family now," Charlene whispered.

Tears dribbled down my own face. "I'm so clumsy. I broke my mother's Christmas ball. I just dropped it like that. I didn't mean to."

"Sh-sh-sh, now-now, it's okay."

"Vivian," Abe murmured, "why don't you come beside me and we'll pray together."

Charlene guided me to Abe. "Good girl, let's just sit here now," she said and set me down between her and her husband. "Let's bring you to Jesus, honey." She palmed my back.

Somewhere between the dropping and the sitting, I had begun to sob. "I'm sorry. I miss my mother."

"Sweetheart, your mamma's passed but you can talk to Jesus."

Charlene took one of my hands and Abe took the other. Each of them rubbed my back.

"Let Jesus have it." Abe pulled me tighter to his side. "Let's pray together now."

Charlene inched in, pressing closer.

"Lord, we bring to you one of your beautiful children, one of your lost children." Abe's face looked pained with concentration. "She has been set afloat on the river like baby Moses and like Moses, Lord, you are going to find her, pluck her from the bullrushes and hold her tight. Jesus, she comes to you now, she lays herself bare at your feet."

His splayed hand moved up and down my rib cage. "She loves you, Jesus," he moaned, "and she is ready."

Noises came out of Charlene that sounded like Arabic mixed with bits that hissed like something hairless.

"Hear me, sweet Jesus," Abe called at the ceiling. "I bring this child unto you. I am your servant, Lord. I live to serve you, Master."

Charlene's head lolled back and her face waved side to side as if she was having a nightmare. Babble spilled and her free arm swayed high in the air.

I had to get up.

Abe's hand moved higher against the side of my breast, coming round. "Take her Lord, take her Lord, take her Lord." Moulding and rubbing.

If he realized, he'd be embarrassed; it would ruin everything if he knew where he was touching. I tried to maneuver his fingers back with my arm. Both his hands jumped to my shoulders, buffing and kneading, encircling my neck then back down. "A lost child, naked in the street, Lord, take her, make her your own."

You're not wearing a bra, my brain commented. *Slutty.* I panicked. *They think I'm slutty.*

One of Abe's hands grabbed my inner thigh just under the hem of my shorts. Brain stunned into silence, my insides teeter-tottered. His chest behind my shoulder, Abe kept one palm on my thigh, the other firmly against my ribs, fingertips kneading my breast. His voice reverberated through my bones.

I needed to stand up.

Charlene's jabbering stopped abruptly. I turned my head to her. She frowned at her husband's hand inside my thigh, massaging my shorts higher. Her hand dropped and hovered in confusion above my other leg.

Abe hollered ceilingward once more: "Say it, Vivian! Say, take me Lord! *Say it!*"

I opened my mouth, "Ohgod—" turned my head and puked orange and red across Abe's lap.

Abe leapt off the bed.

"Oh fuck. Oh god! I'm—" On my feet, I pulled my shorts straight.

Only Charlene sat now, stupefied in the dark.

We were all mute.

The room felt like a stranger's dirty finger wiggling in my ear. Snake-green numbers glowed on the clock radio. Charlene stared hard. When she spoke, it was English but slurred. "Why dit you have hizzand ondu like that?"

I froze, trying to understand, when suddenly it dawned on me: I've been tricked. I couldn't understand when she spoke in tongues—because it was the *devil* talking through her. The hair on my arms bristled and goosebumps ran up my thighs—They *made* me throw up.

I whispered, "Don't touch me." The lanterns outside pulled my gaze. I made a stumbling dash toward the open door.

Tripping over my threshold, I fell into my room and turned the lock. My heart thrashed.

I flicked the light on, staggered backward against the wall and leaned there panting. My feet were filthy and there was something wet on my toes. As I reached forward, I caught sight of the orange and red slime on my arm.

A knock at the door. I jumped, falling back a step.

Not my door. It was the next door. Abe knocked and murmured at the room between mine and theirs. "Sweetheart, it's okay. Don't be embarrassed. You just had too much to drink. It's okay. Let me in, sweetheart."

I flicked my light off, and stood still. *Fuck, how did I get this drunk?* I held a hand over my mouth, scared he'd hear me breathe. I put my ear against the door.

"Vivian, honey, lemme in. We love you. Jesus loves you."

Picking the curtain away from the window, I could see his back and sleeve, my vomit on his leg.

Jesus-people don't make those lizard sounds, I thought. It all made sense now. I sat down in the dark.

"Lemme in, sweetheart. Let me wash you. I'll wash you clean, honey."

Then Charlene's howl. "Abe, what're you doing? That's not even her room. *Abe?*"

"Charlene, simmer down. Y'had too much drink."

"A-a-be! She doesn't . . . Abe. I'm sick too and your place is with me, looking after *me*."

My stomach lurched and I hurled myself toward the bathroom.

7:00 a.m. The desk from under the window was pushed against the door with the television on top. My mouth was thick and sticky. Crawling out of bed, I went to the bathroom. *What time did I go to bed?* Couldn't've been later than eleven or so. The memory of throwing up in Abe and Charlene's room hit me hard and I dropped to my knees, face over the clean shiny toilet. One small dry heave. I rested my forehead on the seat.

Did that fucker really grab my tit whilst leading me to God?

Raising my head, I opened my mouth and stretched it wide, as if trying to pop my ears on a plane. The last thing I remembered with any clarity was the manager, someone called the manager on them. I rummaged until I found my makeup bag with the Ativan and Gravol, dumped one of each in my palm and tossed them into my mouth. *Never drinking again.* My lips pushed under the tap and I sucked back cold water until I remembered something more beautiful than the sound of a motel manager telling off vomit-covered Christians.

I trudged back toward the bed saying a prayer for peace and tranquility and rooted in my bag until I came to a thin lump on the bottom covered by black electrician's tape. Peeling it off, I opened a gnarled bit of Cellophane and plucked out the Holy Spirit: a slightly squashed joint. I climbed back under the bedcovers. As I kissed the joint, I grabbed my purse, flashed *The Flames of Celia Dare* and knew that Jesus still loved me.

It was 11:00 a.m. when I woke again, drowsy but not queasy. When I opened the door, the sun was high and the heat hugged just tight enough to make me feel wanted. Only the cleaning women were out there now. One of them picked up a lone chicken-greased plate as she straightened out the lounge chairs.

Eight

~

No town is too small for a Starbucks, it seems, so I headed for the familiar and picked myself up some breakfast to go. Cigarette, coffee and muffin in hand, I took a wander through the short slim core of Danaville, trying to psyche myself up. I was determined to go back to Annie's but nothing about a hangover engenders confidence in a woman.

I paused in the window of a clothing shop and, shifting from boot to boot, remembered I'd vowed to get a sundress today. A couple bright-but-dull little jersey numbers hung on the mannequins in front of me. Taking a drag off my smoke, I caught the reflection of a young man strolling down the sidewalk behind me. Conservatively dressed, the woman with him had salt-and-pepper hair and an earthy aristocratic face. They turned their heads in unison to take in the sight of me and exchanged glances. Mother and son. I looked back at my own reflection: a mop of stale-popcorn yellow draped around my sunglasses, straggling in a serpentine orgy. Smoke curled up past my eyes and over my head; my Indian Motorcycle T-shirt sat a couple inches over my silver belt buckle. *There's this bitch who's just a fuck machine and she can't get enough.* I had showered for half an hour before I left the motel but I couldn't get the feel of his fingers off my breast. *Fuck y'all*, I thought and chomped the last of the muffin, throwing the wrapper in a trash bin by the curb. The alcohol remorse I had this morning was worse than any I could remember in some time. *You* didn't do anything, I reminded myself, *they* did.

Inside I grabbed two T-shirt dresses and a couple of pairs of non-buttfloss underwear. The store clerk asked if I'd mind putting my cigarette out. I flicked it out the door and she looked vaguely appalled, but said nothing as she hung the dresses up in a change room. She glanced at the stretch of skin between my baby tee and jeans. "That's quite a belt buckle," she commented. "What does it say?"

I looked down. "Lick."

"Oh." Tan cotton trousers and collared blouse aside, she was likely only twenty-five or so. "No point leaving them guessing, I suppose." She held the curtain open.

Inside the dressing room, I realized I'd forgotten to put on makeup. A bit of dark smudge from last night's mascara was about all that remained since my shower. Opening my purse, I put on some lipstick but the face on me looked worse with it than without. I grabbed a tissue from the box sitting on the stubby stool in the corner and blotted my lips a little before I pulled off my clothes. I replaced my sunglasses so that neither the outside world nor I would have to suffer.

The yellow dress hung lank and straight at the sides, almost to my knees. It was sized small but sacklike nonetheless. Gathering material at the waist, I sighed. "Who do you need to impress? Old Bat Annie?"

"What's that?" the clerk inquired, primly helpful.

I pulled the curtain aside. "Kinda looks like shit on me."

Everything about me caused a slight recoil in the store clerk. Maybe the whole town. "I think it looks quite elegant," she said.

Elegant. Who in god's name would look at me and say *elegant*.

I glanced back over my shoulder, pushed my sunglasses up a second, dropped them back down my nose. "Haven't you got anything more . . . oh, forget it. I'll get the blue one too." The idea of putting my jeans back on made me claustrophobic.

"We're having a bit of early heat right now. You don't want anything too clingy."

"Uh-huh." I pulled the curtain and tried the bikini undies on over my thong. Hauling the dress up, I took a gander at them. Kind of cute, baby blue. They didn't show through the dress. "I'll get the underwear too. And have you got any thongs? I mean, ah, like the foot kind? Flip-flops or sandals or whatever?"

Hair balled up in the scrunchy again, old clothes stuffed in the bag with the blue version of the dress and undies, I wandered down the sidewalk in my new red flip-flops and yellow dress, and found myself stopped in front of a hairdresser's. I gazed at the posters of sleek-haired models covering the lower half of the window and tried to remember if I ever looked like that even in Tokyo before I'd started into bleach. Maybe I'd feel better if I got my roots done by a pro. Maybe this is what a girl should do the morning after: get her hair done and buy new clothes.

Inside the salon, Barry Manilow's voice sidled through the air. Not a soul inhabited the chairs. No one was in view anywhere until a redhead walked out from behind a back curtain.

"Got time for a trim?" I asked.

"Sure, what the heck." She looked at her watch. "Don't have anything else till two."

"Maybe a root job?"

She patted a chair and handed me a magazine. Her own hair was verging on fuchsia, up and back in a French roll. No point in judging a stylist by her lid, I supposed. They all have lab fur: too much experimentation.

Overhead, Manilow began to moan at Mandy. "Snazzy tunes," I said into the mirror as I opened the limp-paged hair magazine.

"My twelve o'clock cancelled. She likes Barry." The stylist peered down at my hair part as she reached into her apron. "Whoa, Nelly, those are some dark roots. Explains the rest of it." Sticking a mint in her mouth, she sucked without offering one.

Fingers into my crown, she raised the roots. "Must have to do a touch-up every week or something. Though, some girls like that punky style with the black striping in the under layers. Doesn't seem as if that's what you're goin' for." Then she took hold of the ends and bunched it up to my shoulders. "Would you hate my guts if I said you need more than a trim?"

Looking in the mirror, I mechanically flipped pages and said, "Looks like shit, doesn't it?" I guess this was presumed a rhetorical question because I got no response.

A brunette with jaw-length shiny tresses shot me a smug look from the magazine. I sighed, suddenly exhausted at the thought of my hair, my clothes, myself. I felt as if I were my own cage today, and without bringing my eyes up said, "Ah, fuck it."

She crunched her mint.

Back out on the sidewalk, my head felt inhumanly light, as though it had been transplanted with a hamster's. I may as well have been naked for the sense of security I was left with. Bag on one wrist, I pushed the fingers of my free hand back and through my hair, hands dropping off the ends with a start. I turned my head, phantom strands catching in my armpit. Nothing. Shaking my head, the hairs moved individually, wiggly on my scalp. It felt as though I were doing something obscene in public.

Turning back to the reflection in the salon window, I saw the yellow dress, the dark mid-neck length hair swinging of its own volition. My throat tightened with the fear I had turned into someone's weather girl.

I moved my head again and got another rush: the erotic tickle of movement almost compensated for the weird sense of loss. Past my reflection, inside the salon, that evil Delilah-ish redhead swept blonde like dirt off the floor. I watched the dead hair pile onto a dustpan. Like leaving limbs behind.

I touched the frame of my sunglasses and gawked at my reflection again as if I were a peeping Tom. I didn't know where or who I was, what I was doing. My cell phone rang.

"Vivian? what the hell are you doing, woman?" Erin!

"Hi." I nearly swooned in gratitude.

"What's going on, where are you?"

"I'm in Danaville. I'm kind of hungover and . . ." *Jesus Christ, I'm going to start bawling.*

"Attagirl!"

I could stay at her place tonight. She had an apartment in North Beach, just off Columbus Avenue.

I snapped the phone shut and started back up Main Street toward the car. "Change is good," I said quietly. "Don't be such a *baby.*" An older couple walked by holding hands. Meeting my gaze, they smiled as they passed. It settled me a little, those old people glancing with such open faces. As if they knew me. "You're fine," I whispered. "It's just hair." I copped a few more glances into car windows I passed, watching my reflection. I tried to swagger. *Studied casual,* my mother used to say. I stopped and stared into the window of an insurance broker. "Fuck me," I whispered. "I look just like her."

The bell of the insurance broker's front door jangled and a big-bellied middle-aged man stepped out. Moving onto the sidewalk, he raised his face to the sun then turned it to me. "You weren't looking for me, were you?" he smiled. He didn't look at me like a normal guy would. Either I was losing my mind or this was the face I used to see men give her. *Appreciative.* By twelve I wanted to inspire growls instead.

"Ah no. I just . . ." What, I was just looking at myself? "I had to check something." And I flip-flopped my way up the block toward the car. Throwing my stuff in the trunk, I put the top down. This'll be good. Maybe another coffee. I was parked right in front of Starbucks. I walked in past the faces of coffee drinkers at the tables out front. They glanced up with that same bland appreciation reserved for well-behaved women.

I looked at the ground, meek, all of a sudden. This frank pleasantry from strangers—I didn't know what to do with my face. At the counter I ordered a latte from a young woman who smiled as though we were cousins. Was I going to have to rethink my whole relationship to the world after one goddamn cut and colour? I shoved my sunglasses back over my eyes while

I waited. The guy on the espresso machine gave me a sappy look and I welled up. I'd become girlie and mouse–sized and all these assholes loved it.

I missed the savage crust of my yesterday self. I wondered if my mother ever missed her old self, the ferociousness of a red mouth and black eyeliner.

Yesterday's me was getting shunted out the door like an embarrassing relative. And yet I couldn't imagine ever fitting this new sponge-faced, salon-haired skin either. "Could you put a little vanilla into that?" I asked and forced a smile.

"Sure," the coffee maker said, grinning. "On the house," he added with a whisper.

My eyes rolled behind my shades.

Driving into Annie West's cul-de-sac, I tried to puff up: *You're driving a convertible under a screaming-blue California sky with a cigarette in one hand and a coffee in the other. Fucking fabulous!*

Parked in front of her house, I took a last drag and dropped my coffee in the cup holder, snatched a look in the rearview before I went into the back and opened my mother's trunk to arm myself.

Envelope of glam shots and the photo album in hand, I rapped lightly on Annie's door. No response. I rang the doorbell. Nothing.

Down the steps, I followed the pathway round back. And there she was on a lounger under a navy-and-white-striped patio umbrella, wearing baby blue polyester pants and a pink sleeveless blouse. A hat and sunglasses kept the rays off her face. She wore no makeup but some crooked hot-pink lipstick. It was hard to reconcile this short squat woman with the brazen hourglass in the picture. "Ms. West?"

She jumped and peered round from under the brim of her sun hat. "Yes? uh-huh?"

She didn't recollect me. Incognito, I thought, like a spy. "Hello, I'm Vivian. Are you the Annie West who was once roommates with Celia Dare?"

She squared her shoulders before she pulled a cane out from under the lounger, used it to hoist herself up and angrily limped toward me. I glanced over my shoulder. "Another one of you people was here looking for her yesterday."

"No. I mean, I was actually looking for—"

She stopped three or four feet from me. "Why don't you give it a rest?" She stamped her cane. "You think you can bully me?"

I didn't recall seeing a cane the day before. "No, I'm not, it's *you* I'm—"

"I don't know where she is and I wouldn't tell you if I did."

"I'm her daughter."

"What?"

"Celia Dare was my mother." I ripped into the envelope of pictures, purse dropping on the grass. "Here, see?"

I held up Annie's shot, rope looped over her breasts. She stepped closer, squinting. I looked at the foot causing her to limp and back up to her hands. They were shaking now. Her face tumbled into a soft bewildered pink as she snapped the picture from my fingers.

"Where did you get this?" she demanded in a voice that meant to sound stern but had lost its oomph.

"In our basement. After the funeral."

Annie looked almost frightened now.

"She had cancer," I explained.

Her head quivered a nod. "Cancer?"

I stood mute.

"She's gone?"

Just swallowing.

"She had a baby?"

"Yes."

Inhaling in halting spasms, she put a hand to her neck just before the sobs came. The photograph dropped to the ground and I swooped in beside her, not sure whether I should touch her. Finally I took her hand and cradled her shoulders with my other arm. Moving her back to the lounger, I set her down, and tried to say soothing things: *You're okay, just sit here for a second. It's okay.* She dropped the cane and her hands covered her face as a high soft wail came through. I knelt down in the grass, as if I were trying to get small. Like some kind of apology.

Annie reached for the glass sitting on the end table and took a long gulp then wiped her eyes, shut them tight, then crumpled again. "I missed her so bad," she said. "When did she go?"

"About a week ago." We sat this way, her in the lounger, me on the grass until her chest stopped heaving. She reached a shaky hand over and touched the top of my head. "Y'look like her, like when I first met her." Then she asked where we lived and frowned at my answer.

"Oh god. I need a drink. You want a lemonade or something?" She heaved herself forward. "Goddamn it," she said, reaching for the cane again. "I twisted my ankle last night and I'm stuck using this thing like a cripple. Can you reach that?" She nodded toward the photo of herself and I stooped to pick it up. She took it from me, saying, *"If you got the guts for it* is right. How did you find me? I'm not in the book," as she stood.

Inside we sat across a blonde wooden table, a lemonade and vodka in front of each of us. "You didn't drive that old Valiant, did you?"

"No." I was confused a second. "Oh—she sold that before I was born, I think. This one's almost brand new. She just bought it a couple years ago."

"I guess she didn't go by Celia Dare. She go back to Audrey?"

"Audrey?"

"That was her name before she changed it to Celia. Audrey, uh . . . ?"

"Callwood. Her real name was Josephine Callwood."

"Callwood? Huh, that sounds fancy. She liked for people to think she was classy."

"That's the name on her birth certificate."

"Yeah."

"Are you saying that wasn't her real name?"

West shrugged. I half wondered if she was senile.

She asked what I did up in Canada. I told her, adding, "She didn't approve of the whole modelling, acting thing."

"She didn't?" Annie sipped her lemonade "She sure loved being in front of an audience herself. But I guess when all was said and done . . . church it ain't."

"She tried church for a bit. Thought it was misogynist bullshit in the end."

"What?"

"She was a big feminist activist."

"Women's lib," Annie snarled with disgust. "She was curious about that crap and the Vietnam marches—me, I like a door opened for me. I used to say, you'll be sorry when you get drafted—all that *feminism*. What about you?" she asked suspiciously.

"I enjoy being a girl."

"Yeah." She reached for the pictures, her own shot sitting on top. "Christ, age is a sunovabitch. This goddamn ankle is going to take a coon's age to heel." She stared . . ."Oh for godsake, this was a hell of a night, the night she got this one. What does that say? Can you read that?"

Sinatra's face turned to me and, by heart, I recited, "'You're cruel, baby! But when you're right, you're right. Frank.'"

"She was a real pisser when she was mad. So was *he* for that matter."

"Where was she born? I thought she was from Toronto and then I read she was from Pennsylvania."

"Toronto—no, no, no, whatsits, the ritzier suburb upstate—Scarsdale! Her parents had this real nice house in Scarsdale."

"She was American?"

"Of course. Scarsdale, New York. I think her mother came from money. And the crazy stepfather was a professor in town. She took lots of ballet and piano and singing and all that jazz. She almost became a ballerina. But then she started into the show business type of dancing like they had in the night-clubs."

"Did you work together in nightclubs? Is that how you met her?"

"She waitressed in this bar a few of us used to go to. But she got fired."

"In New York?"

"Uh-huh. I used to go to this after-hours joint called The 92."

"In Little Italy? That's in this book I was reading, this girl who became a mob wife started out working there."

Annie gave me a blank look. "Yeah. Well, it wasn't much of a place but a couple of us girls were dating guys who went there. This fella, Micky D, I used to go around with, he took me in there sometimes. They had this good-looking waitress called Audrey all the fellas liked. I didn't think much of her—*skinny*—but anyways this one night I go in there after work, it was probably three in the morning. You could go any time of night if you were the right people. In those days, stripteasers were special, like celebrities; people knew who we were, we got invitations everywhere and the fellas liked having us on their arms. Anyways, Audrey had these catty blue eyes and Micky D, my fella, said she looked like Elizabeth Taylor. Which was a bit of a stretch. But they liked her, those guys."

"Audrey was my mother? Celia?"

"She had dark hair like yours then." Her eyes clouded back into the place she was before my interruption: "This one night some guy comes in, older square-looking fella says he's looking for Audrey. The bouncer tells him it's a private party but he starts calling, '*Audrey! Audrey!*' She gives the okay and the fella goes over to her but we couldn't hear much until they started yelling. Crazy sunovabitch tried to drag her out the door. The bouncers were on him in a flash, of course, and the fella hollers, 'I'm her father. She's sixteen years old. I'm calling the police.' Audrey says, 'You're *not* my father.' Next thing you know, the bouncers got hold of him. She's screaming, he's screaming. Finally they threw him out. A lot of people got up and left just in case he did call the cops and Jimmy, the fella that ran the joint, brought her to a booth and had a talk with her.

"I say to Micky D, 'How do you like her now, y'pedophile?' He says, 'Why you gotta be like that for?' and goes over to the booth where she's crying. Next thing you know, Jimmy's holding her one hand and Micky's got the other and I'm sitting there thinkin', *She's underage so fire her tush and send her home*. Pretty clear to me. But, then, Teddy the Ghost gets in on the action. Teddy was this, ah, well-connected older fella who used to come in. Micky comes back to me and says, '*You think you can get Audrey a job at the club? They need any singers?*'

"I say, '*Are you* kidding? *She's sixteen!*' And he says, '*Yeah, the whole joint heard. We gotta get her out of here in case the bulls come. Just gotta fix her up first.*' And there's Audrey sitting by herself, so I went over and tried to help her out. I knew a guy looking for stage acts for the carnival so I gave her his number. Low-rent operation but it wasn't bad. A lot of girls danced carnival in the summertime when the clubs were slow. I used to dance the big state fairs—the Royal American and Raynell Golden shows—they did some nice reviews, almost like it used to be in the theatres. Anyway, The Boys got her some ID so she'd be able to work and I didn't see her again till she showed up in Vegas calling herself Celia."

It was Annie's eyes that looked catty to me now. "I heard she ended up doing the geek show at the carnival because it was so rough on the other side."

"Geek show? I don't know anything about that," Annie said, jerking her head no. "She was a dancer. Carnival is a lot of fun. It's not like everybody thinks, real tacky and dirty and this and that. No. A lot of girls were carnival people."

I sat quiet a second, splicing her words with what I'd heard and read, then changed the subject. "Teddy the Ghost, the mafia guy?"

"Mafia guy? Where'd you hear a thing like that?"

"I read it. He was connected to the Gambino family in New York. Teodoro Gossitino?"

"That's crap," she snapped. "He gambled a little, that's all. People like to make a big deal. Too much TV."

"Didn't he go to jail for murder and racketeering?"

"Taxes," she said and hoisted herself out of her chair, hobbled to the counter and poured vodka over the bottom of her glass. "How's your drink?"

My glass was still half-full. "I'm fine. Oh right, he got convicted on tax evasion. I've been reading so much stuff . . . Someone said he was Celia Dare's boyfriend."

"No-o," Annie growled and turned from the counter. "He was like a father to her. A whatsits—avuncular type. He didn't want her working in bars, getting into trouble, you know, he thought she was real smart, the kind of girl who could make something of herself. She told me he wanted to send her to stewardess school. He took her travelling. Florida and that."

"Why would he take her travelling if he wasn't her boyfriend?"

Her face soured. "Because. It was kind of a part-time job for her, being his assistant. Sometimes, these business fellas, if they travel alone, they become targets for speculation. Less problems if you're in a couple then people don't get all funny." She leaned back now as if I was an irritant she didn't want to get too close to. "She came to Vegas with Teddy."

My hand went to my hair, reminding me that I was in disguise. A good spy knows better than to be a pushy bitch. "So . . . I read on-line that she sang with Louis Prima one night."

Her face softened. "That's right. She did that. Keely wasn't feeling good one night and Prima met Celia at one of his shows and she was friends of friends and he asked her to fill in."

"So, she had a good voice."

"She didn't do striptease at first. She wanted to get famous for being a singer and dancer but she was more like an impersonator, you know. She didn't really have her own style. You have to have your own style to get famous singing. She was a good impersonator though. She could do anybody. Sounded just like Keely that one night."

"How did she go from that to stripping?"

"Well," she said, her eyes darting into her drink, her voice rising. "I remember another gal that wanted to be an opera star but her agent told her she'd never make it in opera, that she'd do better as a stripper. Hettie Bay her name was. She married a light-and-sound man in Hollywood; she lives in Palos Verdes. She's quite elderly. Just about all of the girls wanted to be something. You don't just say, *Oh, I want to be a stripper. I can hardly wait to be one of those.* No, you start that way because it's a way you can get a job and then you find out how much money you're making."

The room went silent. After a few moments I said, "And so she dated Frank Sinatra?"

"*No.* I dated him. That's sort of how we connected again. I came out to Vegas for a run at the Silver Slipper. That was a good club to work at—wasn't so much the superstar acts performing but it was an inside-crowd joint, you know. Sinatra would come hang around there or Sammy Davis Jr." Her face brightened. "Very informal, you didn't have to wear a tie so you could be relaxed if you wanted. The first week I was in town, I decided to treat myself to a stay at the Sands—the Slipper didn't have guest rooms so most performers got themselves an apartment a block or two off the Strip. But, like I say, I wanted to spoil myself. I used to go casino-hopping. That's the big sport in Vegas. I'd go here and there, catch the shows, and I was meeting all kinds of people—Keely Smith and Louis Prima, they had the biggest lounge act that ever hit Las Vegas. They were *the wildest.* Whoever had them lost money. You know why? Because the croupiers just stood there—everybody left the tables and you could stand around and watch them free. Nobody played the tables when Prima was on. Lord he was wild.

"And they'd all end up at the Slipper too. I wasn't in town three days when I got invited to have dinner with Frank Sinatra! This was when they were all there at the Sands: Sinatra, Dean Martin, Sammy Davis Jr. . . . when those fellas were around, the whole place was buzzing. So I had dinner with Frank and his friends late one night after the show. And they had their funny way of talking, you know, like surfers and beatniks, calling everyone *Charlie*—Charlie Cool, Charlie Suave, and like that— and everything was a *gasser*. You just wanted to be around them. Dean was so funny. He used to put on this Southern accent and he'd say, *You ain't drunk if you can lie on the floor without holdin' on*. Afterward we all went back to Frank's suite in the Sands and carried on till five or six in the morning. That was normal with him; Frank wanted everyone up playing with him till he said it was time for bed. Nobody minded though—being around Frank, you really felt like you'd made it. He was cute too, big blue eyes—you couldn't see straight when he was turning on the charm. I stayed with him after everyone left this particular night. Big gorgeous suite. Anyway, it was nine in the morning and we hadn't even gone to sleep yet and the phone rang. Frank went out to the other room to get it. Sounded like he was try- ing to smooth someone out a little and then next thing you know he smashes the receiver down and he's slamming things around, *eff this* and *eff that*. There were lots of stories about his temper, guys sued him for assault and so on—it's like all the fury of the world when you're next to it. He came storming in the bedroom and I said, *Who was that? Everything okay?* Well, that did it for me. *None of your effin' business who that was. What are you still doing here anyway, pig?*

"I couldn't move I was so stunned. He yanked the blankets off and pulled me by the hair. He says, *Get your fatass outta my effin bed* . . . I jumped up and got myself together fast as I could. I never had anyone talk to me that way in my life . . . still makes me sick to my stomach to remember. By the time I got down- stairs, I was crying so hard, I couldn't see straight. Then I got to my room and my damn key wouldn't work and I started to kick at the door, like a tantrum, you know, I was so mad. Then this little blonde opens up in her bathrobe. Thought I was losing my mind. She says, *What's going on?* Must've thought I'd been attacked. May's well have, the way I felt. I said, *He called me a pig, Frank Sinatra called me a pig.* I guess that was the worst part. *The singer?* she says to me like I'm nuts. And I start blubbering— maybe I thought she might still be sore at me for sending her to that carnival show. So she says, *You want me to call the po—oh eff the police. What room is he in?* Next thing I know, she's marching us back upstairs. I was saying, *No-no-no, he's crazy, I don't know what he'll do.* And she's banging on his door and we hear him cussing in there and he opens the door and she lights into him. *You so-and-so, you rapist!* I said, *No-no-no. He didn't.* Jesus, I felt like an ass. She wouldn't back down though. So, he says something like, *Who the hell are you, her mother?* And then she tells him to apologize. And then Frank gets this very smug look on his face. He could be a very weird cat, I'll say that much for him. Didn't even look at me. He said, *All right. I'm sorry I haven't laid eyes on you sooner, fireball.* Fireball, he called her. Oh, that made her mad. She said, *There's nothing cool about you, Mr. Sinatra. You're just warm grease.* Huh! I used to tease her about that later when we got to be friends. I haven't thought of that in a while. *Warm grease.* Anyway, he apologized. I was half-scared of her myself."

Annie shook the ice around her glass and took a sip. I looked down into my own glass. Spiked lemonade wasn't sitting very well today. "You were friends after that?"

"Ah, well, a little later. Teddy wasn't around because he had that tax stuff to deal with and she didn't have anyone. This old boyfriend of hers came looking for her, giving her a hard time. Had an argument about his car. Anyway, I got her out of a bit of trouble with him."

"Okie Joe? Was this the candy-butcher guy?"

"Yeah." She looked at me.

I couldn't tell if I'd said something suspicious or if she'd just forgotten what she was going to say. "Sorry. You got her out of trouble with this old boyfriend."

"Yes. I did. He was bothering her at her hotel room and I ran and told Frank about it and also this fella named Johnny that kinda looked after things in town and him and Frank told the guy to take a hike and then we all got to be friends after that. Frank even gave her a part in whatsits, that picture they were shooting. But it got cut. He was good to his friends."

"Johnny Rosselli?"

Her eyes flicked up. "What's that?"

"Was the Johnny who looked after things in Vegas Johnny Rosselli?"

"Yeah. I think so."

"*They* dated though, right? Celia and Johnny?"

She shrugged. "No. I don't know. He looked after her when Teddy went away. We saw him around Vegas and New York. He had an apartment in L.A. She did some lounge singing and then she got into Buddhism or something, met some beatniks and went off to San Francisco. I didn't see her for a while. Then she put together a couple good shows singing and stripping and she was getting kind of famous because nobody else did that then. And then she quit."

"Just like that? How come?"

She shrugged again. "She danced a while and then she quit. That's how it goes. Can't be a stripper your whole life, you know." She looked around the kitchen and yawned. "I think I have to go lie down for a while. This is my usual time to lie down." She set her glass on the countertop.

"Oh. Okay." I looked down at the pictures still strewn on the table and gathered them up.

"It was nice meeting you. I gotta lie down." She led the way down the hall to the front door.

I trailed after her. "Would you have time to chat again? Tomorrow maybe?"

"I'm busy." She opened the door and put her hand on my back. "Good meeting you."

"Maybe I could just come for a shorter time?" I stepped out onto the stoop.

"I'm very tired right now," she said, closing the door as she spoke.

"Could I—" Door shut, she turned the lock.

"Here's your hat, what's your hurry," I muttered, staring at the peephole as it darkened with her eye. Waving sardonically, I turned and fwap-fwapped down the front steps to the car.

Erin opened the door with a kind of bored flourish as if she were raising the curtain on something swell but didn't have the energy to say, *Ta-dah!* She looked the same, short chic honey-coloured hair. "Oh my god, look at you!" she said and hugged me. She leaned back with an appraising eye. "You broke up with Frank."

I reached down for my suitcase. "No. Why would you say that?"

"Oh." She moved back inside the apartment, grinning. "I don't know, it's kind of a girl thing to do: change the hair when you split up with a guy." She closed the door and took a quick eyeball through the peephole. "Just put your bag in the corner. Come on in the kitchen, I'm making us a pitcher of sangria. You want tacos for dinner?"

I followed her in, staring around the spacious creamy-white apartment, the sliding door open to a balcony, the high ceilings, the long hall leading to what appeared to be a decent-sized bedroom. Her living room looked like something out of a tampon ad. A low faux–Japanese style table sat between the cream sofa and loveseat. Sitting on a pale wooden stand that matched the table was a flat broad television. I recognized a painting on the wall from her apartment in Vancouver as well as a hip-high black-and-slate glazed vase she'd bought from Sally at one of her shows. Or rather the stockbroker she was dating at the time bought for her. Big dried heads of ivory and purple hydrangeas exploded out of the mouth with a sense of entitlement.

When I first met Erin, she looked like a mud-flap girl: a long wave of thick platinum hair, body by Pilates and rocketing C-cup implants courtesy of the stockbroker who also paid the rent on her downtown high-rise apartment. She assumed she would become Mrs. Stockbroker until he came to her, two years into the relationship, and announced that he would be wed the following weekend to an equestrian from Southlands.

The following morning, she went out and bought a *Town and Country* magazine and studied the contents before getting herself a three-hundred-dollar haircut and a manicure that brought her nails down to an elegant but sensible length. She hired a makeup artist to show her exactly how to duplicate a money face. From then on she was a honey-haired, big-knockered Audrey Hepburn.

"I don't know if my gut can take tacos. How can you afford this place?"

She glinted as she cut up an orange. "Alimony."

Sitting on a stool on the living-room side of the kitchen counter, I watched her squeeze and drop the fruit wedges into a glass pitcher. "Ah yes. George had a few choice words to say. Something about an insurance policy?"

She rolled her eyes and set her knife against an apple. "What, he didn't mention the Saab?" Off my raised eyebrow, she gave that deep-throated laugh I used to love. It generally meant she'd broken some rule, spoken or otherwise. "The car was in my name. If he hadn't screwed everybody he owed with his Chapter 7 declaration, he wouldn't have needed to put the car in my name to begin with." She poured Triple Sec over the fruit and stirred it around with a wooden spoon. "Anyway, he was cheating on me."

"Did you really change your name to Marcella?"

Uncorking a bottle of wine, she said, "I didn't *change* it. Marcella is my middle name. Why should I be saddled with *Erin* for the rest of my life? I mean, look at me, darling." She gestured at herself. "I *am* Marcella."

"How did you know he was cheating?"

"I was friends with this computer guy. He liked me and he didn't trust George. So he found out for me. This guy knew *everybody*. He asked me one day, if I could meet any celebrity who would it be? And I said Harrison Ford, who he knew, of course. Just like that, *boom*, he set up a lunch date."

My brain ticked over that a second. "So, you went out with Harrison Ford?"

"No." She smiled fondly. "Harrison was always busy when I could make lunch and I was always busy when he could. Harrison was *really* pissed about it. Meanwhile I was trying to get this Internet business off the ground. I had these amazing designs and I thought I could start up an on-line clothing shop. Which George was investing in." She smirked. "He didn't know it, but he was investing. And then everything fell apart. It could have been an *empire*."

Ice in the pitcher, she took two glasses out of one cupboard and ripped open a bag of lime-flavoured tortilla chips with her teeth.

"I thought you were going to be a massage therapist when you came down here."

"I was just so burnt out from catering . . . George said he'd put me through school so I thought massage would be cool. But then on the first day, oh my god, they split us up into pairs. And we had to take off all our clothes. So then this girl, she starts massaging my chest! *Not* my thing. I didn't want to do massage anyway. I mean it's kinda gross, touching strangers' skin like that. I didn't tell George though." She laughed giddily at the thought. "I just skipped class and went for coffee, got my nails done or whatever." She pushed a glass of sangria toward me and we moved our party into the living room. "So, what's with the new 'do, anyway. It's *dark*."

"You hate it?"

She tilted her head. "You could bag yourself a politician with that look. Me, I'm going for a producer. They like blondes." She batted her eyes playfully. "You still haven't told me what the hell you're doing down here."

"My mum died."

"Oh Christ, I'm sorry." Her hand reached over. "When? Jesus, how is Sally? She must be *wrecked*."

"Week ago. And now it turns out she used to be a stripper named Celia Dare."

Marcella choked on a chip then burst into a coughing fit mixed with laughter. "The feminist who ate Vancouver was a peeler?"

I nodded. "Google her. Celia fucking Dare. I came down to try and talk to this old stripper who used to be her roommate but she was about as useful as tits on a bull. I was just getting some juicy stuff and she kicked me out." I stared into my glass a moment. "She slept with Frank Sinatra."

If Marcella were a slot machine, three cherries would have rung across her forehead. "You know what Ava Gardner said about Sinatra: Someone asked her, 'What do you see in that 120-pound runt?' and she said, 'Well, there's only 10 pounds of Frank and 110 pounds of cock.' Did she fuck John Kennedy?" Marcella asked, electrified. "Everyone fucked John Kennedy."

"She booted me out before I found out. She was kind of a cranky old bitch."

"That'll be us in a few years."

I reached into the chip bag. "What was George in the hospital for?"

"He's got Crohn's; didn't I ever tell you that? He was in the hospital every five minutes. So he had yet *another* operation and he ended up going septic when he was home recovering. Every time he got sick, I had to play nursey. So there he is, temperature up to 104 and I call 911: no no no, he doesn't want to go to the nearby hospital, he wants to go to *Stanford*. Then at Stanford he went totally delirious and thought somebody cut off his penis. His sister came to see him and he made her check to see if it was still there. I would've checked for him but he was saying all this weird shit to me." Her voice dropped to a dramatic growl, "'*I* know who you are. And I know what you've done . . .' And there I am, his wife for chrissake, and he hasn't given me power of attorney, he hasn't sorted out his will, there's bill collectors at the door. We were borrowing against his life insurance policy when he was sick before so I forged his name again and got out what I could before everything went to shit." The words rattled off her tongue like stage patter—then that laugh again. I didn't recall her laughter sounding so manic. I couldn't figure out if it was just nerves or actual cruelty.

I wiped sangria and lime salt off my mouth. "You cleaned out his life insurance policy?"

"What was I supposed to do? He was hardly working, his ex-wife was bitching for more child support—what would have happened to me if he died? What kind of man leaves his wife in that kind of position? And the bank account was a *joint* account, so it wasn't *his*. He wants the car back, he wants his money back, he wants, he wants. I have to pay my rent. San Francisco ain't cheap and this is where I have to be if I want to get a decent job. Not way the hell out in Marin County. So now he's threatening to sue. Never should've called 911." She crunched another chip—"Just kidding"—and made a face like a ten-year-old.

The phone started blinking in intermittent red bursts. "I keep my ringer off," she said, checking the call display before picking up. "Hello? . . . Hi-i-i, how are you? . . . Oh nothing . . . Sure, what time were you thinking?" She checked her watch. "Okay. I'll see you then." She put the receiver down with a wince. "I'm sorry, Viv. I forgot I had plans tonight. I've been see-ing this guy I met just down here at Vesuvio's. Well, actually, I met him first at Stanford Hospital—he's the head of cardiology. I was having coffee when I first moved into town and ran into him again." Her eyes lit up. "Recently divorced, no kids. He's so cute—totally naive—I guess from being married so long and hanging out in the ivory tower. I should see if he has a friend I can introduce you to! Anyway, no rush, he's not picking me up for another hour or so. Feel free to hang out here as long as you like. I'll give you the spare key."

Nine

~

ONCE MARCELLA WAS OUT THE DOOR IN AN OUTFIT BEFIT-
ting the trophy wife of a heart specialist, I turned on the TV.
Nothing much on. I tried calling Frank once more. His line rang
a few times and suddenly: "Yeah." Frank has call display.

"It's Viv," I announced with some vague hope that a burst of
joy would bounce back at me. No such luck. "Where are you?
You haven't called me back."

"Busy." He spoke away from the phone. "Sure, gimme
another . . ." Back into the receiver he said, "Really busy."

My gaze drifted around the room. "Are you mad at me?"

Silence, then, "Whatever, Vivian." A DJ's voice traipsed in
the background.

"I'm sorry I didn't call before I left. But I'm feeling less
weird now, not so lost, you know. Which is kind of ironic
since I'm . . . and I found the lady my mother used to know."
Hoots and clapping came through from his end. "Where *are*
you?"

"I'm at the Number Five with Brian, grabbing a beer,
catchin' the show."

"Seems like you're always in strip joints lately."

"Guess so."

Normally I wouldn't care. Rather, I don't care when it's
once in a while. It just seems a bit pathetic when a guy's in a

strip joint every other day like some divorced sad sack who needs a place to cry in his beer.

"Well, I just wanted to check in and say hi. I'll probably be a couple more days here."

"Oh! 'member this chick? She's totally ripped."

I assumed this was directed at Brian. "Bye," I murmured and clacked my phone closed. Staring blankly at the television screen, I recalled a photographer who did publicity shots for strippers telling me that most of them were man-hating lesbians. "You would be too," he said, "if you were stuck with the assholes who hang out in strip joints all day."

Picking up the remote I clicked past old footage of Lawrence Welk squeezing his accordion on PBS to a reality show with three men and three women competing for the fastest tightrope walk over a hundred-foot gorge. The men wore baggy jeans and T-shirts, the women wore Lycra crop tops and tight hip huggers. One of them had on a pair of the striped low-rise jeans currently sitting in my suitcase. I peered at her washboard abs and thought about getting a gym membership.

On A&E, black-and-white snippets of an old nightclub act flashed across the screen. A bullish dark-haired man buffooned around stage, bellowing in broken Italian and English and blowing away at his trumpet intermittently. Beside him a woman in a black taffeta dress with a full skirt and slim bodice folded her arms, a worse than bored face balanced on her long thin neck as the trumpet player jumped around for her attention. The screen cut to the same woman in colour, older and heavier now, with the same short black bangs framing her face. "The thing about Louis . . ." she said. White print spelled her name out along the bottom of the screen. *Keely Smith, singer, wife of Louis Prima.*

I couldn't get away from that name it seemed. Keely described how she met Louis at the age of sixteen, how she adored him and became his fourth wife, and finally how he turned into the cheating, gambling, alcoholic she finally left.

Cut to Louis Prima and the Witnesses on Ed Sullivan, Keely singing clear and strong, Sam Butera blasting the audience with his sax. Cut to the A&E montage and a voice-over announcing, "We will return to *The Wildest: The Story of Louis Prima* in a moment." I had thought *the wildest* was Annie West's appraisal not Prima's usual qualifier. As the documentary went on, I kept hoping my mother would materialize. She didn't. But by the end, when Sam Butera's eyes teared up over Prima's death in 1978, my own tears drizzled down. It wasn't sadness exactly. Closing my eyes, I fell sideways and lay still on the couch a few minutes. Why couldn't it be easier? Why couldn't Annie have just told me the whole story and put me out of my misery. I felt like a kid asking how to spell a word: "But how can I *find* it in the dictionary if I don't know how to *spell* it?"

Grabbing the books from my bag, I lay them around me on the couch. I opened *Pack of Rats* to the photograph of Sinatra and his buddies standing in front of the Sands in Las Vegas. I riffled through the beginning of *Mob Wife*. Snatching the writing tablet Marcella kept beside her phone, I wrote: *Audrey _____? Born 1943? Fake ID. Cecilia D'arelli. Carnival 1959? Did striptease, attacked by marines in Virginia, steals car from Okie Joe. Back to Little Italy? Teddy the Ghost? Travelling with Teddy. Avuncular. Vegas with Teddy. 1960. Annie and Sinatra. Yells at Sinatra. Did Sinatra like Celia, hate her? Okie Joe comes to Vegas. Argument? Johnny Rosselli and Sinatra tell him to take a hike. John Kennedy in Vegas 1960, gets a million-dollar campaign contribution from mob. Showgirls and hookers sent to his room. Celia? Cecilia?*

I stared at the page for I don't know how long trying to paint her picture: My mother in a suite at the Sands Hotel. Morning light coming through the open curtains. I put Annie back in her room, stinging from Sinatra's tantrum, full of guilt for sending a teenager to dance in a cooch show. My mother is so young. Platinum-blonde hair with those late fifties pushed-back curls, dewy skin. She's a ballerina and a tap dancer and her legs are long and pale and thin. She is pissed off that Annie West is in Vegas. But she's angrier at Teddy who leaves her alone while he goes off and does business. Cecilia feels like an idiot standing up for a jealous twat like Annie now. Flipping the page, I wrote:

Adrenaline still surges when she gets back to the suite. Drapes open, morning sunlight cuts the room. Going on ten now and Teddy the Ghost still isn't back. He's been gone since last night. *Had a meet*, he said, but maybe they could hit a late show if he was back in time. It occurs to Cecilia he might've meant right here in the Copa Room—the Summit at the Sands.

Can you get kicked out of a joint for telling off Frank Sinatra? His name is slapped all over the marquee out front, on top of Dean Martin's, on Sammy Davis Jr.'s, on Peter Lawford's, on Joey Bishop's. Seeing their names, it didn't hit her that they could all be sleeping right over her damn head. He's making a movie in town too with all his cronies. Angie Dickinson even.

Served him right though. But Annie probably deserved what she got too. Bitch. When Cecilia heard the banging on the door, she lay there hoping Teddy would answer. Hoping he'd be in the living room on the sofa. He could've come in without her noticing. That's what made him Teddy the Ghost. Teddy Boo. Teddy Spook. She knew damn well though she had to get up and answer it herself.

At least she can hang around all day if she wants. Better than back in New York.

A couple months ago, when she showed up in Little Italy again, she got herself a room in some flea bag. Just needed time to figure out what to do with herself and that car. She parked it two blocks away and kept her mouth shut.

First night in town, she took herself out to a late-night diner for a bite. A couple of tables over was a uniformed cop making eyes. He piped up with jovial comments like single eaters sometimes do. Eventually he introduced himself, asked if he might join her. He wasn't much to look at but he seemed sweet, sort of dopey and bashful. When they got to the bottom of their coffees, he asked if he could take her to the pictures sometime.

"Sure."

"How 'bout tomorrow night? Seen *Psycho* yet?"

"Sure."

After the movie, Cecilia announced that she was definitely off showers. From now on, it would be bubble baths all the way. Officer Ronald laughed and took her hand as they walked.

Over pie and coffee, he offered to sleep on her floor that night if it would make her feel safer. Cecilia raised an eyebrow. She could take Anthony Perkins, she quipped. No guy in a dress was gonna take her down. Ronald told her he'd come to her rescue any time and began to razzle-dazzle her with how exciting police work was in Little Italy. The next night, for instance, there was going to be a big raid right here in the neighbourhood. Could be dangerous. But the law was the law and gambling was illegal.

Cecilia glanced at her watch then looked back at Ronald, suddenly struck with that scrap of information. "Right in the neighbourhood? Where?"

"Couple blocks from here. I've already said too much." He cleared his throat, looked casually away from the prettiest girl he'd ever seen.

"Imagine that."

Seconds after he saw her to her door, she slipped back out, ran up the street and jumped in Okie Joe's car. She found a spot right out front of The 92 and as she rushed up to the door, the bouncer spread his arms wide. "Audrey! What a sight for sore eyes. Gimme that face!" He kissed both of her cheeks.

"Uh-uh—*Cecilia* now."

"I forgot." He grinned. "You go on in. The Boys'll wanna see you—Jimmy and Micky D . . ." In a whisper he added, "Teddy the Ghost just got back."

Inside, it was as if Cecilia had risen from the ashes, a winged thing. Arms opened and encircled her, there were laughter and hugs. Teddy the Ghost looked up from his table. *"Madonn'!"* She blushed as he took her face in his thick hands. "Look at this beautiful Audrey."

"Cecilia. Remember?"

"That's right!" He pointed across the table at Micky D in mock warning. "We made you Italian, didn't we? D'arelli, uh! You thought I forgot, I bet. Cecilia D'arelli."

Micky D bapped the table with his palm a couple times. "That's right. She's family now! Hey, get this girl a drink. Jimmy! Bring some kinda fruity somethin' for Cecilia here."

She grinned and felt her cheeks heat up. Micky D was always friendly but Teddy she recalled as quiet. And fierce.

"Sit down here next to your uncle Teddy and tell me about your travels. What the helluv you been doin' the last coupla months? You didn't show at the restaurant job we got you—I went in there lookin' for you—so this better be good."

She tucked her chin. "I'm sorry. It was just—you'd already done too much. I decided maybe I should see the world and so I got an, um, an acting job working for the carnival." She didn't want him to imagine her nearly naked. Or dirty. Or stinking.

Teddy frowned. "The carnival. *Pthu.* Those carnies are no-good degenerates and bums. The whole bunch of 'em. No honour. No family. They steal from their own."

"Yeah." She nodded. "I got a boyfriend who wasn't very nice and—" *They steal from their own.* "I guess I ran away."

"He hurt you? Huh? Look at me—this guy lay a finger on you? 'Cause I swear—" Teddy kissed his fingertips and eyeballed heaven. "Holy Mother of God, I swear, I'll hunt the sonuvabitch down and break anything on him that moves."

"He just wasn't nice. He—"

Jimmy arrived with her fruity rum drink. "Here you go. I even found you a cherry—Jesus wept! *This* Cecilia. My girl. Look at you! Sweetheart—you look tired."

She smiled weakly, looked across at Micky D and down into her hands. Teddy jerked an eyebrow sideways. Micky and Jimmy excused themselves and made for the bar.

Draping an arm across the back of the red leather bench, he turned himself to her. "You in trouble, sweetheart?"

"In trouble?"

"That carny-bastard get you in trouble?"

"No! Oh no. He tried, but I wouldn't let him. And he got mad and threatened me." She scrunched her eyes shut and opened them again. "I sort of, I took his car. So, I guess I might be in trouble. For stealing." A tear popped from her left eye.

Teddy pounded the table so hard, her right eye spat another. A braying laugh erupted from his belly. She wiped her face, bewildered.

"You took the sonuvabitch's wheels?" He laughed so loud she thought his heart might go on him. "*Bellissima!* That's my girl! She stole his fuckin' wheels, y'hear that, Jimmy? Got what he deserved, the cocksucker—pardon my language. Oh that's rich. You made my goddamn night, sweetheart."

Her chest gushed with swampy gratitude. She rocked sideways and pecked a kiss at Teddy's cheek.

Dropping his arm down onto her shoulders, he bear-hugged her to his side. "He tried to screw you—in whatever fashion—and *boom!* she cuts him off at the knees. Atta*girl.*"

She plucked the maraschino cherry floating on the ice and popped it into her mouth, letting the strong liqueur spread across her tongue. "There's another thing I came to talk to you about. I don't know if this is even—I went out on a date tonight."

"Sonuvabitch better behave himself or he'll be *walkin'* to work tomorrow, won't he?" Teddy slapped the table again.

"Well, he's a cop."

"Jesus, out of the frypan into the fire. What's his name?"

"Ronald Nizzi."

Teddy frowned. "Don't know 'im. Must be new."

"He said they're going to raid a card game in the neighbourhood tomorrow night. I thought—in case you knew anyone . . ."

Teddy rubbed at the hook of his nose, pushed his lips out. "*In the neighbourhood?*" Cracked his neck, then shook his head. "No. Could be a little game somewheres but no way cops could know that thing. Prob'ly tryin' to impress you. Seein' what you know. Good girl though for coming to me. Where you stayin'? You need money?"

"I'm okay."

"Lemme give you somethin' here. This town'll chew you up, you got no dough. You got an apartment?"

"Hotel. Maybe I'll take a drive tomorrow and look for an apartment."

"Take a drive! You still got that sonuvabitch's car? Oh sweetheart." He brayed at the ceiling again. "Leave it here with me. I'll take care of it."

"There's still some stuff in it. I'll just keep it till tomorrow and I'll bring it round."

"*Madonn'* . . . Lose the plates at least." He yelled over his shoulder. "Micky!"

The next night, Cecilia came round after midnight and walked in to Micky D sitting at Teddy's table again, the two of them shaking their heads. Teddy waved her over. He took his cigar out. "Guess who got raided tonight? We had our own mole here and we didn't listen. *Sonuvabitch.* Micky's been bailin' guys outta the joint half the night all 'cause I thought some bull was just tryin' to make time with you." He stuffed his cigar back in his mouth, got no smoke. Micky flipped a lighter for him.

By the time she left, Teddy had insisted on paying Cecilia's rent to the end of the month.

She went out with Officer Ronald half a dozen more times, flashing her eyes wide with wonder at his every word. After each date, she headed for The 92.

Eventually Teddy made her a new proposition: an apartment where she could stay rent free, the stipulation being that she could only spend evenings there. Her job was to be out all day so fellas could play poker. Teddy would pay for dance classes to keep her out of trouble.

Determined to get herself flush with cash, though, Cecilia took another job working at the Starfish beer parlour. Teddy showed up to talk her out of it. "What do you wanna work in a dive like this for? You should go back to school and learn a trade. You talk good—you could do anything. You could be a stewardess. You quit here and I'll send you to stewardess school."

"What's the difference between this kind of waitress and that kind of waitress?"

"What's the—?" Teddy stared. "If you don't know—You could be anything, a model even. How 'bout modelling school?"

It was when Micky D started coming around the Starfish that Teddy got good and hot under the collar. Micky asked her out for dinner and dancing and soon after, the two of them were at the Copacabana. A lot of faces from The 92 were there that night and Cecilia was treated like royalty. Rosemary Clooney took the stage.

Micky was ecstatic. "See, now this broad still knows how to perform, play some real music. I seen Old Blue Eyes in here before. Yeah, Sinatra! Real music. Not like that rock 'n' roll crappola kids are listening too. I'd like to see that 'Jailhouse Rock' bastard sing 'Night and Day.'"

To Cecilia's shock, Micky D could really dance. When Clooney called "Mambo Italiano," Micky's feet cut and chopped the floor, his eyes bugging at the lightning flash of his date's legs, her rubber body bending wherever his lead instructed.

When she showed up at the Starfish next evening though, she didn't have a job. By way of explanation, she was told, "We're overstaffed right now."

"Will you call me when it gets busier?"

"Honey, there's people that think you would be better off doin' somethin' else."

In tears, she headed down to The 92 and waited for Teddy to show up.

"It's good they fired you. That place is a bad influence. What about your family? I wasn't gonna tell you this, but your father came in here again while you were—"

"My stepfather?"

"Stepfather. Whatever the hell. What happened to your real one?"

"My mother kicked him out when I was a kid."

"What—he hit her?"

"Came in here when?"

"When you was runnin' around the country with those carny-whores."

"What'd he say?"

"I toldja, he asked after ya. You should call—"

"Doesn't matter. He's not my father."

"What about your mother? Family's important. 'Specially for a young girl."

"You're my family."

"Ahh, sweetheart . . . but you know, fam—"

"I don't want to talk about it."

"Family is—"

"I don't."

Teddy looked away, addressing the air. "She doesn't want to talk about it. Whaddya gonna do?" He faced her. "Okay. I got another proposal for you. Another job. I got business and no wife. A widower travelling by himself . . . don't look good. Know what I mean?"

"You want to pay me to travel with you?"

"Go home. Sleep good and we'll talk tomorrow."

"Businessmen travel alone all the time," Cecilia said the next evening. Teddy was still in the apartment, the room thick with smoke. He emptied ashtrays, put glasses in the sink, scotch back on the shelf as she opened a window and flopped on the sofa.

He didn't face her. "Well, this one gets a hard time when he's alone."

"Why?"

He looked at the ceiling. "Listen to her with the questions."

She watched his back and waited.

"Because I did foolish things when I was young. So, I got a reputation. When men travel alone, people get suspicious. When they find out one's me, they get extra bent outta shape. *Capice?*" She nodded. "You wanna know what's the smartest thing a girl can do for herself? Don't ask questions." He stubbed out his cigar in an empty ashtray. "Tomorrow I'm takin' you shoppin'. Gonna be winter soon. Girl like you needs fur so she don't catch cold."

All next month, she spent warm in Miami. She *loved* Miami. She had a black-diamond mink coat hanging in her closet but winter was passing her by. Teddy'd got them a glittering gorgeous suite at the Fontainebleau Hotel and she spent her days reading and lounging around the pool, or getting gussied up at the beauty parlour with Tina and Glenda while Teddy slept the day away. Tina and Glenda weren't much older than Cecilia and they happened to be in town doing the same thing: pretend dates with men in Miami to talk business.

It was Tina and Glenda who talked her into bleaching her hair. "Man, them blue eyes of yours! You'd look like Kim Novak if you did your hair blonde. But better! Classier. Or you could style it kind of old-fashioned like Lana Turner. That's comin' back y'know. I seen it in *Harper's Bazaar.*"

Both were bottle blondes themselves and they'd taken to Cecilia—they shortened her name to *Celia* and she liked the sound of it—treated her like a musketeer, a sister, showed her the ropes, winked to her at dinner when the Boys' conversation came to a point when it was time to take a powder. It amused her the way waiters scraped and bowed for him, the way they tripped over themselves. Because of Teddy's money, she figured. One day she'd get rich herself or famous enough to make a waiter scrape.

For Tina and Glenda, there were different dates all the time; a phone call in the afternoon told them what time they would be dining that evening. The girls were to pick out a club or restaurant where they could all go and have a good time. Usually they picked the Eden Roc or the Boom Boom Room at the Fontainebleau. Later that night they would receive a call from the hotel lobby from Steve or Al or Joey. If the men didn't know each other well and needed less Boom Boom and more privacy for their negotiations they'd all check into a motel. The girls never let on to outsiders that when the group took an entire floor of rooms, they would be on one side of the hallway while the Boys were on the other, talking business through the night.

For Tina and Glenda, the rule was no sex with the dates. *Sex is problems.* This shit was too important for problems, Teddy said. If these guys wanted sex, they could get themselves a whore. Keep your mouth shut and look good was all you had to know. One girl had been sent home to Chicago for sleeping with a date.

For Celia, the no-sex rule was irrelevant. Teddy never even attempted to touch her. She was his madonna, his little girl. Generally if he slept at all at night it was on the couch in their suite at the Fontainebleau. He slept in the bedroom during the day when she was by the pool or off getting her hair done.

Oftentimes when those late-night motel negotiations were going on, the girls would have themselves a private party, drinking sweet liquor, dishing movie stars and talking up the pink Cadillacs they planned on having. Celia entertained them with her vision of being onstage one day at the Eden Roc. Or the 500 Club in Atlantic City. Or the Paramount on Broadway. Tina and Glenda would giggle and egg her on, hand her a toothbrush for a mike and demand a show.

Screams and catcalls filled the room when Celia danced the sultry ballet of Cyd Charisse with a chair as her lover. She could do a mean Peggy Lee and the girls would back her as a two-woman orchestra, humming and bumping the tune to "My Man" as Celia belted out *He's not much for looks and no hero out of books, he's my man* . . . shaboom-boom-boom. She took requests. She could do Julie London like nobody's business, and Keely Smith. It wasn't the same doing Keely without her stepfather doing the Louis Prima part though.

Little more than a month passed and *bam!* just like that, the party was over. Teddy had an emergency to take care of in Las Vegas. She packed her bag and cried at leaving her only two girlfriends.

Now here she is at the Sands. She flops back on the bed and closes her eyes. No one to play with. He could've at least spent the first night with her. This town is barely a town. It's eerie is what it is. Ten or twelve hotels in the middle of sand, sand and more sand. Her stepfather told her once that Vegas was run by hoodlums. He used to like talking hoodlums with one of his colleagues at NYU, a criminology professor. Her stepfather thought hoodlums had their fingers into everything, every nightclub, sanitation company, politician, import business— every piece of fruit in the supermarket had mobster prints on it as far as he was concerned.

Kook. Just as well he's out of her life.

She straightens her legs and puts forehead to knees, stretches and palms the bottoms of her feet. The phone rings. She rolls over and plucks the receiver from its cradle. "Where are you?"

"How'd you know it was me?"

"Who else knows I'm here? Where are you?"

"I'm atta phone booth."

"You're always at a phone booth."

"Gotta go to L.A. for a couple days."

"What! What about me?"

"You get your nails done. Go by the pool, they got a floatin' crap game down there. Get it? Floatin' crap game." He chuckles. When there is no response, he says, "Why don't you get your hair done dark like before. It was classier lookin'. You stay in all night?"

"Yes. *Awake*, waiting for *you*."

"You know better than that, sweetheart. Go have a nice drink by the pool and charge it to the room. Go see Frank Sinatra at the Copa Room tonight. He's a pal a'mine y'know."

"I already saw him and I don't like him."

"What's 'at?"

"I saw him in the hall and he's a skinny little creep."

"Ah now, don't be sayin' that. He's a stand-up guy."

"He's an asshole."

"Hey-ey! With the language! Just as well you got away from that Tina and Whatsits. Be a good girl, see a show tonight. You tell 'em Smilin' Jack Entratter at the door and he'll sit you with good people."

"Why don't you take me with you to L.A.?"

"I got a meet. What're you getting funny for? Smilin' Jack is gettin' a call, okay. Same fella used to run the Copa in New York. Get him to take you to Louis Prima in the lounge."

"Louis Prima, the *singer?*"

"Him and the wife. They're playin' at the whatsits. Have a good time, sweetheart."

"But—"

The line goes dead. "*Asshole-asshole-ass-hole.* Fuck, bastard, piss, damn!" she says, flopping back. She glares at the ceiling and closes her eyes.

When she wakes the sun is long gone and the neon lights of Vegas beam and flash outside. Dread sits like a slab of meat in her belly and she thinks she might cry; she has no one now. She misses Miami. She misses dancing with the girls. *Should've stayed with Officer Ronald in Little Italy.* He wouldn't have left her alone. Maybe he would've. Nothing is ever like anyone says. *At least you're not in a doghouse,* she tells herself. She peels away from the bed and flips the light, leaves the drapes open to keep the extra sparkle coming in, ventures into the living room and turns on the television for company while she hunts for a dinner menu. *You've got room service, for crissake. How bad can it be?*

She picks up the phone and orders filet mignon and lobster, a salad, a glass of champagne. And milk. Baked Alaska for dessert. And . . . and, she hates to lose the friendly voice at the end of the line. After she hangs up, she thinks of reasons to call back: ice water, condiments, bread. Of course, madam. Always.

She sits down and stands up. Paces the room. Looks at the phone.

Family's important.

He came looking for her again, Teddy told her. They nearly busted his head open at The 92 but he still came back. He wasn't a complete crumb. He'd be home from school by now. She pictures her stepfather lonesome by the record player, unable to listen to Louis Prima without her. "Serves you right," she blurts just as a knock comes at the door. She smoothes her bed-wrinkled skirt as she goes.

Grinning his "Good evening," a young man wheels in a cart. Celia gestures to the coffee table, stands back and watches him transfer plates and remove covers, before taking out the cheque for her to sign. She adds a fat tip and scribbles in her signature.

"Would you like to join me?" she asks. "I think my eyes were bigger than my stomach."

He stares at her and swallows. "With you?"

"Sure. There's a western on television. You like westerns?"

He looks to the TV. "Boy, do I." She hands him the cheque. He says, "You're—isn't—my boss'd kill me. Thank you though, ma'am."

Alone again, she sits down on the sofa, stares at the spread and clicks on the television with the remote control. She clicks it off and back on again. The remote control at the Fontainebleau was the first she'd ever seen. Stewart told her they came from military technology and one day everybody would have one. Her mother said it was ridiculous, the idea of a person being so lazy—she wouldn't have one in her house. Celia aims it at the telephone, out the window, at the side of her head, fires and tosses it down beside her. Jerry Lewis is on *Ed Sullivan*. She wonders if he's sad without Dean Martin. He looks sad. She cuts into her steak.

By the time she's taken crackers to a lobster claw, a troop of female tap dancers is on with Ed. Celia pulls a long chunk of meat from the shell, dips it in butter and frowns at the screen. "Big deal. Can y'sing?" she barks.

By the time her glass of champagne is finished, she's wishing she were back at the Copacabana, dancing with Micky D. She clicks over to the western. John Wayne. He looks like the kind of guy who'd throw his son down the stairs. She goes for another sip of champagne and finds an empty glass. She calls room service.

A different bellhop this time. He wheels in an ice bucket and pops the cork.

"Do you know Jack Entreeter?" she asks.

"Jack *Entratter*? He's the president of the hotel. And the entertainment director."

"He'd be in the Copa Room right now?"

"Or near it."

"Like a glass of champagne?"

"Excuse me?" He looks around, nervous. "No, thank you, ma'am. But thank you very much, ma'am." He hands her the bill and a pen.

"What time does the next show start in the Copa Room?"

"About an hour. But it's impossible to get into. They've been—oh, what am I saying, I'm sure you'll have no—" He looks down a moment. "My cousin said he helped fix Teddy the Ghost's Cadillac one time."

"Really." She hands him back the bill.

"Yes, ma'am. Said he was really nice."

"He's a prince."

He swallows.

"Good night," she tells him. He backs toward the door and lets himself out.

Strolling to the bedroom, she opens the closet, swishes a hand across her dresses and pulls one out. She marches back in the living room and pours another glass.

An hour later, she's out front in her mink, wearing the diamond necklace and earrings Teddy got her in Miami. The hotel sign lights up its piece of sky with:

Sands

A PLACE
IN THE SUN
JACK ENTRATTER PRESENTS:
FRANK SINATRA
DEAN MARTIN
SAMMY DAVIS JR.
PETER LAWFORD
JOEY BISHOP

A couple stands close by, gazing at the lights as an electric guestmobile pulls up. "I understand you never know which of them's going to be there," the man says to the doorman, examining his cufflink as he steps into the cart. "Who's starring tonight?"

"With our luck," the woman says, "we'll get stuck with Lawford."

Celia watches as the driver motors them toward the casino. The doorman wishes her a good evening. "Off to try the tables tonight?" She smiles, and climbs into the next cart.

Stepping out under the porte cochère, she walks through the doors into an orgy of sparkle and noise, pinging and plinking, shrieks and laughter. Turning around, her head buzzes: the noise, the bejewelled people, painted murals on the walls, crystal chandeliers. She gazes off in the direction the beautiful cocktail girls all seemed to walk. As the heat of the room hits, she opens her coat and follows the mincing steps of their high heels, the flitting royal-blue feathers on their round rears as they carry drink trays down three wide terrazzo stairs into the main casino.

At the bottom step, Celia stands with her mouth open. The room is a bowlful of spinning glistening money. She ambles big-eyed through the tables. Golden light swims, glinting off silk suits and shimmering dresses, diamond stickpins and fox stoles. Expensive bodies perch around green-felt tables, laugh and clap over roulette wheels, blackjack. Faces turn as Celia passes and she meets each and every gaze.

A gambler in a cowboy hat that matches his cranberry sharkskin suit grabs Celia's wrist with his free hand as he shakes dice with the other. "Hey, beautiful, not so fast. You come right in here with Big Daddy Angus and blow his dice for luck."

Encircled in his arm Celia blows the dice.

"Six!" The dealer adds a stack of chips to the pile in front of Angus.

"Oh you *are* my doll. My beautiful doll!" He kisses her full on the lips and she pulls back. He crushes her close.

"I have to go."

"Naw, you ain't. Stay right here."

"No, I really do. Would you let me go, please?"

"Mmm, I got a filly just like you back home. Gonna race her next year. Be a good girl and give Angus another little blow and I'll give you a treat."

Celia smiles sweetly, blows into his palm and waits for him to toss his dice before she slams her palms into his chest, tries to yank herself free.

"*Five!* Honey, you ain't goin' nowhere. You're my good-luck charm." He puts his whisky mouth to her ear again. "Wait'll I get my other hand free, I'm gonna peel that coat off and see the mink without the fur."

"Get your meat hooks off!" She brings her fist back but he hugs and pins her arms.

Smiles and nervous laughter around the table.

"Jackass," she spits, and kicks whatever bony part is closest. The gambler's grin turns cold just as an enormous man in a black tuxedo swoops in.

"Cecilia, is that you? Angus, you been keeping Cousin Celie company! Good man! Here, lemme give you some breathing room with those chips." The big man sets a stack in front of Angus. "Come on, honey, we're late. Thanks again, Angus." He drapes his arm across Celia's back and walks her in a jovial gait from the craps table. "You wouldn't happen to be a close personal friend of a ghost named Teddy?"

"You gave him *money?*" she huffs. Legs shaking, her breath comes in quick snorts. "Goddamn *rapist* and you give him *money?*"

Head high, he smiles to guests as he speaks. "Just an overeager cowpuncher, that's all. I greased you out of his way and he'll give us back twice that in about three minutes. So you're Cecilia."

"I take it you're Smilin' Buddha."

"Smilin' *Jack*, if you want to get technical."

"How did you know it was me?"

"Let's see, I believe the man said, *blonde hellcat with legs up to here and a face that puts Harlow to shame.*" He bends forward to see her legs switching through her open coat. "Yup. You must be the angel who beat up Sinatra this morning too."

"I hate it here. This place is full of creeps."

"Ah, 'she walks in beauty, like the night . . . '"

"Is he coming back tomorrow?"

"He asked me to look in on you. I stopped by your room and you weren't there."

"Where are you taking me?"

"The fabulous Copa Room where you will be thrilled and amazed, thereby changing your entire demeanour. Please god."

He walks her through the doors, where a lush orchestra and a deep crooning voice fall into their ears. Entratter helps her shrug her fur off and hands it to a hat-check girl whose cheek he kisses.

Celia looks her up and down. "No jobs for the ugly, huh?"

Entratter grins and hands Celia a coat-check number on a silver disk, walks her into the showroom.

There he is onstage, the prick. "Call Me Irresponsible" drifts easily from his throat.

Celia stares. Entratter leans over. "They don't call him The Leader for nothin', huh?" He beams at Sinatra.

"Does the room fill up like this every show? Must be eight hundred people in here."

"The room? The whole town. This place alone turned away eighteen thousand reservations the first week. Come on, I'll introduce you to some friends." He leads her ringside. A silver-haired man turns and flashes a smile. He stands to give up his chair.

"Oh look, folks," Sinatra calls from stage as he finishes his song. "El presidente, Jack Entratter's, finally seen fit to bless us with his presence."

Entratter raises his hand for another chair, which arrives at lightning speed. He sets it down for the silver-haired man whom he introduces to Celia as a good friend of Teddy's.

"Hey, Jack," Frank calls. "If y'got something to say, share it with the whole class."

Entratter laughs and yells, "Frank, may I introduce you to the lovely Miss Cecilia D'are—" He leans over to catch the rest of her name.

"Yeah, Celia Dare, folks, my future ex-wife. Whaddya sittin' her down there with that sly fox, Rosselli, before I even got a chance to marry her never mind divorce her. Ladies and gentlemen, the handsome, the shrewd, the brains behind the fabulous Tropicana, Mr. John Rosselli, and a woman who's never gonna lemme forget what a heel I am, Miss Celia Dare. And at the same table, Cyd Charisse, ladies and gentlemen, the magnificent Cyd Charisse is here tonight!"

Celia's head nearly rips itself off her neck. There she is, sitting five feet away. Touching the same table.

Frank grins. "Stand up, gorgeous."

Charisse rises, smiles and waves around the room, sits back down.

"Did somebody say legs?" Dean Martin walks onstage from the wings. "Daddy, make me a scotch before I beg her to kick me to death for the fun of it."

Celia's neck still cranes as Charisse sips her martini, so beautiful, she glows. More than the magazines, more than the movies.

"Ladies and gentlemen, direct from the bar, Mr. Dean Martin."

Celia pulls her eyes back to Martin's handsome Italian mug.

"Hey, how'd everybody get in our room?" Martin asks then sings, *"Drink to me only that's all I aks—ask—and I will drink to youuuu . . ."* He looks from his watch to the conductor. "How long I been on?"

Celia suppresses a laugh. She didn't know he was funny. Not without Jerry Lewis. Rosselli pours her a glass of champagne.

It isn't long before Joey Bishop is on, with a portable bar set up on a cart, and they beckon Jack Entratter up to discuss an urgent matter. According to Frank and Dean, Entratter couldn't remember a line if he was following it down the middle of Fremont Street and next thing you know, a troop of curvaceous showgirls hits the stage carrying the words to a joke for Entratter. His bumbling pleases the crowd no end and once Joey hands him a Jack Daniel's on the rocks for his troubles, he beats it back to the table.

Celia watches him move past the back of her chair to Cyd Charisse who stretches her flute-long neck. Entratter whispers in her ear before he makes his way back to Celia. "Stick with Johnny. He'll take better care of you than your own mother."

Johnny Rosselli turns his suave hawk face and tosses her an easy grin.

An hour later, the show is over and Celia's jaws hurt from laughing. As the lights come up, she notices Rosselli again. He must be older than her stepfather but he is striking. Tanned and iced at once. "I missed Teddy's call or I would've been in touch with you earlier," he says.

"Do you know, um, Cyd? Charisse?"

"Certainly. Would you like—Oh, she's halfway out the door."

Celia turns to catch the last of Charisse and longs for a word. An acknowledgement.

"You'll get another chance—you a fan?"

"Yes! I know all her, her everything . . . Thank you for making room for me tonight."

"Any friend of Teddy's . . . May I have the honour of showing you around town?"

"Don't feel like you have to babysit. I—"

Rosselli's eyes crinkle. "If this is babysitting, it's my kind of after-school job."

"Is it true you can see Louis Prima in a lounge? For free?"

They have another drink together and take a leisurely stroll back through the casino. Every so often Johnny stops to say hello to a cocktail girl, a high roller, someone in silk and diamonds, and Celia marvels at their reverence, the way he manages to make each one feel like she or he is utterly fascinating.

It is coming on midnight when they pull up to the Sahara. Johnny reaches in for Celia's hand as she climbs out of the car. "Prima should be on in a few minutes. We're moving him over to a showroom at the Desert Inn soon," he adds as they head past the camel statues. "He's so damn wild, nobody gambles whiles he's on." They pass the Arabs lounging outside and he hands her through the front doors toward the lounge.

"*We're* moving him? What do you do, anyway?"

He flips his card: John Rosselli, STRATEGIST. "I handle delicate business negotiations."

"Like an agent?"

"I put people together when a deft hand is needed. We're early still. You want to play a hand of blackjack?" In a flash he is by a cage, glad-handing the teller, who passes him a stack of chips.

"You didn't pay for those."

"When you're with me you don't pay for little things like that."

He picks a table, grins to the croupier. "Deal my niece in."

The dealer smirks. "You gotta lotta nieces, Johnny."

"Oh yes. My brothers are prolific men . . ." Cards snap the felt. Celia has a couple tens. "Okay, honey, I'm going to advise you to split," Johnny tells the crown of her head.

Celia tilts her chin up. "Huh?"

He pops another few chips on the table and next thing she knows she has two hands of blackjack going. "Hold on this one," he tells her. "Give him one of these." Rosselli waves his hand across her cards for the dealer. "A little gimme with your finger for this one. Good girl."

The dealer flips her another and she waves a palm over the second hand. The dealer flips his own card. "Winner here and winner there!"

She lets loose a money-squeal. "We won! we won!"

"Jesus, we got a card sharp," Rosselli laughs. An announcer's voice cuts in. "*Ladies and gentlemen, the Casbah Lounge proudly presents the wildest act in Las Vegas: Louis Prima and Keely Smith with Sammy Butera and the Witnesses!*"

Celia's head swings. "Oh no, they're coming!"

Rosselli helps her stuff the chips into her purse. "Oh—" he snaps two back in her fingers "—never forget to look after your friends."

She tips the dealer and smiles before looping her arm through her escort's and clipping toward Prima's raspy bear-voice.

"Hey, you cats out there, you getcherselves ready cuz we're gonna wail you right outta your skins." The band races and thumps behind him. "That's right, keep on smilin' cuz—" Prima's voice revs "'—when you're smilin''" (Keely and the band echo him), "'the whole world smiles with you . . .'"

Rosselli didn't lie. By the time they get to the lounge, there are no seats left. Gamblers head straight for the relentless driving music that beats its way through the smoke and chitchat.

Every pair of hips swivels, every pair of feet tries to keep up. Crowd or no, a cocktail girl makes it to Rosselli in a flash. Smirnoff over ice for him and something fruity for her.

Celia sips. "Mmm, what's this?"

"Let's see, I believe it's vodka, brandy, sherry and a little champagne."

"Has it got a name?"

"An Atomic."

"Because it blows your mind?" she giggles.

"That and for the A-bombs they've been testing out in the desert the last few years."

Celia coughs. "My stepdad says you can get all kinds of diseases from that."

"Nonsense. Government wouldn't do it if it could hurt you." Rosselli nods to her drink, says, "I call them *mousetraps*. Careful how many these cats fill you up with."

She titters. Her eyes bug at the lyrics coming from stage. "He's *dirty!*" she cries.

Rosselli laughs. "You get a licence to be bad in the desert."

She sucks the glass empty and sets it down. "Come dance with me." Pulling him into the crowd, she spins and leaps into motion for "Jump, Jive and Wail" as Prima buffoons across stage and the audience stomps and claps.

Prima hoarses from one song into the next. Twenty years younger and half his width, Keely Smith follows her husband's antics with the perfect poker face. The crowd howls as Prima does all he can to crack her deadpan facade till he suddenly picks up his trumpet and blasts the room alongside Sam Butera's blaring sax.

When the music slows, Celia and Rosselli waltz to Keely's "I Got it Bad and That Ain't Good." Louis thrusts his hips to his wife, looks at the audience and brays, "I got it good and that ain't bad!" He scats background vocals, dances and clowns and Celia laughs so hard her face hurts again. As the song nears the end, a bartender shoves his way through to Johnny and holds a telephone-shaped hand to his ear.

"I have a feeling I'm needed," Rosselli tells her. "You wanna stick around?"

"Okay," she sighs. "Promise to come back?"

"Count on it." He kisses her knuckles. "Jesus, you can move. You're why I can't date young girls anymore."

Rosselli is hardly out of the lounge before a young slickster in a skinny tie moves in on Celia with a sweet drink. "Hey, beautiful. Thirsty?"

"Thanks . . . pally!" She is slick her own self.

Twenty minutes later, she's dancing ringside and Prima is down on all fours howling like a rusty wolf at the blonde with the lightning legs. Keely looks askance and, bored-as-you-please, says, "Sure, but can she type?"

Prima launches into "I've Got You Under My Skin," directing every word to Celia. Keely grabs him by the scruff, "Come on, old man. You've only got so much life left in those knees and I might need you down on them later." The room shrieks as Prima bounces to his feet and lets Keely drag him back.

Celia sponges up every word and gesture and wills their attention back to her. Soon as the tune turns to "That Old Black Magic," she gets her wish. The Vegas version swings with Latin rhythms and, a few bars in, Prima is back downstage singing to Celia, "That old black magic has me in its spell," bending forward to put the mike to her lips for what should've have been Keely's part.

Celia comes close to swallowing her tongue but, looking to Prima's wife, she takes a slow breath and matches her tone for tone. "That old black magic that you weave so well."

"Mamma mia, she can sing too," Prima hollers. Keely looks a little nonplussed.

"Those icy fingers up and down my spine," he goes on.

"The same old witchcraft when your eyes meet mine," Celia and Keely call in stereo.

Prima falls back on his butt, shoes to the ceiling, legs rattling the air as if he's fallen on a live wire. "The same old tingle that I feel inside ('cept for blonde)," he yells.

"When that elevator starts its ride." Keely answers alone now that Celia has no mike.

"Down and down I go, round and round I go, like a leaf that's caught in the tide."

The words take on a whiff of danger as she walks to her husband and, placing a high-heeled foot between his splayed thighs, wails, "I should stay away, but what can I do-o-o? I hear your name and I'm aflame."

To Celia, it's as if she'd crawled through a screen and onto Ed Sullivan's sound stage.

Annie West sees it all. Her eyebrows have been stuck in a permanent arch since she passed John Rosselli on her way in. Annie met him once in New York last year. Micky D introduced her and you'd think the messiah himself had come to town the way everyone kissed his chic tailored ass.

Annie looks around for somewhere to sit or lean. A fella standing near the entrance offers a boost so she can sit on the railing. A drink in her hand now and two others lined up beside her, she perches above the crowd with her legs crossed, tapping a toe in the air as suitors press near, jockeying for position. Annie's busy watching Celia though, feeling crummy.

Annie had lain in her bed in a ball of self-loathing and regret, drifting in and out of sleep. The day was done by the time she woke to a drinks invitation that Sinatra had slipped under her door. "Bring your friend," it said. And, for a while, she felt good again—she and Frank would make up, she and Celia would make up . . . but now she watches and knows she's no friend of Celia's. She heard about the singing, but the dancing—all willowy grace with those long limbs. A ballerina. Like Lili St. Cyr.

When Louis and Keely slow down, Celia's slick admirer

takes the cue to move in close. She staggers just a little and Annie can't tell if it's the booze or if she's tired.

Annie glances around then jerks her head back. She catches sight of him against the bar, looking scruffier than he deserves to be in this expensive company. *Okie Joe?* She talked to him when she went rifling through carnies looking for Celia. She squints to see if it's the same shady bastard. Carnies winter in Florida, not Vegas, she thinks, and stops a cocktail girl, asks her if she knows that fella. *Never seem him before.* Annie looks back and he's gone. A guilt mirage. She turns her attention back to Celia and the guy wiping himself all over her.

Before long, the band finishes up with their usual: "When the Saints Go Marchin' In." The crowd stomps for more and Prima says he'll see them in an hour. He has to go. But not before he comes to the edge of the stage, kneels and puts his lips to Celia's hand. His wife walks off with the band.

Once the performers have departed and the crowd dissipated a bit, Annie hops off the railing. She can hear Celia exclaim over the din, "That was so great! They *are* the wildest!" and lover boy laying it on, telling her she should be up there instead of old ferret-face Keely.

Celia grins. "Keely's beautiful."

"Yeah, but *you're* a barn burner, baby. Come on, let's get some quiet." He puts his hand in the small of her back and scoots her along.

"Quit pushing."

"Sorry, honey, I'm not pushin'. How about another drink?" He flags a waitress.

"Cecilia!" Annie walks over like a girlfriend.

Celia's eyes cool. Annie stutters, "Ah, a few of us are gonna get a bite, you coming?"

"Celia's booked," the guy interjects.

Annie glares. "Nobody asked you, pal."

He looks her over. "What're you, butch or somethin'? She's with me."

The waitress returns and sticks a drink in Celia's hand.

"I don't think she needs another one a'these." Annie plucks it away as the waitress trots off.

"Hey, that's mine." Celia grabs it back; a slight wave runs from her head to her legs. She takes a step. "Who as'ed you anyway?"

Rosselli slips in alongside Celia as though he never left. "I think it's time for dinner. Will you be joining us, Miss West?"

"She's with me tonight, buddy." The young guy pushes Rosselli's hand off Celia.

Celia takes her lips off the straw. "Would everyone quit yanking me around, for cryin' out loud." She sucks the straw back in and mumbles, "Pushy, pushy . . ."

The men fix their eyes on one another, Rosselli's so gunmetal cool that no one speaks for several moments. Annie steps back. Celia glances from one man to the other.

The young guy sets his jaw. "You know who I am? I'm boxing in town this week, buddy. You wanna try your luck with a prizefighter?"

Rosselli doesn't blink. The words drop one stone at a time. "Around here, we fuck fighters."

The boxer straightens. His face reads like a debate. "Ah, forget it. I don't need the aggravation." Annie watches him head for a pit boss and sneer back at Rosselli. Whatever the pit boss says makes the boxer pocket his hands and beeline it out the door.

"How many of these mousetraps you been guzzling?" Rosselli takes the glass.

"Hey, give it . . . *M-huh-house traps*," Celia laughs. "*Eek!* ah, this town's a gasser, daddy!"

"One day in Vegas and listen to the vocabulary." Rosselli sets the drink down and steers her out of the lounge. "Come on, we got a date with some friends."

"You're not meeting Frank and the guys by chance, are you?" Annie trots along through the casino. "Me too! Frank left me a note. You know, he's really very sweet. He has a temper, but he means well—"

"Ah, he's a *punk!*" Celia clips along between them, suddenly noticing her empty hands. "What happened to my drink? Can we get something to eat, I'm *famished*."

When Rosselli escorts Annie and Celia through the restaurant to a table half-full of men, Sinatra stands. "Hey-hey!" He claps his hand to Rosselli's. "The man with the juice! How's your bird, Charlie?"

Rosselli shakes Frank's hand and gives a smile to Sammy Davis as he rises. "I believe you know these lovely ladies," Rosselli announces.

"Swingin'est chicks in Vegas! Have a seat there beside the Brother-in-Lawford," Frank tells them. Celia takes the empty chair next to the already half-cut Lawford. Rosselli plants himself in the chair beside hers and Annie slips round to Frank's side.

Lawford gazes at Celia and Celia gazes across at Davis, remembering him onstage, the power in his voice, the way he leapt and danced in his skin-tight slacks. "Mr. Davis," she slurs as the waiter pours her a glass of red. Rosselli switches his empty glass for hers and asks the waiter to fill up one with juice and a little seltzer for the lady. "Mr. Davis," she continues. "I thought you were just, just . . . Magnificent—*magnificentsville!*" she giggles.

"Well, thank you," Davis says. "What was your name, *mademoiselle?*"

"Watch it, Charlie," Frank tells him, "There's a beautiful broad with your ring on her finger due in town any day now."

Sammy grins, shaking his head. "Come Thursday night I'll be Charlie Jubilant."

"You're getting married?" Celia exclaims. "Wow. Neat."

"*Neat?*" Sinatra repeats. He drains his glass. "Waiter! Another root-beer float!"

Annie titters and leans into Frank. He doesn't reciprocate. Celia glances at Lawford, who is now fully turned in his chair.

"I don't believe we've met." He kisses her hand. "Pete. Pleased to make your acquaintance. What's your bag, baby? You a showgirl?"

He catches her off guard with his very English accent

wrapped round the hipster lingo and she spits a little of her drink as she laughs. "You're funny."

"Am I?" He leans in. "You dig the show tonight?"

"Yup, I dug it."

"God, you're beautiful. Have you got a date?"

"Why do they call you the Brother-in-Lawford?"

"That's Frank's nickname for me. Because Senator Kennedy's my brother-in-law. And Frank's a friend of Jack's and boop-boopy-doop." He bounces his long fingers on the air. "We're all going on the campaign trail once we're done the picture here in Vegas. We're going to make Jack the next president of the United States."

Celia blinks. "So, you're married."

The din around the table rises up with *Hey*'s and *Look who's here*'s. Louis Prima has just come in, trailed by Keely and a stocky man wearing a suit and fedora.

Frank stands. "Don't you got a two o'clock?" he asks Prima.

"Ah, Keely was tired. The man with the juice here had a word and Rickles is gonna do the two. We'll get the three."

The man in the fedora smiles, pleased with himself. His hooded eyes peer around the table. Lawford stands and takes a few steps to shake his hand. The fedora grunts and moves past to Rosselli, shakes hands and slaps his back. Lawford moves to Keely.

Prima points, his mouth gapes. "Hey! Look who's here. The voice. *The legs!*"

Celia grins and stands, lets Prima hug her to his barrel chest. He takes Lawford's chair. Lawford follows Keely and the fedora to the other end of the table.

"Where the hell you come from, kid? Frank! You heard this little gal sing? Sonuvabitch. Just like Keely. And she dances like she's on fire. Whatcher name?"

"Celia Dare." Frank speaks for her. "The broad who loves to hate me."

"D'arel—" Celia's tongue stalls. "I don't even know him."

"So, where you learn to sing like that? How old're you?"

"Too old for you, old man," Keely calls from the other end.

"Twenty-one," Celia tells him.

"See that, she's ancient in Prima years," Keely barks. The man with the fedora pats her arm, whispers in her ear before he excuses himself to the little Italians' room. Seconds after he passes, an explosion erupts from under Prima's and Celia's chairs, ripping a shriek from them both. Celia is on her feet as the fedora belches laughter and continues on to the restroom.

She looks around wild-eyed. Sinatra laughs himself stupid, doing his best to elucidate.

"Cherry bomb," Rosselli repeats. "Sam threw a couple cherry bombs under your seats." Celia looks confused. Rosselli clarifies. "Not Sammy Davis—Sam, the guy who just walked past."

Prima pounds his heart. Keely's face contorts with laughter. She bares her teeth and sticks her tongue out for good measure. "Howja like them apples, old man?"

"You watch it, girl. You could be replaced," Prima pokes a thumb toward Celia who's patting her own heart, laughing as she sits back down.

"Betcher sober now." Rosselli gives her arm a squeeze.

The other Sam reappears, doffing his hat as he passes the length of the table.

Rosselli stops him. "Sam. Hang on. Meet Celia here. Celia, this is Sam Flood. An important man."

Flood shakes her hand, the sapphire ring on his pinky glinting, and gives another meaty laugh. Looking at Celia, he jerks his head toward Keely. "Getcherself in a catfight if y'ain't careful. And you—" he turns to Prima "—do your fuckin' around when it don't affect your family. Getcher balls back down there and leave the kids for that English pansy."

Lawford looks up.

Prima leans to Celia. "You gonna be famous one day, kid. I can smell it." He heaves himself up and makes for his wife.

Ten

~

LATE THAT NIGHT, WHEN MARCELLA CAME IN, I WAS SITTING at her desk, one hand on her computer mouse and one holding up my chin. She tossed herself on the couch, throwing her legs up and over the back.

"Hey," I said distractedly.

"Are you still up? It's what . . ." And she held her watch up to her face. "Ten after *five*? Can you read this?" She pointed her wrist across the room.

"Twenty-five after two," I read from the screen.

"Pretending to be a pedophile so you can get a date with a cop?"

"I was getting the lyrics to 'That Old Black Magic' and I found this old Vegas site. It's got every hotel ever built, what they looked like, what the restaurant specials were. It even says what acts were performing in whatever year you want to know."

"Sounds *very* exciting."

"Are you drunk?"

"Is that a rhetorical question?"

"I even found Annie West—my mother's old roommate. On the Silver Slipper page. In 1960 and then again in '63." I looked back at Marcella. "I'm going to try and see her again tomorrow, so I was doing some research."

Her hand lolled to the coffee table and picked up the writing tablet. "What's this?"

I got up and strode over to her as nonchalantly as possible and whisked it out of her fingers. Sitting down beside her, I glanced over my handwriting and set it in my lap. "How'd your date go?"

"Who's Tiny and Gladys?" she asked, grinning.

I shrugged. "Nobody."

Kicking off her sandal, she needled me in the ribs with her big toe. "Come on. Who's Tiny and Gladys?"

"Tina and Glenda. Nobody. A couple girls I thought my mother might've known. Reading these books and talking to Annie today . . . I'm trying to piece Mum's story together kind of."

"So, you're just making shit up?"

"No. I read a book by this mob chick and she started out when she was fifteen or something being a beard for mobsters—you know, so it would look like they were on a date when the guys were really discussing big drug deals or whatever. I got the impression from Annie that my mother did that for this Teddy guy. She didn't even sleep with him." I looked down at the pad and flipped a page.

"Speaking of which, it turns out he knows the guy who directed *Long Road to Heaven*."

"Who?"

"The cardiologist. —Hey, bunny-bunny . . ." She wiggled her toe into my ribs again. "Could you make us a vodka cranberry?" I got up and meandered to the kitchen, carrying my notes with me. "The vodka's in the freezer. The cardiologist knows him. He also did *Dire Break* last year. Did you see that? Fucking *brilliant*."

I dropped ice in the glasses. "There's still sangria left."

"No, I need vodka! Use the martini glasses. It was *huge*: number one for a month or something. Anyway he's having a party. And he's single. Just broke up with his wife last month so him and the cardiologist have been commiserating. Shaker's over the thing."

"I'm making them Bond style." I poured vodka and juice in equal parts and stirred. Walking back to the couch, I set one down in front of her and sipped the other as I sat. "You don't like the cardiologist anymore?"

"Ach." She swung her legs around and sat up so she could hold her drink. "We haven't even fucked and we've been out, like, four times including tonight. He wanted me to stay over. But I stayed over there last week and the dumb shit gave me some sweats and a T-shirt and fell asleep with me in a hammerlock . . . his goddamn cat kneading my head. He says he hasn't been able to sleep since his wife left him and so I'm supposed to lie there like Raggedy Ann? *I like you so much, I don't want to have sex too soon and ruin things*, he says. Faggot." She picked up her purse and rooted around before she dumped it upside down on the table. "Where the hell . . . ?" She opened her wallet and a cheque along with her driver's licence fell to the table. "I called him a few times when he was in New York last week so he gave me a cheque for my phone bill."

I glanced at the driver's licence: Erin Marcia Wood. "I didn't know you took George's name." I didn't bother mentioning her mutation of *Marcia*.

"Better than *Slaker*. I think the cardiologist is a damn *Christian* too. Can you believe this bloody fundamentalist revival? They've got bands in the churches now and it's a big multimedia extravaganza. And most of them are, like, twenty or something."

Leonard crept to mind, raising his eyebrows, saying, *I told you. She doesn't mean any of it*, I thought in response. *She just likes a good story.*

The next day I drove back to Annie's, armed with a box of chocolate-chip oatmeal cookies, the envelope of pictures, the photo album, the writing tablet, a couple of biographies and a notebook I'd picked up along the way. The heat rose steadily the farther I got from San Francisco and, by the time I reached Danaville, I wished I'd left the top up and put the air conditioning on instead. I'd worn the blue dress I bought the day before and my arms and thighs were turning pink.

Coming up her front steps, I changed my mind and decided to get the drop on her around back again.

She wasn't in her garden. The sliding glass door into her kitchen sat open and I poked my head in. "Annie?" Several pages of a letter sat unfolded on the table beside a couple of thick letter-size envelopes and a shoebox. "Annie?" I stepped onto her kitchen floor then thought better of it and put both feet back outside. Crazy old bitch might come at me with a tire iron. The toilet flushed and feet creaked overhead then down the hall stairs. "Annie?"

"Yes."

"Vivian. From yesterday."

"Yes?"

Seeing her face fall a little at the sight of me, I turned up the wattage and held out the box. At the table, she began stuffing pages back into their envelopes. "I wanted to say thank-you," I said, watching her chuck the envelopes into the shoebox. "For the time you spent with me yesterday. I brought some cookies from the bakery."

She patted the lid down on the shoebox and set it on a chair on the other side of the table before looking up. The suspicious squint in her eyes softened a little as she looked at the bakery box. "Ah. Well, that was nice of you."

"I wanted to tell you, too, I was on the Internet last night and I found this Silver Slipper site and they mentioned you. It was kind of cool seeing your name and I thought, wow, Annie must have some amazing stories and pictures and stuff from those days. Look at what I printed off the site." I held up the pages.

She tilted her head and took them. Her eyes zoned in on where I'd highlighted her name.

"Hope you like chocolate-chip oatmeal." Pulling the box string, I opened the lid and let the scent waft.

"Mmm," she said, looking up, "don't those smell good."

"You were quite the star. You must have danced everywhere."

"Well, sure. Those were some days." Her eyes were back on the printout.

"I found a site about Cuba in the fifties too and Miami and the girls who went back and forth . . ."

"Oh yes. Before Castro screwed up the whole thing. You want some iced tea?"

"That'd be lovely. May I come in?"

"Sure, sure. Have a seat." I set the cookies on the table as she shuffled over to the counter still reading the Web site pages. She took out a couple of daisy-covered glasses. "Oh yes, I remember this girl," she said. "She danced in Havana too. Beautiful hotels down there. It was bigger than Vegas. And everyone would come: doctors and movie stars and politicians even. Those were the days."

"You must have met so many famous people."

"Ohhh, yes." She filled the glasses under the ice maker on the fridge door. "I should get my scrapbook." She poured from a pitcher on the counter. "What's that?" she asked, looking at the notebook I'd taken from my bag.

"I wanted to make notes so I wouldn't forget what you tell me."

"I had a student interview me a few months ago. She was a granddaughter of one of my neighbours and she knew I danced burlesque. I'm proud of it. Why shouldn't I be? It was for a paper she was writing and then she published the story in the newspaper too. A picture and everything."

"Wow."

"Well," she said, setting a glass of tea in front of me, "this gal said burlesque is making a big comeback and the young ones are making their own shows like they used to have in the theatres. But it'll never be like it was."

I took a cookie, pushing the box toward her. "I read that John Kennedy used to hang out in the Havana casinos and in Vegas before he was president. Did you ever see him?"

"Oh sure. He was friends with a lot of those fellas. Frank Sinatra . . . and the sister, Pat Kennedy, was married to Peter

Lawford. When they had their big show at the Sands, Sinatra had parties for him and they would invite a lot of the showgirls. They liked pretty girls around."

"Did you go to any parties with Kennedy?" I asked, munching and scribbling the odd word in my book.

"Uh-huh." She lowered her voice conspiratorially. "I had a little tryst with Frank Sinatra, you see, so I got invited to a real nice one, one night. All the girls liked Jack. Tempest Storm had a fling with him. I wouldn't've minded myself."

"Did my—did Celia?"

"No." She pushed out her bottom lip and shook her head. "She didn't care for him."

"Why?"

The corners of Annie's mouth dropped into a *god-knows* mug. "She could be kind of proper sometimes. She came from that sort of uptight family, up in ah . . . I wanna say Rochester, no . . . ah . . . *Scarsdale*. Yeah, it's very *bourgeois* up there." She ducked her head as she chuckled. "Celia was seeing this beatnik fella for a while—except you weren't supposed to say *beatnik*, you had to say *beat* or else it showed you were *square*—and he called her bourgeois all the time and she'd get very touchy about it and she said to him one time, *The only people who say bourgeois are bourgeois.* I thought that was very funny. He was from the same type of family as hers but he liked to affect this low-down coloured talk. A lot of the fellas did, 'specially if they were into music." Her hand drifted to the shoebox and sat on the lid a moment. I reached into my bag. Setting Judith Exner's book on the table, I pushed it toward her. "Did you ever meet *her?*"

Annie looked at the cover. "I don't . . ." Squinting suspiciously again, she read the quote: "I knew them when the dream of Camelot was real . . ."

"She went by Judy Campbell then," I said.

"Yes." She nodded slowly. "You're reading this, huh?"

"Did you ever meet her?"

She nodded again and looked at the back cover. "We knew many of the same people."

"That stuff about the FBI sounded scary. Did she ever talk about it?"

Annie put the book down and reached for another cookie. "She thought the whole world was jealous because she was so damn beautiful or something but she was really just a pain in the ass. She thought nobody knew about her and Kennedy but everybody knew. Everybody knew about him and Monroe too. And Jayne Mansfield and Angie Dickinson. She was at that party, Angie Dickinson. I think. She was in town anyway. That's where Celia met him but she didn't like him."

"Kennedy? Who did she like? The beatnik guy?"

"He was later. She had a big crush on Dean Martin. But I don't think he was there that night. She got disappointed when he wasn't there."

"So they were lovers, her and Dean?"

"Oh no. She wanted to be though. She even came with me when the guys had their show in Miami so she could see him. I was headlining at the Gaiety then—where Zorita used to dance."

"Who's Zorita?"

"Who's *Zorita*?" Annie repeated, flabbergasted. "What do they teach you kids? Zorita and her snake. You know! She was in that movie, *I Married a Savage*. I met this young gal who told me that when she was a kid, her mother was a stripper and she used to hang out backstage. Zorita would say to her, *Hey kid, you got your ice-cream money today?* and she'd say no. Zorita'd go get her snake, take her by the hand into the club, walk up to a table with several couples at it and say, *Give me a buck for the kid or I'll throw the snake on the table!* After three or four tables, Zorita'd wrap the snake around the kid and she'd take it back to the dressing room."

"Was Celia stripping then, when you were in Miami?"

"No, no. She was trying to be a singer but she didn't have much direction, just drifting around with me—I made her audition for a musical when we got back to New York so she'd stop moping. A tribute to Carmen Miranda. She got it too."

"Wow. A Broadway show?"

"Off-Broadway. This crazy producer that had a thing for Carmen Miranda financed it. What was his name? Stark— Michael Stark. Celia wore a wig and pretended to be Portuguese because that's what he wanted. She used a fake name too, Rosa something."

"Rosa Ramos?" I blurted. I dove into my bag and pulled out the mini-album, flicking to the shot of the sandwich board outside the theatre. *For the Love of Carmen.* I slid it over. She picked it up and held it away from her eyes. "Where'd you get this?"

"It was in my mother's things."

She grunted. "Rosa Ramos. Just as well no one knew her real name. Tanked. Carmen's corpse was barely cold and this goon was trying to do a musical about her."

I imagined my mother with fruit on her head. "Why was she moping? Because of Dean?"

"Everything. No job, no man . . . I know lots of times when he wouldn't come down to the parties, he'd say it was because he had a girl up in his room but really he was just watching westerns. Shirley MacLaine even says that in her book. You read her book?"

"Judy Campbell says that too. She said he wasn't very virile."

"Oh sure, just because he didn't want to get in bed with her. I think he was plenty virile, he just wasn't a skirt chaser. He always thought his wife was foolin' around on him."

"Campbell said he used to enlist her to spy on his wife."

Cookie in her mouth, Annie nodded and pointed toward me until she swallowed. "Same with Celia. He wanted her to call his house in the middle of the night. He was a strange cat. He might've even done that with Shirley MacLaine, I can't remember."

"I guess the rest of the world never knew about Campbell and Kennedy until they made her testify." Annie stared at the photo of her and Celia by the pool. "Like my mother," I added. "Didn't they try to make Celia testify against John Rosselli?"

Annie put her hand to her forehead as if she were experiencing heatstroke, closed the album.

My mind dashed for a change of subject. "Did she ever see her stepfather again?"

"I, I'm . . . She didn't want to see him."

"Did something weird happen between them?"

"No . . ."

"He must've tried again if he found her once."

"She didn't get along with either of them. That's enough now."

"I didn't mean to . . . Can we look at your scrapbook?"

"I have things to do." She reached down for her cane. "I'm busy. And you shouldn't come back again because I won't be here. I'm going out of town tomorrow to visit my daughter."

She was kicking me out for good. My eyes started to brim with tears before I could get a hold of myself. "I didn't mean to offend you. We can talk about whatever you want."

Hearing the croak in my voice, she let the cane drop. She squinted at me. "What are you getting all weepy about, I've got things to do, that's all." She raised her hands and let them drop on the table, muttering, "Christ in a crapshoot . . . Listen, she was fine. She did some singing and then she spent time in San Francisco being a beatnik and then some singing striptease and she quit. And had a baby. That's all there is. I—" Her hand moved to the shoebox again. "Okay, listen. Maybe you should . . ." She fidgeted with a ragged corner of the top. "I found these in the basement because you got me thinking again and I read them last night. Maybe you should take them." She lifted the box onto the table and set her fists on top. The two of us stared at it. "She wrote me quite a lot from San Francisco so maybe you can get to know her like that. And then you'll feel better." Her hands dropped on either side of the box and she pulled it to herself. "I went a little cracked when my mother died too."

I sat in the car in front of Annie's with the shoebox in my lap. Glancing at the house I wondered if she was really going to see her daughter or if she just wanted me to disappear. The old cardboard gave under my hands and I loosened my grip a little. Lighting a cigarette, I flipped open my cell phone and realized I'd turned it off the night before. I pressed it into life again.

Two messages. From Frank. He sounded smashed out of his tree. "Who do you think you are? When I met you, you were depressed and nowhere and I gave you happiness and compliments and picked you up till you felt better and now . . . (indiscernible slur) got a little money in your pocket . . . (indiscernible slur) . . . it's fuck off, Frank . . . don't need Frank anymore. No business with Frank. Fuck you." Click. I saved it for posterity. Message number two: Frank. "Vivian! Pick up the phone! Pick up . . . I know you're there. You think you're such hot shit? There's girls lined up to get with me, *lined up* . . . (slur slur)."

A beep came through. I answered. "Viv?" Frank, live.

"Hey."

"I think I left you a message last night. I was drunk and . . ."

"I'm heading home tomorrow."

"You are?" He sounded relieved. "I'm sorry I haven't been very understanding about what you're going through, it's just that—when you're fucked up, I'm fucked up. It'll be better when you get home."

"Yeah." I ran a hand over the shoebox as though it were a kitten. "Have you ever dated a stripper?"

"*Dated?* No. Why? You getting insecure, baby? You know we don't even really look when we're in peeler bars."

"Why wouldn't you go out with a stripper?"

"Where you going with this?" he asked warily.

"You sit and watch these women but you think they're beneath you."

"Shit, here we go. You're sounding just like your mother."

"Yeah. Okay, well . . ."

"It'll be better when you get home."

"Yeah."

On the way back into town, I stopped at a gas station. Inside, next to the cash was a rack of CDs: Country Oldies, Best of the

70s, Hooked on Classics, Best of Sinatra, Best of Shania Twain. I picked up one called *Songs for Goodfellas*—Mario Lanza, Tony Bennett, Bobby Darin, Louis Prima, Dean Martin. Everybody. I went to the counter with that and *Big Band Babes* and paid for my gas.

Sitting just down the hill from Marcella's in Café Greco on Columbus Avenue, the Goodfella Songs still coursing through my head from the drive back in, it hit me again that Frank knew nothing about my mother's trunk. And now I had a second box I didn't want him to know about. Maybe he was right. I was being unreasonable.

I looked out the window. The street was loaded with Italian restaurants and cafés but my mother would've hated this area. For its history anyway. A couple doors down was Vesuvio's, the old beat-writer hangout. She hated Kerouac and the rest of them; just a bunch of misogynist jerk-offs, she said. She loved to quote Truman Capote's appraisal: *Kerouac doesn't write, he types.* To which I'd reply, "What do you care what that bitchy *faggot* said." I never quite got over her use of the word once in reference to me. When I refused to get involved in sports at school I overheard her say to Sally, "Terrific. Despite all my best efforts, I've gone and raised myself a female faggot." *Female faggot* was Germaine Greer's slur for wimpy women, I later discovered, *female eunuchs*. For once Sally took my side. "Christ, give her a break. I'm not exactly running the six-minute mile myself." My mother had started jogging. "At least you're good with a drill," she said. Sally laughed. She generally waved off what she didn't agree with. Me, I lay awake stewing and rehearsing: Now, if she says this, I'll just say that, and if she responds like so . . .

I sipped my coffee now, shoebox in my lap. Still hadn't opened it. Instead, I'd opened a book I'd spotted in the window at City Lights. *Straight from the Fridge, Dad: A Dictionary of Hipster Slang.* I read until I got up my nerve.

The envelopes were all postmarked but one. I rifled for the earliest.

March 27, 1962

Dear Annie-Fanny,

Greetings from the land of beats and honey! How's it going, baby!

Well, we made it. We're in Frisco. Kevin and I are sleeping in the Volkswagen out back of this really cool house on the edge of the Haight. Kevin says it's kind of a flophouse and everybody comes and goes so we'll probably have a room inside soon.

Ernie and Dinah are sleeping in a tent beside the van. So far it's pretty cool. We pool our resources and have little campfires in the backyard for dinner. I know you think it was stupid of me but I'm glad I sold my car. When I told Kevin I got it as a gift from Frank, he flipped his wig. I explained it was for having a part in a movie. Kevin said it was just as well my part got cut because that Hollywood lifestyle with fancy cars and things is so bourgeois, but I think he's secretly jealous. Last night we were lying in the back of the van and he said, "How'd you meet all these old dudes—you hung out with Sinatra!" We were smoking reefer. Oh, by the way, I keep using your line from that time in Kevin's parents' basement when we were at the play rehearsal and you said, "No thanks, I have to drink later." Everyone laughs their head off. Anyway Kevin wanted to know what Frank was like, so I said he was very generous but had a bad temper. Then he asked, "Did you get it on with him?" I said no, of course not. (I didn't say that you did.) So, then Kevin said—get ready for it—"Man, so, is it true he hangs with gangsters? In the papers they said he was tight with Lucky Luciano and Bugsy Segal. You ever meet Bugsy Segal?"

Bugsy Segal! I said, "Oh sure. Not much of a conversationalist. Kinda dead." Ha ha! Kevin said he thought I look like a gangster's moll with my white-gold hair. Which kind of bit my rump. Just like when Katie, his idiot ex, said I had a Marilyn Monroe dye job. After that creepy night with Marilyn and creepy Old Man Kennedy at the Cal-Neva, I don't want anyone comparing me to that fried-up mess ever again. Have you seen her around? Promise me if I ever get like her you'll shoot me. I'll shoot you too. Deal?

Anyway, I also told Kevin I had a friend named Teddy the Ghost and he'd heard of him too, and Sam Giancana. I told him Sam goes by Sam Flood when he's in mixed company. It kind of blows his mind that I know all this stuff. He said he also knows quite a bit because his uncle is a cop and he talks a lot about mobsters. His uncle thinks that Robert Kennedy is going to take them all down. Kevin said, "Ha! Can't take those cats down, they're like shape-shifters. I think that's how you got infused with that holy barbarian soul of yours." That's from Jack Kerouac. I don't know what it means, but it makes me laugh. Then he wrecked it and asked if I ever got it on with Sammy Davis Jr. And he figured I said no because I was prejudiced. "Does that make you uncomfortable, the idea of getting it on with a colored guy?" I told him no—it was because Sammy was married and don't be stupid.

Then he wanted to know about my last old man. I said, "Boyfriend, you mean?" He laughed like crazy: "You're so square, it kills me." I felt foolish but he said he meant that I was cute. He said, "I love every corner on you." Ha ha. So then I told him about nutty Michael Stark. I still have his ring on my necklace, which I showed him, and then I said, "But he went crazy and stabbed a guy for insulting me. So he went to jail."

Kevin thought that was even more of a riot. And then he said I was beautiful. It makes me want to cry when he says such nice things. It's like he really means it. He said when he kisses me he tastes God! I don't know what that means either but it sounded sweet. Oh, Annie, he makes me so happy.

So here goes. You probably already figured it out but I'm not a virgin anymore! I feel strange saying that out loud. Writing it out loud? Kevin was pretty bug-eyed when he found out it was my first time. He figured I must've been doing it with Teddy and for SURE with Michael Stark. Maybe it is weird that I never did it with Michael. But lots of girls save themselves till marriage. Kevin says that's bourgeois. But he was flattered that I picked him to be my first, though. I know he was.

I know you don't like him but Kevin thinks you're terrifically funny. And righteous. And that you laid the foundation for me to lose the shame that society tried to inflict on me when expressing the joys of my body and mind.

I guess I better go now. Kevin's up. I'm sitting on the back porch of the house and I can hear him talking to Ernie and Dinah. This truly is a family of friends. It's so great.

I miss you, supremely, truly!

Love,

the Cisco Kid

PS I'm learning to rejoice in the expansion of the soul instead of being caught in the prison of consumption. It's great!
PPS I guess I should send this to New York. I don't know if you're still in L.A. or not. Maybe I should send it care of Johnny's place?? Also we don't have a phone. (gasp! choke!)

                                                    April 12, 1962
Dear Annie Gitcher Gun,

Well, Kevin and I aren't living in the van anymore. This lady and her daughter left, so we have a room in the house. Ernie and Dinah packed up their tent and moved into the van. They prefer it to the house, they said, because they feel free. I think I told you in my last letter that we don't have a telephone though. It makes me nervous. What if there was an emergency and we couldn't call an ambulance? Or something worse, like I miss Annie so bad I want to beat my head with a hammer?

I do like this city, though. Dinah and I have been the happy wanderers. We cruise around through all the neighborhoods—South of the Market, the Castro, Fisherman's Wharf—while Ernie and Kevin study writing. They read tons of Ginsberg and Kerouac. Plus they've been getting into Gary Snyder and Lawrence Ferlinghetti. They're writing their own poetry now.

At night, we build a fire in the backyard and roast wieners for supper. Ernie plays guitar and I sing. It always kills everyone when I do some Peggy Lee or Dinah Washington song and I twang it up all country-and-western. Kevin has started accompanying us on a xylophone that the little girl who used to live in our room left behind. And Dinah whacks the bottom of a cooking pot. Sometimes everyone in the house is out there with us. I guess I'm trying to talk about fun stuff right now because I actually don't feel that fun. I don't know if I'm being a bourgeois jerk or what.

This morning (well, afternoon, we hardly open our eyes till noon or so) we were sitting round the kitchen table, drinking coffee. It was me, Dinah, Ernie and Kevin. Dinah and I said we were going to get dressed and explore the city some more. Then Ernie pipes up and says, "I think you girls should make breakfast." I thought he was kidding so I said, "I ain't hungry yet, Pa." And then Kevin said, "For us, baby. Ernie and I've been talking and there's got to be some changes around here. I think you girls ought to sweep the floor and make breakfast for us. You've got to do more than consume as we create."

Dinah and I looked at each other and Dinah squealed, "We create!" and I said, "I told you last night that I want to sing at the next Poetry Follies."

Kevin said, "Baby, look at me. You don't contribute by competing with Ernie and me for time and space. There's a guy coming over this afternoon who knows a guy who used to be roommates with Jack Kerouac. He's going to teach us how to compose our poetry in such a way as to entrance the common mind. This should be a welcoming place." He pulled me onto his lap and touched a finger to my nose like I was a child. He said, "I know you got a lot of attention from being pretty and flashing your legs. But that was another place, one where people were happy to consume you. They worked soulless jobs in order to consume you. It's like Whither goest thou, America, in thy shiny car in the night? Nowhere, man." He's always quoting this stuff and I don't know what he's talking about. He said that he and Ernie want to beatify the square world and set them all on a quest for meaning. Then he reached into my blouse and pulled out the diamond ring that nutty Michael Stark gave me and said, "This thing was used to purchase you." And he YANKED it right off my neck and said, "I want you and Dinah to make us all breakfast to show solidarity and then I think you should go down to a pawnshop and hock this. For us all."

So, I said, "This was my ENGAGEMENT ring. And I do so contribute," but I felt like bawling all over the place. It seemed so mean of him, especially in front of everybody like that. "You're talking with ego now," he said. "The ego is self and the self is an illusion." He pointed out that Ernie hocked his horn to help us buy the Volkswagen and that the horn really meant something—music!—whereas my ring was just evidence that I was once a whore. He actually SAID that. And I just squeaked, "What?" like a mouse that was already eaten. Just because nutty Michael Stark gave me a diamond ring does NOT mean I'm a whore. Then he slapped my butt and pushed me in the direction of the fridge. How can he be so sweet and then so mean to me?

We made breakfast, Dinah and me—we did the dishes too, then left Kevin and Ernie to await their writing guru. Jack Kerouac's roommate. Oh BROTHER. We went down to the Tenderloin where all the pawnshops are. Dinah was pissed off and scuffing her feet along the sidewalk, which drives me crazy. Dinah has a voice like Minnie Mouse on helium. "I don't know about this floor-sweeping shit," she says. "Once your old man starts hounding you about keeping his floor clean, it's over. Last night Ernie wanted me to have myself a lollipop while he meditated. That's the third time." Which made me sick because it reminded me of Okie Joe. Remember I told you about him using that expression. Dinah didn't think I knew what it meant so she made an O with her lips and stuck her tongue in her cheek to demonstrate. She can be quite crude.

"He claims it helped his mind drift to the uncharted nooks of beatitude . . . He can kiss my beatitude goodbye if this keeps up." Then she asked, "How much bread you think we'll get?" I didn't want to think about it. It didn't seem fair. But it's not as if I was ever in love with nutty Michael Stark so maybe I was just being a baby. Dinah thought we should go into a few places and see who was the highest bidder. The money offers were all over the place, everything from one-fifty up to two-eighty and then Dinah haggled them up to two-ninety.

She said we should tell the guys we got one-fifty. I felt bad about lying because the money's supposed to be for all of us. Two hundred, I said. I think she was kind of disgusted with me because she said, "Fine. But you better stick with the story. Don't you sell me out just cuz he gives your button a tickle." I know I tease you about being crude but when you do it, you still sound clever and it's funny. Dinah just sounds gruesome.

As we left she asked me, "Whaddya think that rock set him back in real life? Had to be a couple grand at least." I made the mistake of saying he gave me a sable stole too and she whistled and said, "Guess you got lots of stuff to hock if things don't pan out."

And then I remembered the pearls that my stepdad gave me. They're in the velvet pouch at the bottom of my suitcase. Stewart's a jerk and a pill but I'm never giving up those pearls! What if Kevin goes through my stuff? And then I start thinking about everything I left in Johnny's closet—my mink, the stole, my dresses, my cashmere suit, the rhinestone pumps, my beautiful satin-bowed slingbacks. If they knew they'd call me a capitalist glutton pig.

Dinah had on black dungarees, a black turtleneck, these scruffy tennis shoes that she just dyed last week. She dyes everything she wears black. Her feet are tinted black from the dye. I started getting paranoid about my capri pants. They're black but they probably cost more than her whole wardrobe and I had this yellow sweater on too. It's as if they can't stand color. Can't you reach enlightenment with a bit of color?

Never go to the Tenderloin. It's completely disgusting and seedy. There's nothing but rundown buildings and all kinds of crummy characters kicking around the sidewalks. I was bugging a bit and I said, "Let's get out of here and go treat ourselves to a nice lunch."

So that put a bulb in her lamp again. We found a little café, nothing terribly swish but still pretty rich for Dinah's blood. She kept her hand on the door as we came in as if she thought the ceiling might crush her for the sin of even coming in the joint. She said, "Look at everyone. They're so bourgeois." So I said, "Let's just sit. We'll have some wine." I figured maybe if I got her a little drunk she'd shut her trap. I just wanted to be somewhere NICE for a change!

We sat down at a table and Dinah picked up the menu. "Holy shit!" she squealed. LOUD. "I could cook us dinner for a week for this kinda dough." She is so loud and squeaky at the same time. Like a kicked rat. And then she looked around and said, "You think any of these people was ever so broke they lived on rice for two months?" I stopped feeling bad right about then. It was my damn ring! I said, "How 'bout we pretend that we only got the one-fifty. We cooked breakfast, swept the damn floor . . ."

She was up for that. By her third glass of wine she DUG that café. And all I could think about was getting my hair done. You should've seen my roots. I looked like a skunk in negative! Even old Dinah got excited. She'd never been in a beauty parlor. Her mother cut her hair. Or her friends. So, after lunch we got our hair done.

By the time we got home the guys had already left for the Follies. Did I tell you about the Poetry Follies? It's like a vaudeville night with readings and jazz and comedy sketches. Like the way you said the burlesque theaters used to be in New York. Except with poetry.

We got dressed up so we could go surprise them. I thought maybe we could go dancing after or something. When we got to Harry's Drink there was a poet onstage and the jazz guys were playing while he did his thing. I was feeling all girlie and pretty again so I started casing the joint for signs of Kevin. The poet was finished and everyone snapped their fingers (that's what they do instead of clapping) and I thought I'd hear Kevin because he always yells when he likes a poet but I couldn't find him and then they announced the Dynamic Dueling Philosophers and two poets got up: a skinny guy and a chubby girl with dark hair. It took me a second. Katie? Goddamn Katie and she was holding Kevin's hand!

I tried to find Dinah but she was sitting in idiot Ernie's lap necking her brains out. And then they started in on this poetry-battle thing. Katie said something like, "He despises the thought of thought. From a She that Is. He wants a boudoir baby . . ." I suppose that was supposed to mean me? I don't remember much more except where Kevin said, "She needs to get behind, to worship at the altar of poetry, of her man and her soul." And Katie told him, "It's better to die on your feet than live on your knees." It was like the argument they had that time in the basement at Kevin's parents' when we were going to do that play and she was quoting from Simone de Beauvoir and he was doing Kerouac and saying that de Beauvoir just ripped off stuff from Sartre. It's all this philosophy crap I don't know anything about and now there they were making fun of me onstage. God, even Dinah and Ernie knew all the jokes and when to laugh and when to snap their fingers. When their crummy duet ended, Kevin dipped Katie and bit her neck. Everybody snapped like crazy. He BIT her neck!! God. And then they went back into the audience, holding hands! When I went over I didn't even know what to say because I didn't want Katie to have the satisfaction of seeing me mad. Remember her hair was light in L.A.? Now it's pitch-black. She smiled at me and I wanted to bash her in the face, I swear.

Kevin said, "Hey, you got your hair cut." He pulled me onto his lap and he said, "Did you spend all our bread, you bad girl?" And then he bit my shoulder. With the same teeth he bit her with! Ew. "You catch us goofin' onstage, baby?" Then he told me that Katie just moved up here too. "She's gonna crash with us for a while." Crash with US!! Then he started yapping about how Katie worked the phones for a bookie just before she am-scrayed and how us girls had a lot in common. ?? I said I had to go to the bathroom and pulled a Houdini instead.

You should be supporting, not competing, he says. Except for fatassed Katie. Katie can take the stage. Mind if Katie moves in? She's having a hard time. Asshole. Ass Hole.

So here I damn well am back home. Annie!! I don't want her in my place. I HATE her. She insulted you (remember when she said you had silicone boobs?) and she insulted me and him too. God, you must be sitting there saying I told you so. I can just hear you—"That crumb is a no-goodnik from Creepsville."

I just don't know. I know I'm overreacting a little. Kevin's right. I can be a child sometimes. I put my desires and needs ahead of others and let the SELF get in the way of my enlightenment.

I know I want to be here in Frisco. I think this is where I HAVE to be right now. I'm growing and learning. Maybe I have something to learn from fatassed Katie even. I find THAT hard to believe. If I meditated more I'd probably master this whole situation.

I better sign off. They'll be home soon and I need to pretend I'm asleep because I'm too cranky to be Zen about it right now.

Love, Celia

xoxoxoxo

PS Miss you miss you miss you miss you miss you miss you.

May 2, 1962

Dear Annie,

How's it going, my darling, my dearest? As I told you on the phone, that fatassed Katie moved in here a couple of weeks ago. It seems like a couple of years. Did I mention that she has a fat ass? And that she's a self-involved know-it-all jerk? And that she's thoughtless and rude? Take this morning for instance. There she was, scraping a piece of burnt (because she's too self-absorbed to notice the smell of smoke) toast over the sink before she put a dump truck of butter on it (which contributes to her FAT ass). Meanwhile I'm trying to get around her to make some coffee. She made no attempt to get out of my way. She said, "Want some toast, Celie?" Celie! Who does she think she IS?? I ix-nayed that little offer. So she says, "Oh, I think I might have eaten your yogurt last night." I didn't say anything. If I don't keep my yap shut with her, I mean if I say one thing, I won't be able to stop. It'll be like an A-bomb.

I was pleasant. I poured her a cup of coffee. Then old Fatass says to me, "You know, Celie . . ." Celie AGAIN! There was a dirty butcher knife sitting on the counter and all I could think was how good it would look lodged in her melon. Anyway, then she said, "It seems counterproductive for us to be living in the same house like this and not speaking to one another."

Counterproductive? She has no IDEA! So I sat down and stirred my coffee and kept myself very pleasant looking as she took MY rosehip jam out of the cupboard and SLATHERED it onto her toast. Then she sits down at the table and she says, "I know we got off on the wrong foot, back in L.A. I said some things I shouldn't have but I know now that I was mistaken." Well, that was good of her. "You have a very pretty face and a sweet voice and when you're not addressing me, you're really quite joyful. I understand what Kevin sees in you."

I hate her I hate her I hate her. Oh my god! She's knocking at my door.

Well! Madame Fatass just had the nerve to ask if she could borrow my black bra! MY bra?? Is she crazy? I said I was wearing it. Full-time. My other one was wrecked. I have to get out of this house right now or I'll boot her one. I swear it. I'm going to see if Dinah's in the van. Talk to you later, lambchop.
xoxo

~

May 10

Oh my god, I just found this in my underwear drawer. I thought I mailed it! Well, guess what. That damn Katie has hardly been home in a week. She stopped in the other night when we were out in the backyard having our campfire (just in time for dinner, of course) to rhapsodize about Conner, the righteous colored guy she met. He plays stand-up bass, she said, in the Fillmore in a place called the Jumpin' Joy. Now when she's not down at the club with him, she is at his apartment reading her crappy poetry as he strums accompaniment. (He must realize she needs all the help she can get.) She's trying very hard to sound hip. She told us Conner was a soul brother in the deep end of jazz. "Man," she kept saying, "listening to him just fries my wig" and then, between mouthfuls of our hot dogs, she said it was time we all got more hep to the city's grooving Negro scene instead of living like a bunch of hypocritical flapjacks who wouldn't know hep if it bit 'em in the ass.

OH BRRRROTHER!!!

And then she said, "'Hepcat' and 'hip' are derived from a West African tribal language in which hippicat means 'man of wisdom.'"

Three cheers for Katie the anthropologist.

Kevin said, "Cool," at first but then he got fidgety. Finally he blurted out, "You should be careful hanging out with this cat, Katie. I mean, I don't have a problem, you getting tight with a colored dude, but you know, a lot of people do. You could get hurt. Look at those Freedom Riders, man, they're just fighting for the right to ride a bus up front and the cats are getting a shit kicking."

Katie said, "What's your point, Kev?" And he said, "Nothing! Man, no point. I'm just saying someone might get a little hot about it." She said, "Someone?" in this smart-alecky tone.

Who the HELL does she think she is? She's convinced the whole world is just itching to jump her bones.

I complain too much. I should mail this letter and quit my damn bitching. It must be boring. I wish you were here. Make that goof-off agent of yours get you a gig in Frisco! Maybe I'll try and call you again next week. It's just that, as you probably figured, I'm not too flush lately. And I feel like a jerk calling collect. But I'll write more soon. We're supposed to go down to the Jumpin' Joy and see this Conner clown play. I'll let you know how THAT goes.

xoxo

Love, Celia

PS I'd kill for room service right now.
PPS I'm still not very enlightened. Ha ha.

May 15, 1962

Dearest Dollface,

So, I think I told you about Conner? Well, guess what. We all went down there tonight. Me, Kevin, Ernie, Dinah and Katie. Conner put us on the guest list and they seated us practically ringside. PS The Jumpin' Joy is strictly colored people. We were the only white faces in the room.

Katie said it was a high-tone place, so I finally got to wear the one half-decent dress I brought with me. The band was pretty good. And the place was actually nice. I don't know what I was expecting. I guess because a lot of colored people are poor, I thought a colored place would be rundown or something but it was actually snazzy.

Kevin was driving me crazy. He kept addressing every guy he saw, including ERNIE, as Brother. Ernie kept smiling like he thought he was about to get knifed any second, plus he seemed really worried and jealous about Dinah. Every time she turned her head he'd follow her gaze, and if she was looking at a colored guy (and who else would it be?), his hand went up her thigh, and he'd stick his wormy little tongue in her ear.

To be honest, Kevin and I weren't speaking. We still aren't. Mostly because I wrote a poem this past week, and I made the mistake of showing it to him. He laughed and said, "Baby, you're so WASP." I ripped that page right out of his hand and I said, "You know, Kevvie, YOU didn't exactly claw your way out of Harlem. The only people who use the word 'bourgeois' ARE bourgeois." And I pulled on my long johns and yanked the blanket off him and took the pillow and right before I left I said, "YOU are oppressing me." Then I slept on the couch. Which is where I am again right now.

But anyway, I'll tell you about what a jerk Kevin is being later. Tonight was so MOTHERY! The band just filled the room with this yummy jammy jazz. It was so good, I forgot I hated Katie for a minute. You should see that Conner play. He's kind of crazy-looking with these long wiry arms and it looks wild the way he cradles the bass with them and he has LONG bony fingers plucking away the whole time. Apparently people call him Scarecrow. No kidding.

Anyway soon they played softer and an MC came out onstage and announced the first act. Then this teeny little colored chick with a crazy smoky voice sashayed out and launched into a rendition of "Love Me or Leave Me." Oh Annie, she was SO GOOD!! When she sang that line about regretting instead of forgetting with somebody else it made me all lonesome for the stage again. I clapped like mad. If I can't do it myself, I may as well show lots of appreciation.

The band completely changed tempo. They had these wicked horns and it was sort of, I don't mean to sound prejudiced or anything, but it was jungley sounding. A troupe of dancers hit the stage. Real hoofers! Their feet were POUND-ING and they had these terrific silver dresses with slits, which made their brown legs look beautiful!

Oh man! The sound of their feet, I swear it swept right through me. I couldn't take my eyes off them. I was holding

my breath for fear they'd disappear. It felt so good to see a
real band and real show people, you have no idea. Their heels
slammed and cracked the beat and then suddenly the dancers
parted and formed a sort of tunnel. And this WOMAN
stepped out way at the top of the tunnel and started walking
toward us and I got a tingle from the top of my head to the
bottom of my feet. There was just one spotlight and it was on
HER. She threw her hip and she hit a note that blended so
thick with the horns you couldn't tell what you were hearing
until every left foot onstage stomped. Like an exclamation.
And everybody froze, the musicians and dancers, and all that
was left was that WAIL of hers. Then she stopped. Like someone turned off a siren. And it was dead quiet. Then she
hollered, "He said to me," and suddenly the band came back
in and she sang, "Big Leg Woman, keep your dresses down."
Oh Annie, it was something else! Do you know this song? The
way she sang it. Oh my god. And her figure! She had on this
gold shimmering number with slits and it rode up every stride
she took downstage, these big powerful thighs like she was
daring us all and she just bawled it—"Cuz I got somethin'
under this dress, daddy, make a bulldog hug a hound." I
wanted to cry she was so good. When she hit the edge of the
stage she ripped open the front of her dress and let it drop.
Underneath she had on a tiny gold skirt that kept flipping up
over this great big muscular behind! and she'd be running her
hands over herself and she was glinting and gleaming like
crazy. The whole audience stomped and pounded the tables
and I felt like I had to hold my head so it didn't explode! I was
running in my chair! The chorus girls were still frozen in
those lusty poses they struck earlier, but compared to the
singer, I swear they looked like Olive Oyl. Then she started
weaving her way through them, singing all the while, and
she'd pause and slap a dancer right on her backside! And her
voice went full throttle when she sang, "He likes the way I
shake my great big fat behind." Her big fat behind made Katie's
look like a pancake.

Belting some more, she tore her skirt off like it was nothing and tossed it over Conner's skinny little noggin. And then she headed back toward us in a gold G-string! When she got to the edge of the stage again, her fingers shimmied all over her halter top and she sang, "You can bet your bottom dollar, honey, ain't a cherry in this house." (Oh my god!!!) Her top hit the floor and there she was in nothing but pasties and a G-string as the band slammed the last note. The stage went dark and it was so quiet. And then very softly she sang: "He said, You oughtta keep what you got wearin' down. Girl you make a bulldog hug a hound." The room went BONKERS! Oh man, I was on my feet with them.

Katie barely clapped. Maybe she was sore because this colored girl made a big ass look FANTASTIC! She gave me the craziest look though—sort of smug or something with this forced pinched smile like the Pope's dog just shat on her front lawn. Finally I said, "What's the matter with you?" And Katie said, "Figured you'd like her." I looked around the room and threw up my hands. So, then killjoy Katie said, "Miss Peaches is headlining. That's who I'M waiting for." Miss Peaches is a nickname for Etta James. Big deal. I mean, Etta is a big deal but now I didn't even want to like her. And, actually, she was almost anticlimactic after that "Big Leg Woman." Talk about devil-may-care. She was devil-may-fuck-himself!

Anyway, the whole show was great. Katie stayed behind with Conner, and the rest of us walked home. I was going to use the pay phone to call you tonight but Kevin threw a fit about it. "For chrissake," he said. "It's three in the morning. You shouldn't be wandering around alone this time of night."

I said, "Maybe if we had a phone at home like normal people, I wouldn't have to."

"Here we go again," he said. He always acts as if I'm a spoiled princess or something.

If I were a spoiled princess, what the hell would I be doing with HIM? So I said, "Oh fuck off, Kevin, I'll do what I like." He said, "Real nice, Celia," and stormed off home. Oh and he told me to sleep on the couch because he didn't want to be woken up. Golly gee—WHO'S the <u>BABY?!</u>

You weren't home after all. So here I am on the couch. I wouldn't give that jerk the satisfaction of getting in bed with him. He can go piss up a rope for all I care. And suck on the soggy end!

May 16. Morning. Okay, Afternoon. 1:35 pm to be precise.

Kevin says that singer was a stripper. I said, she was a SINGER! Kevin said in the colored clubs a lot of the girls strip and sing as well. Is that true? I guess that's why Katie gave me her You-WOULD-like-her face. She has this thing about me having been a showgirl. And you being a stripteaser. As if it makes us low-class women or some bull like that. She's always quoting Simone de Blowhard at me.

Anyway, I thought I'd add this last bit before I mail this. At least Kevin and I are speaking again. He said he was sorry, he just worries about me being out alone late at night. That was nice. I don't know why, but I keep thinking about my mother lately. Stewart said she was sick. What if she really is? Most of the time I hate her, but what if she's sick like her sister was? Maybe I don't hate her. I hate Stewart. He could've stuck up for me, he could've made things right. But he was too busy trying to save his own skin, the chickenshit bastard. I wonder if they're even together anymore. And if they're not, she proba- bly blames me like she did with my real father. She was as mad at me for not telling her everything he did as she was at him for doing it. Why doesn't she ever believe me? Why can't she love me no matter what? I hate her for that. I really hate her for it. But I don't. God, what if she's sick? I don't know what to do. Do you ever just miss your mom even though there's noth- ing there? Why can't I just stop it? I'm being depressing again. Sorry. Mostly I miss you, my dearest, sweetest, bestest friend.

Love, Celia
xoxo

May 18, 1962

Dear Annie,

I've been thinking about what you said last night. About me singing and dancing like that girl at the Jumpin' Joy. I think you're right that it would be a good gimmick but I don't know how to put this, I hope you won't be insulted—but I just can't. For one thing, I want to be taken seriously as a singer. I know they sort of did take that girl seriously to have her open for Etta James. But maybe colored people are different that way. I know I know, Tempest Storm opened for Sammy, but Tempest is still a stripper. It's not as if somebody goes to see her for her terrific talents. Please don't take that wrong. YOU have talent, you really do. You're so good with the audience. I love when you do your Mae West's sister bit. You've got it DOWN. It's just that I studied voice and classical ballet half my life and I want people to say I've got a great voice, not great boobs. Not that they would ever say that anyway. Which is another reason I can't be a stripper. Look at me!

Oh boy. I don't think I'm going to mail this. Off to the underwear drawer with this one.

May 19

Annie, Annie, I can't stop crying. I finally called my mother. It was so horrible. I called collect from Cecilia D'arelli. I don't know what I was thinking. She doesn't know who that is. I yelled, "Mother, it's Audrey," and the operator scolded me and said, "Ma'am, please. You're not allowed to speak yet." And then I heard my mother cough and I knew it was true. She is really sick. The operator asked her if she'd accept the charges and she said yes. And at first I was thrilled. She said yes! I said, "Mother, it's me. I'm in California." And she didn't say anything. I said, "Mom?" and then her voice came and it was like acid. "Disappears for days at a time. Is that where he goes?"

I wondered if she thought it was some stranger named Cecilia who was having a fling with Stewart or something and I said, "Mother, it's Audrey." She said, "I know who it is. He told me he found you in New York. What did you do with him?" I didn't know what she meant and I said, "Stewart? Nothing. He said you were sick." And then she said something so horrible. I can't stop crying. She said, "And you thought you'd wait long enough that you could come back here and pick the bones." I couldn't speak. She said, "Neither of you is getting a dime out of me. Not one dime. I don't want you in my . . ." and then her voice cracked and then really faintly I heard her say, "Oh god," before the line went dead.

My hands were shaking so bad. I tried to call you but there was no answer. It feels like rocks in my throat. How could she hate me so bad? I'm so stupid. I'm getting the paper wet from crying.

No matter what happens to me in my life I'll never forget you, Annie, ever.

Love, Celia

xoxo

May 20, 1962

Can you believe this Marilyn stuff? I bought a newspaper this morning and you know how often I do that. But she was right on the front page, this picture of her with Happy Birthday, Mister President as the headline. Have you seen Dean? It said that she skipped town on the picture she was doing with him, and went to New York to sing "Happy Birthday" to Jacky-boy (as you would say). The Chinaman at the corner store where I bought the paper said, "You see her on TV? I saw. No goo'. She look like drunky snake in her eye." I love the Chinaman. But this is so bad. It's so embarrassing when you've met the person and you know she's a mishmash. In the paper, she looks stoned out of her tree. I could just die for her. I mean she's embarrassing anyway, the way she puts on that simpy voice. But THIS! Do you think she'll get fired? You have to get in touch with Dean and tell me EVERYTHING. And tell him I said hello. No don't. Oh go ahead. I haven't seen him since that night we all had dinner with Marilyn and Frank and the old man at Cal-Neva. Every time I think of that night, how messy Marilyn was, saying she was going to call Mrs. Kennedy and tell her everything—I get the heebies! And now here she is stoned out of her gourd in front of the whole world.

To top it off, Katie came over today. I was sitting at the table reading this thing about Marilyn and feeling crummy and in the back door comes Fatass. Who barely lives here anymore, thank god, but she still acts like she owns the joint. She waltzed in and headed straight for the fridge, poured herself some Kool-Aid and sat down at the table. She saw me reading about Marilyn and she says, "Looking at your hairsake?" I just turned the page. THEN she says, "It's a funny thing, you chicks who go out of your way to look like sexpots and strippers and all that, you know, and then when it comes down to it, you can't get it on. I mean, it's like a psychosis when you think about it." I am not kidding. She said that! She looked stoned—on weed not booze. Lately, if she comes in and she's high like that I can just stare at her, pick a point on her forehead and stare at it the way Johnny does when he wants to scare guys and she gets all freaked and leaves. I sat back and got to work on her. I had one of these yummy pastries that Dinah bought when she cashed her welfare check yesterday—Raspberry Cream-cheese Hamfists—they are to DIE for. Anyway, this was the last one and Katie gets the munchies really bad when she smokes, so I took a bite and sighed like I was having a climax or something. Then all of a sudden, I noticed her eyes. You know how usually your pupils get big with weed, well, hers were like pinpricks. And then she says all syrupy, "It's okay. Kevin told me."

"What?"

She gets this poor-you look on her ugly squash and she says, "I know that you don't ball with Kevin. And that your mother didn't want you. It's classic really. A lot of girls, when their fathers do things to them as kids, they grow up like you, bleach blonde, very sexualized, you know, like Simone de Beauvoir says, 'Shut up in a boudoir, her wings are clipped and it is found deplorable that she cannot fly.'" I kid you NOT. She actually got all teary-eyed for me, like I was pathetic! I didn't know who I was going to kill first. Kevin was up in our room practising on Ernie's guitar. I wanted to go kick his teeth in. I said, "Who said I don't do it with—"

She cut me off. "It's okay. I SEE you. People think it's bourgeois uptightness with girls like you, but I understand. You are sexualized externally but not intellectually." I said, "Stop SAYING that! Girls like me! Girls like YOU. What's your problem?"

I couldn't take it anymore and I ran upstairs and threw open the bedroom door. Kevin practically jumped out of his skin. I said, "Your ex-lunatic is downstairs saying that my father did something to me when I was a kid and that's why my hair's blonde and we don't do it!"

Kevin put up his hands. "Whoa, I don't know what you are talking about."

"Did you tell her about my mother? That was PERSONAL! That was between me and my OLD MAN. Not my OLD MAN'S ex." He gets all wiggly and nervous and he says, "I might have told her you didn't get along with your madre, but that's it. She's yanking your chain."

Whenever she sets foot in this house, there's some kind of crap for me to deal with. I said, "I want her out. For good." He kept telling me to chill and calm down and come let him hold me. I said, "Goddamn Christ, Kevin! Either she goes or I do." I meant it. He just gawked and so I said, "Fine. I go then." I started dragging my suitcase out of the closet. He grabbed me and said, "Whoa . . . What's all the shootin' about? Come'ere." And he hugged me and told me to stay there and he'd go talk to her.

I snuck halfway down the steps. First I heard him say, "What's goin' on, Katydid?" I hate it when he calls her that.

And she said, "Ke-e-ev. I think I might've upset your old lady."
Her voice went quiet and I couldn't hear a damn thing. A few
minutes went by and then suddenly Kevin yelled, "What're
y'doin' that shit for?" And Fatass said, "Quit wiggin'. It IS
beatitude, man. It opens you." Kevin said, "This guy is bad
news" and she said, "You're just jealous, daddy. Go play with
your girl; I'm gettin' outta here before you stomp my buzz so
bad I gotta throw a funeral."

   I'd like to throw a damn funeral. A minute later Kevin was
at the foot of the stairs saying to me, "She's fried, man.
Scarecrow's been doing H with her. She's been snorting for a
while now. Today's the first time she mainlined." I didn't even
know you COULD snort heroine. "She's an idiot," I said, but
Kevin got all sympathetic and said she was just experimenting.
So I said, "She's a heroin addict, all the more reason you
should get her out." He said, "I don't think abandoning your
friends is the right thing to do when they're in trouble." So I
said, "Did you tell her we don't get it on?" He said, "Does that
sound like something I'd say?"

   So now we're supposed to act like a family and look after
Junk-head Katie. Kevin thinks we should INSIST she comes
home for dinner every night. How grand. Fuck fuck fuck!
Maybe she'll OD and solve all my problems. Ew. That was
mean. I better go. I don't have much else to say. I wrote
another poem last night. I'll spare you though. Write me back.
You never write. And I hate calling collect.
   I miss you.
   Love, Celia
   xoxo

June 2, 1962

Dear Annie-Fanny,
   Sorry I haven't been writing much lately but I've been at
the Follies practically every night. I started going so I wouldn't

have to be home so much with Fatass. Although a lot of the time Kevin goes over to Conner's place. He's trying to force-feed Katie a truer form of crystallized beatitude, he says. I don't even care anymore. I think I told you about the Follies—those are the poetry nights and they also have music and singing and short comedy sketches. Lots of sarcastic ones that make fun of politics and squares and television. Those are my favorite parts. I'm turning into little Miss Popular because I know all kinds of inside stories. Like, for instance, I told some of the guys that I heard the reason J. Edgar Hoover left Meyer Lansky alone is because Lansky has pictures of Hoover in a dress! It's probably not true but it's hilarious, and they did this sketch called "Tea Party at Hoover's." It brought the house down. They even did one of Hoover dressed as Marilyn and he sang "Happy Birthday, Mister President." It was a scream.

Mostly it's the jazz boys I've been hanging with, a trio that backs the poets. They heard me sing once and now they keep hounding me to sing with them every night. One night I gave in and did "Love Me or Leave Me" just like that colored singer at the Jumpin' Joy. I was so excited to be singing again. Kevin didn't even show up. I'm not even sure if I dig him anymore. He said he didn't come because Katie had a breakdown and they needed time to examine the self. Brother. Dinah and Ernie didn't show either. They've been going off for lots of parties in Oakland. I guess they have new friends out there.

I love singing again but in a way it makes me feel lonesome. I wonder if I'm pining for lights and action and New York and Las Vegas and I feel bad because then I feel shallow. Last night, I was lying in bed with Kevin and said, "I think I'm going to read my new poem tomorrow night. Will you come down?" He didn't even answer me. I said, "Seems like you don't hear a thing that comes out of my mouth anymore." And he said, "Baby, I wish you'd think about someone other than yourself. You haven't once asked how Katie is. You're like this bottomless . . . sponge for attention and fuck if I'm not trying to keep someone from dying in the midst of it."

Then he tried to get it on with me. After THAT. I told him to go slam the window on it.

When I told the guys in the band about wishing I could be a poet as good as the others, the sax player, Gordy, said, "But you ARE poetry, Celia." I could have kissed him. I'm starting to think I dig Gordy more than Kevin. The embarrassing part is that my poem is for Kevin. He now says he'll come. He'll probably end up bringing Katie. I can sing in front of a loungeful of people in Lake Tahoe or Las Vegas but Katie comes around and I feel like the original loser.

I guess I'll just mail this. You say you love my letters but I feel like a boring whiny old drip.

Love, Celia

xxoo

PS I have a confession to make. I DID kiss Gordy. Does that count as cheating?

June 3, well, technically 4, 1962

Dear Annie,

I'm in JAIL for chrissake! They let me have some paper, and Linda, another lady who's in here, gave me a pen. She's a lady of the evening. We're in a holding cell together. Hold on.

I just asked Linda and she said she prefers to be called a working girl. Lady of the evening's too bourgeois. Linda says hi. She said she's heard of you, Annie! You're my famous best friend! She said she saw you in Los Angeles once but she can't remember what nightclub. I wonder if they'll mail this for me. Linda's a riot, she keeps calling the cops or guards or whatever they are "lousy screws." I'm glad she's here. I guess you're wondering how I got my skinny ass in here. (Linda keeps saying I have a skinny ass. I don't know how I feel about that.) (Actually there's another girl in here from Harry's too. She's in for possession of marijuana but she's passed out on the floor right now.) Well, I read my poem tonight just like I said I would.

I went down to Harry's early. I dressed all in black. And
Lorne, the gut-scraper (a violinist—he calls himself the gut-
scraper), tugged at my beret and said, "The kitten-hipster
cometh. She's icy-cool now, daddy." And then I got
embarrassed and said, "I knew you guys were going to bug
me. My dress is in my bag for later if I sing." Lorne tried to
smooth my feathers. "No, it's great, it's like you're goofin'
on us. It's like a spoof." I said, "Thanks loads," and I took a
cigarette out of one of their packs and they teased me about
THAT too. Gordy grabbed it out of my mouth and said, "Uck!
It's like a nun giving head." "For chrissake," I said. "I smoke
funny. I dress funny. I'm bourgeois, la-di-da."

Gordy said, "Oh, don't get all bent. It's cool how you do.
You got one costume for your poetry and one for your singin'.
You treat this dump like a real club and I mean that in the
most monster way." Gordy's such a honey. He said he was
talking with his uncle who blows around New York and played
with Rosemary Clooney, and his uncle said Clooney's such a
grape hound, sometimes she can barely stand up when she's
on. Gord said he thought we should do a bit where I burlesque
Clooney. He said, "You could wear that nice dress of yours, all
sweet and square, but you're stoned, see, and you talk to the
audience and sing and you cuss out the band . . . It'd be crazy."
How would the audience even know who I was? I wondered.
And Gordy said, "We'd announce you. And you'd do one of
her big ones, 'Come On-A My House' or 'Mambo Italiano'
and then you could dance too but you'd trip it up, see."

That Gordy. It turned me to mush that he thought up a
sketch just for me.

I was supposed to be third up with my poem but Kevin
still hadn't shown and I asked the fellas in the Castro the
Friendly Ghost sketch if we could switch spots. They said yes
and then it was an hour later and STILL no Kevin. I wanted to
die. And Gordy felt sorry for me and that was TRULY humili-
ating. You know, when you dig a new guy and the old guy
ditches you? Anyway, I'd had a couple glasses of wine so I just

said, "Screw it!" and went to the mike. My poem is called
"Rifling." I had it all memorized (everybody does their stuff by
heart). Just as I said the first line, guess who stumbles in the
door with his arm around Katie. I got all tripped up and had to
start over again. This is how my poem starts,

Rifling
Again, I am rifling through music, listening for you.

Kevin and Katie hung at the back of the room. I was on
the verge of bombsville so I FORCED myself to take the mike
off the stand and turned to Gordy and the guys to help me get
my courage again. You would've been proud of me. Then I
turned around and sat on the stool and tossed my head back
and I just DID it. The rest goes like this:

Tracing your outline through each chorus,
letting each note cascade over my head.
The lyrics dripping down my throat.
Only when the sun has crawled away does
your heart unravel, loosening, floating and I am
allowed to hunt you in you.
Until daylight tracks its way home. Climbing
through windows, seeping under doors, tightening,
its raw light forcing me back to hide and listen.

I KILLED, Annie, I really did. Everybody was snapping
their fingers like crazy. Maybe they just felt sorry for me but it
felt really good anyway. (Linda is reading over my shoulder
right now. I wish you could meet Linda. She's very nice.)
Until it quieted down and I heard someone kind of snort like
I was a real jerk or something. I looked over and guess who.
Kevin was putting his hand over her mouth and laughing. I
felt as if my face was on fire. I didn't know where to look and
sweet Gordy winked at me and put his arms out. I got a hug
from him but I wanted to do a Houdini in the worst way.

Except I promised the guys I'd sing. I decided to just go get a drink and try to think of the coolness of the good people and pretend there was no Kevin. But then he grabbed me, the creep. "Hey, babe! You did your little poem. You looked cute in that beret."

I said, "What was so irrepressibly funny to Katie?"

"Ah nothing. It was a gas when you were doing those Vegas moves." And he tossed his head, imitating me! VEGAS moves? Then that fuck-faced Fatass sidled over and SHE said, "Atta chick, Celia. You can take the girl out of the burlesque but you can't take burlesque out of the girl." They both laughed. And no I didn't murder them. I said, "You two wouldn't know burlesque if it bit you in the ass." And then I stormed back to the stage and told Gordy I wanted us to do the Clooney bit NOW. I marched straight to the bar for a glass of grape and downed the whole glass as soon as it hit the counter! Kevin came up to me again and said, "You're not hot, are you? She just never saw a poet go in for all that drama is all."

Can you believe!? I said to the bartender, "Hit me again, pally," and then I reached for my bag of clothes and started thinking Rosemary Clooney into my voice. I sang a little in the bathroom to make sure I had it.

Gordy introduced me. He said, "Cats and kittens, flap your ears cuz I'm about to introduce you to someone very special. Here now, the goddess of grape, the original bottle baby, stopping in to sing us a treat on her way to detox—Miss Rosemary Clooney." I had on my ice-blue dress (still do) and I left the black beret on and I grabbed the mike and said, "Thank you, you beautiful San Franciscansans." And then I turned around to Gordy and he looked so cute I said, "And you! You bump your gums too much, pally. I'm sober as a whistle, baby, straight as a, a, whaddycallit." Gordy looked so happy and I looked into the crowd and lit into them. "All right, you crazy cats, you righteous . . . sons-a-bitches . . . we're gonna shake it up in here. And if you're very very good, I'm gonna letcha . . ." and I looked back at Gordy and said,

"One-two-three-four—'Botch-a-me, I'll botcha you and ev'ry-thing goes crazy!'"

I was good, Annie! I don't mean to sound conceited, but I really WAS! I was strutting around and flirting with the room and singing "'Bah-bah, botch-a-me, bambino. Bah-bah-bo, bo, boca piccolino. When you kiss me and I'm a-kissa you. Tra la la la la la la la la loo!'"

The crowd whooped and clapped and some of them were even singing along! I don't know if I was just stoned on the sympathetic vibrations or the wine but I was FLYING! I imagined where Katie and Kevin were even though I couldn't see them and I thought "Fuck you!" but I yelled, "Kiss-a me!" and tossed my beret. I kept hearing Katie somewhere in the back of my head: "You can't take burlesque out of the girl." And the next thing you know I slipped a shoulder strap down. The room went mental.

And then I took the other strap down and I yelled, "Let 'em have it, boys" to the band. I was on FIRE and I plucked Gordy's cigarette out of his mouth and took a drag and I blew the smoke at the audience. By the time I sang, "'If-a you squeeze me and I'm a-squeeza you,'" I was shimmying out of the dress. I kicked it to the side and I was dancing and singing in my slip.

You should've been there. I had my thumbs looped in my slip straps and I was stretching them like suspenders while I sang. This shaggy poet-cat jumped up and jived with me! I just laughed, and shoved him back in his chair and he LOVED it. They all loved it! When the song ended they were pounding the tables and screaming for more. I said, "You want more, you little devils? Whatchu wanna? Uh? You wanna, you wanna 'Come On-A My House'?" The band launched right into it! What I didn't know was there was some little weasel reporter in the back of the room. I don't know what the hell he was doing there. So I kept belting it out—"'Come on-a my house, my house,'" and I slipped right out of my slip! There I was in my bra and my lacy French-cut drawers and my slingbacks (the ones you talked me into getting in L.A.). Oh my lord, Annie. I feel like a skinny little nothing most of the time but suddenly I was the curviest road this side of the Rockies and I thought, Fuck you, Fatass, and the next thing you know, one bra strap was down and then the other. I did it like YOU. I turned my back to the crowd and I plucked the straps and stretched them sideways, and slid the bra down to my waist. Then I crossed my arms and faced them.

   That fink reporter must've made a call. When I got to "Come on-a my house, my house, I'm gonna give you everything," I threw my arms in the air right as the BULLS walked in! They blew the whistle and the band stopped. I stopped. Everything stopped. Then every cat and chick in the joint suddenly remembered their stash and tried to get rid of it. They jammed into the bathrooms and ducked out the back and there I was with my arms crossed, trying to grab my slip. Next thing I knew, a cop yanked me by the arm and said, "Zat 'sposed to be poetry, miss?" and told me I was under arrest for indecent exposure and contributing to the delinquency of minors. Contributing? He doesn't know the half of it. One of the girls screamed, "Leave her alone, pig!," which was very sweet of her. Gordy and the band were slammed to the wall and getting their pockets and pant legs frisked. Harry was cuffed for selling booze to minors and everybody and their dog was getting ID'd. I was worried they were hurting Gordy. And they were really manhandling me too. I was still NAKED except for my undies and this pig was dragging me to the door and I said, "Would you let me cover up at least?" (Linda's getting mad reading this over my shoulder.) The cop says to me, "You shoulda thought of that before you decided to expose yourself," and slammed my wrists together and snapped his handcuffs on. "I betcher folks'll be real proud." Then the fink reporter who I'm sure started this whole mess ran up with his pad and pen and started BOMBARDING me with questions. "What drove you to take off your clothes, Celia? Are you a prostitute?" What a jerk. There I am in my slingbacks and drawers and the cop is pulling me out on the STREET!! Talk about indecent exposure. And that rat face reporter was running alongside me and he said, "Celia, how long have you been singing? Can you impersonate other singers or do you just naturally sound like Clooney?" Which was kind of nice. Outside, a couple of the poets were spread over the bull carts and everybody was yelling, "Fucking pigs!" I even heard people singing "We Shall Overcome"! Man, it was cold though. How come California gets so cold at night? Even in summer. If this happened in New York, at least it'd be warm.

Who's out on the sidewalk with her arms folded? Katie. She was shaking her head and handing me this I-told-you-so face as they brought me to the car. I kissed my fingertips at her with a loud smack the way Teddy used to do. The photographer was yelling, "Celia! Over here!" Flash flash. (Linda thinks this part sounds cool.) Then this very sweet young cop ran up with a blanket and said, "Jesus, cover the girl up," and he wrapped it around me before they stuck me in the back seat. It was scratchy but better than nothing.

I saw Kevin come out just before we took off, yelling like a madman. "Beauty is truth and truth is beauty. That's my girlfriend, man." I was pretty touched actually. The fink reporter ran after him. I bet Kevin was sorry he opened his mouth.

When we got down here to the station they demanded ID and of course I didn't have it. I said, "It's in my pocketbook, you goon." My bag was still on the floor at Harry's. Poor Harry himself sat there waiting to get booked. I felt bad for him. He had his head down and his hands cuffed in his lap. I apologized while the guy who arrested me banged out my name on the typewriter. I said, "I guess I got carried away, Harry." Harry said, "S'alright, honey. Who knew lookin' so good was a crime." He's very sweet.

I said to the cop, "How come I'm under arrest for something that happens every day in nightclubs all over town?" And he said, "For one thing, they don't got a licence for this type of performance. For another, you got totally naked on your upper half." (He was a real genius that guy.) I said, "Pasties? The rest of the boob, no problem, but the pink part in the middle, that's criminal. Is that what you're saying?" I was feeling like a freedom fighter all of a sudden. He says, "I don't make the rules, lady. Address?"

Then Kevin came charging in. A cop stopped him first but then he ran over to the desk and he had my pocketbook, my dress, and slip and everything. He said, "I got here quick as I could." And suddenly I was happy. "Kevin! You CAME." I was still in my blanket and I jumped up and hugged him in it. Kevin said, "What gives? What's the charge?" And I said, "Nipples. What did that reporter ask you?" Kevin said, "Shit, THAT guy. I told him you were a jazz singer and an outlaw and tonight you shed light on our existence by baring yourself before god and man. Like Buddha."

He was very excited that he got to talk to that reporter. It made me feel less excited about what I did. I don't know why. Then Kevin said, "I'd bail ya, baby, but all I got's eight bucks. Katie's got three." Then I felt even less excited. I decided I better bite the bullet. I said, "Go home and look in the bottom of my suitcase. There's a velvet pouch with some pearls."

He got this funny surprised look as if that was a very strange thing. "I never told you because they're sentimental to me and I was waiting for an emergency." He didn't say anything. I guess he was mad. I said, "Kev, please! Just pawn them and get me out of here. They'll set bail tonight." And the cop said, "Morning."

"What! I can't stay here all night!"

The cop didn't give a damn though. He just wanted my ID. Kevin finally said, "Okay, babe. I'm going to go back to the house and do like you said." And he left. He didn't even kiss me goodbye until I asked him to. He came back and kissed me like it was a big chore. Then that crummy cop said, "Won't be seein' him again." I said, "You don't know what you're talking about. He's my BOYFRIEND!" So, now I'm waiting. At least they let me put my clothes back on. Kevin hasn't come back yet. I think maybe I should try to sleep. Where the hell is Kevin?? I guess the pawnshops are still closed.

June 4. Morning.

I'm awake. Not that I slept anyway. You know me, I can't sleep in my own bed half the time never mind a JAIL cell. A different cop just came by. He was older and very nice. He slapped the morning paper up against the bars to show me and guess who's on the front!!! I have to send this to you. You won't believe it. The headline says, "Debauchery or Botch-a-me?" with a picture of me handcuffed with my arms over my boobs and I'm giving the Teddy kiss-off! They got that on film! Oops, I have a CALL!!

I'm back. I can't goddamn believe this. I don't know whether to scream or cry. Or laugh, it's so stupid. I'm so STUPID! The cop was very nice though. He said, "We don't normally let detainees receive calls but it's about your bail. And this seems crazy to me, pretty little thing like you being in here." Anyway, the call was Kevin. He said, "I'm not coming down." I said, "Didn't you find them?" "Katie's pregnant," he said. What the hell's that got to do with the price of eggs? I said, "So? Where's Conner?" And then Kevin said, "Conner! Sonuvabitch is too busy shooting up to get it up." ?? I just about gagged. He said, "Baby, try to understand. You were my girl, but Katie's my soulmate. This country's no place to raise a kid, you know, with Cuba and the A-bomb and everything. We're thinkin' about Mexico. You're a gone chick, baby. What you did for us is beautiful." And he hung up. Then the old cop was patting my shoulder. He didn't hear but he knew all right. He said, "Life's shit sometimes, kid." I guess I'm pretty typical and ordinary and it IS all shit when you get right down to it. So here I am. Stuck in a jail cell. Truth is beauty, beauty is truth—What a load. Oh god, now I AM crying. Even Linda already got bailed out. And the other girl from Harry's threw up so they just took her somewhere else.

3:30 p.m.

Jesus, Annie, you won't believe this but I'm on a plane now. The cop came back right after I stopped writing you and said someone arranged for my release. Whatever that means. A lawyer. I've never seen him before in my life but he's sitting right beside me now. His name is Leonard Trigliani and he said he was designated as my legal counsel. By John Rawlston he said. I was racking my brains trying to think where I knew that name and I finally remembered that you said Johnny uses it sometimes. In Florida, didn't you say? Anyway, he put me in this very sharp Cadillac and said, "Your Los Angeles belongings have been shipped back to New York City where I will be accompanying you this morning. You have a reservation at the Plaza." Actually, that's when I remembered about Johnny because he stays at the Plaza sometimes. I just can't figure out how he knew. Somebody must have seen the paper and told him. Oh boy, this picture of me in the paper. This is quite a hangover, waking up to this. Anyway, then Leonard Trigliani took me by the house so I could get my stuff, and suddenly I didn't want any of it. The house looked so dank and dirty from the Cadillac. I just wanted to go home. The only person I'll miss is Gordy. I can hand you this letter!

Midnight.

I just got to the hotel. I tried to call but you're not there. The lawyer was right. All my stuff from Johnny's in L.A. is here in the closet. God, I'm glad I never brought my mink with me to San Francisco. Imagine if Kevin hocked that. I'm going to have a hot bath. Fine, I'm a bourgeois princess. Oops, the phone!

I thought it was going to be you but it was Johnny. He said, "I leave her alone five minutes and look what she does." It was so nice to hear his voice. I said, "How do you always know where I am?" And he said, "You think I don't know anyone in San Francisco? Besides, you exemplify the moral depravity of the nation's youth. How could I resist?" Then he asked me if I was really going around with a commie—the article in the Chronicle is loaded with Kevin shooting off his big yap. I thought maybe Johnny would be mad at me but he said, "No, honey, of course not. I just thought you should be in New York with Annie instead of that place of mine. Things are a little hot in California." Anyone who knows him or Sam G is getting a lot of hassle right now, he says.

I don't even feel bad, you know. I keep thinking I should feel embarrassed because I was in the paper practically naked but I feel sort of excited. Isn't that goofy! Johnny says you're coming home tomorrow. I'm glad he got me a room for the night. It would've been lonely to come home to the apartment without you there. I can't wait to see you!

Love, Celia the Flasher

xoxox

As my gaze eased up from the page, the snort of the espresso machine shoved me back into my own reality. Suddenly the clatter of dishes, the chatter and laughter of teenagers and old men as they stirred their coffees all felt so jarring. I pushed the heels of my palms against my eyes and tried to imagine what a man could say to make a woman hate her daughter. My foot kicked out reflexively and heads turned as the chair across from me jumped back.

My chest heaved and I swallowed, terrified I was going to start crying right there in the coffee shop. To Josie it had never mattered what I did: I was the most miserable cunt imaginable and maybe she couldn't stand me but she never stopped loving me.

At the bottom of the box was an old *Time* magazine. June 18–25, 1962. The cover featured a grainy reproduction of mayhem: cops and young bohemians. Among them a thin blonde wearing nothing but heels, handcuffs and a pair of French briefs. It was my mother. On the cover of *Time*. I flipped it open to look at the credits or the story but all I could find was "Outside a San Francisco coffee house." Maybe here, along Columbus Avenue. How could they have her on the cover of a magazine and not give her name? There were about a dozen people in the shot and I wondered if one was the fink reporter. A folded piece of newspaper fell out as I flipped through. The bottom half of the *San Francisco Chronicle*'s front page: *Debauchery or Botch-a-me? Celia Dare exemplifies the attitude of our disaffected youth in coffee house raid.* Kevin sounded as unbearable in the news as he did in her letters, but there was nothing directly from her. It described Dare's "disdain of social mores and conventions" with her depiction of Rosemary Clooney as "a booze-soaked call girl." Celia, it said, was "the product of divorce." A psychiatrist spoke on the dissolution of the American family and its repercussions as evidenced by a higher incidence of prostitution, drug use and disregard for public decency. *Time* had more shrinks and crime statistics along with the prophecy of doom.

"Excuse me," I said to a guy clearing the next table over. "Do you know if Harry's Drink is still around?"

He said he'd ask the manager and came back a minute later to tell me it used to be down off Divisadero about twenty-five years ago but it was long gone now.

As I put the letters and magazines back in the shoebox, another page fell out, torn from *Good Housekeeping*. Page 111. *What's it REALLY like to be an AIRLINE HOSTESS?* "Even if you're not particularly interested in being a stewardess, you might like to know what, besides glamour, the job consists of." Criteria for landing the job seemed to be mainly looks and a "pleasing personality." It mentioned the pay, which wasn't enough to keep one in cabbage soup and that the marriage rate was notably high. "Over 50 percent of the girls resigning from one major airline give matrimony as the reason." Teddy the Ghost must have made a real impression on her. On the back was an ad for Tampax. Beneath a picture of a model kicking off her high heel, it said, "Today's smart girls

never let the time-of-the-month interfere with fun and freedom. Why do you? Why don't you change to the comfortable,
dainty way of sanitary protection . . . its special shield never
lets your fingers touch it. What could be daintier for changing and disposal?" My mother's thinly veiled disgust at the
sight of her own hairy legs came to mind. Bleaching them on
her bed. Sally's hoots of laughter. Cell in my hand, suddenly
I was dialing. When Sally answered, I was paralyzed for a second. "Sally? It's Vivian." My voice echoed clunky in my skull.
"I'm in San Francisco."

"Vivian . . ." She paused. "What are you doing down there?"

"Figuring it out."

"Oh." She laughed uncertainly. "Are you by yourself?"

"I'm staying with a friend. I found Annie West. I just read a
bunch of old letters Mum wrote to Annie and . . . and you
should see them. They're so—she's only eighteen. I guess she
wanted to be a stewardess too, and there's this crazy *Good
Housekeeping* list of qualifications and, ah . . . I thought of you.
I don't know why." I looked out the window onto Columbus
Avenue, the steady stream of traffic and tourists, urban profes-
sionals who could afford the rent and the beggars who couldn't,
pleading for change.

"Oh. Yeah, she did. She said that. Funny now, isn't it? Are
you okay? Vivian, I'm sorry I . . ." She trailed off.

"So, Annie West, she kind of kicked me out when I asked
too many questions—Mum dated this mobster and was friends
with this other one—did Mum ever date Bobby Kennedy? Is
that who the heart's from?"

There was a moment of silence. "Sounds like you probably
know more than I do."

After we said goodbye I wanted to erase the whole phone
call. At least I hadn't told her when I'd be back. I didn't want to
see her. I didn't really even want to talk to her. And what help
was she anyway? I should probably go buy a Bobby Kennedy
book now. I took out the pad from Marcella's apartment and
reread the last of what I'd written. Louis Prima and Sinatra. All

of them around the table. I pulled out *Pack of Rats* and riffled through the dictionary of hipster slang. I looked up things I'd heard Prima say on TV the night before. I peered at Judy Campbell's memories.

Eleven

~

WHEN SHE OPENS HER EYES, CELIA IS BACK IN HER SUITE under the bedcovers, still in her dress. With the blackout drapes closed, she can't make anything out. She snaps the light on, squints at her wrist. *Two o'clock?* Her head is fogged in. She remembers only bits and pieces. After Keely and Louis left for their next show, everyone kept drinking and joking. The casino hopped. She remembers going to the Silver Slipper with them, Frank on one side of her and Johnny Rosselli on the other—she learned to shoot craps. She and Frank were laughing. He hadn't seemed so bad last night. She remembers coming back in a guestmobile, Frank and Johnny crowing like roosters at the rising sun and her laughing until she got hiccups. Johnny brought her into the suite, made her drink a glass of water. It was the next day already and still no Ghost. "Where's Teddy?" she asked him. "He disappeared on me."

"Ghosts'll do that."

Celia giggled, then started to cry. "I'm all alone."

"What am I, chopped liver? You just had too much to drink. You let Johnny tuck you in. Teddy'll be back before you know it." He gave her a tissue, took her hand and led her into the bedroom.

The maids had turned down the bed and she stared at the open triangle of bare white sheet before she sat, the ice blue of

her dress flouncing around her. Taking the chocolate off the
plumped pillow, she peeled off the wrapper and stuck the candy
in her mouth, sighing as it melted. Rosselli lifted the covers
until she dutifully folded herself under.

"You're *really* nice." She reached up. "You've been nice to
me the whole—all night."

"You're family." He kissed her forehead and said good-
night.

"You're going?"

He sighed and walked to the wall, pulled a chair over. They
both looked out the window at the orange sun making its way
around dusky little Vegas.

Now she's awake again, the chair is back against the wall,
Rosselli's gone and the drapes are closed. She shuffles into the
bathroom, winces at her reflection and sits down to pee. *What
do people do during the day in Vegas?*

Back in the bedroom, she unzips her dress, holds the bodice
to her chest and makes her way to the glass doors, sticking her
nose through the drapes. The sun pierces. A few guests lounge
around the pool, some in short sleeves, most in slacks. Cocktail
girls stroll. No floating crap game though. She opens the doors
to let some air in. She'd thought it would be like Miami, hot all
year-round. Ducking out of the curtains, she drops her dress
and heads for the shower.

It's three by the time she has herself in a chaise lounge,
daiquiri in one hand, movie magazine in the other. She's just
read that Sophia Loren uses olive oil to keep her skin beautiful,
when a voice bellows, "Hey, Dare, whatcha doin' down d'ere?"
A few heads turn. It calls again, "Hey, Celia, I Dare ya!"

She looks behind her but the light is too bright. Soon, a
shadow blocks her sun and she lowers her sunglasses. "Hi,
Frank."

"Hey, baby, what'sa matter? Am I back in the leper colony?"

She shades her eyes until she can make out an orange shirt
and black trousers.

"Come join the party, have a few laughs and keep Annie company."

"Um, no—thank you—I think I'll just stay here."

He drops down on his haunches. "What's your clyde, baby? I thought we made nice last night. I thought things were copacetic between us."

"I'm about to have breakfast."

"So, have it at my place, for chrissake." He looks at her magazine. "You shouldn't be reading that junk anyway."

"I'd like to be by myself right now. But, thanks."

He is quiet a second, then, "You got a problem with that broad? It was Annie said I should come get you. She woulda come herself but she says you don't like her."

Celia shrugs. "I'm just not up to company right now."

"Jesus Christ, drop a grudge." He stalks off.

She closes her eyes and wishes for Miami. She misses Tina and Glenda. And the Fontainebleau. And her bikini.

An hour later she is back in the room. She calls the front desk for messages. Nothing. A moment later, the phone rings. "Hello, my lovely. It's Johnny. How has your day been?"

"Hi-i-i . . ." It isn't Teddy but something about Rosselli smoothes her. "I've just been lying outside, reading. I saw Sinatra."

"He told me," he chuckles. "You make a guy work. You don't even like Annie."

"What do you know about it?"

"You said so last night—you called her a liar. Actually you said *deceitful*, which I thought was a mouthful for a girl in your state. Then you said you don't like Frank cuz he treated her bad."

"Well, no one should—I don't have to explain myself."

"You don't. Plans this evening? If not, may I escort you again?"

Celia sits up. "Yes. I'd like that."

"Terrific. Eight-thirty? We'll have dinner and catch a show."

She puts the receiver down and digs her fingers into her hair. Reaching her arms up and back, she stretches, releases a primordial squeal at the ceiling then skips to the radio on the wall and runs the dial up and down until she finds a classical station.

Sitting down on the floor, she bends forward and begins slowly stretching her body, pulling at each muscle until it aches.

After a manicure, a pedicure and an hour of fussing her hair into a French roll and her face into Frencher makeup, she puts on two petticoats, holds her strapless red dress up and stands in front of the bedroom mirror swinging the skirt, relishing the weight of it. She slips into her gold-toed pumps then does a fox-trot, dipping herself, high-kicking and flashing enough leg to make her mother shriek.

The phone rings and she flings her dress across the floor, herself across the bed. She slaps the receiver out of its cradle and a throaty man-voice hits her ear.

"Hello there, I'm lookin' for Celia. Z'at Celia?"

"Yes."

"Celia, honey, this is Louis Prima. We met last night in the restaurant."

"Hi, Mr. Prima!"

"*Louis* to you, sweetheart. Honey, you ain't heard nothin' from Keely, did you?"

"Keely? No, why would I hear from her?"

"Ah, well, Keely ain't feelin' so hot and she might need someone to do a little vocalizin' in her place. And you gots vocal. You consider doin' a couple songs with me in the lounge tonight?"

"*Tonight?*"

"Yeah," he rasps. "You can sing like nobody's business and hell if you can't jump."

"*Me?*"

"Yeah, you. How's aboutchu do the midnight show with us—crowd needs a pretty girl up there or they all gonna take an exit."

"Keely won't mind?"

"You'd be helpin' us out. I had to do the last couple shows by myself last night. When she took off with Sam, she—"

"Sam Butera?"

"No, d'other Sam—"

"Sammy Davis."

"No, the Sam that threw those fireworks under our chairs."

"Lot of Sams around here."

Another wheezy laugh from Prima. "You got stage experience, don'tcha?"

"Um, yes. A bit." If high school musicals count. And the sideshow at a carnival.

"I knew you musta. This'll getchu lotsa people watchin'. Who knows who gonna see!"

"Oh my god. This is so nice of you, Mr. Prima. And Keely. Tell Keely thank-you."

"Stop callin' me mistah, you gonna give me a rash. Meet me at the Sands lounge round eleven and I'll clue you on the show."

Celia puts the receiver down. She jumps up and down on the bed and screams, "Me! Me! Me!" over and over. She stops and looks at the phone. Her stepfather would drop dead if he knew. Stewart'd jump right up on the bed with her.

A speck of desolation creeps inward, spreading like lava until she starts to jump again, harder, higher. She forces a giggle until it's real.

Over dinner she tells Rosselli every word of her talk with Prima. She's too anxious to eat; her fork raps a backbeat against the rim of her dinner plate. Rosselli reaches across and stills her hand. He tells her to be careful.

"*Careful?* I'm going to be *good*."

"We should get you over to the Sands soon. Maybe get a shot down your hatch so you won't be nervous. How old are you, Celia?"

"Twenty-one."

He sips his vodka.

"What? I am. I was born in 1938."

"Very good. Don't suppose you recall your birthday too, do you?"

Her face reddens and he raises his hand. "Never mind. I

hope Teddy gets you out of this town soon. Before they ruin you." He waves to their waiter.

In the lounge, they find Prima sitting on his own with a glass of something amber over ice. He stands when he sees them. "Miss Celia and the Great John Rosselli."

Johnny shakes his hand and nods. Prima rubs at the back of his neck. "So. So, you two gonna have a—?" The waitress slips in before he can finish. "I was thinkin'—" he takes a folded piece of paper from his pocket "—'bout makin' you a list, but no point cuz I just call out what's cookin'. You know, 'That Old Black Magic'—you done great with that last night. You jump in when you know 'em, sing backup with the boys or you can dance. And ah, you wanna do a solo? You up to doin' 'I Got it Bad'?"

"You paying her for this?" Rosselli's cool eyes burrow.

Prima looks at him. "Huh?"

"Oh, you don't have to pay me, I just—" she stammers.

"It's work, isn't it? Isn't this about work, Louis?" Rosselli keeps his gaze on Prima.

"Sure, John, I'm gonna pay her. What kinda dough we lookin' at? How's about—"

Celia opens her mouth, but the sound comes out of Rosselli's. "I think three's fair."

"Three *hun'red*? Dems a lotta nuts for one squirrel."

Celia shakes her head. "Johnny, don't be—" She stops. He still hasn't blinked.

Prima rubs his neck again. "Hey, what we gettin' all serious for, baby? We in *Vegas*!"

"What's Keely think is fair, Louis?"

"She thinks like me, John: three hun'red's a good deal for a performer like this gal here, last minute and all." He downs his scotch and wipes his mouth, keeps his eyes to himself. "Okay, I'm headin' to the Casbah, catch me a catnap before I hit the stage. You comin' or should I meetchu a'quarter t'twelve?"

"She'll meet you."

Celia grasps the bulk of Louis's arms and kisses his cheek. "Thank you so much for this chance. You won't be sorry."

Rosselli slides the ice around in his glass of Smirnoff.

She sits, looks at him. "What was *that*?"

He pushes his lips out and down, says nothing.

"I've only been working for this my whole life, for crying out loud!"

"And that's a long long time," he muses.

"Why are you being like this?"

"Married man. You don't want to get in the middle of that."

"What, so he just wants to, to—*do a little hey-hey*?"

"*Make* a little hey-hey." He smirks.

"Some people think I have talent, you know."

She huffs and looks away until he asks, "How old do you think Keely was when he took up with her? Sixteen." He gazes out to the casino. "She had talent too."

Celia's eyes flick as she sips.

Less than an hour later, the Casbah Theater Lounge buzzes with Prima's announcement. "And tonight's special guest: New York's fabulous Celia Dare." Blood roars in her ears at the sound of her name, and the zoom and pound of the band courses up her legs.

As the curtain opens, the audience seems to be talking more amongst themselves than anything. Prima waves the curtain closed again. Five seconds later, it opens and the audience continues to babble and gawk. He closes it again. Finally the crowd catches on and whistles and stomps till Prima opens up. "You awake now? You kids bettah perk up out there—Yeah, that's it, smile when you say my name," and with that he starts into "When You're Smilin'" and Celia chimes in backup with the Witnesses, trying to get the feel of Keely inside as the voice falls out. But she just can't keep up that sly calmness and by the time Prima slips into "Just a Gigolo," Celia is out-goofing them all. Butera pulls one hand from his sax just long enough to hand her a couple maracas.

She shakes the bulbous rattles a minute or so then stuffs them in Louis's back pockets. He clowns a giant "Oh" as if he were getting molested *but-good*. His ass-end rattle-shakes a rhythm and Celia jives with him. She spins off and dances around Butera as he lambastes the Casbah with his sax.

Louis stands centre stage, turns round and round: "Anybody seen a good-lookin' blonde?" He bends forward, stuffs his head between his knees and tries to look up Celia's skirt as she jumps him from behind, vaults across his back, petticoats flying under the screaming raspberry of her dress. The audience claps and roars her full of euphoria.

Annie is in the lounge, watching from a table this time, her mouth open. *This kid can do anything.* She's a natural, aping Prima's big-galloot moves.

Annie's escort, Ike, lights her cigarette and whispers, "Those things'll kill ya," in her ear. She takes a long drag, turns her head and blows smoke in his face. He growls. A tingle up her neck, Annie glances over her shoulder, scanning the people at the bar, jolts when she sees his face again. For chrissake, that *has* to be him. She nudges Ike. "See that guy over there in the brown sport coat, the one that needs a haircut? He look familiar to you?"

Ike looks over. "Seen him yesterday. Some drifter hittin' me up for a job at the Riv. Probably just stick his fingers in the wrong pot and end up in the desert with a busted head. Sent him packin'."

She nods.

When it comes time for her solo, Celia closes her eyes and sings "Night and Day" as though she were back home in her living room, sitting on the piano, her parents' friends ready to applaud. She opens her eyes only when Louis starts horsing around—"Night *and* day, whatchu think I'm made of?" Soon he has the beat loping a little faster as he starts harmonizing with "Up A Lazy River."

Not only is Rosselli watching from the bar but she can see how many famous kissers are in the crowd too—Shirley MacLaine and Milton Berle. When she catches sight of Cyd Charisse, her stomach turns. She feels foolish suddenly, the audacity of performing in front of a dancer like Charisse.

Prima catches the look on her face and tries to follow her gaze but sees someone else entirely. The band takes his cue into the shuffle-beat of "Baby, Won't You Please Come Home" as Prima substitutes *Baby* with *Keely*.

The music continues to thump and Celia freezes. Keely is standing right next to Charisse, healthy as a country girl and damn pissed off. *Why is everyone such a goddamn liar?* She pulls herself together. Striding to Prima's microphone, she harmonizes with "Cuz your big daddy is fawwl-lin apart . . ." Smoke curls across Keely's blank stare. Soon Prima bellows, "My baby's here! She's feelin' better. Sam-there-boy, call up Keely with that-there horn-a-yorn, call my baby home to Papa. Get 'er marchin' on to me."

Butera's sax howls into "When the Saints Go Marching In," but Keely doesn't move.

Her breastbone ready to crack, Celia dances and claps her way off the stage, as though she is heading into the congregation at a revival meeting. The crowd parts. She heads straight for Keely.

When she gets there, Celia throws her hands in the air and kneels before Keely, arms outstretched, fingers flicking heavenward. Keely shakes her head no.

Celia stands, looks into the other woman's eyes and hears Keely say, "He can't do this to me, he can't do it anymore."

She takes Keely's hands and says, "I'm just a poor stand-in while he waits for the real thing."

Keely lets herself be led onto the stage, where the gang of them outwail even the best Southern Baptists. Louis gets down on his knees in front of Keely, genuflecting, bowing, prostrate. Celia dances a walk around them, eyes closed, arms flailing.

The Casbah explodes, every voice and foot onstage and off rejoicing.

When the curtain closes, none of the performers speak. Louis takes Keely in his arms and Celia floats out into the lounge. She wanders through the chattering and cackles of the crowd, the clinking of the slot machines and hears nothing. Weightless.

Annie catches her by the wrist. "My god, that was *fantastic*. You were hotter than hot, girl!" When Celia doesn't respond, Annie introduces her date. "This is Ike Epstein, he manages the casino at that Riviera. Ike was just saying we should take you for a drink."

Celia gazes past them. Finally she says, "Annie, you and I aren't going to be friends."

Ike tugs Annie's arm. "She ain't worth your trouble."

"Gimme a minute," she tells him and jerks her arm loose. "Better yet, why don't you call me tomorrow."

"Broad doesn't want nothin' to do with you." When Annie doesn't budge, he throws up his hands. "I *ain't* callin' you tomorrow." He makes off toward the craps tables.

Celia wanders toward the front doors. Annie goes after her. "Just—please, I—" Celia stops and faces her. "I know I'll never be able to—" Annie swipes her forehead in frustration. "Listen, I'm really sorry for the place I sent you. I didn't know how bad it was. But I have to tell you, I think I saw that Okie Joe character in here. I heard that you had a falling-out with him and I thought you might want to know."

Celia just stares.

"I met him when I came around to find you at the Sherman show. He told me you were gone and he seemed pretty hacked about it. I saw him in the lounge last night and then again while you were singing."

"You want to chase me out of Vegas now?"

Annie's chin begins to quiver.

Celia heads for the doors, leaving Annie limp-limbed in the middle of the casino. Rosselli comes up from behind and hands her a crisp white hankie. "Don't worry," he tells her. "She's just emotional right now: her first big break and getting caught in the middle of someone else's marital problems. She'll come round."

"No. She won't." She dabs at her eyes.

"How's about you let me buy you a pink lady?"

Annie blows her nose. "I think I'll go to my room, catch up on some beauty sleep."

"Sure?"

"Yup." She looks at the hankie in her hand.

"You keep that."

Back at the Sands, Annie opens the door to her room and takes a last look down the hall just as Celia swishes around the corner, striding down to her room. A man walks twenty or thirty feet behind her. Celia searches her purse for the key. The man slows and the hair on Annie's arms stands up. Just as Celia turns the lock he steps in and slaps a hand over her mouth.

"Celia!" Annie screeches.

He shoves her in and slams the door behind.

"Cecilia!" Annie reaches the room and starts to bang. "You sonuvabitch, open this door or I'm callin' the cops." She pounds and kicks.

A murmur, then Celia's voice, tiny and scratched. "It's okay, Annie, go away."

"No! Celia, you come out here. I'm not going anywhere."

"I'm okay." Her voice is quivery.

Annie runs up the hall and grabs the house phone. "I need someone with a key at room 502. Please! It's an emergency!"

Celia's shoulders are against the wall, an arm against her windpipe. She can see the glint of a pocket knife from the corner of her eye. Laboured breaths come in and out.

"What a good little actress you are . . . *It's okay, Annie,*" Okie Joe squawks. "*You go 'way.* I guess all thieves gotta be good actresses, huh?"

"My boyfriend's in the bedroo-kh . . ."

He cuts off her air. "Oh, boyfriend!" he calls. "Are you home? He must be sleepin'. Can you breathe or am I leanin' too hard?" Face red, she is choking. "Oh, don't go dyin' on me." He lets up a little, switches the knife to the other hand and begins pulling pins from her hair. "I like it better down. And I like it dark, the way it used to be before you got all uppity and whorey." He grabs a handful of hair and yanks her toward the bedroom. "Vegas Vegas Vegas . . . I just can't believe my luck."

She cries out and falls on one knee.

"Quit whining or I'll slit your throat right now and god knows, I got every right to."

"I can pay you back and you can get out of here before he comes. I have money."

He hauls her along. "I'll bet you got money if you can afford this joint. You hookin' these days? You used to be nice when I first met you. Remember that?"

The phone rings. "Teddy," she says, her voice tears and gravel now.

"Who's Teddy? He got my car?" He kicks her legs out from under her. "Let's getchu down on the floor just like old times. You were happy then, livin' in a doghouse. Suited you."

"Teddy!" she screeches at the phone. "Please don't hurt me. He'll kill you. Teddy the Ghost. He'll kill you—" The ringing stops.

He starts to chuckle. "What the hell's Teddy the goddamn *Ghost*? He your pimp?"

Men's voices in the hall now. A little laughter, growing louder until they stop right outside. " . . . yeah, *on*stage. With Prima—Rosselli said she killed." A light rap on the door. "Celia. Baby, it's Frank."

She and Joe look toward the suite's front door. Joe sits on the floor, his back against the bed and hauls her shoulders back against him, her head under his chin, the knife at her neck.

From the hall: "Frank, maybe the girl just don' like you." Celia recognizes the Southern drawl Dean uses from the Copa. "Maybe we should just go find you a girl who *do* like you."

"I just thought it'd be a nice gesture to have a little celebratory cocktail, that's all. Awright, fine. I'm leavin' her a glossy." The sound of something sliding under the door.

Then a woman's voice shrieking down the hall, "*Frank!* Frank, wait."

"Who dat?"

"It's Annie, y'blind sonuvabitch. Could see those Charlies from Albuquerque."

Annie's words come in a rush. "Frank! She's in there—some guy's got her in there!"

Then from Dean: "Well, if we're interruptin', then what the hell we—"

"No! He pushed her in there. I saw him . . ." She bangs on the door. "Celia!"

Inside, Celia and Joe face the door. He *shh-shhes* into the top of her head. She feels his muttering jaw graze her hair and suddenly the gaunt bony face of her first singing teacher floats in her eyes, her voice in Celia's ears as she tried to coax corrections. *Enunciation is important, Audrey.* It finally hits her, that's who Okie Joe reminded her of, the familiar way he stuck his tongue a little too far between his teeth whenever he pronounced *th*.

Joe mutters above her head, "That bitch is never gonna leave."

She listens to the murmur against her skull, feels the rhythm of his jaw, tenses her shoulders under him, waiting. *Enunciation is important.*

"Now, you tell th—"

She slams the top of her head against Joe's jaw. His teeth cut the tip of his tongue and he howls. She howls along with him. Then clamps her teeth onto the fleshiest part of his knife hand.

"He's *hurting* her!" Annie shrieks in the hallway.

"Get out of the way," Frank yells and slams his skinny shoulder into the door.

"No offence, Frank . . ." Dean pulls him aside and gives the door a shoulder check.

The door cracks but holds until both men hurl themselves together.

Okie Joe does his best to slap her head off his hand, his wrecked tongue lisping blood, before he drops the knife. Celia snatches it up, pushes herself off the floor.

Joe lunges and grabs her ankle. "'ou fugging bish." He yanks hard and she falls as the door crashes open and Annie, Frank and Dean charge into the bedroom.

Annie rushes Joe and kicks her silver pump into his jaw. "You goddamn pig-shit-bastard," she screams. Celia wriggles free.

Joe punches back at Annie's legs. Frank pulls Annie back and boots Okie Joe in the stomach with his polished black dress shoes. "What're you? A fuckin' *rapist*?"

Joe grabs hold of Frank's leg. "Geg off me, 'ou peech of shi' . . ."

Frank looks at Dean. "What'd he say?"

Annie's face is covered in sooty tears as she helps Celia, who stares disconcerted at the little pocket knife she still grips. Funny how much bigger a thing looks when it's at your throat.

Frank grabs Okie Joe by the back of the head.

"Wai', jus', sop, sop!" Joe yells, holding his hand up.

"Whoa, there, Frank. Pally's got somethin' to say."

"She shole my car, and ah my mo'ey."

Wrapped in Annie's arms now, Celia interjects. "No! *You stole! You* stole everything I had. I took it back!"

"ying' bish, I—"

Frank boots him. "Don't call her that. You took, she took it back. Sounds fair."

Dean slips his arms around Celia and Annie. "Why don't I take you ladies up to my room." Celia is glued, her eyes wild on Joe's gory face. "Come on, honey." Dean gently pulls her along like a high heel snagged on carpet. They head for the bedroom door. "Good night all," Dean calls over his shoulder.

"Hey, Dago, where y'goin'," Frank gripes.

"You got this under control, there, Frank. It's your kinda party. Come on up and join us when you're through."

A quiet tap at the broken door as someone else comes in. Dean glances. "Ah, Mr. Rosselli, you handsome devil. Me and the girls is cuttin' out but Frank here's in for round three."

Pausing, Rosselli reaches for Celia just as she bends to pick up Frank's picture, a stupefied look on her face as she reads, *Celia, You're cruel, baby! But when you're right, you're right. Frank.* She drifts from the room and Rosselli pushes the broken door closed after them.

Noon the next day, there's a rap at Annie's door. Annie puts her robe on and opens up to Rosselli, a newspaper under his arm. He's changed his clothes but he looks as if he hasn't slept. He comes in and orders them some breakfast and coffee while he waits.

Eventually both women come out with their dressing gowns and faces on. Johnny hands Celia an envelope with Prima's three hundred as he pours coffee. They eat and make disjointed small talk. When breakfast is finished Johnny sets his paper beside Celia's plate. "You might want to have a look at that."

On the front page in bold print: MAFIA BIGWIG BUSTED and a mug shot of Teddy. *Teodoro (Teddy the Ghost) Gossitino was arrested and charged with one count of first-degree murder, two counts of racketeering, three counts of tax evasion . . .* Celia's mouth hangs.

Johnny fidgets with his napkin. "He called last night but I didn't want to say anything, what with your big gig and all."

Celia glares. "He called *you?* He couldn't call *me?*"

"He had one phone call to take care of you, business and himself." He gives her wrist a squeeze and says, "The murder rap is crazy, never stick, but the tax thing . . ."

Celia pulls her hand back and rests her fingertips over her eyes.

"He doesn't want you visiting, he doesn't think it looks right."

Johnny and Annie trade looks. Celia's shoulders start to shake and Annie says, "Honey, don't worry. You have friends; everything'll be fine."

Celia takes her hands down. "Why is everyone such a liar? *Oh, I'll look after you; Peggy Lee used to dance carnival; you're the kinda girl I wanna marry; I just got in with the wrong crowd; Keely's sick! Don't you worry!* When someone starts moving their fucking lips, I should worry!"

Johnny's face registers something like amusement. "He also told me to keep an eye out that you don't use foul language. He doesn't want you to sound low class."

She picks an untouched piece of toast off her plate and throws it at him before slamming into the bedroom. Johnny winces. "Ah, she'll be okay. I gotta see about getting her another room till we figure out what to do. Should probably get her back to New York."

"I'll be moving into an apartment on Paradise Road tomorrow," Annie says. "She can bunk with me."

"Unless we have her declawed, I don't think you wanna live with her. She talk about her family?"

"Just that they didn't get along. Same's a lotta girls around here."

Johnny gets Celia moved into the Tropicana but she won't speak to him. She won't answer her phone and she won't come out of her room. She puts the *Do Not Disturb* sign up.

After three days, Sinatra agrees to give it a shot. He taps at her room. "Baby, it's Frank. You all right?" She doesn't answer. He sets his voice on snake charm. "I know you're in there. I'm worried about you, baby, s'not good holin' up like that for too long. Start seeing pink elephants. Trust me, I been there."

Celia rests her forehead on her side of the door, loneliness getting the upper hand on anger.

"Baby?" With no answer still, his voice starts to edge up. "Whaddya got to be so reactionary for? . . . I'm sorry. I should be more understanding about what you're going through—it's just that—seeing you fucked up, I get fucked up."

My phone rang. I jumped.

"Where the hell *are* you?" Marcella.

Still in Café Greco and it was dark out. I stared down at the words on the page, and saw my Frank smeared all over Sinatra.

"*Hello-o!*"

Disoriented, I checked my watch. Nine o'clock. "Uh, I'm just on my way. Sorry, I should've called."

"Shit, Vivian. I thought we were going to hang out tonight."

"Yeah, we are. I'm almost there. I'll see you in a minute."

I closed my phone, eyes still stuck on my handwriting. Fanning the pages back, I shuddered, remembering the sense of my own foot kicking Okie Joe's face to a bloody pulp. "Jesus, what is wrong with you?" I muttered, and closed the tablet.

Once, before I left home, I told my mother an ugly dream I'd just had, hoping for help in deciphering its meaning. "Who *dreams* dreams like that?" I stood in her office in my T-shirt and underpants, still shaky from the looming sense of indifferent violence, my role as voyeur rather than participant. "What does that say about me?"

"What were you doing again?" she murmured without turning her head. She'd already been awake some time and was hunched over her desk, marking papers.

"You're not listening," I said testily. "It was like watching a play. *I* wasn't even *in* it."

"Whenever you dream, you are all the characters." She looked up at me. "You play them all."

Twelve

~

"Why would Frank Sinatra give your mother a car?" Marcella asked as she stared at TV and ate a bowl of low-fat frozen soygurt. On screen two average-looking women underwent radical plastic surgery in preparation to compete for who was the prettiest. "I'm thinking I might get lipo done on my gut."

I glanced at her belly. It was flatter than mine. "Because he gave her a part in *Ocean's Eleven*. But it got cut out. And the books all say he was giving his buddies parts in that thing right and left, paying them with cars and stuff. In one of the letters, she *said* he gave her a car."

"Look at her tits." Marcella sucked on her spoon as she watched the screen. "Like grapefruits on a whippet. Mine are better than that. Do mine look that bad?"

I sat at the opposite end of her ivory couch with the shoebox on my lap. Glancing over the letter in my hands, I said, "First you're bitching that I haven't spent any time with you and now you're glued to this so-called reality shit."

"You should talk. You make up so-called reality about your dead mother in cafés when you could be here with a real live person doing real live things. And now you're going to fuck off back home to be with that fuck-up boyfriend of yours." She stared at her bowl for a moment then glanced at me. "Sorry. George's lawyer sent me a letter. They're threatening to deport me if I don't return his car and his lithograph and his fucking espresso machine and blablabla. Easy for him and his big-shot lawyers. How am I supposed to compete with that? I phoned that asshole computer guy and he's not returning my calls. He gave me an investment cheque a little while ago and the bank just told me it *bounced*. Do you think they could seriously deport me? I mean, that account was *joint!*"

I folded my mother's letter. "I don't know." Picking out the *Good Housekeeping* page, I reconsidered the plight of the airline hostess. On the other side, beside the tampon ad, was part of another article, "Why They Are Afraid to Marry." *Six basic fears that may drive a young woman to flee in panic from what should be the happiest moment of her life.*

"Why is he doing this to me?" She slammed her bowl on the Japanese table. She rubbed her forehead and dropped her hands. "Are you really going to do this porn-from-home thing? What does the porn guy think you can make?"

I shrugged. "The numbers keep changing. I've heard every-thing from two grand to ten grand a week."

"Fuck. We could do that. You could bring your stuff down here and we could do that."

"Why don't I go have a shower and we'll go out for a drink. My treat."

She brightened slightly. "Okay. There's a place down the block that's not bad. I've run into this A&R guy from Sony there a couple times. Can *you* sing?"

I rummaged for my toiletry bag. When I got to the bath-room, the idea of a shower beating me down was too much. Plugging the drain, I ran hot water for a few minutes and dumped in some of Marcella's lavender bubble bath. As I turned off the taps, I could hear her on the telephone. "Yes . . . but . . . I thought you were screwing around on me. I know I'm messed up, I should have kept on my meds, but George . . ." She gasped to get her breath. "I'm so scared. You're the only man in the world I thought would never abandon me and every time you went up to Vancouver—but I *thought* you were—and every time you got sick, it felt like you were leaving me again. Please don't hate me. I realize more and more that I need therapy. A lot of this is because my serotonin levels are so messed up. I need to get back on the Paxil and I need to quit drinking. But every time you threaten me . . . I *will* . . . you're right. I just get scared . . . Of you and of my life and having anything good in my life . . . I'm really trying . . . I'm not bad, I'm not malicious. I love you . . ."

Early next morning, with a hangover not strong enough to slow me down, I packed up and scrawled a thank-you note. Marcella's earplugs and sleep mask blocked all from her personal universe but did nothing to spare the world her snore. Outside in the hall, I slid the spare key back under the door and headed to the parking garage.

Marcella needed Paxil—my anxiety was so bad, I was scared I might throw up. I wondered if this was how dogs and cats feel before an earthquake. I didn't want to go home. I didn't want to stay. Seemed like I accomplished nothing by coming down here and yet the idea of home, of film sets and Sally and the house and having to find a new agent, auditions, Frank—none of it was drawing me. The guilt over my disinterest made me feel worse.

I called Leonard. "Hey," he said, his voice dull. "You're up early."

I checked my watch. 8:00 a.m. "You sound weird." Great. If anyone was supposed to feel like home and hope, it was Leonard. "What's the matter? You sick? Are you sad?" I punched the cigarette lighter in and took out a smoke while I waited for it to pop.

"I don't want to talk about it."

Fidgeting with the electric window, I lit my cigarette. "What did you do, crack up my car?"

"No." He sounded like a wet Kleenex.

"Well, I'm on my way home. I'm going to try and see if I can do the drive all in one go."

"Why?"

"I miss you too, fuckface."

"Sorry."

"I can't afford another hotel. I should have a cheque at the agency when I get back but most of it's going to go to my Visa bill and my rent . . . the phone bill." Leonard was quiet. "Tell me what's wrong when I get back?"

"I think I need a shrink."

"Maybe we could get a group rate. I better go. God knows what it's costing me to use my cell down here. I'll talk to you tomorrow."

Once I was on the road, I changed course and headed off on Highway 26 to Danaville. Maybe if I just came clean with specific questions then we'd be square with each other and I wouldn't be playing games and she wouldn't need to be evasive and I could feel good about the whole thing. I didn't even have her damn phone number. How could I have left without her number?

Coming into her cul-de-sac, I pulled up in front of her house and wrote:

1. When did you and ~~my mother~~ Celia become roommates? Vegas? After T was arrested?
2. Where did red heart come from?
3. Did Celia date Bobby Kennedy?
4. Why wouldn't Celia's mother talk to her? Did she talk to her stepfather?
   I flipped through Judy Campbell's book.
5. Did Celia like Peter Lawford? (Nobody likes him in books.)

Maybe Annie would respond better if I said *Celia*, if I didn't make it so personal. In reality I had no idea why she'd shut down all of a sudden.

A taxi pulled up in front of my car. Annie's front door opened and there she was dragging her suitcase onto the stoop. I threw open my door and rushed over to her.

One look at me and she pursed her lips. "I told you no. I'm going to see my daughter."

"Could I get your phone number and maybe I could—"

"Phone number's unlisted."

"I just have two questions for you," I pleaded, "three, it'll only take a second." I took her arm and her bag as she hobbled out on her cane.

"Don't help me. I'm not some old cripple. Just twisted my ankle and if it wasn't for you . . . don't help me!" She shook her shoulder free.

"I'm sorry. It's just that my mother's gone and it's too late to ask her and I really appreciated you letting me see her letters but in some ways I just have more questions like, like did you guys become roommates in Las Vegas when you were working at the Silver Slipper?"

"Yes," she said, exasperated. "I told you that."

"Oh, ah, I'm sorry. And in her letter—why wouldn't her mother talk to her? What did Stewart—he's the stepfather, right?—what did he say that would make her mother hate her?"

The cab driver had got out of the car and was holding the back door for her. I couldn't recall ever seeing a cab driver do that for me. Not in the sluttiest outfit I owned. "What do you think?" Annie huffed. "Her mother was jealous of her. That's how it always is. He told the mother, I don't know, that Celia kissed him or something. He took her to Elmo's for her birthday and her mother was out of town for a funeral or something and her mother didn't like it. *Okay?* Now, let me get my plane."

"Elmo's? Is that the El Morocco? She told me she went there for her sixteenth . . . but . . . okay," I chased her as she started walking again. "So, she dated Bobby Kennedy? You said she didn't like John. Did she like Bobby?"

Annie stabbed a look at the sky. "Well, if she dated him, she must have liked him." Reaching the taxi, she grabbed hold of the car door and started to maneuver her way inside.

I took the cane as she sputtered and cussed. "And there's this Tiffany heart with gold inlay. Was that from him? Judy Campbell got notes from Jack Kennedy and he just signed them *J* and I thought maybe this heart was from Bobby be—"

"Yes! Okay. She liked him. He liked her. And he gave her that piddly little heart. You want to hand me that?" She grasped for her cane. "I'm gonna miss my plane." Throwing the stick in beside her, she slammed the door shut.

"When was that?" I yelled as she rolled away. "Have a swell trip, y'old bitch." The cab turned a tight U in the cul-de-sac and sped off down the road.

I don't recall much of the drive back. I played oldies CDs. I bought another somewhere along the way called Music to Watch Girls By with Andy Williams and Tony Bennett, and yet more Louis Prima. When Doris Day sang "Que Sera, Sera," a song I'd always found unbearable, I cried. I played it over and over, *When I was just a little girl, I asked my mother, what will I be* . . . wiping my eyes with tissue when the going got too blurry.

Soon my head was taken up trying to imagine what Annie's apartment in Vegas looked like. Paradise Road. Nothing's the same in Vegas. It's not as if I could head there now and get any idea of then. Where did my mother fill in as a showgirl? What did she do all day, all night when she wasn't working? Sit around in that apartment and watch Jack Paar? Mum loved Jack Paar. She thought every talk-show host since paled in comparison—no one else was so clever or sensitive or had the guts to get up and walk off right in the middle of a show because he disagreed with the studio. She loved his ability to say fuck you to foolishness even if it meant losing everything.

After work, Annie comes home to her Paradise Road apartment. Television blares *The Jack Paar Show* in front of Celia who sits on the couch, one eye on the issue of *Good Housekeeping* in her lap, the other on Paar and his singing basset hounds.

"Hey, kiddo." Annie closes the door behind her. "Catch!" She tosses the spare key. "I was thinking: you should keep it on you. Girl got her place robbed the other day and they used the key right out from under her mat."

Celia looks back at the hounds' drooping eyes as Paar tries to convince them to sing "Love is a Many Spanieled Thing." "I thought there wasn't supposed to be any crime in Las Vegas."

Annie rolls her eyes. "Oh, no-o-o. Usually they drive a guy *outta* town before they put a new part in his hair."

"Jonathan Winters was on tonight. He was a riot."

"I can never decide if he's a genius or a retard." Annie heads to the kitchen, uncorks a bottle and pours. "What're you reading that rag for?"

"It was on *your* coffee table."

"I cannot be held responsible for the reading materials of previous tenants."

"There's a thing in here on what it's really like to be an airline hostess."

"Don't start that again." She holds up her glass. "Want one?"

Celia nods and reads aloud. "'*Even if you're not particularly interested in being a stewardess, you might like to know what, besides glamour, the job consists of.*'"

"Only thing more glam is dumping bedpans."

"'*A girl must be single; from twenty to twenty-seven years old, five feet two to five feet eight inches; and from 100 to 135 pounds. She must pass a physical examination and psychological tests designed to find out whether she has a stable, pleasing personality.*'" Celia stares at the page a moment. "A pleasing personality test?"

Handing her a glass of wine, Annie plunks down. "They don't call it the *cock*pit for nothin'. It means, can you say, *Yes sir, whatever you need to relax, Mr. Pilot, sir?*"

"You're disgusting. '*She must also be attractive. Usually she must have two to four years of college . . . starting salary may be as low as $70 a week, with small yearly increases until, after seven years' service, a ceiling of $95 a week . . .*'"

"Or you could haul off and be a cocktail waitress thereby tripling your salary. Hmm, what to do, what to do? I told Frank about your waitress-in-the-sky thing. *She's a nice kid*, he said, *but man, how can she be so stupid when she's got what's she got right in the palm of her hand?*"

"What's that 'sposed to mean?"

"It means Phyllis McGuire started spending time with Sam Giancana. And he tore up a hundred-grand worth of gambling markers she ran up. Date the right fellas and can the stewardess crap."

"Who's Sam Gianwhatsits again?"

"Sam Giancana. Sam Flood. The weaselly-lookin' one with the droopy eyelids that Frank runs with. The one crazy for the cherry bombs."

"Oh him. He's rich like *that*?"

"Sure is, sister." Annie sipped. "Shit, I almost forgot: they need a chanteuse over at the Dunes show tomorrow night. Wanna sing?"

"Everyone's topless in that show."

"Except the comedians and the chanteuse. You wanna do it?"

"I don't know."

"Christ, it's the Dunes! It's a classy show. Don't be so puritanical, this is Vegas for godsake; every woman in town's topless."

Celia stares into her glass. "All right."

"The *enthusiasm*. I thought you'd be thrilled. You get to sing on your own—your own numbers." Annie stands up. "I gotta get ready. You still coming tonight?"

"Yeah. I'm sorry, I'm just—I want to be respected as a singer and I don't know if—not to say that you're not respectable but you're more comfortable with . . . Never mind."

Later that night Celia and Annie walk into a private room at the Sands where Frank's soiree is being held. Frank's taste is all over the joint in the form of orange and black, and the bar is loaded with Jack Daniel's, Chivas and the fixings for martinis. A strictly inner-circle crowd. Sammy Davis is there and Lawford, Tony Curtis and Janet Leigh, Shirley MacLaine, Juliet Prowse— Celia's head spins as she walks in—but no Dean.

A handful of flashy girls, as Celia's mother would call them (skirts a little tighter, décolletage a little lower, false eyelashes a little falser) are positioned around the room chatting with the men. Frank descends on Celia as soon as she's in the door. "Baby, you made it. Come here and meet a pal a'mine." He takes her coat and pulls her with him across the room, leaving Annie to hang up her own. Plucking a martini from someone's hand along the way, he puts it into Celia's. "Here, kid, have a little gasoline."

A man in a pinstriped suit with thick tousled hair and big white teeth smiles as they come toward him. "Jack," Frank calls, "meet Celia Dare. Celia meet my pal, Senator Jack Kennedy."

She's heard of him, though she thought "the Senator" was only a nickname. Kennedy extends his hand. Frank slips away to join his new girl, Juliet, skim his fingertips along her jaw and kiss her temple. Celia looks for Annie as she shakes the senator's hand.

"Celia, I saw you onstage with Frank and the fellows. I think my sister was a little jealous." His thick Bostonian accent is almost a caricature.

"Who's your sister?"

"Pat Lawford, Peter's wife. No woman wants to see someone so beautiful and agile too close to her husband."

The Brother-in-Lawford. Kennedy tilts his head to her as if he's never had such a scintillating conversation.

"Robert Kennedy. Is he related to you? Wasn't he part of Senator McCarthy's crew?"

He smiles. "Yes, he's my brother, Robert." *My brothah, Rahbeht.*

"Quite the witch hunt he took part in."

"Communism doesn't worry a pretty, young girl like you?"

She blinks at him, sips the martini, wincing against gin. "Persecution and book burning don't worry a pretty politician like you?"

"Well, aren't you just fine." Kennedy laughs overloud. "Do you have a political affiliation, Celia? Perhaps I could change you into a Democrat if you'd let me take you for lunch tomorrow."

"My stepfather says your brother was a political whore working for McCarthy."

"Oh, I like you, Miss Dare." His tone sounds as though he might offer her candy any moment.

She glances around for Dean again. "My friend's not feeling well. I should check the powder room." She forces up the sides of her mouth and walks away.

"Hey, baby, how's your clyde?" Sammy catches her wrist in his slim dark fingers.

"Smokey! Come dig something over here." Peter Lawford takes Sammy's elbow and tugs him. The conspiracy in Lawford's voice pulls Celia in close to hear, "If you want to see what a million dollars in cash looks like, go into the next room; there's a brown leather satchel in the closet; open it. It's a gift from the hotel owners for Jack's campaign."

Sammy stops. "No thanks, Charlie. There's some things a one-eyed Negro does not need to know." He spins and smacks into Celia, breaks into nervous laughter. "Sorry, baby, I gotta learn to turn in the direction of my good glimmer."

Lawford moves back to Celia just as Annie sidles up. "I saw you talking to my brother-in-law. He digs you. You better get back over there before some other chick cuts your grass."

"No, thank you, I'm fine," Celia says distractedly.

Annie smiles at Lawford. "Pete the Pimp strikes out. Poor you, honey, poor you." He shoots her a withering look and moves off to catch Sammy.

Leaning in close, Annie says, "Apparently four girls are going to entertain Jacky-boy in the other room tonight. Every colour of the rainbow. *Four.*"

Celia glances over at Kennedy who's chatting with a show-girl from the Stardust now. "Entertain as *prostitutes?*"

"They're not doing it for their health. And," Annie whispers, "did you hear about the dough in the closet? I betcha Giancana's got a piece of that. And I bet Johnny arranged it."

"He's not even in town, is he?"

"He's *somewhere.* Jack better watch he doesn't get himself behind any two-way mirrors. He's been cattin' around with Monroe and that Judy-chick too. Where you going?"

"Home. I don't feel that social tonight. Dean's not here, is he?"

"Frank said he's got a date."

"Dean's always lying to Frank. Maybe he's not feeling in a party mood either."

Outside Dean's door, Celia hears guns, cowboys and Indians. She decides he won't answer if he's indisposed and knocks. A loud sigh from inside before the door opens. "Sweetheart! Thought you was Frank comin' to gimme a punch in the mouth for not showin' up at his shindig. Come on in."

"You don't have a girl in there?"

He holds a finger to his lips. "Just me and the Duke shootin' us some Injuns on the idiot box." The two of them plop down on the sofa.

"That Kennedy guy was there."

"Uh-oh. No, sugar, you cuddle up with Uncle Dino and stay far away from them there snattle rakes. Getcherself bit and . . ." He muttered inaudibly and put his arm around her like a pet. "I 'spose I should admit to you that Cyd's on the other station. She's with Astaire dancin' around *The Band Wagon*."

Dean smells like home. Like Stewart, she realizes with a start. "S'okay. I've seen it." She looks at the screen a moment. "Do you ever read *Good Housekeeping*?"

"Sure. Helps me determine my figure flaws."

"I read an article today on how a lot of girls are afraid to get married."

"How come I never met me one a'them?"

"Said one of the reasons is *a girl's unconscious rejection of her womanly role as a homemaker*. They never said anything about her fears that her husband's going to have four wild girls brought to the Sands for him."

He watches Wayne lecture a young cowboy. "Probably never said anything about her thinking she'd rather have a go at her husband's manager either."

"Oh god, are you still on this kick about Jeannie?"

"My wife spends an awful lot of time with my manager. You think about that." He takes his arm from around her and sits forward. "Honey, be a sport and call Mort's place. You can hang up if he answers. 'Course, if he doesn't, then you gotta call my place."

"It's two in the morning."

"Come on, sweetheart."

"You're crazy . . . Should I get a manager? You think Mort would represent me?"

"His hands are full with my wife."

"Those who don't trust generally can't be trusted."

"I finally get a teenage girl in my room and she turns out to be a sage." Dean slumps back.

"I'm twenty-one." Celia slips her arms out of her coat sleeves, nestles under the heap of fur and drowses from John Wayne to watching *The Band Wagon* with Stewart.

I stood pumping gas into my mother's car, reading one of her letters to Annie, the part about the pearls. She called him Stewart, never Dad. Her real father, she told me, left when she was tiny. Four years old or something. He was 4F and, as one of the few men left on the block, during the war, he helped out the women alone. He really helped out the women alone.

Her mother was jealous of her. That's how it always is.

Nancy! I finally remembered her mother's name. She rarely spoke of her and when she did, she said "my mother" never "your grandmother."

I took my receipt from the pump and got back in the car.

Audrey lies in bed listening to her parents bark at one another in their room. Her mother's had a migraine all day. She had been so looking forward to Valentine's Day—"To some sort of romance from my husband and what do I get from you. A suitcase? That's your gift to me?"

"You've been complaining about that old bag. I thought—"

"You thought you'd get a pearl necklace for your daughter and a bag for your old bag so she can get the hell out of Dodge."

"Don't be ridiculous. You've been harping on about your luggage: having to hop on another plane to see your sister carrying *this ratty luggage*. And the necklace—Audrey just got a part in her *first* professional ballet—"

"It's the chorus, for godsake."

"It's the corps de ballet and it's damned impressive. It's the first big step in her career. The pearls were a little celebratory gift from *both* of us. To show our pride."

"*Pearls? Pearls* are a little gift? *Please*, Stewart."

"You're getting hysterical. We talked about this."

"About *pearls?*"

"Sometimes I get the feeling you're too busy competing with her to be proud of her."

"Don't you dare put that on me. You buy a string of pearls for a fifteen-year-old girl and *luggage* for your wife and I'm the bad guy?—Don't touch me. Just leave me the hell alone."

Audrey swallows and stares into blackness, scared he'll walk out and never come back. She listens to his feet moving down the stairs as she touches the strand at her collarbone. She raises them to her lips and bites their milky roughness, then undoes the clasp.

The door to her parents' bedroom whines open under her knock and she hears her mother's sniffles, the bedclothes rustle as she turns. "Go away."

"Mother? It's me."

"Audrey, please, let me be."

"Can I come in just for a second? I was thinking, these pearls, they're really pretty but they're too grown-up for me." She stands over the bed looking at her mother's shadow against the pale sheets. "They'd suit you better."

A derisive grunt. "Because I'm an old crone."

"No. They just—"

"Audrey. I appreciate the gesture. Please go to bed. I don't want your pearls."

She heads back to bed, crunching the pearls in her fist, wishing them to a powder. A light knock and she sits up again.

"Are you sleeping?"

She doesn't answer.

"I can hear you breathing."

She sniffs a chuckle.

The door opens and Stewart comes in and sits on the side of her bed. "I guess you heard all that. Your mother's under a lot of strain with your aunt being sick. It's just frustration at being so helpless in the face of it all and I'm not handling it so well either. I'll make it up to her. And in the meantime I know she wants you to have those pearls. Despite what you heard. She told me. That's why I bought them. Okay? I'm very proud of you."

"I feel like she hates me."

"Don't be silly. She loves you. I'd say almost more than *I* do but that's not possible. Don't worry about our fights. They've got nothing to do with you.—Hey, *The Band Wagon*'s on television right now. *The Late Late Show.*"

"All right."

Stewart takes the pearls from her hand, fastens them at her nape.

Celia shows up two hours early at the Dunes. She introduces herself to the orchestra members and makes sure they have the music to "My Heart Belongs to Daddy" and "Cry Me a River."

Later, she watches from the wings as the chorus girls dance, the jokers joke, the strippers strip. Annie's right, every girl in Vegas is half-naked. Big deal.

When her time comes, the MC announces *the musical stylings of New York's delightful Celia Dare.* She slips out into the spotlight, lets the boom of the orchestra fill her breast as she sets free lyrics she's known since she was a baby almost. Her voice sails into the audience who, so surprised by the auditory resemblance, goes catatonic. By the time "Cry Me a River" ends, the room is alive with chatter. There's no mistaking the sound of Julie London.

The stage manager catches hold of her as she comes into the wings. "Jeez, kid. Annie West wasn't fooling. I heard how hacked Keely was when you did her numbers with Prima." He laughs. "Great gimmick. Don't hear too many female impersonators. Er, impressionists! Girl impressionists. Love to hear what your own sounds like." He pats her on the back and walks off.

My own? It hadn't occurred to her she'd been using anything else.

Annie's contract is nearly up at the Slipper, Frank and the guys have gone to L.A. and Celia is soon bored with filling in. She and Annie sit in the apartment watching the news. Now that Kennedy's campaign is in full swing, and Frank's renamed his crew the Jack Pack, their fundraisers are all the talk. "I thought Frank didn't like that name Rat Pack," Celia says.

"He doesn't. He tried the Clan for a while but it didn't sound so good to Sammy."

"Are we part of the Rat Pack?"

"I think you have to have a dink."

"What about Sam Flood? Or Giancana or whatever his name is."

"I think he's got his own: the Whack Pack."

Celia giggles and smacks Annie's leg. "You think that stuff's true?"

"Didn't you see him on TV last year, those hearings with Robert Kennedy and he kept taking the Fifth?"

"I was too busy biting the heads off chickens. Wait! I remember one night in The 92, a trial was on TV and the Boys kept calling some guy a cocksucker."

"That was the Senate Committee racketeering thing."

Celia recalls a gangster sitting at the courtroom table under a bad hairpiece and sunglasses as a lawyer asked him if it was true he disposed of people by having them stuffed in a trunk. The gangster took the Fifth on each question, chuckling as he did. The lawyer asked if he was going to tell them anything or just giggle like a little girl.

"Giancana's *that* guy?" She looks at Annie. "I thought the Boys mostly own hotels and stuff."

Annie shrugs. "Just smile and look pretty's what I say. *Thank you for the fur coat, sir.*"

Celia picks at her nails. "Do you think I'm just a female impersonator?"

"What!" Annie nearly spits wine down her sweater. "Who said that?"

"The stage manager at the Dunes. And then he corrected himself and said *impressionist*." Celia scans Annie's face. "I sing standards. Everyone sings those songs. Why is it when Frank sings, or Sammy, nobody calls it a gimmick?"

"Sammy told me once Frank got on him years ago, told him he was emulating him too much, that it was flattering and all but Sammy should get his own sound if he was gonna be big. Personally I think Sammy sounds more like Vic Damone."

Celia gives her a pleading look.

"What's wrong with a good gimmick. Everyone's got one. Look at Dean with his drunky bit, his Southern drawl—he's from Stubenville, for chrissake. Sammy talks like he's an Englishman half the time onstage and he's a coloured kid from Harlem. Far as I'm concerned, we gotta up the gimmick factor and put together a real act for you."

Soon Annie is booked to headline at the Gaiety in Miami and asks Celia to come along. They stay at the Riviera and Celia phones around hoping to reconnect with Tina and Glenda. No luck. Frank and the guys are doing another mini summit at the Fontainebleau.

At dinner one evening, Frank introduces her to Bob and Don, a couple of producers from Warner Brothers. On any given night, one or both are happy to escort her through Miami's nightlife. They take her to see Jerry Vale at the Eden Roc, Martha Raye at the Beachcomber, the big musical production numbers on the translucent stage of the Latin Quarter, where pretty girls in minuscule costumes dance up a storm. In the Latin Quarter, Celia's eyes drift then settle on a familiar face one table over. Looks like Jacqueline Kennedy. Once the show is over, she excuses herself and heads for the pretty stranger.

"Hello. I'm Celia Dare. I just realized, you're a friend of Frank's! I think I met you in Vegas."

The woman makes a pleasant face. "Hello. I'm Judy."

"That's it—*Judy Campbell*. You're the girl dating Jack Kennedy."

Campbell shoots a look round her table. "You're mistaken. I've had occasion to meet Senator Kennedy but—he's a married man."

Celia blinks nervously. She's gotten so used to parenthetical marriage the last couple months that she hadn't considered discretion. "I must be confused. I'm sorry to have interrupted your evening. Nice to see you." Retreating to her table she asks Bob and Don if perhaps they could all head over to the Gaiety and pick up Annie, get a bite to eat.

Don's eyes flash. "Isn't that where Zorita used to dance with her snake?"

Celia sighs. "Yeah-yeah." They are out the door before she can do up her coat.

At the Gaiety, they catch the tail end of Annie's act, before the chorus girls do their goodbye dance. While they wait for Annie to change into civilian clothes, Bob and Don take the opportunity to chat up the other strippers, tell them about the dearth of pretty girls in Hollywood, how producers are always scouting for new talent.

When Annie comes out, cloaked in her mink, dark curls spilling from her updo, she suggests they all head to Ricco's for a late dinner, and that perhaps Celeste and Barbie should come along. Annie doesn't care for Bob and Don and their *would-you-like-to-come-up-and-see-my-celluloid-etchings* bullshit, so bringing along two tomatoes seems the ideal way to get a free dinner without even having to talk to one's benefactors.

They've just ordered the wine when a voice calls out, "Jesus Christ, it's Westerly Wind, and the Daredevil." Frank. Next to him is his girl, Juliet, her long dancer's legs folded under the table against his. At the same table is none other than the woman not-dating-Jack-Kennedy. Frank sends them drinks.

Annie nudges Celia. "Sitting between Judy and Frank, that's Joe Fish."

"Who's he?"

"Joe Fischetti—Al Capone's cousin. The Fischetti Brothers run the Fontainebleau."

"Al Capone's cousins run the Fontainebleau?"

"Sure. You can bet him and his pals contributed to Jacky-boy's campaign too."

"If Robert Kennedy is trying to crack down on—why would they—"

"Because if they get Jack in, he's theirs. He'll call off his brother."

Celia hears Stewart's voice: *Mobsters are like boa constrictors. Once you're in, you're in till you're dead.*

A few nights later, Frank and the guys throw a farewell party to mark the end of their Miami Summit. Celia and Annie arrive at cocktail hour and already the place is jammed. Annie spots Joe Fish talking with Judy Campbell again. "Hey, they're with Skinny D'Amato." She pulls Celia in their direction. "You've got to meet Skinny. He owns the 500 Club in Atlantic City and one of these days we're gonna get you on that stage."

"Oh, please. I don't want to have to talk to her."

"Well, I don't either. She's always announcing that she prefers the company of men; probably yodels it down Jacky-boy's pants every chance she gets."

"She's going to hear you."

"Fat chance. She prefers the voices of men. —Hey, Skinny!" Annie's tone melts into honey.

A hard-eyed Italian turns around. "Look who's here. West is East!" He kisses her cheek and gives her a hug, his body shivering against her in playful ecstasy.

She grabs his face in both her hands. "Skinny, you gorgeous hunk of man. You gotta get down to the Gaiety. I'm only there a couple more nights. In the meantime, meet my best girl-friend, Celia Dare."

Judy saunters off to join Frank and Sam Giancana.

Smiling to herself, Annie links her elbows with Skinny's and Joe's elbows. "So, boys, what's cookin' these days?"

At dinner, Annie and Celia sit with Frank and Juliet. Judy

Campbell has taken the seat next to Dean, which puts a scowl on Celia.

"So Frank," Annie says, "how do you know Judy? Sam Flood sure seems fascinated with her."

Frank shoots her a look. "She's got a little class, West. Lotta guys are attracted to that sorta thing."

Annie smiles. Juliet glances toward Campbell who is tilting her head to Dean. With a little heat in her tone, Juliet inquires, "Yes, but how *do* you know the lovely Judy, Frank?"

He flicks his cigarette at the ashtray. "Parties. Here and there. She was married to some deadbeat actor a few years ago."

"What exactly does she *do?*"

He shrugs. "Family's got money. She paints a little, Sunday artist."

"Oh. An artistic party girl," Juliet purrs. "How *intriguing.*"

Annie ups the ante. "You know who she looks like? Jacqueline Kennedy. Hmm, Miss Campbell is pals with Jack Kennedy too, isn't she, Frank? Didn't you introduce them?"

Frank glares. "West, you don't know fuck all so maybe you better shut your trap."

"I rather like listening to Miss West," Juliet interjects. "I find her thoughts insightful and her voice melodic."

"Broads are ruining my goddamn appetite," Frank growls. He throws his cigarette into the dregs of his Jack Daniel's and leaves the table.

Annie bats her eyes at Juliet. "Sorry. That woman just gets on my nerves."

"Pat Lawford can't stand her either," Juliet replies. "And you don't want to hear what Dean's Jeannie has to say."

Annie gazes over at Judy, scattering perfect subdued laughter like petals over Dean. She looks back to Juliet. "Perhaps we're just jealous," she offers. Their eyes lock as both blurt a stereophonic "Na."

After dinner and three umbrella drinks, Celia heads for the dance floor where Dean foxtrots with the artistic party girl. "May I cut in," she asks.

Judy looks mildly appalled. It seems Celia has been a boor again. "My feet are getting a little tired anyway," she says and coasts away on a cloud of grace. Celia deflates.

"You must have been hankering for a dance real bad," Dean says as he takes hold of her. "I should've come for you earlier instead of trying to con poor Judy into being my wife-spy."

"I thought *I* was your wife-spy."

"You didn't like the job."

"I'd do whatever you wanted me to." She gazes up.

"Be careful what you say to an old man. I got a weak heart."

Celia rests her head against him. "Do you fly out tomorrow?"

"Yes, ma'am. Got some recording to do in Los Angeleeez . . ."

"I've hardly seen you. Are you having an affair with her?"

"Judy?" Dean smiles. "I'm too tired for that."

"What does Sam Flood do?"

"He's a businessman. And none of your kinda business, so do yourself a favour and stay away from businessmen. Find yourself a nice dentist."

A lump in her throat, she excuses herself to head to the washroom.

By four in the morning, the crowd is down to a smattering. Celia concocts excuses to stay until she notices Dean heading for the door. Annie catches hold of her elbow and hangs on. "Let's get back to the hotel. Last call for the Annie Taxi."

"Don't!" Celia wobbles in her shoes. "Where'd he go? You made me lose Dean!"

"You've had a little too much bug juice, lambchop. Come on—"

"No! I have to talk to Dean. Frank knows where he is."

"Come on, you can call Dean tomorrow. You'll thank me in the—Jesus!"

Celia yanks free and stalks over to Frank.

Minutes later, she weaves her way down the hall to Dean's room.

~

As she sits on his couch, a nightcap in hand, Dean raises his glass. "Drink up and be somebody," he says.

Celia looks into her scotch and tries to think of what to say. "Remember I was talking about getting an agent?" She concentrates on not slurring. "I'm going to New York soon and I'm going to get one—I wanted to get your advice."

"Well, there's a few guys who handle dancers and chorus girls . . ."

Her eyes suddenly brim. "*Dean.* I'm not just—you don't take me seriously. You don't get it . . . Judy doesn't love you. Not like I do."

He sets his drink down. "I think we gotta get you some coff—"

"No, I think I love you, Dean." She dumps a little of her drink in her lap.

He takes her glass away. "You don't wanna be in love with an old man like me. You need a good sleep's what you need."

"I want to be with you. Take me to bed. Please. Dean?"

He sighs. "Trust me, I don't deserve the honour."

"No. Stewart, stop saying—"

"Stewart? See—"

"Why did you bring up Stewart? It's none of his business. He's . . ."

"I'm going to put you in a taxi."

"No! Please don't send me away, please don't send me away . . ." She's crying flat out now.

"Okay, okay. You're okay." He pats her back.

She gasps and punches weakly at his chest trying to talk through sobs. "I—I—I love . . ."

"You wait right here." He comes back with a pill bottle. Dumping one into his palm, he says, "Maybe I should just give you half a' one." She cries harder. "Na, this is an emergency; open wide." He lays the tablet on her tongue and feeds her water.

Just swallowing the pill seems to calm her. He holds her hand and she flops against him.

"Too much excitement for one night. Come on now, let's put you to bed and your ol' pal Dino is going to sleep on the couch."

"I don't want you to sleep on the couch," she croaks.

"Sure you do. I snore. Hell, you might snore your own self."

Celia jolts awake. It's two-thirty in the afternoon. Still fully dressed, her shoes are on the floor. Dean and his things are gone. A note sits on the night table: *Goodbye, sugar. Had to catch my flight. Knock 'em dead in the Big Apple. Dino.*

She wants to crawl into a swamp. The last thing she remembers is Dean tucking the blankets under her chin, and lullabying her good-night with "Return to Me." His melancholy voice is wrapped around the ache in her skull now. She reaches for the phone.

"Oh, baby," Annie moans sympathetically. "Come on back here and we'll order room service. I'm a little hung myself."

"I want to die. I *propositioned* him."

"You and whose army. I'm impressed though. I heard he could be a real rat but I guess he considers you a lady."

"He considers me a child. A trampy child."

"You just got the booze guilts. You'll feel better after some breakfast. You know what Frank says, *I feel sorry for people who don't drink. When they wake up in the morning, that's the best they're gonna feel all day.*"

Back at the Riviera, Celia announces she can't be in Miami a second longer. "I've humiliated myself—all those people who saw me stoned out of my tree last night."

"Everybody there was smashed. I necked with a bellhop in the elevator. He was on his way to bring someone their breakfast just as I was getting home. That's Miami."

Celia insists.

"Can't you hang on three more nights?"

She shakes her head.

Annie sighs. "I'll give you the keys to my place."

Thirteen

~

CELIA LIES ON THE LIVING-ROOM FLOOR OF ANNIE'S apartment, listening to Dean albums. Crumbs and bits of oily dried-out food are strewn on the coffee table and rugs. An old bread crust digs into one of her arms—she concentrates on sucking up all discomfort as penance.

Bumps and foot scuffles come from the hall. "Just drop it here. Great." Annie's voice. Then a knock. "Celia? Celia Do-da-Dare, you in dere? . . . Shit . . ." Louder knocks and muttering. "Christ! I said leave me the key if you go out." Dean starts into "Volare" and Celia drizzles as she sings along. Annie pounds harder on the door. "You *are* in there. Celia!"

By the time Celia answers Annie is ready to bite her face off. "Were you just going to leave me standing out here?" She struggles a suitcase through the door. "Help with my bags or so—"

Celia grabs one, eyes puffy, nose red. "I thought you weren't home till tomorrow."

"You just been lying around here, mooning over some decrepit old whorehound?" Annie swishes through the apartment in a flourish of ermine and hair. "How'd you feel if he screwed you and went home to his wife. Huh?" She looks around. "Jesus . . . And another thing, if you're going to lie down and die every time a man rejects you, do yourself a favour and put a gun to your head now. You go around actin' like a man's the main course and you're doomed. Treat 'em like dessert."

Celia wipes her nose. "Sometimes a person has to grieve, you know."

"Oh for Pete's sake—mooning is for suckers. Meanwhile someone's been contemplating your career and I think it's me." Annie pulls a newspaper from the strap of one suitcase and tosses it on the coffee table. "There, take a gander. It's circled."

Celia picks up the paper. *"Open call for tribute to Carmen Miranda . . . female singer between 25 and 35 . . . able to dance and sing Samba. Portuguese an asset . . .* So? I can't speak Portuguese and I'm not twenty-five."

Annie rips the needle off Dean's drone and hangs up her fur. Celia looks her up and down, the tight skirt, the tighter angora sweater. "You went on the airplane with your boobs sticking out like that?"

"Why is it people with flat houses are always casting stones?" Annie glowers. "This sweater introduced me to a very nice lawyer, for your information. I was also invited to see the inside of the cockpit. What did *you* do today?"

Celia sets the paper down and stares at her bagging socks.

"Exactly. But you're doing something tonight. You're going to learn to do Carmen Miranda as well as you do Julie London."

"I don't want to be a female impersonator."

"Oh, yes you do, missy. And I know just the gal to teach you. Go have a shower. I'll order us some Chinese."

Two hours later, they stand outside an apartment one floor up. High heels clip toward them and the door is opened with a flourish by a petite olive-skinned woman wearing a jewelled turban, a silk kimono and feathered mules. Her ruby lips part and both she and Annie exclaim, *"Dahling!"* as they kiss cheeks.

"Simone! Meet Celia; Celia, Simone."

"Precious, aren't you pretty!"

The voice, the hands—this is no girl. Celia recoils slightly but follows as Annie launches into descriptions of Miami, her Mae West act, the boas and hats she wore and last but not least, the need for a teensy-weensy favour. "Celia here is a fabulous singer—"

No. Scratch that. My mother could never stand transvestites. They gave her the squeams. She felt mocked by them on every level. I think I liked the idea of my mother learning to drag from a queen.

Turning off at Grants Pass, I pulled into a strip mall and headed straight for the music department at Wal-Mart where I rooted around until I finally found Carmen Miranda in the Easy Listening section. From what I remembered of her, she wasn't all that easy. I drove across parking lots and headed into Applebee's for lunch.

A couple of years younger than me, the waitress had my old-colour hair, mixed with a little more ash, and a slow easy gait. She called me sweetheart and said "Uh-huh" each time I said thank-you. As I ate my Sante Fe Chicken I read liner notes on the short life of Carmen Miranda and scribbled into my notebook.

"I don't want to be a female impersonator anymore."

"Oh, here we go. You don't *want* to be in the chorus, you don't *want* to be a showgirl, you want the spotlight—you-youyou—well, here's your damn chance! . . . think I'm going to support you forever? Go have a shower and get dressed, you're making me nauseous. Tomorrow we're getting ourself some Carmen Miranda albums and you're going to get this damn job."

By night Annie's booked doing her Mae West show downtown. Days, she spends with Celia arguing presentation, material and hair colour—early Carmen was dark, later Carmen blonde. They nearly come to blows over the essence of Miranda.

"Bigger!" Annie barks over Celia's vocals. "Vivacious like a hot tamale! . . . use your arms! . . . It's World War Two and your country's counting on you to be the Brazilian ambassador—*win* their *hearts!*"

"You're making me a caricature."

"Carmen *was* a caricature. *Tutti-frutti!* The Brazilian Bomb-shell! Hollywood loved that fiery-Latina shit. They wouldn't *let* her be anything else. And soon the Brazilians went from loving her to hating her for making them look like dopes. She was the highest-paid woman in America and she was wearin' eighty pounds of fruit on her head. What is that if not a caricature?"

"People don't believe I'm Italian. You want them to think I'm Brazilian?"

"Yeah. Well. We'll wig you. Should use a Portuguese name too."

"What difference does that make?"

"You should even talk with a Portuguese accent for the audition. Directors are morons. They have no imagination. If you act like a Portuguese and quack like a Portuguese . . ."

When the casting director calls her name, Celia comes on-stage wearing a dress of Annie's chopped in half and taken in, a dark wig piled high on her head and bangles on either wrist. Jittery from lack of sleep and too much coffee, she introduces herself to the two men sitting down front of the empty theatre and hands sheet music to the piano player. Annie sits in the back.

As the music begins, Celia bounces her hip and sings, "'Would you like to spend a weekend in Havana? . . .'"

The two men in the seats up front, director and choreogra-pher, are motionless. When the last note plays, the pianist turns an eye to Celia and winks.

"Rosa Ramos?" asks the director, tilting his long angular body toward her.

She nods.

He pushes glasses back up his nose. "Got an agent, sweet-heart?"

"Nope."

"Picture and resumé?"

"Nope."

He exchanges looks with the choreographer who asks, "Any theatre experience?"

"Chorus mostly," she replies, hiding behind a Portuguese accent as if it were a bush.

From the start, Michael Stark, the director and producer, looks moony-eyed at Celia, worrying over her voice, the chill of the theatre, the draft on her throat. He takes her for dinners to discuss the role, drapes her shoulders in a sable stole to ward off cold. He once knew and loved Carmen Miranda, he says. He wanted to marry her but she wasn't interested in domestication. That is, until she married that wife-beater who never deserved her, until the studios and agents gripped her so tightly her heart gave out. Now that she's gone, Stark says, he's going to make damn sure the world knows what part they played in her demise.

The first time they go to dinner, Celia arrives without the wig. He asks that in future, she wear it in his presence. She listens intently and speaks little.

"But what about the marquee? Christ, I didn't think this through. I thought you'd be able to dump the Ramos after you got the part," Annie says later.

"I tried. He said, *Rosa Ramos is who you are for the duration of this production.* He calls me Carmen most of the time anyway. Last night he took me to the cinema. He's got this projectionist friend and after the last show, they ran *Springtime in the Rockies* for us—you know, with Betty Grable and Carmen Miranda. And he kept pointing out his favourite dance moves, the expressions on Carmen's face—except he'd say *your* face. I thought he meant he wanted me to learn that look but then he says, 'And look at your legs. Grable's don't hold a candle to yours.'"

Annie is incredulous. "This bastard's buggy."

Celia shrugs the way a person might at a wealthy cross-dressing uncle. "Maybe it's like method acting."

Stark picks Celia up and drops her off after each rehearsal. When a young man in the chorus is seen kissing her hand backstage, he gets fired. After seeing Celia to the door of her apartment building, Stark calls minutes later from a phone booth to make sure she's reached her suite and again two hours later to assure himself that she is readying herself for bed, gargling with salt water, avoiding caffeine, eschewing cigarette smoke.

The night before the musical opens, Celia falls asleep on the couch and wakes with a yelp as Annie comes in the door. "It's just me, hon."

"I was dreaming about my dad." Celia falls back into the cushions. "My real one. I think. Except he looked just like Michael Stark. He was pushing me on this tall swing in the park and I was going back and forth in these great big swooshes. And sometimes I looked down and my legs were long but when I remembered my dad was there, they were little like I was a kid and I had to keep remembering I'm *Audrey* or . . . or I don't know what and my dad kept saying, 'Don't tell Mummy.' And then suddenly Cyd Charisse was there and she reached out with a cigarette like she was going to burn my leg but my dad—or Michael—gave me one last push and I went shooting off into the air."

"You're just nervous. You'll feel better after tomorrow night."

"I hardly remember him. My mother never talked about him after he left."

Her father is with Mrs. Kent, the widow next door, again. Audrey's mother thinks it only right that her husband help out around the neighbourhood. Flat feet shouldn't have kept him from serving his country on the home front. The Japanese capitulated two years ago but still, most weekends he is the Lonely Lady's Handyman. Thin and frail, Mrs. Kent needs him the most.

The evening her mother sent her to collect him for dinner, Audrey walked through Mrs. Kent's open front door, calling *Daddy* as though it were a question. She expected to hear nails being hammered, the growl of a saw, but there was only the dulcet tones of Bing Crosby on the radio.

As she neared the kitchen, soft murmurs mixed with shy giggles. Feet shuffled on linoleum. She could see shoes moving, snatches of bodies passing in and out of the door frame. As the song ended, it was as though they were eating something awfully tasty in that kitchen, *mmm*-ing, and lip-smacking. Audrey stood small and awkward in the entrance as The Andrews Sisters started "Near You" and her father held Mrs. Kent and sang into her ear, "*It's like heaven to be near you . . .*" They danced in a slow rocking circle.

Mrs. Kent gazed dreamily over her handyman's shoulder only to see a curious four-year-old. She pushed him away. Audrey's father cut in with "Hi, honeybun. We're just taking a break from work, goofing off a little. You want to dance with me too?"

She grinned and went to his hands, stepping onto the toes of his shoes. After a few turns, he picked her up. "We better go see Mother, shouldn't we? Well, goodbye, Mrs. Kent. Screen door ought to be fine now. Let me know if you need anything else."

Mrs. Kent's hand flitted about her temple. She didn't meet Audrey's eyes.

As her father carried her down the steps, he said, "Mrs. Kent is very lonely since her husband went away to fight the Germans and sometimes she misses dancing the way you and I get to do. So now and then I cheer her up and we dance around the kitchen like this," and he twirled in circles down the side-walk as he carried her. "The problem is it makes Mummy sad when I dance with other ladies—she likes all the dances for herself. So I don't tell her." He stopped and kissed her nose. "I think you better not tell her either because if she gets very upset, I might have to go away and then we'll all be sad. See?" She nodded. "Good girl."

Audrey's mother, Nancy, was a bit funny when they came home. She looked at her husband as though she thought he might have stolen pennies from her purse. From then on, when-ever Audrey's father went to Mrs. Kent's, he was told to bring his daughter along.

Sometimes the three of them dance. Sometimes Mrs. Kent gives her crayons and paper and asks her sit out on the back porch with the dog and draw his portrait.

She's seen them kissing. Mrs. Kent likes to kiss; her mother doesn't. Audrey doesn't talk about it.

One day, Audrey comes inside from Mrs. Kent's porch and is surprised to see they aren't dancing. Audrey is in the midst of opening the icebox when she hears a light rap at the front door. She can see the top of her mother's head through the door window.

Audrey looks through to the parlour where Mrs. Kent and her father are on the sofa: Mrs. Kent's blouse undone, her father touching her brassiere, making that noise as though he's eating cake.

Couldn't they all just dance? She reaches up to the counter and turns up the radio.

Nancy walks quietly into the kitchen. Audrey twists her fingers, glancing from her mother to her father as he bites into Mrs. Kent. In a voice that sounds to Audrey like the devil, her mother growls, "You goddamn whore."

She grabs her daughter by the arm and yanks her from the house.

"You knew all along." Nancy hauls her down the sidewalk and up the walkway of their own house. "All along, you never said a word." Pulling her up the front steps, her hands shake as she stops and grabs her child's face. "How could you betray me?" And slaps her.

Opening night, even with comps to reviewers, friends and relatives, the theatre is less than half-full. Stark hits the streets out front asking passersby if they would like to see the finest Brazilian performer to ever hit the American stage. Some take him up on it, some laugh—"Sure, pal, like I wanna spend my night watchin' some broad dance with bananas on her head."

Between strays off the street and the friends Annie brought, the audience is fluffed to a little over half capacity.

When Celia comes out for her curtain call, the crowd is checkered with a few diehard Carmen aficionados on their feet while most clap politely from deep in their seats, relieved that the night was a freebie. Stark rushes to her onstage, his face wet with tears, his arms cradling a monstrous bouquet. She takes the flowers and Stark's hand and together they bow.

She is sponging off her makeup when he opens her dressing-room door.

"Michael," she says uncertainly. "Do you have notes—"

He raises a hand to quiet her and, getting down on one knee, takes a deep and shuddering breath. "These past weeks with you have been the most glorious of my life. And I believe they have been the doorway to a love and a joy few people will ever know." Taking a small velvet box from his pocket, he flips the top. "Carmen, I have always loved you. If you will marry me I promise to bring you joy each and every day of our lives together."

"Oh my goddamn Christ!" Annie shrieks later at the apartment. "This guy is the original loser! What did you *say?*"

"I didn't know *what* to say. I think I lost my accent even. He said, *Don't answer me now. Think about it. And have the sort of sweet dreams a woman has knowing she is truly loved.* Then he slipped the ring on my finger and left."

"So where is it?"

Celia goes into her purse and opens the box.

Annie whistles. "This sonuvabitch is cracked."

"I'm scared to lose the accent now. What if he goes funny?"

"Goes?"

The next day, Annie trots to the door and steals the neighbour's paper. "Hang on to your bird, vee are turnink to zee t'eatre section undt see vat Herr Warner said about zee extravaganza."

Celia stands in her housecoat, wringing the belt.

"I saw Albert Warner there so he should—There we go." Annie's eyes scan the text.

"Out loud, please."

"Oh. Ah. Well, the caption is, 'Let Sleeping Dogs Lie.' *For the Love of Carmen is the new musical by first-time director-producer Michael Stark and God help us if it's not the last. The play, to put it kindly, is a love letter to the former toast of Broadway,*

Brazilian superstar-cum-has-been Carmen Miranda. Stark would have better spent his time and money on a truckload of graveside flowers . . . Oh boy . . . all right . . . blablabla—*cast in the lead is newcomer Rosa Ramos whose uncanny ability to capture the once-beloved voice of Miranda is overshadowed by her . . ."*

"Keep going," Celia says.

*" . . . her, at best, mediocre acting skills. While singing, it's as though Ramos can feel the grip that must have taken Miranda's heart once she realized the world didn't care for her worn-out tutti-frutti camp. But once the music—*Honey, he's a cocksucker and everyone knows it."

Celia drops her head against the back of the sofa. "Just read it."

"—once the music stops, Ramos truly is the walking dead. But to be fair, her soggy attempts at emoting are difficult to qualify since this wet dog of a script soaked cast, orchestra and audience alike in a drooling damp." Annie tosses the paper. "Jaded old hack."

Celia sighs. "Least nobody knows my real name."

"No, you were good! I'm sure the other reviews will be better."

There are only two other reviews and they are no kinder. At the theatre that night, there's a message from Stark saying he will not be in attendance. The cast wander about like hapless zombies.

After the players limp through a second night's performance, fifty-one audience members mope to the exit. Backstage, the dreariness has become a black joke. The cast decide to go out and get blotto.

As they come out the back door, one of the chorus kids makes a show of checking first to see if there are tomatoes to be hurled. Except for a man in a trench coat, the coast is clear.

"Audrey?" the trench coat calls softly.

"Sorry, Mac," a chorus kid bellows. "Ain't no Audrey in this dog-and-pony show."

Celia's feet are paralyzed. The others trip past.

"Audrey. I knew it was you."

She stares a moment then unearths her feet.

"Honey, please. Just five minutes."

She freezes again. Her stage-husband comes back and drapes his arm across her back. "You okay, Rosa?"

"Go ahead," she says. "I'll catch up." Soon she is alone with him. Stewart steps toward her.

"I'm not coming home."

He nods. "She's sick. Same cancer as her sister."

Celia stares down the alley.

"Audrey, you should come home. At least for a visit."

"She doesn't want me there."

"I know things were lousy before you left and you got the brunt of it but—"

"She threw me out. And you let her."

The back door opens behind them. Annie pokes her head out. "There you are! I thought I—sorry, did I interrupt something?"

"No." Celia's voice falls icy flat. "Everyone's gone up the street for a drink. You coming?"

"Yeah, sure. I'm comin'." Annie clips down the steps, eyes flitting toward the guy. "Don't have to tell me twice."

"Audrey."

"I'm not Audrey anymore."

"For godsake, we all made mistakes. Can't you—"

"No, I can't. Go home and look after your wife."

Stewart is speechless a moment. When he sees her shoulders slump, he reaches out for her. Celia lets him hug her a moment. "I should've handled it better," he says into Celia's hair. "I shouldn't have let things get so out of hand."

She pushes him away when she starts to cry. "I can't. Please, just leave me alone." Reaching behind her for Annie's hand, she rushes off down the alley.

When they reach the street, Celia buckles and Annie hails a cab. They spend the rest of the evening at the apartment in front of the television, Celia's head on a pillow in Annie's lap, a blanket heaped over her body as though it weren't warm enough to wander around in pasties.

The funeral for Audrey's aunt had been in Chicago. Nancy stayed on but she thought it best that Stewart and Audrey go back and leave her to sort things out, pack up her sister's belongings.

Back in New York, Audrey took the train into town after school for ballet rehearsals and afterward, she and Stewart would head to a restaurant. They spent hours talking about politics, the future, analyzing dreams. It didn't look like her mother would be back in town for a while so Stewart asked what she wanted to do for her birthday.

"Don't suppose you'd ever take me to the El Morocco, would you?"

"Big bad Elmo's, huh. We could arrange that."

The day before her birthday was Saturday and late that afternoon, Stewart presented her with a suitcase-sized box. Inside was a new dress, slim-fitting emerald, silk and strapless, with a matching bolero jacket.

She gulped at the sight of herself in the mirror. Nancy wouldn't approve. When she came out of her room to show Stewart, he spun her around. "Spectacular! Put your pearls on!"

They drove into town that evening, Audrey in her new dress and Stewart in his tux.

Seeing the finery as they came through the front doors—the elegance of the clientele against the rich decor—she went weak in the knees. First dinner: duck à l'orange. Baked Alaska for dessert. Later: champagne and the main attraction—beautiful sun-kissed Harry Belafonte onstage. They waltzed to his crooning, and salsaed to the calypso beat.

Come two in the morning, Stewart took the keys back from the valet.

"Are you sure you're okay to drive?" Audrey asked.

"Definitely. If we go fast enough, we're bound to cut a straight path."

Back at the house they drank more wine and jived to Louis Prima albums. Outside, the sky paled to blue and Stewart suddenly remembered. "Jesus, I rented Rita Hayworth for you."

"Well, get her out here!"

"I mean *Gilda*. I got it at the same place I bought you the reel of *Singin' in the Rain*. Stay there, I'll go get the projector and we'll watch it against the wall."

Minutes later, the two of them lay on throw cushions staring at Hayworth.

The sun had begun its pink rise over the hills outside as Gilda's melancholy voice strummed "Put the Blame on Mame, Boys . . ."

Lying in the cushions, her voice low and scratchy from too much time awake, Audrey sang along. Stewart looked over. "Hayworth once said, 'They go to bed with Gilda and they wake up with me.'"

"That's sad," Audrey croaked. "Do you think she was lonely?" Hayworth and Glenn Ford argued somewhere in the distance when her lids fell shut.

She opened her eyes to a foot nudging her ribs. "Get up."

Her head throbbed. Early-morning sun lit the room and Hayworth was gone. The reel on the projector spun, loose film flapping. With Stewart's arm around her, she couldn't move. Suddenly he sniffed hard and sat up, glanced unsteadily about the room and up at his wife who stood in her overcoat, jaw clenched. "Get off my floor," she said evenly.

"Mother. When did you get back? I thought you . . ."

"Five minutes ago. Caught the first flight out to make it home for your birthday."

Stewart stood up and rubbed his arms. "Audrey wanted to watch *Gilda* for her birthday."

"So I see." Nancy's arms were stiff, her mouth, her throat.

Standing too now, Audrey squinted in the hangover bright. Stewart picked up cushions, tossed them to the sofa. "Thought you were staying on till Tuesday. I could've picked you up."

"Tough when you're caught with your pants down, isn't it?"

Audrey tried to focus, decipher her tone. Adrenaline coursed through her arms. The green dress? The outfit was too flashy.

"We'll clean up, Nancy, don't worry," he said with a sigh.

"*Please*. Look at yourself, Stewart. And her with all that black makeup."

Audrey took a step toward her. "Mother?"

She glowered at her daughter. "Think you're clever, don't you?"

"Nancy," Stewart said. "What are you doing?"

"Opening my eyes and taking a good look around," she said, turning to him. "What a ride you've had."

"What's going on?" Audrey finally asked.

"Get out of my sight," Nancy said flatly.

Audrey paused. Her mother glared at Stewart, who suddenly looked thin and uncertain. Audrey moved past them up the stairs. On her bed she sat rubbing fingers over the Christmas-ball finish of her dress as she listened.

From Stewart: "What in god's name are you *thinking*?"

The sound of a match striking.

"I'm worried about you, Nancy."

Her mother gives a clanging fake chortle. Then says, "Stop saying my name, please. Out of your mouth, it sounds like a sickness."

"Perhaps from your point of view, it looked peculiar—"

"That's right."

"We fell asleep like that because . . ."

"Do tell."

"We went into town and had dinner and some champagne. It's her sixteenth birthday after all. Then I brought us home and she was a little wound up still—she wanted to watch a movie."

"So you thought you'd watch a striptease film with a sixteen-year-old girl?"

"It's hardly a—Hayworth takes off her *gloves*. Look, Audrey really wanted to see *Gilda*. I didn't want to be a crank about it."

Silence. Then, "Audrey wanted to."

"Yes. Her heart was set on it so I asked Eddie to see if he could get us a reel."

"You were *entwined*. I came home to my husband entwined with my daughter."

"Well, I—Jesus—she cuddled up to me in the night, I guess—don't make such a production out of this, Nancy."

Upstairs, Audrey's face was ashen. *Cuddled?* Heat prickled up the back of her neck. She couldn't recall cuddling.

"*Cuddled up?* My daughter made a pass at my husband? Is this what you're saying?"

"I'm sure it wasn't a pass—"

"I told you. Spending the time you do with her is unnatural. I told you that—the pearls and the singing and carrying on at parties. And what did you say?"

"Listen, Audrey's mature for her age and because of that, she often seeks more stimulating conversation with adults. It's noth—"

"You said it was *fine*. I was crazy. Nancy's always crazy. You brought this on!" She started to sob. "Why, why can't things ever be right for me?"

"No, no. Come here, sweetheart."

Audrey shook, her flesh red and jumping. *I'm sure it wasn't a pass.* Why would he say it like that? His arm was around *her.*

Later, Stewart sat in the chair against her bedroom wall. He stared at the floor before he spoke. "Your mother and I think it would be best if you left the house for a while."

Audrey's eyes opened wider.

"Everything will be fine. We just need to take a bit of breathing time. Your mother's cousin is in Brooklyn and my sister, of course, is here in Scarsdale. You might miss a bit of school if you stay in Brooklyn but there's more room and you'd be closer to your rehearsals."

It won't be fine, she wanted to say. *Why didn't you tell her to shut up? Why didn't you say she was wrong? You* picked *Gilda.* But she stayed mute.

He looked away. "I know it's hard to understand, but this is the best thing."

The next morning, Nancy stayed in her room while Stewart drove Audrey and a small suitcase to the train station. Her aunt would be expecting her, he said. Handing her what cash he had in his wallet—twenty-seven dollars—he promised it wouldn't be too long.

She sat down on a bench and let the train to Brooklyn leave without her. And the next and the next. She didn't think of the ballet rehearsals themselves but she did think of that Italian girl in the corps with her. The one who lived all by herself in Little Italy. She knew something about everything. She would know.

Celia sits up suddenly from Annie's lap. "I'm going to say yes,"
    "To what?"
She reaches for her purse. Opening the small velvet box, she slides the gold band from its groove and slips it onto her finger, heads off to bed.

The next day they are up at noon. Celia, chipper and buoyant, has gone to the store for bacon, eggs, fruit, milk and bread and begun a whopping breakfast for the two of them.

Eyes catching on the diamond that glints off Celia's finger, Annie tries unsuccessfully to make light conversation. She takes to reading yesterday's paper and announcing snippets instead.

"Looks like Jacky-boy took another primary."

"Uh-huh," Celia says brightly as she scrambles eggs in a bowl and pours the whole mess into hot grease. Annie flips the radio on as Celia lays bacon, eggs and orange slices onto plates. The toast pops. And then, "In other news, theatre director Michael Stark has been arrested on charges of aggravated assault." Celia's hand stops in mid toast-grab. Annie turns up the volume. "Stark allegedly stabbed theatre critic Albert Warner late last night in Manhattan's Stork Club. Warner is listed in satisfactory condition. Stark's bail will be set pending psychiatric evaluation . . ."

Celia tosses toast on the table with something just this side of a slam before she slumps in a chair. A resigned blast of air through her nose, she thumbs the ring.

Annie pats fingertips to her lips a moment. "I think Warner had it coming."

Fourteen

~

IT WAS 3:30 IN THE MORNING BY THE TIME I DRAGGED through the door of my apartment. It felt foreign, but then so did everything lately. Sticking my face into my bedroom, I flipped the light on, relieved the bed was empty though it looked slept in. Not that I make my bed much but the crumple right now seemed alien, impertinent. Catching some movement by my dresser, I let out a yelp and knocked my head against the doorjamb. It turned out to be me in my mirror, my short dark mop reflecting back as the most foreign thing of all. I watched my hand as it ran through my curls. Some part of my brain had expected my old self to resume where it left off before I drove south. I turned the light off.

In the bathroom the toilet seat was up. More impertinence. I looked at my reflection over the sink. I was a stranger in my own mirrors.

I left the light on and relit the bedroom as I passed. I turned on lamps in the living room. On the desk, my laptop sat open and an empty beer bottle loitered beside it along with a dishtowel tossed across a crumb-scattered plate. Some little gizmo was attached to the top of my computer screen. On closer inspection, it turned out to be a webcam. The machine was off, but the camera lens stared. Snatching the dishtowel, I threw it overtop.

In the kitchen, a couple more empty beer bottles sat on the counter. A chip bag. My shoulders jumped and warbled and agitated me. The bottles and bag agitated me. It's not as if he wasn't here all the time anyway—*what's the big deal?* I went to the counter and put the empties in the cupboard under the sink, chucked the bag in the garbage.

I don't know where to sleep, I thought. I can't sleep in that room. I had a peculiar itch in the back of my mind that the girl in the mirror was going to watch me sleep. The webcam would watch me watch her. "This is what happens when you drive for sixteen hours," I told myself. Sitting down on the couch, I reached for the remote and turned the television on, hoping commercial voices and canned laughter might soothe me.

My cell phone went. It was going on four in the morning.

"I'm sorry. Did I wake you?" Leonard. "I figured you'd turn it off if you were sleeping."

I told him that I'd just got in the door.

"I had a nightmare."

"Me too. Or I'm about to. Want me to come over?"

"You will? Yeah." He sounded so grateful, it made my heart ache a little. I rummaged in my mother's trunk, picked up the heart and stuck it in my coat pocket. I looted some sweats and a T-shirt from my room, set the trunk in the hall closet and covered it with an old blanket before I left.

Leonard's apartment door was unlocked and he sat on his bed. "I didn't think you owned pyjamas," I said from the entrance to his bedroom.

"Eunice gave them to me." He looked up and his head jerked back. "Holy shit! When did you do that?"

I glanced upward at my bangs. "Couple days ago." I shrugged. "I'm in flux." I dropped my stuff to the floor and flopped on the bed beside him. "Eunice is Mrs. Whoserface?" Touching at the royal-blue piping of the shirt, I gasped. "Are these *silk*?"

"It's not like that!" he said and hugged his knees.

"They're nice." I tugged the hem and let him go. "What'd you dream?"

"I was at the back of the bus and I had a coffin across my lap and you were inside and people kept turning around and looking at me. They wanted to take the lid off and I wouldn't let them and there were only three stops to go. Three minutes, I kept saying, if I can just keep them away for three minutes." Leonard has an obsession with threes. When his mother was three months pregnant she was diagnosed with some kind of uterine cancer. The doctors wanted to operate but it would have meant aborting. They told her there wasn't any point in carrying to term anyway, that children in these situations usually die before the age of three. She was a devout Christian and she refused. Leonard was born, the cancer progressed and she died when Leonard was three months old. His father couldn't bear to look at him and he was raised by his grandmother until he was three years old when his father remarried. I have a lot of recovering Christians in my life, it occurred to me.

"On your *lap*?"

He nodded. "It was like this." He brought his hands out to his sides. A three-foot coffin. "And it had leather straps at either end so I could carry it."

Laughing, I said, "That's the trunk—my mum's trunk."

"Oh. Yeah," he said softly. After a pause he took a sharp breath as though he was about to speak and then didn't.

When Leonard gets like this, I stay quiet. It's a delicate operation. It's as though he's a little kid on the end of a wharf with a fishing line in his hands, waiting for some bold swimmer to take the bait. He keeps trying until he catches one by the lip. It takes patience. After several yanks, Leonard said, "She's mad at me for not staying tonight."

"Mrs. Whosits?" I asked. He nodded. "Did you sleep with her?" A long pause, one fruitless yank and then, "Yes. But I didn't want to stay there tonight. And now she thinks I only want to be there if she's paying me. And that's not true. I'm starting to think I . . . She's beautiful, so it's not that—but she's twice my age, practically."

"*Practically.* I assumed she was seventy or something, playing bridge."

He looked perplexed a second. "They don't actually play bridge. Her and her friends just say that. It's code for, let's get together and eat and get drunk and yak. It's a euphorism."

"Euphemism."

"Can you not do that when I'm like this?"

"Sorry. That's a good one, actually. All the nice words that mean *drunk* should be called euphorisms. Euphoria-isms? So, she's not seventy."

"She's fifty-four." He got up and went to his dresser, brought back a snapshot. "That's her there." In the photo, he stood in his full catering attire (tuxedo shirt, bow tie and black trousers) behind three women sitting at an umbrellaed patio table.

He pointed to a brunette, olive-skinned woman with large dark eyes and a full laughing mouth. She was beautiful.

"Has she had loads of work done?"

"No. She's Italian. Her maiden name is Delucchi."

"She's married."

"Widowed. I just feel weird. I'm scared I've got a mommy complex or something."

I examined the picture again. "She doesn't look mumish. And she sure doesn't look like yours." Leonard's current mother, his stepmother, was married once before she met Len's father. She divorced her first husband shortly after she found him in bed with a man. Which would explain why she chose John Wayne's double for number two. She seemed perennially frustrated and wanting. Except to her face, Len never referred to her as Mother or any of its variations. Always Edna.

"I looked up Germaine Greer on the Internet," I said, "and she's got a thing for boys now. Young ones."

"What's your point?"

"I don't know." I shrugged. "She kind of slagged off dykes and fags a bit. I don't why my mother was into her. I read somewhere that she wrote a sequel to *The Female Eunuch* because women had gone from having no cunt then to being all-cunt now. Something like that. Today's girls are nothing but their sexuality . . . ?" I waited for an argument and didn't get one.

We slept in Leonard's bed that night. As I closed my eyes, I reached across and squeezed his wrist, told him to have good dreams. "Just stay out of the box," he whispered and left his wrist in my hand.

The next day I drove downtown to the library. Trudging up escalators through the cavernous, echoing pseudo-pantheon of the main branch, I headed to the political science department and asked if they had anything on Bobby Kennedy. The librarian pattered away on her keyboard and directed me to two sets of shelves, one with books and one with videos. Videos hadn't occurred to me. I pulled three Bobby books and stood over the videos, agog, before I chose two on 1960s history—one on the relationship between Bobby and Martin Luther King Jr. and one the mutual loathing between Kennedy and Lyndon Johnson.

On the way home my cell phone rang. According to the call display, it was me calling.

"Are you home?" Frank.

"I'm in town," I said. "I'm on my way home now."

"Why didn't you call me?" he asked, incredulous. "Your bag's here, you're not."

I didn't feel like it seemed an inappropriate answer. I didn't know why I didn't feel like it either and I didn't want to discuss it. "It was three-thirty in the morning when I got in. I was just about to call you. It was early when I got up and then I went to the library and there's no reception in there. You're not even allowed to use your cell."

Silence.

"I'm sorry, Frank."

"The only time you use my name these days is when you're pissed off at me or you're scared I'm pissed off at you." He exhaled. It was silent again except for a faint clatter in the background. "So when are you coming home? I'm at your place."

"I know. I'm about six blocks away. What are you doing?"

"Show you when you get here." His tone levitated a little.

I shut my phone, turned off Burrard and detoured down West 5th. Toward my mother's. Just to check.

Out front, the agent's sign still stuck out of the ground like a tongue. The house stood in its comfy-yet-stately grace, patiently waiting for someone new to embrace it.

When I set the key in the lock of my apartment again, it still seemed as though I was entering alien territory. And yet I resented Frank's being there. He was tapping away at the keyboard of my computer; that's what he'd been doing when he called. "Hey!" he yelled as I dropped my books and movies by the door. "Viv." He stopped at the top of the hallway. Flipping on the light to get a better look, he continued slowly toward me. "What the hell did you do?"

"I cut it."

"I see that. It's brown." He sounded as though I'd had a sex change.

I smiled. But if it were possible, if it would have made me feel normal again, I would've reached up and unzipped, peeled this skin off me like a wetsuit. My old self would've grabbed hold of Frank and ripped his fly open.

He touched my hair, then took my hands and stood back from me as if making sure everything else was where he'd left it, pulled me to him and hugged me. Our bones didn't seem to fit together anymore and when he kissed the side of my head I couldn't tell if he said "I miss you" or "I missed you."

All the same anyway. I missed me too. I thought of my mother jumping on a bed in Vegas, forcing herself to say ha ha until glee crept in and the laughter was real. Frank said something about my hair and how it would take him a while to get used to. I think he said he wished I had told him, as he took my hand and led me down my hallway. My mother kept jumping on the bed until I remembered I'd made the whole thing up. Maybe I'm made up right now, I thought. Maybe my brain is in a jar somewhere getting poked with a stick.

"We're all set up," Frank told me, squeezing my hand.

"We're on Brian's network now." He sat at my desk. Onscreen was an instant message that read, "Wish I could see U. If U send another picture, I'll send a present. One that takes batteries!"

"What is *that*?"

"This is Papi Chulo. He thinks I've got long blonde hair and that I shaved my pussy yesterday while I was talking to him."

I blinked. "Can't he see you with the camera?"

"No, I told him I'm new to this and my camera isn't working yet. He's only seen a still shot of you." He giggled to himself and clicked to show me a photo he'd taken of me a couple months back wearing black lace lingerie and a Lone Ranger mask that he bought me for Valentine's. He looked up now, as if he needed desperately for me to say he did good. He typed, "U are bad!! :)"

"How girlish of you," I said. "How did you two hook up?"

"It's part of Brian's network: jerkflirt.com," he said, gaining momentum. "What we have to work on is conversion and retention—we've got to convert guys who are surfing the Net into members on our site and then retain them as members. There's different ways to do it. Once the webcam is turned on, you can talk to thirty guys at a time and that's free for them, but if they want to see you naked then you go into a private chat room and they pay six bucks a minute." His fingers jabbed at the keyboard. A second stream came up, this guy's name was Naughty_Boy. "Even without making videos," he said, "just instant messaging and doing private shows in here, we should make a minimum two grand U.S. a week. But I can't turn the camera on yet, for obvious reasons." He spoke rapid-fire, as if he was on something.

"What does he mean," I asked, "see another picture of you?"

"I e-mailed him that Polaroid of you in your red G-string. And he sent us a cashmere sweater."

"This is—Frank, you're moving too fast. You just sent this guy a picture of me with no mask or anything. One of my private pictures? Fuck."

"Don't freak out. He's in Salt Lake City. Probably a Mormon."

He clicked on *Margo* in the list of available models. A blonde
girl in a black-and-white checked bra and G-string suddenly
appeared onscreen, a stack of sex toys beside her and a keyboard in her lap. The video stream was slow and shuddering
like homemade animation, ten or fifteen frames per second.
"See, once we get you in front of the webcam, this is how it
should work." A long stack of instant messages from names like
Slaveboy and FatMike jammed the screen, the old ones disappearing as new ones jackhammered in. FatMike wanted her to
rip her stockings for him. The stockings cost her twenty bucks,
she said, and she wouldn't rip them for less than a fifteen-
minute private. In private, she said, she would show him whatever he wanted. Slaveboy wanted her to speak to him on the
mike. She would only do audio in private and she could only be
dirty in private. There were censors watching.

"I mailed Slaveboy a pair of your dirty panties for fifty
bucks," Frank blurted as he typed.

"Ew. Really?" I looked down the hall toward my laundry bag.

"What? What's the big deal, I can buy you ten new pairs for
that."

"How do you even know he'll send the money?"

"It's already sent. It goes through a third-party processor
into our account. Once these guys see you live, your panties'll
be goin' for a lot more. 'Specially dirty ones." He stopped
typing and looked up at me, a bit breathless. "You wanna turn
on the camera and do some?" He licked his bottom lip as if he
were next up for a line of coke.

"Can't you . . . I just got home. Don't you . . ."

Bewildered, he looked at the screen. "I thought you'd be
excited. I set it all up myself."

I sat down on the couch. "It's great. You did great." My voice
was flat. I remembered an essay I'd read in an issue of *Penthouse*
I bought for Frank once. It was written by a former madam and
addressed a female reader. The way to keep our men happy, she
said, was to make a fuss over them. Tell your man how impressed you are with his accomplishments. Men like to feel as

though they are smart and capable, and pleasing them means reinforcing that. "Do you ever get sick of hearing how pretty you are?" she asked. "Well, he never gets sick of hearing how competent and clever he is." I dangled that in front of my mother once. She quoted Margaret Mitchell. "I'm tired of saying, '*How wonderful you are*,' to fool men who haven't got half the sense I've got, and I'm tired of pretending I don't know anything so men can tell me things and feel important while they're doing it."

It would be worse if he left. Worse if I were alone inside and out. "I could never have figured that stuff out by myself. It looks complicated." I tried to put a rise in my tone.

"Took some doing." Frank typed a few last words, closed the connection and came and sat by me on the couch. "I don't like it when you're gone," he said and picked up my hand. "We get all clumsy. We forget how to take care of each other."

I grabbed hold of him around the neck. "Hug me," I told him. "As hard as you can." I couldn't feel it. With one arm round my shoulders, he used the other to scoop my legs before he stood and carried me off to the bedroom. Once he'd laid me down on the bed, he went to the dresser and lit the candle. He'd never done that before. He touched the motorcycle helmet that had been collecting dust since his bike broke down two years ago. When we were first dating we'd drive out to the country on that bike. Roaring down Highway One was the best foreplay I'd ever experienced.

When I woke, there was a note saying he'd be back in a couple hours.

I went out in the hall and rooted for the notebook. My mother sitting alone in a Scarsdale train station. She would be in the carnival soon. Marines would try to rape her. Okie Joe. I looked up from my bed into the dresser mirror. It reflected back to the mirror above my headboard, the picture in the picture in the picture: her in the train station, me at the airport. I can see her anger and tears and mine and her mother's and all of us with our fists clenched.

When I landed in Tokyo on my way to modeldom, the agency had no bed ready for me. The girl I was replacing wouldn't be leaving until the following afternoon. I was given the choice of sleeping on the pullout couch at the office or staying at the agent's place. I was scared of her looking at me, constantly appraising me, and I chose the couch. The agency was actually an apartment where four models lived on the off-hours. When I woke the first morning, a raggedy-looking girl was at the foot of my pullout, jamming clothes into a knapsack. "Hi," she said, glancing up irritably. "Don't mind me. I'm just getting the hell out of here. Did Miko try to get you to stay at her place last night?" I said she had but that I'd wanted to be with the other models. She chuckled derisively. "Smart move. If you'd slept there you would've woken up with her hands down your pants like the last girl did. Fuckin' dyke." I was used to other descriptors for lesbians, adjectives that suggested dyke-as-saviour not rapist. She looked around herself then zipped her bag with a rip as though she were gutting a deer. "And whatever you do, don't let them touch your hair. I used to have hair like yours, now look at it: perms and layers and . . . *fucked*." She had rock-and-roll hair, nothing like the coifs of fashion magazines.

Once she left, I wandered the apartment. The two bedroom doors were closed. The other models were sleeping behind them in bunk beds. It was only 7:00 a.m. Saturday. There were white notes stuck to the walls in various places, warning us not to touch this or that appliance or face a fine of two thousand U.S. A sheet of rules and regulations had been left for me outlining the fines I would be subjected to were I to break said rules. I was already in debt for my first month's rent, my plane ticket, my composite card and I was expected to work until such time as the debt was paid. Were I to leave town, or change my appearance, change agencies, appear late for a booking, not show for a booking, behave poorly, dress poorly, steal, swear, take drugs, or anything else I'd been doing ad nauseam since my first period, I would be fined. A slam of bleakness hit me.

I would stay there and wear their clothes and model their beer and do whatever it took but I'd die before I'd go home with my tail between my legs. It took me three months in the end to pay off my debt, pay my rent and fly myself home. I kept sane by way of Leonard; writing him long letters, calling when I thought I could pay for five minutes and still manage to eat. I'd rant and rave by pen or telephone, say things like, "If I don't get out of this shit-hole soon I'll slash my wrists. They've got cockroaches the size of cats (I threw a giant Italian *Vogue* at one last night and the *Vogue* bounced. I swear to Christ!), when you walk down the sidewalk, big-assed rats run back and forth in front of you from the stinking garbage to the restaurants and every five seconds the slant-eyed bastards are trying to get me to drop my gear for everything from screwdrivers to smoked-eel ads. What the fuck is that? *Hello?* Where's my *Elle* cover? . . . And if you ever breathe a goddamn word about any of this to my monster, I'll shish kebab your balls!"

I imagined Audrey now in the train station. I'd given her a friend in Little Italy. Someone who'd know how to get her a job so she wouldn't have to go home. I wanted her to have a girl-friend so I wouldn't feel lonely.

Dumping my tote bag on the bed, I spread out the books and opened *Pack of Rats* to a bit about the opening for *Ocean's Eleven*. Maybe Sinatra invited her. Maybe she was there at the Fremont Theatre. And then what? Where was Johnny? I cracked *The Chic Mafioso*. Judy Campbell stayed at his pad in L.A. when she was in town. Mother probably did too. Rosselli orchestrating murders on one page, and on the next having boys over from the Catholic orphanage to swim in his pool. He had been a movie producer once. He lunched at the Brown Derby. There was a picture of the big-brown-hat-of-a-restaurant in a couple of the books. I can see my mother in there. Her, Johnny and Annie gabbing and stuffing their faces. The Derby was right across the street from the Ambassador Hotel and its nightclub, the Coconut Grove. She must have been salivating to get on that stage. Johnny could've got her a job singing in the lounge at the Ambassador. At the Cal-Neva. Meanwhile he was working out details to off Castro. JFK won the election that year and he made his brother Attorney General. Then Bobby went right after the men said to have put his brother in office. It's all true. It's all false. One book says a guy's a deity, another says he's a demon. It struck me that biographies said more about the biographer than the subject.

Just like when Katie, his idiot ex, said I had a Marilyn Monroe dye job. After that creepy night with Marilyn and creepy Old Man Kennedy at the Cal-Neva, I don't want anyone comparing me to that fried-up mess ever again. Have you seen her around? Promise me if I ever get like her you'll shoot me. I'll shoot you too. Deal?

Celia's been staying at Johnny's place in L.A. the past few weeks. Thanks to him she's got an agent now, Marty Sugar. Sugar's got her booked for a week singing in the lounge at the Cal-Neva Lodge. Sinatra's there too, in the midst of buying a piece of the place named for the fact that it straddles the California/Nevada border. Sitting pretty on the north shore of Lake Tahoe, the Cal-Neva is elegant but rustic with a real log exterior, stone vestibules and floors, a monstrous A-frame lobby with a stone fireplace and thick wooden beams. There are guest rooms in the main building and chalets for the fat cats and celebrities out back. The fun is its duality—the state border runs through the enormous fireplace and the king-size outdoor swimming pool: gambling on the Nevadan side, hotel and entertainment on the Californian. "You can violate the Mann Act without even going outside," Sugar joked as he gave her the booking details. Celia wasn't amused.

Her second night at the Lodge, Frank invites her for dinner. Annie is supposed to join them but she hasn't shown. For now it's just Celia, Frank, Dean, Sam Giancana, Joe Kennedy Sr., and Marilyn.

Celia sits between Marilyn and Dean. This is the first she's seen of him since Miami and she's squirmy with the memory.

Frank orders wine and gossips with Giancana while Monroe directs her conversation to the Kennedy patriarch.

Dean acts as though Miami never happened. "Well, don't you look like a million, sweetheart. I betchu sound like one too. I'm gonna get me in that there lounge to prove it."

She smiles. "Frank says you fellas are all buying into this place."

"A boy's gotta keep up with his investments or all he'll have left is his charm."

Marilyn giggles and leans into Old Man Kennedy. "I thought you said that boy of yours would be here tonight. He was going to explain to me the relationship between a commander-in-chief and a legislative body."

Kennedy's gruff voice butters over. "If he doesn't show up, my dear, I've got a few legislative suggestions for you."

Marilyn gives his arm a light swat.

"I taught those boys everything they know."

"Really? What about . . ." and she whispers in his ear. Old Joe roars. Marilyn titters and gulps her martini.

Celia catches a glimpse of his hand on Marilyn's thigh and leans to Dean. "Is it true about Marlene Dietrich and him?"

"Now y'see why she switched to girls."

"What's doin' over there?" Giancana growls across the table. "You guys got the beautiful broads and I'm stuck over here with this skinny shit." He elbows Frank in the ribs.

Dean chuckles. "Give old Sam a kiss now, Frank. And don't skimp on the tongue."

Giancana cackles, and gives Frank another jab as Dean continues. "Now, you girls probably don't know this but see that nice sapphire pinky ring on Sam. That's an engraved promise ring from Frank. Those two fellas been going steady for what, three, four years now?"

Sam laughs so hard he nearly swallows his cigar, coughs and pats his jacket for a lighter. Leaning over the table toward them, Monroe oozes a breathy "I don't know what you heard, Dean, but these boys are all *man*."

Celia's eyeballs roll, wondering if Dean's had his wrinkly bits against her too. "Frank? You heard anything from Annie? She said she'd be here yesterday."

He snorts. "You broads . . . one day you can't stand her, the next you're cryin' at her door." He looks to Dean. "Charlie, where's Sam at?"

Giancana makes kissy lips.

"Not you, y'crazy bastard. Sammy's comin' up in from L.A. still, isn't he?"

Giancana rolls ash off his cigar into the tray. "Burns my ass, sharin' a name with that fuckin' nigger weasel."

Dean shrugs. "I thought he was driving up this afternoon."

"Mr. Gi—Flood." Celia does her best to keep a pleasant even voice. "I really wish you wouldn't say that word."

"Excuse me." Giancana stuffs the cigar back in his mouth and barks around it. "—sharin' a name with that *darn* nigger weasel."

Frank tastes the wine. He nods and the waiter pours round the table. "Sam don't mean anything." His voice is caramel-glazed. "He's just shootin' the bull. See, Sam, Celia over there is one very loyal girl. Some guy says something about one a'her pals—*shoop!*—right for the throat! And she's got a lotta teeth."

Giancana shoots her a smile. "Hey, how'd you feel about a little trip to Cuba? I gotta job for you."

The table roars.

"Don't tease." Marilyn puts her cheek to Celia's. "I like her. Did you hear her sing last night?" She takes Celia's hand and clutches it to her heart. "She makes me cry.—You do, I caught some of your first set and when you sang 'Comin' Through The Rye' . . . something in your voice . . ." Her eyes shine as if a flood might come through all that paint and wash her away.

Across the table, Giancana says, "Why don'tcha hold my hand like that, I'm cold."

Monroe's look doesn't waver, it pleads and sends a flash of panic through Celia's as though she's just heard a missing child scream.

Frank's voice barrels in. "If you girls are gonna keep that up, I'll have to ask you to go to my room."

Marilyn laughs and drops her hands, keeping one woven through Celia's, resting them between the chairs. A sudden thought of her mother splashes across Celia's mind. Sick, her cool hand clutching, cancer eating away at her grip. A spasm jolts her.

Marilyn clutches tighter. "Oops, was that me or you?"

"Excuse me, I just felt dizzy a second. Probably just need to eat something."

"Hello, kittens!" Annie. A mink stole wrapped around her beaded dress, she looks like hedonism personified. She comes up behind Celia's chair, kisses her cheek.

"You were 'sposed to be here yesterday."

"I couldn't get on the plane—there was a *bomb* threat! Didn't I call you? It was just—I'll tell you later. Swear to god, there's a damn bomb threat every other day lately."

Dean stands. "Here, lovely, let me rescue you from the threats and accusations of a cruel world." He embraces her. "Ahhh . . . Annie West, the place I want to be buried."

Frank makes no pretense of rising. Annie sits next to Dean.

Old Man Kennedy leans in. "I don't think we've been introduced. I'd remember you."

"Aren't you sweet." Annie tosses him the sort of smile she reserves for people she'd enjoy more if they were dead. She switches her gaze to Giancana. "Judy sends her regards."

"Campbell?" Frank asks. "Where's *my* goddamn regards,"

"Judy," muses Giancana. "Where'd you see her? Washington?"

Marilyn tenses. Celia's finger bones crunch under the pressure.

"Yes, I was in D.C. for a short engagement and ran into her at the Mayflower."

"Seein' that boyfriend of hers again." He chomps on his sogging cigar. "Sonuvabitch wouldn't be nowheres if it weren't for me."

Marilyn leans over Celia's menu. "What did you say you were going to have?"

Annie smiles sweetly to Giancana. "She's got her own apartment in L.A. now. I ran into her again on the street just outside her new pad yesterday—just after all that bomb-scare stuff. She seemed a bit shook up and I was feeling rattled myself so we went to Romanoff's for a drink."

Giancana grunts, "I *bet* she's shook up." He trains his hooded eyes on Joe Kennedy Sr. "People gettin' harassed all over the country, guys gettin' deported."

"He wasn't a supporter of ours," Kennedy mutters.

Giancana's head turns slowly. "If there's no support, you'll know it."

"Okay, we already chewed this fat," Frank intervenes, picking up his menu. "Let us masticate upon a lovely slab of beef."

A waiter slips in beside Monroe's chair just as Kennedy's hand is nosing its way up her dress. "Madam?" the waiter asks.

"I have to go to the powder room." She pulls at Celia.

"I'll have the lamb," Celia says and lets Marilyn take her to the ladies'.

She shoves through the door, letting go of Celia and opening her purse as she goes. She rifles for a pill bottle, fusses two capsules into her hand and tosses them down. A tiny Mexican washroom attendant offers her a drink of water. She swallows and hands the glass back. She turns her back on her reflection, and her fingers form a cage around her eyes.

The attendant offers a tissue. Marilyn shakes her head and hands her purse to Celia, who stares at it, flummoxed a moment, then opens it and removes a ten-dollar bill. "Would you mind giving us a minute," she says, handing over the money.

With a nervous smile, the attendant murmurs, "Certainly, miss," and leaves.

A sudden yowl from Marilyn and she slams a hand on the counter. "Stupid bastard."

"Maybe Dean could switch seats with you."

"What?" She reaches for another tissue. "Not Joe. His crummy son of a bitch." She dabs at her eyes. "Two *years* I've been seeing Jack. I should call his wife . . . I'm—I'm getting a divorce and then what will I be . . . single, white and a hell of a lot older than twenty-one." She throws up her chin. "And now he's fooling around with . . . Who the hell is *Judy Campbell?*"

Celia shrugs. "She was seeing Frank for a while too. She had her picture in the gossips once with Sam—this Sam . . ." She waves in the direction of the dining room. "Maybe it's not true about her and Jack."

Marilyn turns to the mirror. "Look at me." She touches the skin under her eyes. Her hands follow her gaze down over her breasts to her stomach. "I'm *fat* and old. Old and fat." She glances at the other woman's reflection. "H'old are you, Sheila? . . . shh . . . Celia?"

"Twenty-three."

"Twenty-three. Twennnny-threeeee." She stares at her own face. "Ten, eleven, twelve years younger, ten, eleven, twelve pounds lighter. They take big bites of me every day and still how fat I am . . ." She opens her purse and takes out the pill bottle, flips off the cap.

"You already did that." Celia tugs at her pearls. "You took your medicine."

Lids falling sleepy down her eyes. "I did? A little dab'll do ya," she says and tosses the bottle back in her purse, plucks out her lipstick. As she runs the tube over her lips, a knee buckles and, throwing one hand down to catch herself, the other draws a red slash down her pale powdered chin. "*Shit.* I'm so stupid, and ugly and—"

The restroom door opens and the little attendant pokes her head back in. Marilyn drops the lipstick. "Stop looking at me! *Stop it, stop it, stop it.*" The attendant bolts back out.

Celia pulls some tissues and comes to her side. "Look at me." Her arms limp, Marilyn turns. Plump tears roll. "They put me in a crazy house a few months ago, you know. They put me in a little room in a straitjacket and left me there to rot while all the people came by to stare at me like I was in a zoo. One after another."

Celia's throat knots. "Don't cry." She puts the Kleenex to Marilyn's mouth, "Spit." She runs it gently under her eyes. "You're too pretty to wear all this makeup." Marilyn swallows, eyes to the ceiling. Celia turns the tissue over and wipes off her chin. Reaching for the lipstick, she finishes with a new red bow on Marilyn's face.

"You're very sweet to me." Taking Celia's face, she sets a full kiss onto her mouth just as the door opens, then gently taps her forehead against Celia's before she walks past Annie coming into the restroom.

Annie gawks at the closing door. She pivots to Celia. "She practising for her lifeguard ticket or what?"

Celia pats her lips.

Annie cocks an eyebrow. "*What I Did on My Summer Vacation* by Celia Dare."

"She was just saying thank-you."

"Uh-huh. I heard she and the great Lili St. Cyr were lapping each other's shores once upon a time. I guess it's true."

Celia tsks. "Don't be disgusting. It wasn't like that at all."

"She's a bombshell all right, a walking goddamn minefield."

"She's just scared and lonely like everyone else."

"Well, well, well. One kiss and suddenly she's sittin' alone in a dark theatre watching *Gentlemen Prefer Blondes* over and over . . ."

"Would you stop? I just feel bad for her. She's like this *infant* and these guys—those guys out there . . . do you think Dean ever slept with her?"

"If I said yes, would you never wash your mouth again?"

Celia leans against the counter. "She ate two of those Nembutals when she first came into the restaurant and she already seemed a little stoned. Then she swallowed two more when she came in here. And *then* she forgot and went for more. Isn't anybody taking care of her?"

"She'd prefer to be someone's fuck-dolly. There was a rumour goin' around that Giancana had her sleep with some French diplomat and taped the whole thing for blackmail."

Celia makes for a cubicle, slams the door shut. "You always wanna believe the worst."

Annie takes the next cubicle. "I'm a realist."

Celia flushes the toilet. "She's a messed-up child."

Annie flushes, the noise almost obliterating her loud snort. "I already got one child to take care of." They step out of their respective stalls and eyeball one another.

"I'm not a child," Celia blurts. "I can take care of myself."

"I know you can, kid. Just humour me."

Celia marches off to the sink. "A day late and you didn't even leave me a message."

Annie leans against a stall, a smile playing on her lips. "Does this mean you were worried about little old me?"

"And since when do you hang out with that asinine Judy Campbell?"

"Speaking of which. You want the dish or not. Campbell gave me an earful."

Celia's eyes flick.

"She was a mess. We're sitting in Romanoff's and I'm making small talk like I know everything. Next thing you know, she says, *The FBI showed up at my door.*"

Celia stares.

"She says, *They asked me if I know Sam Giancana. One of them said it was an organized-crime investigation like I might be involved.*"

"The FBI?"

"The FB goddamn I. I said, *Did they ask about Jack?* No, she says. And then she says, *Oh god, everybody knows. Even Winchell knows. Jack said not to worry, that 'Sam's working with us.'*"

"*We* know Sam," Celia says. "Are they going to show up at *our* door?"

"Campbell's picture's in the paper with him for chrissake! And she's screwin' ol' Jacky-boy. Everybody *does* know."

"Why would Sam and Kennedy meet?"

Annie shrugs. "Castro?"

The two women jump as the washroom attendant pokes her nose in. "Miss? S'okay I'm coming back?"

Celia glances at her watch. "Shit. I've been in here twenty minutes."

Annie walks toward the door. "Ain't life grand when you got the guts for it."

By four in the morning, Celia has finished her last set and gone back to her room.

She sits on her bed. She stands up, sits down, looks at the phone some more. Picking up the receiver, her hands shake so fiercely, she lets it drop in her lap until the hotel operator's voice comes on. "Could you place a long-distance call for me? Scarsdale, um . . . Never mind." She stuffs the receiver back in its cradle. It rings back.

She jumps and runs into the bathroom. Door closed, she turns on the shower, takes off her dress and goes about removing her makeup, humming, brushing her hair. She grabs the wall for balance and closes her eyes.

Reaching back into the shower, she turns the water off, opens the door. The ringing starts up again. She marches to the phone and centres herself. "Yes?"

"You *are* there."

"Johnny." A mix of relief and disappointment. She sits on the bed, puts a foot up and rests her chin on her knee. "Where have you been?"

"Business."

"I haven't heard from you in almost two weeks."

"If it's an emergency, leave me a message at the Desert Inn."

"Is it true Judy Campbell had the FBI at her door? Did they ask *you* about Sam?"

"They ask me all kinds of things. I think they got their wires crossed lately. Just when you think you're all on the same team, everything goes haywire."

"How do you know her?"

"Known her since she was a kid. Anything unusual happening at my place?"

"Nothin' much. Couple perverts moved in across the street a few weeks ago. Kept trying to cop a look."

"In the apartment *directly* across? They say anything to you?"

"No . . . what?"

"Anyone come to my door?"

"No. Think it's you they're watching? Why would they be watching *you*?"

"No one's been at my door then?"

"Just electricians a couple weeks ago—something happened with the wiring in your building. Anyway, it's fixed n—"

"You let *electricians* in?"

"They were from the building."

"They didn't by any chance look like the *perverts* from across the street, did they?" Celia is quiet. He sighs. "This is why I don't want you in Vegas right now—they got Sam's name in a black book says he can't set foot in any Nevada casino. They've been going after Phyllis, too."

"The McGuire Sister Phyllis?"

"You might wanna think about using a phone booth at home. And keep quiet about Sam being there at the hotel."

She tugged at her bottom lip. "Everything's okay, right? You haven't done anything."

"Of course not, honey. Don't worry. Everything's jake."

After she hangs up, Celia puts on her dressing gown and looks out the picture window into blackness. The dark of the evergreens surrounds and clutches. It'd be seven New York time. Sitting back on the bed, she puts the phone in her lap. Eventually she asks the operator to place a call to Scarsdale. She holds the receiver with both hands, trembling with each ring. After six or seven, a woman's voice answers. It sounds like her mother's but raspy and far. "Hello," the voice repeats.

She hangs up.

She creeps down the hall to Annie's room.

It takes several knocks and self-identification before Annie's door opens. "What are you doing in your nightie, get inside before we have a troop of mashers out here." She closes the door. "That crocked bitch Monroe phoned here twice thinking I was you. *Sheila, you know Jack*, she says. *I don't know what to do.* Since when do *you* know Jack."

"Isn't Peter here yet? I thought they were friends."

"Lawford's an asshole. If Pat's not here playing wifey then he's likely off trying to dip his noodle into every soup in the joint . . . What's the matter, you look like hell."

She sits and blows her nose. "I don't know what to do with myself."

About to say something smart-ass, Annie shuts her mouth.

"It's been two years since I left home and I'm nowhere. Just some stray they let sing in their lounges once in a while."

"Think these pricks would let you touch their stages if you were no good?"

"I called my mother." Her face crumples.

"What did she say?"

"I hung up. I couldn't speak. It's like my whole life. I'm sitting there mute and eventually I'm just going to hang up."

"Come on, honey. Don't be a jerk. You've done a hell of a lot! You sang with Louis Prima and Keely Sm—"

"Keely hates me."

"Keely hates everyone right now. She just left Louis."

"They split up? Cuz of me? . . ."

Annie rolls her eyes. "Not that you ain't some kinda wonderful, but Louis's been poking everything in heels for some time now."

"I've been thinking maybe I need to get away from all this for a while. I met a girl who told me she was about to do this new play. It's small and the money stinks but she really cares about it. Maybe if I was playing a part where I was *saying* something to the world, maybe I'd feel *right*. Instead of just goofing off."

"Is this about Marilyn?"

"In the bathroom, she said it's like they take big bites out of her every day. I think it's her taking the bites and they're making her sick."

~

Hardly a breath after she and Annie have rung in 1962, Celia starts rehearsals in Los Angeles for the play she read about in the paper; a modern adaptation of a Greek comedy about two men who try to build a new society based on a utopian world created by birds. It's small but, she thinks, significant.

Kevin, the casting director and lead actor, has offered his basement as a rehearsal space. His parents' basement to be more specific. Celia plays the leggy "Flamingo" as well as a member of the Greek chorus.

Annie watches from the corner of a ratty old couch as Celia, feather boa dangling off her head and down the back of her jewelled ruby-coloured bodysuit, does her best water-bird strut. Kevin plays up his character's lascivious underpinnings by groping Celia as she coos past.

Katie, "The Iris," plants both fists at her waist. "Kevin, I think you're missing the point. This play is about the sleazy world of machismo politics and patriarchy and, man, you're celebrating it, not exposing it. Bad enough your hand is always on the Flamingo's ass—but you want her to make like it's cool, like her purpose is to be stroked by you."

Kevin groans. "Oh man, baby, you always got somethin' to say. This play is about enlightenment, escaping the ruins of a bourgeois civilization, not being so stultified by our upbring-ings that we can only stumble . . ."

"This is about bourgeois politics yes, but it's about expo-sure. You're not supposed to be a goddamn hero, man, you're supposed to be like John Kennedy: too much money and power and capitalist piggery."

Annie cocks an eyebrow at Celia. The rest of the cast begins to slump, some taking a seat, settling in for yet another showdown.

"Kennedy, man!" Kevin stalks the length of the basement. "Kennedy is the best thing the bourgeoisie has ever offered the beat generation—that cat is righteous, he's opening the world to the coloured man, he's saying yes to civil rights. You just don't like the fact that if the dude was here right now, *he'd* rather touch Celia's ass than yours."

One of the Greek chorus groans. "Why don't you two fuck and get it over with."

Katie glares. "Not if my box was left empty for a century. Simone de Beauvoir said, *No one is more arrogant toward women, more aggressive or scornful than the man who is anxious about his virility.* This whole play is just an excuse for you to ball some showgirl with a Marilyn Monroe bleach job. No offence, Celia, but an actress you ain't and if Kevin wasn't such a gash-hound you'da never got in the door. You *or* your friend with the silicone pals."

"Honey, please," Annie coughs. "Sometimes the Lord giveth till it hurts."

Kevin cuts in. "Katie Katie Katie . . . if it ain't the bourgeois calling the bohemian black! *Women should be emancipated and valued* and bla bla bla but when it comes right down to it, you're just an uptight June Cleaver zombie-bitch."

"Don't call her a bitch!" Suddenly a cacophony of chirps and calls from the chorus.

"She *is* a bitch. Kevin has *vision.*"

"That showgirl shit *is* a form of oppression—"

Soon Katie loses all patience and walks out the door. Eventually the rest drift off until there are just five left, including Annie still in the corner, smirk on her face. Celia has flopped beside her. Kevin paces. His pals Ernie and Dinah light a joint, take a drag each and hold it out for Annie, who puts up a hand. "No thanks, I gotta drink later." The offer moves to Celia. She shakes her head.

Kevin takes the next haul. "Man," he sputters through held smoke, "maybe if we'd all had a little reefer to start with, this division could've been avoided . . . This town is eating itself and dying of its own poison."

Celia's eyes flick to Kevin. "I think so too."

Kevin takes another drag. "You're a gone chick, baby. The world just don't know it yet." He reoffers her the joint. She takes it, tokes, and falls into a coughing fit. Annie smirks some more.

"Somebody put on some music," Kevin demands, smoke pouring out of his face. "I need jazz to think. I need Miles, man, I need Coltrane."

After the debacle in the basement, Katie refuses to return to rehearsals, citing, "All oppression creates a state of war."

"Is that Simone Bouvier too?" Celia asks Kevin at a greasy spoon in West Hollywood.

"De Beauvoir. Yeah. That's her problem, she shoulda been reading more Nietzsche."

"Who is she anyway, de Beauvoir?"

"French chick. Scammed all her ideas from Jean-Paul Sartre."

"Oh. He's . . . ? You must think I'm really . . ."

"Half-hipped? I can get you on the ball, darlin'. These cats are all great philosophers."

"You don't think de Beauvoir is a great philosopher?"

"I think she was the old lady of a great philosopher. She supported great philosophy and sometimes that's more important than being one yourself."

"Oh." Celia picks at her nails. A small boy wails at a nearby table and she watches his mother try to settle him while she wrestles the baby against her chest. Celia gazes from the woman and her children to the man across from them. Fork in hand, the man stabs a look at Celia. She jerks her face back to Kevin's moving lips.

" . . . raw, unschooled. But you have the heart of a holy barbarian—which is what you need in a family of friends."

She bites off some egg on toast. "Is that what I have now?"

"Indeed."

"I like that."

"Good. Cuz when Katie said she was out, Sherry and Irma backed out too. I think we can expect more dropouts. So, this kick ain't happenin'."

Celia's face drops. "Is it my fault?"

"Naw. Katie used to be my old lady. You can dig." She nods at her plate. He goes on. "Katie's all right; she's just bent out of shape about being a chick sometimes. She's not comfortable in her femininity. And then *you* walk in with that fine frame of yours . . . *all* girl."

Chewing, Celia grins. He crows with delight. "You kill me, baby. I'm keepin' you!"

"So he wants to go to San Francisco! He says it's a sacred scene and everybody's diggin' it!"

In Johnny Rosselli's apartment, Annie watches Celia's rapturous face. "A sacred scene? Horny Kevin, weasel-faced Ernie and dopey Dinah?"

"Don't be like that. I thought they were cool."

"Do you think Kevin actually believes he's coloured? I mean, does he look at those white people claiming to be his parents and scream in horror or does he figure he's adopted?"

"Lots of guys talk like him. Frank and Dean talk like him."

Annie grunts. "I thought Katie's quotes were better . . ."

"*Katie!* Katie said you had silicone boobs!"

"Well, you can hardly blame her for wondering. All is not gold that glitters and all is not tit that titters. All I'm saying is Katie had his number."

"She's just jealous. I want to do the Poetry Follies with Kevin."

"What are you going to do for money? Rhyme all over someone?"

"I'm selling my car."

"Your car? So you can run off with that skinny little turd?" Annie shakes her head. "Maybe it's me who's jealous. Might be the last I see of you."

"You mean you won't be my friend anymore if I go with him?"

"What if I say no? Don't answer that. Of course I'll be your damn friend. I just mean—I'll miss you. Outlaws don't phone home very often."

Leonard called. "What're you doing?"

"Right now . . . I am flipping through *On the Road* and one of my mother's letters," I said, still on my bed, fenced in by books. "This dork she went out with was a Kerouac freak. And I'm looking through the *Women's Book of Quotations.*"

"You still writing about your mum?"

"I used to use this stuff to fight with her and now I'm using it to . . ."

"Build a shrine," he said. "Eunice just called. She asked me for dinner and I said I had plans with you and she said to bring you along."

"You scared of her now?"

"No. Can you come or not?"

Frank's key turned in the lock. "No, I just got in and I've hardly seen Frank. We're going to hang out." My glance shot around the blankets and I shoved the letters back into the shoebox and stuffed it under the bed. I pushed the notebook under my pillow. Frank walked past the door and waved on his way to the bathroom. Shoving the phone between my ear and shoulder, I tossed books into my tote bag. "Can I give you a call tomorrow?"

As I hung up, Frank came in, set a stiff shopping bag on the floor and sat down at the foot of the bed. He picked up *On the Road* still lying in the sheets. "This book's awesome," he said. I said the same thing to my mother when I was twenty, though, at the time, I actually thought it was a juvenile piece of crap. The female characters bored me. They had no teeth.

"Capote said Kerouac doesn't write, he types," I said.

Frank tossed the book back on the bed. "What the hell is that supposed to mean?"

"I read that Capote and Jackie Kennedy hung out a lot in the sixties. He had an apartment in the same building as Bobby Kennedy in New York."

Frank blinked at me. He reached for the bag. "Look what I bought for my girl," he said, grinning. First he pulled out a black-and-turquoise feathered cat mask.

"Wow," I said, taking it. Little jewels crested the eye holes. The feathers were a mix of long loose downy bits and stiff quills. I held it up to my eyes.

"Nice. It's good with your new hair." He squinted. "Why did you do that anyway?"

"It's just hair," I said, dropping the mask away. "It was all dry and dead. And I just wanted—" I shook my head "—to be . . ."

"It's okay," Frank said reassuringly as he patted my thigh. "You could be like a slutty librarian now."

I looked at the next gift he took from the bag: a purple vibrating dildo. Next a pink rabbit toy with a bunny face on the shaft and vibrating ears at the base. Last what appeared to be a strap-on rubber dick. "What's this?" I asked, picking up the pleather harness.

"Lotta guys really dig a girl in a strap-on," he explained. "They like watching her touch it and they like watching her use it on another girl." I gripped the rubber shaft of the dick portion. "See," he said, "I'm getting off right now." He picked up the feathered mask from my lap and fastened it to my face as he kissed me. "Oh hang on, let's do this right," he said, got up and lit the candle on the bookshelf. He touched the dusty helmet he'd bought me again.

"Thinking about getting a new bike?" I lay back and scissored my legs like a cricket. He cradled me a moment, then picked me up and turned me so my head was at the top of the bed. "What are you doing?" I giggled.

"I want to see your pussy lit by candlelight."

We spent the rest of the afternoon and evening in bed. Frank had brought a bottle of wine as well as some cheese and baguette with him and he brought it all in on a cutting board for us between rounds of lovemaking. He'd never been so attentive, so adoring and curious about every angle of me. Not since we were first dating, and maybe not even then. My apathy disappeared with a vengeance and I realized it was depression that had taken me so far away.

As we rested and reclined, drinking Shiraz and giggling like fiends, Frank pulled the notebook out from under my pillow. "What's this?"

I snatched it back. "Nothing."

"Baby's got a *secret*," he sang. "Come on." He held out his hand in a gimme.

"It's, you know, mother-daughter depression-shit. See?" I fanned the pages of handwriting.

"Huh," he said, losing interest. "Well, I guess it's cathartic. I was worried when I first saw you today but you seem way better, actually."

"I'm sorry I didn't call when I got back. I—"

"It's okay," he cut me off. "I'll probably totally lose it when my mum and dad go. But we're good now, right? That's what's important." He reached for the second bottle of wine and the corkscrew. "Hey, does the wireless card for your laptop work in here?"

"God, you are merciless. You're just dying for me to—"

"I just want to show you how this one girl treats these guys. She reminds me of you. Every time a guy types some demand in the free-flirt space, she *slams* him. She's like, *Look, buddy, this is my time and I do what I want. Shut your mouth and be a good slave.*" He filled up my glass.

"Really?"

"You *like* that idea!" He put down the bottle and took off at a run for my laptop.

By midnight, I was somewhat smashed and Frank had the computer set up on an end table at the foot of the bed. Webcam bulging up off the top of the screen, an auxiliary keyboard sat in my G-stringed lap as Frank giggled over the streams of instant messages from the twenty or thirty men who had logged on to chat with me. They asked to see my feet, my ass, my tits, my shoulder blades. Someone named Squirrelly asked if I'd draw a heart on my belly for him in lipstick. When we're in private, I'll do anything for you, I typed, laughing. My mother's San Francisco letters flitted through my head. Her big broad grin. *"You want more, you little devils? Whatchu wanna? Uh? You wanna, you wanna 'Come On-A My House'?"* I saw her throw up her arms, her breasts bare, the crowd cheering and the cops blowing whistles . . . *I keep thinking I should feel embarrassed because I was in the paper practically naked but I feel sort of excited.*

GuySmiley said I looked too nice to be in a place like this, that I looked smart and corn fed. Frank cackled and made rude remarks. "At least he didn't say you looked cornholed." I told him to bugger off. GuySmiley said I was an angel. "Oh shit!" Frank laughed. "Smiley wants to go private. He wants to buy ten minutes."

"How much is that?"

"59.99 U.S.! Plus tax. Wanna?"

GuySmiley seemed like a decent way to start. Frank tapped some keys and a still shot of me replaced the moving picture with the note *This model is currently in a private show.* Now it was just GuySmiley instant messaging. "Lucinda, Lucy Lucia," he typed.

My name had been Dori but now as a brunette, I was Lucinda. "Hi Guy. How R U?"

"Did you know that Lucia is the saint of light?" he typed.

"No. How lovely."

"U are lovely. Wish I could see ur eyes. Will u take off the feathers?"

"I'm a secret. Would you like me to take off my bra?" I could see my own giddy face on the screen moving in jerking pixilation, turquoise feathers dancing across my forehead, my black bra and undies under a sheer black blouse. Frank's face split with joy.

"Not yet. I just wanted to talk without others," GuySmiley said.

"That's sweet," I typed. "Are you married?"

Frank shook his head and slashed his fingers at his throat. I ignored him.

"My wife died 2 years ago. U look like her."

I gave an oops face to Frank.

"Didn't mean to be a downer," Guy typed. "U have a pretty mouth." And it went on like that for ten minutes. I felt bad for Guy. He told me sometimes he fantasized that a woman's fingers caressed his face until he fell asleep.

Once his time was up, we went back into the free-for-all chat room. The instant messagers asked if I had toys. I wasn't ready for that yet. I said I didn't have any tonight. Take off your panties and touch yourself, one asked. A few minutes later, Hardboy bought five minutes. He typed what you'd expect: Show me tits, Lets see ur ass, Do U like anal?

Then back in the public forum. The instant messages continued. Do U have high heels? Will U dance for me? I want U so bad. U are an angel from heaven. Back and forth, I went from one-on-one in private to trading messages with fifteen or twenty at a time.

It seemed ridiculous that this, dancing and jumping up and down on my bed naked, showing strangers my feet, telling them to get down on their knees and worship me, was worth three hundred bucks an hour. I was comfy in my own bed, doing only what I wanted and they adored me. Who wouldn't feel excited?

While Frank slept, I couldn't. It was three in the morning and my adrenaline rushed. I had made close to four hundred U.S. and Rosemary Clooney was belting it out through my frontal lobe, *Come on-a my house, my house, I'm gonna give you candy . . .* I sat in the living room with the shoebox and looked at *Time* magazine, the photograph of all those kids outside Harry's Drink. My mother kissing off the world as young hotheads lay face down on police cruisers, hands cuffed behind them. "Youth Culture—Oxymoron or Brave New World?" the caption read. I tried to imagine what her show would've looked like. Did she just impersonate one singer per show or was it a medley? I imagined her shopping, choosing costumes and wigs that could easily peel off and reveal another singer underneath. Julie London's long red tresses could come off to reveal Rosemary Clooney's blonde, which could come off to reveal my mother's own hair styled like Peggy Lee's. And what were her buddies doing? The jig was up with Judy Campbell and John Kennedy. Hoover tracked mob ties and rattled his sabre with a vengeance. He told Bobby who told Lawford who told Sinatra that there'd be no more buddy-buddy. Sinatra no longer spoke to Lawford. Kennedy didn't speak to Sinatra or Giancana or Judy. Bobby had mobsters deported. And poor old messpot Marilyn staggered from guy to guy until she tripped and drowned in a puddle of booze and pills. In the end, Joe DiMaggio, her ex, arranged the funeral and the Kennedys weren't invited. I pictured DiMaggio sitting at the back of a bus, her coffin across his lap and all the Kennedys turning around wanting to take the lid off.

After San Francisco, Celia's celebrity grows. She weaves together her chanteuse impersonations with striptease in a way that's never been done. There is cachet to seeing a Celia Dare show. To be ignorant of Celia's buzz lands you face first in Squaresville.

She gets mentioned in Winchell's column; Louella Parsons calls her a one-gal phenomenon. Even old Hedda Hopper slides her in, referring to Celia as a strange little songbird who can't wait to moult before your eyes.

Flowers come to her backstage, jewelry, invitations to dinner, to Paris, to marry. Restaurateurs invite her to dine in exchange for an autographed picture. She opens for stars at the El Morocco, the Eden Roc, Latin Casinos in Jersey, Camden and Philadelphia.

Celia and Annie have moved into a roomier apartment in the Village. There's a bedroom for each of them and a third for their clothes. They buy a colour television too, though most everything is still black and white.

They sit on the sofa one afternoon in front of *As the World Turns*. Celia frowns at the writing tablet on her knees. She had just got back from her first stint as a headliner at the Latin Casino in Miami and proved she could pack a house. Now she wants to build her own baby: a event on Broadway at the Paramount Theatre. If she bills it as a charity event, she could probably get half the celebrities she knows in on it. She could call it *Celia Dare and Friends: A Return to Vaudeville*. She just needs a backer.

"Do you think it's too much me asking him to finance this?"

"Johnny?" Annie sticks a spoonful of yogurt into her mouth. "Nothing's too much for Don Giovanni."

"*Don Giovanni*," Celia snorts. "Why doesn't he call back then? Do you think he's asking Frank?" Celia's idea for the Paramount show is to have herself and a couple others as regulars with a different major star each night of the week's run. They can sing a song or tell a few jokes, whatever they feel like. The audience would never know who might show—just the way they billed the Summit in Las Vegas: *Starlight starbright, which star will shine tonight?*

"Asking Frank what? If he'll show? He'll show. Christ, I hate yogurt." Annie slaps the container down on the coffee table. "Make me do sit-ups today, okay? Ah forget it, I'll just smoke." She reaches for her pack.

"Then why doesn't he phone back? Sammy said he'd do it. They're shooting a funeral scene today for *Robin and the Seven Hoods*. I've never been to a funeral. You?"

"*No.*" Annie's eyes are on the television. "Jesus."

Celia looks to the screen. *As the World Turns* had been obliterated with a slide that reads *CBS News Bulletin*. Walter Cronkite's voice breaks through. "*In Dallas, Texas, three shots were fired at President Kennedy's motorcade in downtown Dallas. The first reports say that President Kennedy has been seriously wounded by this shooting.*"

By dinnertime, Celia and Annie are still in their nightclothes glued to the TV, switching channels every so often and chain-smoking as news anchors refer to Lyndon Johnson as "President Johnson," correcting themselves if they err. News anchors announce the arrest of Lee Harvey Oswald, suspected communist sympathizer, in a Dallas movie theatre.

Oswald's picture flashes. "How do they know he's a communist?" Celia asks.

Across the room Jacqueline Kennedy moves like a pink ghost before the cameras. "For godsake," Annie complains. "Why doesn't she change that suit . . . bits of him all over her."

Three days later, the country is still veiled in tears. As the television screen fills with the solemn procession of the president's casket from the White House to the Capitol rotunda, Annie asks, "Do you mind if I turn this? I need a break." Flipping the channels, each network covers the casket but one. She stops. An anchorman's voice announces the transfer of Oswald to the Dallas County Jail.

"He's been shot!" shouts a reporter over the scene. "Lee Oswald has been shot! There is absolute panic. Pandemonium has broken out!"

Celia slaps her hands over her mouth. On the floor in front of the television, Annie falls back on her butt. The camera shows the assassin of the assassin.

"Jesus Christ. I know him," Annie gasps. "I mean, I don't *know* him but I know he owns some dump in Dallas."

"What do you mean?"

"Maybe I'm wrong. I don't know."

In the days that follow, the press reports that Jack Ruby, a Dallas strip-club owner, killed Oswald out of love for his country and a deep pity for the president's widow.

Fifteen

~

I DREAMT I WAS ON A STAGE DANCING WITH BOBBY KENNEDY. My mother and Eunice and Len were in the corner playing strip poker. Bobby kept nudging me toward the camera. There was a camera on the dresser in the wings. Suddenly the dresser was huge and my mother was tap dancing on top with Gene Kelly, her thumbs in her slip straps. I woke up at noon and Frank was gone. I had a vague memory of him saying he had to go over to Brian's to learn how to do something or other. I didn't care, I wanted to kiss Bobby. In my dream, I wanted to kiss him because he had come back for one performance only.

I staggered into the kitchen and put coffee on, visions of my mother and Eunice Chelsey playing strip poker dancing through my head. I had a terrible longing for my mother to have danced with her heroes. Most of those nightclubbers did charity events. Sammy Davis Jr. did them right and left. If *Celia Dare and Friends* was for charity, they'd have come out. If Johnny sponsored it. They did what they were told where mobsters were concerned.

In the spring of '64, Celia's show opens with a mini-summit of Frank, Dean and Sammy, middles with Carol Channing and ends with Cyd Charisse and Gene Kelly. She dances a softshoe with Kelly as the two of them sing "The Doodlin' Song." Seated in the front row closing night is Gene's friend Bobby.

After a week straight of sellout shows and rave reviews, Celia is having drinks with her benefactor. "Peter Lawford brought Bobby Kennedy backstage afterward. He had such a soft voice. I was expecting this ruthless bastard the way people talk but he was so shy."

"Kennedy?" Johnny's pale eyes slice across the table. "Those guys are all pigs."

"They say you get a lot of action yourself, Don Giovanni."

"*Don Giovanni.* If it weren't for that prick-mick persecuting Italians, my name would never have even been in that publication. Italians are who Bobby-Civil Rights-Kennedy targets. Look what that bastard's doing to Hoffa—wiretapping his lawyers, bugging the jury—one long breach of civil liberties!" Polishing off his vodka, he rattles the ice and points a finger. "You stay away from Bobby Kennedy."

"I could swear you're jealous."

Shooting air out his nose he raises a finger to the waiter, who scurries off. "I don't want you getting loused up by that little shit. Look what he did to Marilyn. Him and the brother both. Treated her like a whore."

"I thought that it was only Jack."

Johnny waves her off.

"He came backstage—I'm not having his *baby* for godsake!"

"Don't even joke. Makes me sick. That man will never touch you."

She's a bit flabbergasted. "It's Lawford that hits on me, not Bobby."

"Lawford's just covering for queer."

A few weeks later Celia and Annie are on a double date at Le Club. Celia's escort is a high-rent criminal lawyer, Annie's a shifty-eyed character reminiscent of Micky D from the old 92. Another guy who makes his living off vending machines.

"Look at the bastard," the lawyer gripes. "Kills me. They make like clean-living Catholics going to church, playing touch football, meanwhile they're chasing every skirt in the country and now you got this one banging his dead brother's widow."

On the dance floor, Bobby and Jacqueline Kennedy shake it up. The two had come with Truman Capote, who'd gone off and left the couple to themselves.

Celia watches them cling to one another, hypnotized. Her brief conversation with Kennedy backstage still echoes. "Mr. Attorney General," she said. "Or should I call you Mr. Kennedy?"

"Just call me sonuvabitch, that's what everyone else calls me," he jokes, his voice thin and shy, his eyes lined and sad.

The self-deprecating boy in him has roamed in her mind ever since. She watches him with Jackie and she wants to hug her too. "They're just looking after each other," Celia declares.

The lawyer guffaws. The vending-machine owner joins in and pulls Annie closer, saying "This girlfriend of yours, she kills me."

Annie smiles wanly.

Leaning across to Celia, the vending guy corrects her. "He's getting his rocks off is what he's doing. This guy is capable of the kind of bullshit a girl like you shouldn't know from, so, maybe it's good you don't. But lemme tell you, there's a lotta guys just waiting to piss all over this fuck." His thumb stabs toward Bobby.

"*Eh!* Ladies present," the lawyer reminds him.

"Excuse me," he says. "I get riled."

"I'm going to go powder my nose," Celia announces. Annie joins her.

In the ladies', Celia leans against the counter. "Can't believe I let you talk me into this."

Annie touches up her lipstick. "You said you were sick of married men hitting on you. These guys are single."

"Wonder why. Christ. Every guy who wants to date me is either married or a low-life. And only the creeps want to go out in public with me."

Annie takes out her eyeliner. "Yup, even when they're single—the so-called legit boys only want to see you in private. In public they trot out these Chanel-suited ice queens like Jacqueline *Bouvier.*"

"What's the difference between me and Annette Funicello, is what I want to know. She cavorts around some beach movie in a bikini and sings dimwit pop music and nobody treats her like she's anathema."

"*Anathema.* There's a twenty-five-center."

The outside door to the restroom opens and closes.

Celia comes face to face with the reflection of Jacqueline Bouvier Kennedy just as Annie says, "Everybody's anathema to somebody, I 'spose."

The widow's eyes have the same haunted quality as her escort's. She looks in the mirror at Celia. "That's a fair assessment."

Annie steps into a stall.

"Mrs. Kennedy, I'm Celia Dare," she stammers. About to extend her hand, she stops and washes them. The attendant hands her a towel. "I'd like to offer my condolences and—I guess there are no words. I had the pleasure of being introduced to Bobby—Robert Kennedy—not long ago and I'm so glad you have each other right now."

The bathroom is silent. The attendant waits for more wet hands. A flush from Annie's stall and her door opens.

Mrs. Kennedy's cool face forms a smile. "Thank you, Miss Dare. Bobby mentioned your show. He said you were wonderfully energetic."

Annie heads for another sink to rinse her hands.

"Oh . . . Thank you." Celia tells her.

"Pleasure to meet you, Miss Dare."

"And you," Celia says as Jackie heads into a stall.

Outside the washroom Annie bats her eyes at Celia. "Oh and by the by, Jackie, how *is* your brother-in-law in the sack?"

Still in my robe, I poured myself a bowl of cereal and tossed the video that showcased memories of 1964 and '65 into the VCR. Lyndon Johnson wins another term as president and tells the country he intends to save the South Vietnamese from communists; a flashback shows JFK's funeral and Jackie addressing the nation in a breathy childish voice not so dissimilar from Marilyn Monroe's; Mohammed Ali still calling himself Cassius Clay; the Beatles with their so-called long hair in front of mobs of screaming, crying girls; the rush to get to the moon for a gawk at a gravel pit; six days of rioting in Watts; Miss America grinning pure and wide and white; go-go boots, miniskirts, polka dots galore.

Frank showed up in the middle of it. "Been working?" he asked.

"Isn't it weird to think of the Stones on the same top-ten list as Petula Clark," I commented. He frowned at the fires onscreen now, police turning their hoses on blacks in the street.

"Booking lots of private dances?" He was fidgety and a little overexcited as seemed to be his general state since he got our jerkflirt.com connection.

I turned the tape off. "I haven't even looked at it."

He sat down at my desk and went directly into the site. I sighed and wandered over, peered over his shoulder. The home page asked if he was interested in flirting with live guys, live girls or live she-males. "I didn't know they had guys," I said and reached over his shoulder to click on the name *Cazzius*. A young guy with a tribal armband tattooed around his slim bicep appeared. He looked about eighteen. He had thick blonde hair and a stoned smile as he lolled on his side, his hand in his underpants. Names like BigDick and Sugarman asked if he was bi or gay. He tapped at the keyboard on the bed beside him: Bi. "Next time I buy a lotto ticket, I'll have you in mind," BigDick said. Cazzius typed a smile. They asked how old he was. Twenty-one. Where was he from? Halifax. They asked if he read and what he was reading. *"Zen and the Art of Motorcycle Maintenance."* Then he lay back and rubbed his black bikini front again.

"You should touch yourself more," Frank said to me. I reached over and clicked on another model. A bored angry-faced guy named Diamond. Each one looked more bored than the last. Frank clicked back over to the girls. I recalled the weather-girl wannabe saying how important it was for a woman to look friendly and approachable.

"Have you noticed there's no black people on this site?" I asked.

"They're under *Exotics*." He clicked on Sabrina and suddenly onscreen, there was Sienna, the girl with the question-marked repartee from Nevermind. Her false eyelashes batted back at us. Up on her knees, she stretched her rubbery young body and showed off a bejewelled belly button above a pink lace G-string. She ran her hands up and down her thighs before she sat back down and grinned. "Watch her go, babe," Frank said and went to the kitchen. "She's been making about three grand U.S. a week doing this stuff and then another fifteen hundred from this other site where guys can download videos of her fucking Brian or whoever." I heard a cork pop and Frank poured wine. He brought glasses back to the desk and both of us watched Sienna. Lojo typed: "U so hot, I lick u clean." Sienna typed, " :) "

"Can u flash u pussy 4 me?" Lojo asked. "Only in pvt," Sienna answered and licked her finger as she gazed doe-eyed and smiling.

Frank maneuvered me into the desk chair. "She was asking about you when I was over there. She thinks you are the hottest thing she's ever seen. She does, Viv, she wants you like you wouldn't believe. Even more when I told her you did your hair dark. She said, *Oo, we'd be like a twin duo?*" Frank imitated her light questioning voice. He put the glass of wine in my hand.

"What time is it anyway?"

"Cocktail hour." Pushing his face into my neck, he ran his tongue up my throat. "God, it turns me on to think of you fucking her with that strap-on." He picked me up and carried me into the bedroom, stopping only long enough to light the candle on the bookshelf again.

The news is unbearable. "Today in the Watts neighbourhood of Los Angeles, a riot erupted when a Negro man was arrested by a white police officer for reckless driving." The cameras pan over smashed windows and flames as looters rush from supermarkets and appliance stores. A woman cries on the sidewalk as children cling to her thighs.

For six days and a hundred and fifty blocks, Watts burns in Celia's living room. She hugs her knees remembering stories about Vegas hotel managers who drained swimming pools when a Sammy Davis or a Dorothy Dandridge dared to break the water's surface. She's getting depressed again. What's the point of having a microphone if you're never going to yell something big enough to rearrange a redneck's brain? There's Freedom Fighters and then there's me.

When Annie comes home that night, she hears Celia in the kitchen singing, "Another bride, another groom—"

"Hello, kidlet!" No response but repetition, a little deeper, a little more constricted. Annie hangs up her coat and heads past Dinah Washington spinning on the record player.

Cigarette in hand, Celia looks up from the table with a bluesy, frowsy, sleepy-eyed wink. "Hey baby, how's your bird?"

"Plucked, chicky, how 'bout yours?" Annie opens the fridge.

The song ends and Dinah starts into *Where is my daddy, with his big long slidin' thing . . .* Celia duets it with feeling. Turning in the light of the fridge, Annie looks at her. "You're not."

On her feet, Celia moves languid across the kitchen floor as though getting the walk might get her the voice. "I just have to get the smoky throat right. I can't get that thing, that smoky raspy—like how a cat would sing." Strolling back to the table, she grabs her wine and takes a slug before she drags off her smoke. "If I smoke a lot my voice gets a little more rasp." She steps closer to Annie and sings, "Where is my daddy with that big long slidin' thing . . . ?"

"Sharesies if you find him?" Annie snatches her cigarette, takes a drag and shoves the refrigerator closed with her rump.

Pouring a glass of last night's champagne, Annie grabs buns and peanut butter out of the cupboard and sits at the table. A sip from her glass, she gives a flat-champagne grimace before speaking. "I don't know how to tell you, sugar, but you ain't black and that might be the intangible quality you're looking for. Washington's voice is lower too."

Celia lights another cigarette. "Julie London's voice is this low. So's Peggy's."

"Even if you get her voice—reach me a knife while you're up?—no matter how long you lie in the sun, you ain't gonna get her skin."

"Walnut-shell juice! You can tint your skin with it," Celia announces, her voice giddy as she hands Annie a butter knife. "Make me one too."

"You're kidding, yes?" Annie asks, incredulous. "*Why* do you want to do a Negro act?"

In the dining room Celia changes the record. "Maybe I should start with Ella. She sounds more like a white girl anyway and then I could ease into Dinah," she says and waltzes back into the kitchen to "Our Love Is Here To Stay."

"How hard you been hittin' the sauce? You *cannot* do a minstrel show!"

Celia continues to dance slowly around the kitchen, smoking, eyes at half-mast trying to soak up the vibe. "It's a *tribute*. My contribution to the civil rights movement."

Annie slathers peanut butter on her bun. "You're smashed."

"I did Carmen Miranda. I even learned some Por-tu-guese," she says Hispanically.

"Maybe by morning, I won't need to explain how asinine this is."

"That's why the lady is a tramp," Celia trills, hitting Ella's line pitch-perfect.

Annie pushes the corners of her mouth down as she chews, with a *not-bad* nod.

In the end, Annie lets herself get juiced on Celia's excitement. She hauls out whatever might be useful, gives her a lead on a makeup artist who knows her way around henna and walnut-shell juice. "I used to date this jazz musician and I remember him saying that coloured singers tend to come in after the beat. White singers are more on the beat or even ahead of it. He liked the way the coloured girls did it cuz it sounded cooler and more confident."

Celia sucks up every tidbit she can get her ears on. "What if I do a singer from each decade. I could talk about each one's struggle, you know? I've gotta bring up more through my nose with Billie. She'd be good to start with: parents abandoned her, worked in a brothel, recorded all this stuff with Benny Goodman and never saw one dime in royalties. And the heroin. I could end the set with her hauled off to jail and take off the white gardenias, slip out of that dress and then have somethin' a little more Dinah underneath."

"And you gotta have chorus boys," Annie adds, slipping into Mae West mode. "Prop players. We'll dress them in black."

"Yeah!" Celia squeals, beside herself with anticipation. "They'll be the bulls who arrest me, club owners and husbands, and drug dealers."

"And at the end," Annie says, "They'll pick up your naked little body and hold you up to the heavens! You still need a six-ties chick. How do you feel about Etta James?"

"I saw her at the Jumpin' Joy in San Fran."

"Well, then you know you're half her weight. But, who cares, it's the spirit you want. And on a practical level, if you do Etta last, you could have your own hair. She's got the same plat-inum as yours."

Opening night found the Copacabana filled to capacity. Word of mouth had spread about the show's rehearsals and some thought this would be the show that would make Celia Dare a household name. She had special invitations sent out to Mr. and Mrs. Robert Kennedy along with Jacqueline Bouvier Kennedy and Peter and Patricia Lawford, Frank and Mia, Dean and Jeannie Martin, Sammy and May, Cyd Charisse and Tony Martin. Cyd and Tony couldn't make it; Dean had a show in Vegas; Sammy and Peter were in London.

Annie and Johnny are down front. Frank's daughter, Nancy, shows; Walter Winchell comes. Somebody says that Annette

Funicello is there with Frankie Avalon. Members of the press, black and white, are scattered throughout. Two of the Supremes are in attendance. They say Etta James might show. Bobby Kennedy and Gene Kelly sit ringside.

Backstage, Celia paces through the opening act, biting at her nails, tugging at her wig.

Once she hits the stage though, she is *on*. Every note, every step, every *every*, comes off smooth as the orchestra that accompanies. Celia doesn't get a sense of the audience until, clothed in nothing but hot pants, go-go boots and pasties, her tinted body is hoisted into the air.

When the lights go down there's an odd pause until the hands of Senator Kennedy slap together, a big-toothed grin on his face. He is joined quickly by Kelly and the rest of the audience. There's an anxiousness in the room, the uncertainty between the lightning and the thunderclap.

Celia sends a couple chorus boys out to mingle and listen. The only sure thing is that members of the Negro press have all left. One of the Supremes was overheard saying it was *interesting*. Johnny and Annie tell anyone in earshot that Celia is a genius.

Eventually she dresses and joins the room. Annie barely gets a hug out of Celia before Johnny steals her away to the dance floor. Pulling her to him, he says, "Well, my darling, you were magnificent. You've become an incredible performer."

"Thank you." She looks past his shoulder to the other couples dancing. "It's not over yet. People decide what to think when they read the papers."

"Who gives a christ what those cage liners say." He twirls her deeper into the crowd. "Teddy would've been proud. I half expected him to bust out just to see opening night."

"What do you think the coloured press will say?"

"I see your nigger-loving senator pal is here."

She looks over her shoulder. "He's a friend of Gene's. I hardly know the man."

"Sam's rotting in Cook County because of that sonuvabitch."

"Please. Not tonight."

"I'm just saying it's not right. After everything Sam did for—"

"Excuse me, may I cut in." Kelly smiles off Rosselli's shoulder.

Celia grins a thousand watts.

Johnny does his best imitation of gracious and moves off, only to be grabbed by Annie and whisked back onto the floor. "When you gonna learn to let a fella lead?"

Celia looks into Kelly's smiling face. "I'm so pleased you made it tonight."

"It was the young senator from New York who was most insistent. I jumped at the chance, of course, because I like being seen with you. The last time we danced, my name ended up in every rag in New York."

"Oh sure." She gives him a swat. "Talked to Miss Charisse lately?"

"You're not even going to bite on that senator remark?"

"Fine. Aren't the former president's wife and the married Bobby keeping company?"

Kelly sighs in her ear. "Bobby always took care of her when Jack was busy. So it fell to him when Jack passed. He's really rather fascinated by you. He thinks you're—how did he put it?—*a brave and cerebral performer.*"

"Does he now?"

"Come join us for a drink." Kelly dances her in sweeping turns to the table he and Kennedy share. Bobby rises. Kelly steps to the side and, keeping hold of her hand, he bows, presenting her. "Senator Robert Kennedy . . . Miss Celia Dare."

Bobby stands uncertainly, arms hovering at his sides. She reaches out and he envelops her hand in his. "Thank you for the invitation Miss, uh, Miss Dare. It was, uh, it was an extraordinary production."

Her second introduction to the senator and much like the first, she is struck with how slight his frame is, his nervous stutter. Nothing like his brother.

"Might I be so bold as to ask you to dance?"

On the floor, he calms. "Do you like Benny Goodman? I'm

terribly fond of Goodman. Especially the songs Peggy Lee sang with him."

She sings, "Why don't you do right," into his ear.

"Oh my goodness," he chuckles. "I was raised a gentleman but if you keep that up . . ."

Over Bobby's shoulder, she catches sight of Johnny back at the table. His head is tilted to Annie's prattle but his eyes shoot directly into hers. She bares her teeth playfully and flicks her hand as though he were a bug. Setting his jaw, he heads for the door. Celia's first impulse is to dash after him but it's all so ridiculous.

"Sorry, what was that?" she asks.

"How long will your show run?"

"We'll see what the critics think."

He moves his mouth to her ear. "'Seek roses in December, ice in June; Hope constancy in wind, or corn in chaff; believe a woman or an epitaph, Or any other thing that's false, before you trust in critics.'"

Turning her head, she almost meets his mouth and they both avert their gaze. "I take umbrage with the woman part."

"Byron."

Celia puffs on a cigarette, studying a pile of dishevelled papers. "Nothing in the regular press. What do you think it means?"

Annie pours them another cup of coffee. "Except Winchell. Winchell liked it."

"Read that thing in the *Advocate* or whatever it's called again, the bit about savages."

Annie riffles until she finds the review. "*As American Negroes, are we meant to feel gratitude that a member of the whiter-than-white community has seen fit to romanticize the darkest periods in the lives of our most talented jazz artists? That a mediocre talent, from whom no one would hear a peep were she not undressing, feels the need to elucidate to the world how susceptible Negroes are to the seduction of narcotics is more evidence of the clearly racist agenda in New York's theaters and nightclubs . . .*" She lights another cigarette. "The blacks are pissed that you're white and the whites are too chickenshit to say a word."

The doorbell rings. "Are we home?"

"What the hell," Celia addresses her slippers. "Perhaps it's a singing Molotov cocktail."

Annie scampers to the door and returns carrying a long white box. "For Miss Dare," she announces, setting it in front of her.

Celia runs her eyes over the length before she takes the lid off. A bundle of lush pink roses. Plucking the card, she reads, "'They have tried their talents at one or at the other and have failed; therefore they turn critics. Samuel Taylor Coleridge.'"

"Roses from a dead guy," Annie clucks. "How romantic."

Celia looks up quizzically. "Johnny?"

"Didn't look like he'd be sending roses any time soon last night. And poetry? I doubt it."

She reaches for the phone and calls her agent. "Hey, Marty . . . Just sitting here looking at these gorgeous roses . . . No, I thought maybe you . . . Yeah, I saw." She shoves at the newspapers. "But Marty, the point was a tribute and if the Negro community . . . I'm just . . . okay. Bye."

Phone down, she looks at Annie and recites: "'Controversy can lay a golden egg. You threw down the gauntlet, now go after their goat.'"

"What the hell's that mean?"

Celia shrugs. "I pay him 10 percent. I'm sure it means something."

That evening, the Copacabana is packed again, loaded with mainstream journalists. Two mentions come out the following day. The *New York Post*'s story is more about diatribes found in the Negro press than Celia's show. Supposedly they had called for comment but were unable to reach Miss Dare. The closest thing to an actual critique is the *New York Times* remark that the show is more likely to give one pause for thought than a desire to dance.

As the engagement goes on, the attending crowd evolves: academics both black and white come to observe her as a phenomenon. Anxious students approach her for the school paper.

"I've researched you and your roots," an earnest young woman tells her. "People forget that you began as an activist—baring your body as a way of laying the naked truth out for the world."

Small-theatre actors try to engage her in an examination of the show's artistic significance. "Doesn't intent override reaction?" asks one hungry-faced young man, his eyes ferreting into Celia's, his hair cut in such a way that he could be mistaken for Ringo Starr's brother. "I'm doing my thesis on art, society and community reaction. What *is* rock and roll? Does the alienation of some necessarily mean the illumination of others? I mean, when you examine the lyrics to 'Help!'—"

"Honey, can I get a word." The Copa's manager puts out his hand for Celia.

"Excuse me," she tells the student. "Good luck. I'm sure it will be fascinating."

Trotting alongside him, she moans, "How do they even afford to get in here?"

"You're telling me." He leads her to a quiet table. "Listen, kid, I love the hell out of ya but packed house or no, this show's bombing."

"Excuse me?"

"Where the bar's concerned, I mean. It's killin' us. Your agent called about doing a hold-over on account of the crowds but, sonuvabitch, these little bastards don't drink. They scribble in their notepads and say, *The thigh bone's connected to the knee bone. How do I get me an A and screw this singer-broad without spending any dough?*"

"Screw me? I thought they wanted to stick me in a jar next to the dead babies."

"You're a good girl, Celia, you do a real nice show. But for me, an up-type show is better, no drug overdoses. No politics." He curls his lip at the crowd. "Look at the little fuckers . . . ordering water and coffee."

1966: Timothy Leary; *Tune in, turn on, drop out*; Martin Luther King; Ku Klux Klan; one-man rocket launcher; space race;

happenings are what's happening; theater of the absurd; LBJ and Ladybird; Malcolm X; burn your draft card; Watts; *burn baby burn*; the Warren report; Twiggy; Chargex; topless; bottomless; Bob Dylan; psychedelia; communists; Stokely Carmichael; napalm; Dupont; Victor Charlie; *One-two-three what are we fighting for?*; Beatles; Billy Graham; more popular than Jesus Christ; *Are you like that: living in a vacuum, no purpose, no reason, no challenge, just existing?*

The sun was up when Frank woke me. I was on the couch, someone's version of Bobby Kennedy splayed across my chest. The television was still on. The documentary had ended and the picture was in fuzzy limbo. I could make out a news broadcast. President Bush explained that the U.S. involvement in Iraq was as a liberator not a conqueror; they were going to win hearts and minds and bring democracy to the people.

"What are you doing?" Frank looked from me to the TV. "Didn't you come to bed?"

I couldn't remember. I'd been drunk the last six nights running. We were raking in the cash. Frank said I was a brilliant enticer, a master manipulator. More popular than Jesus Christ.

"I don't like it when I wake up and you're not there," he pouted.

Colour and sight and sound squiggled through my head. My dreams were psychedelic. "Five-six-seven, open up the pearly gates," rang loud against the back of my skull while Billy Graham drawled from a London stage at my forehead: "Are you living in a vacuum, no purpose, no challenge, just existing?" No reason, no vacuum, just challenge, flopsy, mopsy and cottontail. I felt nauseous.

"I need a piece of toast." I swung my feet down on the rug. "How do I get my money for this stuff I'm doing?"

"What do you mean *my* money, Kemosabe?" He grinned. "I showed you our account last night, remember. We've already cleared almost three grand American."

Are you living in a challenge: all vacuum, all pearly, all sixes and sevens?

~

"You look like shit," Leonard said to my back from his couch. I was in his kitchen.

"Ah pipe down, y'big flirt," I said.

"Seriously, Viv. It's one in the afternoon for chrissake, what're you pouring wine for? And you're into this shit you're into and you *look* it. I thought you cut your hair and went back to your natural colour because you wanted to . . . and you're just . . ."

"When the hell did you start casting the first stone, pally?" I sat down on the couch and handed a full glass to him.

He shook his head a bit maniacally, I thought, as he said, "You're fucked. I'm fucked. It's all fucked."

"It's a glass of *wine*. Relax. I did some X last night and I just need to mellow out." I exhaled slowly in the hope it might entice him to do the same. "So. Tell me what happened."

His look of incredulity dissolved as he considered his own problems. His head shook again with something in the neighbourhood of bleak fear. "I went over there last night."

"To Eunice's?" I asked. The wall opposite us was no longer blank. Len had painted it an evening-sky violet. A hooded man stood in profile. It was hard to tell if the intention was a monk in prayer or the Grim Reaper contemplating his navel at dusk.

"*Yes.* And—ah, forget it. I can't . . ." He sucked a breath and hurled it back out. "Maybe everyone's right. Maybe I'm a fag."

"I read that somebody saw Bobby Kennedy in a nightclub necking with Rudolf Nureyev." I attempted to hand him the second glass of wine I'd poured.

"No," he said sternly as though I were about to pee on the carpet. "Okay, I was over there and we were drinking—The only time I ever do it with her is when I'm drinking—And we start making out. And we're down to, well, we're taking off our clothes and she was rubbing her chin against my shoulder and I was a bit turned on but then I was getting kind of turned off . . . grossed out in a way because . . . she has . . ." He paused, embarrassed. I wasn't sure for which of them. "She has whiskers, kind of. Definitely, she has whiskers and she was rubbing her chin against my shoulder. And then," he sighed, "she opened her blouse and she pushed my head down into her boobs and put one of them into my mouth." Len's face flushed red back to his ears. "And I started, you know . . ."

"Suckling?" I offered cheerfully.

"Yes." He looked as though he'd been betrayed by the masses and I'd just joined the club. "Yes, *suckling.* I was suckling like a baby and she's old enough to be my mother. And, and I was totally *doing* it, you know? It was a *mother* thing."

"Len, it's no big—"

"Would you let me finish? And so I started to get freaked out because all I can think is, I'm fucked up. This is just like Mrs. Eisman. 'Member Bonnie Eisman?"

"And how." Len's stories about Mrs. Eisman kept me sane when I was in Tokyo. My letters to him described rats and cockroaches. His told me about his friend Donna's mother, Bonnie. Donna and her mother went to Burnaby Foursquare Church, the same one Len's family went to. When Donna went off to university, Len and Bonnie became close, I gathered, as a sort of consolation for her empty nest syndrome. Len would go over there and drink tea or sometimes they'd go to the symphony together. Eventually Eisman made a pass at him. Meanwhile on the other side of the planet, I sat in crowded anterooms, usually in a bikini, waiting to audition for some drain cleaner or laxative commercial as I read Len describing his third-base grope with Mrs. Eisman at which point he had drawn the line. He simply couldn't bring it on home. Mrs. Eisman flew into a rage. Hiking up her pants, she stormed into the kitchen, called one of her other swains and made plans to go away for the weekend as Len stood in the doorway, bewildered. When she hung up he apologized. She said, "I'm sorry too, Len. But you just can't take a woman to the edge like that and turn back. I have my needs. Sex is a normal bodily function. Like having a bowel movement." Huddled over the pages I burbled into laughter. My name was called by a small young Japanese woman:

"*Bibian.*" I continued giggling right into the audition room where I was led with four other models and told to dance like crazy *gaijin* (which I thought meant *American*, was later told meant *foreigner* and still later told meant *barbarian*). I credit Len with landing me a job that got me out of debt and paid for my ticket home: a billboard for cherry-scented tampons.

"So, I stopped it," he told me now. "I said, I can't do this, I'm sorry. And she jumped up and took off into the kitchen, just like Mrs. Eisman, and I went in there thinking she was calling a guy but she wasn't, she was crying. Like *unconsolingly*. And I started apologizing. And she was saying, *I'm an old stupid woman*, and then she touched her chin and she felt the whiskers, and then she screamed, *Oh god. I forgot to shave. I'm getting electrolysis. You must think I'm hideous.* And I said it wasn't that, even though it kind of was, but not really, and I felt like shit but I couldn't handle it. Her emotional stuff, I mean. I got freaked out. I said I had a dentist appointment, but she knew I was making it up . . ." He sighed and stared at the floor a second. "A couple hours later, I got a call from her. She said she took pills and now she changed her mind and she didn't know what to do and I told her not to go to sleep and to drink coffee and then I went over and the ambulance was already there. She had this look on her face like the way dogs look at the SPCA. And I caused it. She's okay now, but fuck . . . it went from an idealic-type situation to *this*."

"Len, she was probably depressed before you showed up . . . and it's *idyllic*."

He turned his face to mine and looked at me for what seemed like forever.

"What?" I said with a half laugh. "I don't mean to be a hard-ass but she *was* your employer. If she was a man, my mother and her cronies would've been saying how he abused you and took advantage because he had all the power and money. *She* had all the power and money. But she was depressed."

He hadn't turned his head. He hadn't blinked. He finally said rather matter-of-factly, "I am taking responsibility for my actions."

"Excuse me?" I replied a bit defensively.

"I've talked to the Benedictines."

"What is that? An antihistamine?"

"The Benedictine *order.* Benedictine monks? I'm going to join a monastery."

"Oh, come off it. You're not even Catholic. You've been listening to too much Leonard Cohen."

"'It is better to abandon practises if they are not assisting one to greater openness and love of God and neighbour.'" He rose and returned with a printout of some monk page from the Web. I took the paper from his hand. Monastic living was explained in its different forms. Celibacy leapt out at me both for my rejection of it since age fourteen and Len's general practise of it. *For those who choose to embrace a monastic life in a more formal way, in a monastery or hermitage, monastic spirituality includes celibacy,* it said.

I looked up at him, searching for words, then back at the page. *Many married and single Christians outside the formal setting of a monastery also look to monastic spirituality as formative for their lives, passing days or weeks each year there, participating in the prayer, silence and work, and for the rest of the year living ordinary lives. These people are often called oblates, from the Latin word meaning to give oneself as a gift.*

"Are you going to be an oblate?" I asked, a bit spooked. I snatched what I could from the printout. "Len, it says right here, *Monastic spirituality is not a running from but going toward.* And *you,* buddy-boy, are running from." I nodded as though that settled it. I gave a short burst of laughter. "You're not going to be a goddamn monk."

Len was silent. Already participating it seemed.

Sixteen

~

1966. CELIA AND ANNIE SHOW UP AT THE APARTMENT DOOR, Annie doing a last double check of her cleavage. She got drunk with Truman Capote one night last week at Le Club and now they're about to be his guests at a Kennedy party. Celia looks down at her shorty black-and-white vinyl dress, wondering if it's appropriate. Suddenly the door opens. It's Bobby. Celia hadn't expected him to open his own door. "Miss Dare, what a surprise." He doesn't look surprised.

Annie introduces herself, and catching Capote's eye, slips past to greet him.

Standing in the foyer, Celia lets Bobby take her coat and the graze of his fingers on her arm reminds her that this is a bad idea. "I can't wait to meet Ethel." She's officially a phony now.

"Ethel and the kids are at Hickory Hill for the weekend," he tells her. "Uh . . . did you receive the flowers, by the way?"

"Flowers? . . . With the Coleridge quote? Those were from *you?*"

"I didn't sign my name?" he laughs and the air feels clunky and nervous.

Her chest starts to thump. Great, this is all she needs. A few moments of silence and then he says, "Well, why don't you come on in and I'll fix you a cocktail." He steers her toward the front room where other guests are sitting around talking and drinking. Benny Goodman plays on the hi-fi now, Peggy Lee doing the vocals on "Where or When."

Bobby pours her a martini.

"Thanks. You must've been a little boy when this song came out."

"My mother used to dance to it in the kitchen with me."

Celia's four-year-old self watches her father waltz with the neighbour.

"Dance with me," he says.

"No one else is dancing."

"Maybe we'll instigate a house hop."

They both look around the room. Maybe dancing isn't the best idea. She looks for Annie but she's busy with Capote, and Jackie Kennedy has joined them. Celia's eyes stick on Jackie's long cool-looking limbs, everything precise and in just the right place. Annie looks slack and fleshy by comparison.

"Do you mind if we have a seat?" Celia asks. "Maybe I'll feel more like dancing after I finish my drink."

"Sure. Of course. Let me introduce you to my sister-in-law. Have you met Jackie?"

"Sort of."

As they move toward them, Jackie appears to be exchanging more words with Capote than Annie. *We're just a couple of strippers to her*, Celia thinks. *Why are we* here?

Next afternoon, Celia sits over lunch with Johnny. "When did you start running around town with a punk like that," he rants.

"I shouldn't tell you *anything*. I'm not sleeping with him, for godsake." She's starting to wonder if part of her enjoys pissing him off. "Truman Capote was there. So was Allen Ginsberg. Both *faggots*, as you would say—you think he's sleeping with them too?"

"Kennedys'll fuck anything with a pulse."

"You make me feel so special."

He drums his fingers. "He's got a lot of enemies. Don't get caught in the crossfire." He glances past her shoulder and stares with disgust. "Christ, that piece of shit's in *here*."

She sighs. "Which particular piece of shit is it now?"

He nods behind her at a man seated in the corner. "One of Hoover's. And I think it's you he's tailing. He was lurking around at the Copa the night you closed. See what happens when you spend time with a prick like Kennedy!"

She rolls her eyes. "First its Hoover then it's Kennedy. Maybe you're just paranoid, Don Giovanni."

"Christ, I hate it when you call me that."

She holds his glance.

"I'm retired," he snaps.

Celia stretches her neck with nonchalance. "So, where's your gal Judy these days?"

He leans back. "Hell if I know. I don't want to talk about Judy. I don't want to fight with you. We haven't seen much of each other lately. Let's be nice."

She flicks one nail against another. "It pisses me off when you say all a guy wants is to get into my pants. Like there's nothing remotely interesting about me."

"I think you're very interesting." He touches her fingertips. "Given a chance, most men would want to swallow you whole."

"Nice recovery," she says, rolling her eyes, and excuses herself to the bathroom.

The man behind her rises and follows. In the hall, he catches hold of her.

She turns. Looks at him. "*Stewart.*" She jerks her arm away. "For godsake, I—What are you *doing* here? I told you, I—"

"Please, Audrey, just give me two minutes."

"Don't call me Audrey," she snaps. "Does my mother know you're here?"

"She's gone."

Celia stares.

"She died. Almost two months ago. I'm sorry I didn't get word to you," he says, "but after the last time we spoke I didn't think you'd want to be there." His hand goes out to her again.

"*Don't.* Don't touch me and, don't—look, if you'd been

man enough to stand up to her in the first place, maybe things would've been different."

"I understand you're angry. A day doesn't go by that I don't think of how things could have been. It breaks my heart to see you live this sort of lifestyle and to know I'm partly to blame."

"How *dare* you. I am a *singer*. People respect me. Know whose place I was at the other night? Senator Robert Kennedy's. He sent me flowers. We were invited by Truman Capote. Don't you ever take credit for who I am or what I've accomplished."

"Excuse me, the lady's not interested in your company."

Stewart turns. Eyeing Rosselli up and down, he looks to Celia. "But you're interested in his? Just because he's wearing a silk suit doesn't mean he's not a sow's ear."

Johnny grins. "Honey, you go ahead."

"No. You—" she points to Stewart "—go home. Please, just go back to Scarsdale."

He looks from Johnny to Celia. "Don't turn your back on family. You lost your mother this way, don't lose me. We're family. We need one another."

Her pulse jumps in her neck. "No. We don't. I needed you once and where were you? Just stay out of my life."

Nobody speaks. Finally Johnny puts one foot forward and Stewart sticks a hand out. "I can take care of myself, buddy."

A mild shrug from Johnny, and Stewart says, "I shouldn't take credit? Dance lessons, voice lessons . . . you'd be nowhere if it weren't for me. Fine. Forget it, *Audrey*." He strides through the dining room and shoves his way out the door.

Celia stares straight ahead. Johnny reaches, as though he's about to pick up a broken bird.

"Please. If you touch me now, you'll have to scrape me off the floor. My mother's dead."

"Oh god. I'm so sorry, honey."

"Yeah," she says softly.

"I guess you're not going home for the funeral."

"It was two months ago."

He sighs. "I'm sorry. Maybe you should come back with me to L.A."

"I have to go to Palm Springs," she tells the floor, her voice flat and distant. "Then I'm booked at the Sands."

"I'll fix that. People will understand."

"I'm just going to keep moving. I have to go to the ladies' now."

One bright L.A. morning in May, Celia walks into Harry Drucker's in Beverly Hills where Johnny's getting a haircut. She winks to the barber. Johnny's eyes are closed. The barber stands back as she sneaks up behind, covers Johnny's eyes and drawls, "Reach for the stars, daddy."

A smile creeps across his face. She giggles. He pulls her round and onto his lap.

"Very nice," she commends Harry as she pats Johnny's hair.

"Did I tell you I was going for a haircut last night?"

"*Oui, monsieur.*"

"Such a good little spy." Swatting her butt, he sets her back on her feet. "Stand there so I can look at you. How long you in town?" Harry steps in to take a last few snips.

"Week. Marty got me a *Starring-For-Three-Nights-Only* at the Grove . . . You don't seem very surprised."

He winks and tugs the sleeve of her suit jacket. "I'm glad you're here."

They've talked on the phone most nights since Stewart's reappearance. She could hardly stand a day without his voice. Without, it felt as if she might spurt away like a shot balloon. She takes his arm as they come out of the shop. "You look good," he says.

"I am good. I'm gooder here with you," she flirts and, then, embarrassed, changes the subject as they stroll up toward Rodeo Drive. "Why did you move to California?"

"These damn Rosselli lungs—they started finding signs of tuberculosis in me, so when I had a chance to go into business with some fellas out here—"

A guy in a suit heads straight for them. As Johnny moves to step around him, the guy says, "Filippo Sacco."

Johnny shoots the man a glance and moves past.

"What'd he say?"

Rosselli doesn't answer. A few steps farther, a man with a crewcut heads toward them, arms open. "This has nothing to do with you personally, John," he says and offers Rosselli a plain manila envelope. "We got nothing against you."

"Go see my attorney," Johnny snaps without breaking stride. "I don't know what you're talking about." The two men bracket Rosselli and Celia now, keeping pace.

"You want your girlfriend to take a walk while we chat?" the bracket on Johnny's side offers. "Cuz right now, we're the only ones who know about this."

"We want to talk to you personally," Celia's bracket explains. "We can meet up in Ventura. Nobody will know." He drops his voice. "It's a matter of national security."

"Go see my attorney," Johnny repeats, keeping a firm hold on Celia, eyes straight ahead.

The men fall behind. Celia looks over her shoulder as the men smirk to one another. Johnny jerks her close. "Keep walking."

"What the hell was that?"

"Nothing."

Back at his apartment, the manila envelope is now waiting on the doorstep. Johnny steps over it and the moment they're inside, calls his lawyer. He paces the apartment, won't speak until a knock comes at the door.

Holding the envelope addressed to Filippo Sacco, the lawyer sits down and opens it in front of them. Inside are two yellowed photographs, one of a young woman and the second of a boy about four years old. "That's my mother," Johnny says. "And that's me."

Celia's guts twist. She keeps quiet.

"Anything I got a record for in Boston, I don't think they'd bother. They could go after me as an illegal alien, but why? And why's he saying, *It's a matter of national security?*"

The lawyer slides the pictures back in. "What are you thinking?"

"Cuba. And if that's the case, I wanna let someone inside know. If this thing gets out—it's not getting out through me."

"We should take a trip to Washington," the lawyer says. "Don't use the phone." He looks around the room. "Tomorrow morning. First thing."

Rosselli nods. Celia's never seen him nervous before.

An hour later she and Johnny sit on a log at the beach and bite into a couple of deli sandwiches.

"Filippo," she says.

"Audrey," he answers.

"Does hearing your old name give you the creeps too?"

"Goddamn shock to the system."

"How do you think they know?"

He shrugs. "There's a guy I have bring money to my family in Boston. I got a record there, so I can't go back. Maybe this guy cracked."

"You weren't born in Chicago."

He shakes his head.

"Must've been something pretty bad they wanted you for in Boston."

"I was a kid." He squints at the sand. "I'm too old for this shit."

"So this is about you and Sam and the CIA?"

"See why I hate those fucking Kennedys? Here I am helping the country fight communists and that little shit is breaking my balls."

"Maybe he doesn't know."

"People I work with don't do that sort of thing. You play straight, make money, everybody's happy. *These* pricks—nobody knows which end is up. Now I gotta make sure they know I'm not going to sell anyone out."

"Who? The government?"

"Everybody." He sighs. "I was six years old when I came here from Italy. I came out of the dirt and here I'm wearing silk and diamonds. This is a great country. I'd do anything for this country."

She digs her bare toes into the sand.

"I just want to play golf."

"You should take off your shoes."

Sun on his face, he looks craggy and tired. She leans over and tugs at his laces. He makes no move, so she gets off the log, kneels in front of him and pulls off his shoes, rolls off his socks. Staring at the water, he doesn't seem to notice. Celia grabs him by the ankles and yanks his feet to and fro over the grains. Giving her a half-hearted smile, he says, "If there ever comes a time you can't find me, check the airport. That's what they do when they get rid of a guy. Leave his car at the airport like he left town."

Her head jerks up. "Who does? That's not funny. Don't say that again."

She plants herself back on the log, rummages in her purse, takes out nothing and closes it. "I haven't seen Bobby Kennedy in months."

They have dinner at La Dolce Vita that night. Rosselli points out the Friars Club in the windowless mustard-yellow building across the road. He likes to go there for a sauna now and then. Maybe play a game of cards with Milton Berle. Or George Burns. Frank or Dean when they're in town. It's relaxing. A men's den.

"Maybe you'd like to go there after dinner?" she suggests over veal scaloppini.

He shakes his head. "I just want to go home and get to bed early."

He looks so old. "Why don't you come home with me," she pleads, gripping his hand as if he might evaporate.

Taking him into her bed that night, she clings and inhales his breath, giving him hers as if it might buoy him, save him from being sucked into the blackness. "I love you," she tells him. "Don't disappear." He buries his face in her neck, says nothing. He leaves at daybreak.

~

Three days later, her last morning in town, she wakes to the phone and Johnny's "Hi, sweetheart."

Gravel is still in her voice. "Why didn't you call me? Where were you?"

"New York. Everything's fine. False alarm."

"New York?"

"Had a meet with a guy. It's fine. No national security."

She looks at the clock. "Why are there FBI agents following you around then?"

"Ah, casinos."

"Taxes?"

"Everything's fine."

Rolling onto her side, she flicks at the pillowcase. "I have a flight back to New York today."

"I guess we'll just miss each other. I'm on a flight out this afternoon."

"Maybe I could postpone my trip."

"No, I'm in and out. Stopping in L.A. then I've got some other business. Listen, can you do me a favour? There's a package there I want brought back to New York tonight. Can I send a guy round?"

"I guess. Is it big?"

"Na. Just a little gift box. It's a shirt for a friend. The guy'll tell you where to drop it."

She sighs. "Okay. Is . . . Are we . . ."

"What's wrong?"

"We just—we were *together* the other night. And it doesn't seem like you even—"

"Aw, honey. I don't know what I would've done without you. But you've got to get back to work and I have to do the same."

She kicks off the blankets and stares at the ceiling.

"You still there?"

"I should let you go. I'm sure you're busy." She hangs up then dials.

"Hello, my lovely," Annie breathes in her vixen voice.

"How's tricks in the land of Hot and Vacuous?—Hey, I saw Johnny out last night."

"Where? I just got off the phone with him."

"Elmo's. He was out with Betsy Duncan."

"Who's Betsy Duncan?"

"Nightclub singer. You know her."

"I thought they weren't seeing each other anymore."

"You know John, always got something on his arm. Since when do you care?"

"I *don't* care. It's just weird is all. He went out there because of his legal shit, and next thing you know he's picking up tail and club hopping?"

"Don't tell me you jumped on that old dog."

Celia fiddles with the phone cord.

"The Silver Fox fucks again." There is a click in Annie's ear.

By the time Celia's in New York, Johnny's back in L.A. She calls him to say she dropped off his package. He says he'll be heading to Mexico that evening. Giancana just got out of Cook County and is about to exile himself.

"I've never been to Mexico . . ."

"You should go sometime. You'd like it." Silence. Then a sigh. "What now?"

"How could you be with me like that and then just . . ."

"You know how my life is. I've got business."

"Annie needs the phone, I gotta go. Have a ball." She hangs up.

"Was that Capote?" Annie takes the lighter from Celia and fires one up for herself. "You didn't just say no to a party, did you? I *liked* the one we went to."

"Fine." She pushes the phone across the kitchen table. "You go then."

"Fine. I will."

"He told me about Bobby's affair with Candace Bergen. *It was in all the Paris papers,*" she mimics.

Annie flicks her ash into the tray. "What're you so hacked about?"

"Everything."

"Long as it's not the goddamn war. Ran into Betsy Duncan yesterday and she said Johnny was raging on about how we're trying to fight communism and these asshole protesters have nothing better to do but—blablabla."

Celia chomps the inside of her cheeks. "Well, tough. Because Vietnam is what's hacking me the most."

Annie studies her a moment, a half smile on her lips. "You knew what he was like."

"Who? Bugger him. I disapprove of this war. That's how I feel."

"Awful passionate all of a sudden."

"I've always felt this way. In fact, I'm going to a demonstration this afternoon in Central Park." She pokes at the newspaper between them. "Martin Luther King is going to be there."

Annie looks at the paper: America is engaged as a liberator not a conqueror; soldiers are there to win the hearts and minds; a general explains the Vietnamese don't value life the way westerners do; America will liberate them not only from communism but from their own barbarism.

"And maybe I *will* go to that party," Celia barks. "Go rip into Ol' Bobby Sox for not speaking out more."

"Won't that just piss Johnny off all to hell?" Annie grabs the phone. "You know Truman will berate you for hanging out in the park with a bunch of longhairs in bad footwear but them's the breaks."

"Tell him you're going with me."

"Fat chance."

"If you don't go with me," she says, brushing toast crumbs off her housecoat, "I'm going to tell him that not only did you sleep with that bartender he likes but that he gave you—"

"Shut up!" Annie tamps her cigarette out.

In Central Park, Celia and Annie make their way past small patches of pro-war sign carriers—*Anarchy Cannot Be Permitted in the USA; Fight Communism and Red Termites; End Hanoi Sanctuary*—and join the mob of antiwar demonstrators. Thousands are already there with more coming every minute. Onstage Phil Ochs strums "I Ain't Marchin' Anymore"; the crowd sings along.

Annie stands in her fox fur, arms crossed, hair under a turban-wrap, face covered with the biggest cat's-eye sunglasses she could find. Celia's in flats and a pea coat; she didn't want to look too bourgeois. There are a few long-haired, beaded sorts around but a lot of square-eyed academics too and women who look like teachers and secretaries, regular sorts.

Stop the Bombing; End U.S. Aggression; Draft Our Boys to School Not War.

"Who's NOW?" Celia asks.

"Us unfortunately."

Celia points out the sign: *en—oh—double-u for Peace Now.*

"Oh. I don't know. I think they're some women's group."

"What's their bag?"

"Bunch of dykes. The day men stop picking up the cheque and buying me jewelry is the day I firebomb their headquarters. Broads'll get us all drafted if they don't shut their yaps."

At the mike, a young man tells the crowd it's important to sing, to speak, to scream protest at the destruction of life. A few yelps and yips answer. "Girls and boys for peace, may I introduce to you the surreal and psychedelic Allen Ginsberg."

Celia's head turns. "He was at that party, remember?"

Balding, bearded Ginsberg comes centre stage in a white kaftan, a red sash across his shoulder and chest. The sound system begins to crap out as he plinks finger cymbals and suddenly the crowd utters a collective om.

"Oh Jesus, here we go." Annie pulls her coat tighter.

Ginsberg chuckles. "Little changes in this world if we don't insist on it. Insist, people. As my esteemed colleague mentioned, sing, scream, *Howl!*" The crowd wolf-calls.

"America," he continues, "I've given you all and now I'm nothing. America two dollars and twenty-seven cents January 17, 1956. I can't stand my own mind. America, when will we end the human war? Go fuck yourself with your atom bomb . . ." Feedback from the mike.

An eruption of cheers. Several yell out, "'I don't feel good don't bother me.'" Everyone seems to know the words.

"There must be fifty thousand people here," Annie grumbles, "and I don't see a single man I'd sleep with."

"Crabs," Celia reminds her flatly.

Annie moves to put hands over her ears but cups Celia's mouth instead. "Say that again and I'll smother you in your sleep. Jesus. I hate this shit."

"America—" Ginsberg's voice pierces then drones "—I used to be a communist when I was a kid . . . I'm not sorry. I smoke marijuana every chance I get. I sit in my house for days on end and stare at the roses in the closet . . ."

"What do you think that means?" Celia wonders.

"He's a stoned communist queer."

Young women with peace symbols painted on their cheeks snake through the crowd handing out pamphlets. Celia cranes her neck, peers up at the trees where a few people have roosted, some with cameras. "They said on the news that Johnson has FBI watching all the protest stuff," Celia says. "Do you think there's FBI guys here?"

Annie shrugs and turns her soured puss back to the stage. To Celia's left is a scraggly guy in a stars-and-stripes shirt under a black leather jacket. He wears an Uncle Sam top hat and holds up a sign: *Make Me Not War.* To her left, two young guys have a banner: *Dow Shalt Not Kill.* As the one nearest turns, his eyes brighten. "Hey, you're not Celia Dare, are you?"

She smiles. "Have you seen my show?"

"Far out, man! Hey!" He shoves his partner in sign carriage. "Hey man, it's Celia Dare!"

The other guy stares. "Holy shit, it is. My brother's gonna bug. Maybe you could sign our sign!" They lower the banner and pat their pockets for a pen. "Crazy, man. We're from L.A.! We tried to get into your show."

Celia signs with a flourish.

The first one keeps gawking, his lips mashing one another

before they open. "Too bad it's so cold. You wouldn't have to wear that coat."

The crowd explodes in cheers and shrieks. She hops up and down. "What's happening?"

"Right on!" the anti-Dow guys holler. "Want a boost?"

Soon she is up on their shoulders. Two men onstage set a fire. "What are they doing?"

"Burning draft cards."

She half expects sirens, police to appear out of nowhere. But the cards go up like any other bit of paper and ashes scatter in the breeze.

"Toke?"

She looks down to the joint held up. "Why not? We're all going to hell anyway."

That evening, Annie and Celia sip wine in Bobby's apartment. This time Ethel is there, her two youngest children upstairs with a nanny, the rest of the brood at Hickory Hill.

Capote and Annie twitter over the afternoon's march to the United Nations Building. Annie giggles. " . . . and guess who slipped off down a side street. My footwear wouldn't allow for anything that would constitute a march . . ."

Meanwhile Celia has got to talking with Jacqueline Kennedy by the fire. Intimidated at first, she's now at ease as Jackie leans forward with interest. In person her voice is fuller, richer; not the wispy childlike one she uses on television. Celia tells her about the men in the trees.

"Wouldn't surprise me." Jackie taps a nail lightly against her glass. "Damn warmongering lunkheads."

Celia gazes over Jackie's linen trousers and blouse, the elegant tilt of her chin. She repositions her hand, lengthens her fingers, tries to match the expensive grin.

Bobby comes to perch on the arm of Jackie's chair, thick hair flopping at his forehead, front teeth rabbitting as he grins. "Hello, ladies. Did Celia tell you she used to dance ballet. Jackie wanted to be a ballerina once."

Jackie waves a dismissive hand, the colour in her cheeks rising.

"A *ballerina*. Jeez, kiddo, don't sell yourself short." This from a newly arrived Ethel. "You could've been a soccer player with those feet."

"Who me?" Crossing her legs, Jackie's size 10 foot bounces lightly as her face throws a perfect smile to her sister-in-law. "No, I'm not terribly sporting. I believe I'll refresh my drink."

Bobby stands as she rises and strolls smoothly through the other guests.

"Hello, I'm Ethel," she says, extending her hand. Then to Bobby, she adds, "You're not planning to run away with this cute little—what is it you do again, dear?" She looks back to Celia.

Bobby sighs, muttering, "The senator's wife, ladies and gentlemen . . ."

"Excuse me? I don't know what the girl *does*."

"I'm an entertainer," Celia interjects.

"You know, with that bleached hair, you remind me of the late great Marilyn Monroe. Did you know her? Bobby knew her. Didn'tcha, Bob?" He exhales through his nose. "Aww . . ." Ethel polishes off the last of her drink. "Bobby feels bad."

Bobby glances past his wife's head and gives an imploring nod across the room.

Looking a bit resigned, a woman strolls over and links her arm through Ethel's. "A Kennedy girl with an empty glass, that won't do." She trades Ethel's empty for a full one. "Here, have a G & T. And when will you ever show me those photographs . . . ?" She looks back at Bobby and mouths, "Soda," as they go.

"Excuse, ah . . . My sister can always, ah—Oh, I didn't introduce you. That was Eunice. Where are my manners?" He pushes hair off his forehead. "I'm sorry."

"If you'd really like to do penance, maybe we should talk about the demonstration."

With a mournful groan he looks ceilingward. "A room full of combat and she wants to talk war. Miss Dare, I promise to take you for the most mouth-watering lunch at which you may shove questions down my throat until I asphyxiate if you'll just give me a break tonight."

A week later, she takes him up on his offer.

"More and more people are showing up at these demonstrations—they're burning our flag in Europe. Seems nobody likes us."

"Welcome to my world," he smiles. "I'm asked frequently at press conferences about how I feel regarding this, ah, draft-card burning." Seeing the turn of her mouth, he stammers and picks up his wineglass. "I don't agree with it personally but I understand it as an action taken by a person who feels very strongly."

"The Kennedys are seen as a family who stand up for civil rights and the poor but—"

"I do. I have. I've worked very hard at programs in this city—look what we've been doing in Bed-Stuy. We've been—"

He stops as her hand moves an inch closer. He clears his throat. "I know I wasn't too forthcoming about my position in the past, but lately I've made it quite clear. Furthermore I've made it clear to Johnson. The man hates me. *You people think the office of the chief executive is some kind of Kennedy dynasty. Well, it is not. I'll destroy you and your dumb-ass dove friends.* I went to Paris in January and met with the foreign minister and Johnson was ready to kill me."

"Was that where you had dinner with Candace Bergen?"

The waiter sets plates down, asks if either of them would like fresh ground-pepper. Bobby stammers in the negative then drums his fingers as Celia smiles a yes, allowing more and more pepper for the pleasure of watching her dinner companion's agitation drag on. Waiter gone, she eyes her filet mignon, hoping it will still be edible.

"What an odd thing to bring up in the midst of a conversation ostensibly about peace."

She shrugs. "It was in the papers."

Bobby blinks rapidly. "Miss Bergen is an acquaintance of mine and she was there working. We had dinner one evening."

"This filet is fabulous. You were right: melt-in-your-mouth."
She makes happy eating noises. Bobby saws at his meat and
flexes his jaw.

The next afternoon, Celia picks up the phone to, "A protest.
How do you think I felt to hear that someone I care about is a
traitor to her own country?"

"Oh for god's sake, don't be so dramatic."

"Think you would be where you are, have what you have if
the communists ran the shop?"

"How do you know I was there?"

"I know you been running around with that runt-bastard
who put Teddy behind bars. This would kill him if he knew."

Annie comes back into the apartment with the mail and
tosses a package on Celia who mouths, *Johnny*. She looks at the
package in her lap. "Bobby wasn't even—"

"Don't contradict me," he bites through. "They just threw
Hoffa in the can a few weeks ago. A union leader, a guy who
worked for the common man. That prick has been persecuting
from the beginning, 'specially anyone whose name ends in a
vowel: the McCarthy committee, the McClell—"

"McCarthy was chasing commies. I thought you—"

"*Don't* play with this. *Capice?*"

Her eyes shift back to Annie who nibbles her thumb now as
if it were popcorn and Celia the late late show.

"I don't want you spending time with this guy."

Her voice small, she starts to explain. "I only saw him
because—"

"No more. That's the end."

"You can't tell me who I can—"

"I can't? Don't be stupid."

Jamming the phone between her ear and shoulder, she rips
open the package. A slow breath from Johnny before his voice
comes through again, softer. "Still there?"

Sliding her hand in, she pulls out a book: *The Enemy Within*
by Robert F. Kennedy.

"This isn't a nice man. People think he had something to do with Monroe's death."

"She killed herself. She almost did it two weeks before at the Cal-Neva."

"If anything ever happened to you . . ."

She flips the book to see a photograph of Bobby with Ethel and their seven children. There are nine or ten of them now. She traces a finger over the hollows under his earnest eyes.

"I know it seems as if I don't care for you lately, but my god, I do. I've been so busy."

"Okay."

"Okay? S'at it?"

She opens to the title page. "I'll talk to you another time. Just leave me be for now." She puts the phone down.

"Fuck a duck," Annie says. "I could hear him from over here."

Celia reads the inscription aloud. "*For Celia, 'No Legacy is so rich as honesty.' Affectionately, Bobby.*" She looks up at Annie. "Did you tell him I was out with Bobby?"

"What am I, nuts? This is one messenger who don't wanna get shot."

"So he can screw any knot in a tree but I'm 'sposed to sit around with my legs crossed?"

"'Course not." She waves toward Celia's copy of The Enemy Within. "Honesty ain't all it's cracked up to be. The secret to being a girl: Just smile and nod. Either that or pull a National Velvet and start wearing pants."

"Terrific." The phone rings. "If it's for me, I'm not home."

Annie picks up. "Hello . . . no, she's not . . . hi, Bob . . ." She flashes wide eyes at Celia. "Okay . . . I'll let her know."

"He's married," Celia says and drifts down the hall to her room.

The next afternoon Celia comes out of the shower in her robe, wet hair slicked back. "You gave me an idea for a new show."

Annie looks up from her romance novel. "What'd I say?"

Dropping her bathrobe, Celia stands in the middle of the kitchen in a pair of oversized trousers and a men's undershirt.

"You goin' off to join the Friars Club or what?"

She runs a hand over her hair and sings, "'*Danke schoen, darlin', danke schoen . . .*'"

"Wayne Newton?" Annie grins despite herself.

"Him and . . ." Celia sings, "'*I love . . .*' Hang on," changes keys, "'*I love I love I love my calendar girl . . .*'"

"You're going to do boy-drag? Granted, the balls haven't dropped on Newton or Sedaka, but Jesus wept. Have you told your agent about this?"

"Not yet. I can't think of a third."

"You could go a little more butch and do Deitrich." She cackles to herself.

"She does wear pants." Celia drops her voice an octave. "'*Falling in love again . . .*'"

"Probably got a bigger dick than the other two . . . 'Course, hers goes in a drawer when she's done."

Marty Sugar arranges for her to break in the act up at Isy's in Vancouver, sharing the bill with Sammy Davis Jr., then work her way due south as headliner. Bags under his eyes, thinner than ever, Sammy has just come home from London where he was shooting a comedy with Lawford.

In his dressing room, Celia opens a delicate gift box. She lifts a slim gold lighter out just as he pokes a cigarette between his lips. "'The Flames of Celia Dare,'" she reads aloud. "Oh Sammy, this is too much."

"Not for you, baby. Dig the blue diamonds? Just like them crazy glimmers of yours."

"Charlie Lavish. Heard you bought yourself a new Rolls. You're going to put yourself in the poorhouse."

He grins as she lights his cigarette. "I work harder than any-one I ever met. I deserve nice things. I deserve to see the pleasure on my friends' faces when I can get them nice things."

"What does May think of all your toys?"

"You didn't hear? Splitsville."

Celia winces.

"I was Charlie Crestfallen for the first while but it was for the best. I'm a swinger, that's who I is, baby. And May, well, she weren't."

"So you've been raising hell with Pete in London ever since."

"Yeah, well, Pat gave Pete the hook too. So we're a coupla bachelors. Speaking of which: Looky what I brought us." He reaches inside his jacket and takes out a flat gold case, flips it open to reveal a mirror and a glass vial. He dumps a small heap of white powder onto the mirror. "Stuff's more pure than any driven snow you could know." He takes a gold blade from the lid and cuts it into lines then offers her the first. "Have a toot."

She looks past the straight white ridges on the mirror to his anxious elbows hopping, the vague grey tinge to his brown skin.

"Okay, I'll go first." The mirror is back under his nose before she can speak. He sniffs and shakes his head with a delighted gasp. "And after the show we'll go to a disco and frug the night away. There's some tasty little go-go dancers down at this joint on Pender." Passing the case back, he eyes Celia's wig of man-hair, the sharp black suit. "You could make out like a bandit wearing that getup."

She pauses too long again. He takes the coke back and snorts a second line. "*Woo!*" he shouts at the ceiling. "They should just call this shit *more* cuz that's all I want."

She flicks her lighter a couple times, thinking.

After Vancouver comes San Francisco. The disenchanted from all over North America have flocked to the Haight-Ashbury intersection, as if that tiny pocket of the world would save their souls. The neighbourhood hangs and flops now: long lank hair next to matted beards and Afros, beads, bongo drums, baby-filled papooses, peace signs on foreheads and bare bellies and, everywhere, heavy lids drooping over bloodshot eyes.

Celia spends most of her stay just outside town in Palo Alto bringing the house down at Nero's Nook in the Cabana Hotel then on to the gorgeously gaudy just-built Caesars Palace in Vegas.

Her first night in town is Dean's last before he heads back to L.A.

"Sammy looks like shit," she says when they catch up for a drink. "Lawford's always stoned and screwed up and he goes right along with him."

Dean sips his scotch, puffing his Lucky Strike. "Don't worry about Sammy. He's just blowing off a little steam. 'Specially in Canada and England—the girls don't care what colour he is."

"Does Frank know he's into the drugs so much?"

"Ahhh, *Frank* . . . Sammy would cut off his balls for *Frank*."

When she first came to Vegas, Dean's stage booze was apple juice. Now he's sucking back scotch morning till night. He's getting a nose that could guide someone's sleigh. "Everything's changing," she says.

"When Momma dies, a little bit of God dies."

Her chest seizes a moment, she studies his face.

"My mother died at Christmas," he explains.

"Mine too."

"Guess it's going around. You ready to divorce your wife?" He smirks. "Frank's getting ready to toss Mia."

"They just got married for chrissake!"

"This is the way the world ends, not with a bang but a whimper." He reaches into his jacket and pulls out a bottle of pills and sips one down. "Percodan?" he offers. "Great for what ails ya." She shakes her head. "At least one of us is pure." His eyes drift about the lounge. "I wonder sometimes what woulda happened if I'd taken you up on your offer that night. If I woulda been washed in the blood of the lamb. Probably woulda got you dirty."

"I should get back." She pats the armrests of her chair. "Maybe we can catch up in L.A."

"Yeah. You do that. *Baby.*" Calling after her, he adds, "Hey, come do my little TV show when you get to town. You wouldn't believe what they pay me to get out of bed."

In L.A., the Coconut Grove is booked solid. On her night off, she heads to the Factory. Lineup outside, the doorman opens the door wide for Celia. Inside, lights are flashing, go-go girls are dancing in birdcages. "Soul Man" wails from the sound system. On the dance floor they're doing the frug and the pony but what catches her eye is Frank's Mia in the middle of it all with Bobby. His eyes crinkle and he's smiling his bunny smile as he dances. Mia hops like a sparrow in front of him. His eyes catch Celia's. When the song ends, he heads over.

"Hi!" He leans in to be heard over the sound system. Celia glances about as though someone might be taking notes. "I, ah, I heard you were in town," he says. "I've been reading your reviews—I, ah, especially liked the one that said you challenged America to acknowledge the plight of the castrated woman."

"I liked that one too. I thought the feminists would hate it. My agent promised!"

He smiles. "I think it's time I caught a show referred to as *arch and sardonic* by one crowd and *far-out* by another."

Laughing, she rests her hand on his arm, pulls it back. They each shift foot to foot.

"You should. Come to my show, I mean. You and Mia. I'll save you a ringside table."

"That was—Mia and I are just friends. Not that you, ah . . . I'm actually here with Rudy."

"Oh, I didn't mean. Sure. Bring whoever you like. I'm, ah— I'm sorry I didn't return your calls. I was—"

"Busy. Yeah."

They nod, avert their eyes. "Rudy? Is she—"

"He. Nureyev. The dancer? You should come say hello."

Turns out all four of them, Bobby, Rudy, Mia and Celia are staying at the Ambassador. They make a date to head for sand and surf that week, three of them determined to hit the nude beach. Nureyev thinks Celia's hesitation is hilarious. "She okay onstage with music but without, she is squeak like mouse," he says, pounding his steel thigh.

Taking the elevator up, Rudy and Mia get off on the fourth floor.

"Well," Bobby says, stopping at Celia's door. "I hope you'll be up for the beach."

"Thank you for this evening."

"It was a pleasure. I worried I might never see you again when you didn't return my calls. Not that you owe me any— never mind. Sweet dreams." He moves back a couple steps before he sticks his hands in his pockets, turns and heads for his own bed.

Inside her suite, she wafts through to the bedroom, a little giddy. The phone rings.

Johnny. He can't dictate to her and she is going to tell him so. She sits on the bed. The ringing stops. Resumes. She plucks the receiver as if it might burn. "Hello?"

"Hey, baby. How's your clyde?" Off her silence, "It's Frank. You forget me too?"

"'Course not. I haven't heard from you since Christ was a kid. How are you, daddy-O."

"Daddy's hacked. You seen Mia? She's in your neck these days."

"She's got the lead in a scary movie! I saw her tonight."

"Scary all right." His voice is angry and morose at once. "She was 'sposed to stay in New York and do a picture with me. 'Stead she fucked off west. She say anything?"

"Yes . . . she said that she misses you."

"Don't con a con, kid. She don't miss me. She don't give a shit."

"Yes, she does. She just doesn't want to live off your name."

He snorts. "How the hell y'think she got the lead? Where'd you see her?" Frank knows all about the Factory. Peter and Sammy are part owners. "A discotheque? Her and a bunch of goddamn free-love longhairs?"

"No. When I came in, she was dancing with Bobby Kennedy and then I joined—"

"She's two-timing me with that little shit-for-brains."

"They were *dancing*. I was dancing more with him than she was."

"I don't like that either. Johnny know you're with that prick?"

"I'm not *with* him. And Johnny's not my keeper."

"Well, I'm Mia's and that's it for that broad. She's deadsville far as I'm concerned. Tell her I said so." He hangs up.

Two days later Mia brings Bobby, Rudy and Celia to a nude beach she knows out past Pepperdine, Celia and Mia in dark wigs and sunglasses, Bobby and Rudy sporting fake goatees and baseball caps. They wave to people as they drive, giggling and blowing kisses.

Not long after they've reclined under the sun, Mia springs a leak. Frank's lawyer served her with papers that morning. Celia's throat seizes. About to offer condolences, she blurts her conversation with Frank instead, wrapping it in apologies.

Mia bites a nail. "I should have stayed in New York, I guess. I should've been a proper wife. I don't even know what that is."

Celia looks at her tiny childlike body, the big sad eyes. The four of them lie back against the log and stare at the ocean. Only Mia and Rudy are naked. Celia has on her bikini bottoms and can't get up the nerve to take her top off in front of Bobby who's still not out of his shorts either.

Finally Rudy announces it's time for wine and opens a bottle. "Goddamn. Don't remember some cup." He shrugs and takes a belt, passing the bottle to Mia, who sips pensively.

"I used to want to be a pediatrician," she says, wiping a tear. "Maybe Asia and Africa. Look where I end up: pregnant with the devil's baby."

"Oh god, Mia. Does he know?" Bobby asks.

Mia manages a smile. "Not that devil. Satan. He's co-starring in the picture I'm on . . . I'm performing in these chunks of capitalist piggery and I'm the wife of the most decadent man in America . . ." She plucks at the rock on her finger, flashing like a lighthouse under the sun. "I think I need to contemplate, find some kind of truth in my soul. I need to go to India."

Celia stares at Mia's elfin feet. "What's in India?"

"Maharishi Mahesh Yogi."

Celia glances to Bobby for enlightenment.

~

Bobby and Rudy sit at the table reserved for them and Celia makes a meal of flirting with both through the earlier part of her act. Dressed as Wayne Newton, she grabs Nureyev's face and, just before she pulls off her mustache, kisses him on the lips. The room erupts.

Come four in the morning, Bobby walks Celia to her suite again, the two of them giggling.

"Does everyone know about Rudy? You're not afraid people will think he's your lover?"

He smiles. "With the reputation Kennedy men have?"

At her door, they stop. Bobby stammers something inaudible, looks down the hall and takes Celia's hands. "I wish I weren't leaving in the morning," he tells her.

Guilt winds around inside her. "I'm savouring your book a little at a time. You're a wonderful writer."

"It's not high art but I suppose wiretapping's the closest I come to creativity." Glancing down the hall again, he suddenly puts his mouth on hers.

She kisses back, grasping his arm. He pulls her in by the small of her back. As his lips part to kiss her more deeply, she turns her head. "I'm sorry."

"You're involved with someone?"

"You are."

He smiles sheepishly. "'Most dangerous is that temptation that doth goad us on to sin in loving virtue.'"

"More Shakespeare?" she sighs.

"When faced with reality, steal another man's poetry." He takes his hands from her shoulders. "Would you—I'm sorry," he says. "Good night."

Seventeen

~

I SAT ON THE COUCH WATCHING A CLIP OF AN OLD *Merv Griffin Show*: footage of Norman Mailer being cuffed by police in Washington followed by Merv's studio interview. "I felt it was very important to get arrested to protest the war in Vietnam, which I think is an obscene war. I'll repeat myself, I think it's more obscene than all the dirty four-letter words that all the dirty American authors pour into all the dirty books that you ban in your libraries. I think this war is more obscene in one minute in the mind of General Westmoreland than all those words put together because we're burning children over there, we're burning children we've never seen."

Hoots and mutters from the studio audience as I picked up my phone. Leonard was in my ear with an invitation. I pressed the VCR's pause button and said, "You're not going to be a monk, so shut up about it."

Silence. I looked down at my toes, laced with toilet paper to keep them apart as my Rascal Red polish dried. Leonard wanted me to drive out to Westminster Abbey Mission with him to see the Benedictine monastery. "I can't go anyway," I told him.

"Why? Are you hungover again?"

"I feel sorry for people who don't drink. When they wake up in the morning, that's the best they're going to feel all day."

Silence. "Frank Sinatra said that." More silence. "Frank made me an appointment to get acrylic nails done. My Frank, I mean."

"You can't go with me to investigate how I can use my art to contribute to peace and truth in the world because you need fake nails so you can sell more pornography to pathetic soulless perverts, is that what you're saying?"

"Well. Yeah. Oh for chrissake, Len. Have you talked to Eunice?"

"Yes. I was over there this morning. I brought her some soup and a little painting. I wanted to tell her that she inspired me spiritually."

"Eunice, you and your mental instability have inspired me to hide out in monkitude."

"I've always been interested. *The first awareness of a vocation to the consecrated life is often seen and discerned in early childhood."* He was reading from that goddamn Web site again.

"Watching *In the Name of the Rose* thirteen times suggests obsession not a calling." I hobbled on my heels, wet toenails splayed upward, sat at my laptop and Googled "Benedictine monastery." The Sisters of Benedictine came up first. *Have you considered a lifetime dedicated to serving God and the people of God? Maybe you have what it takes to be a Benedictine woman.* My eyes drifted up to the webcam sitting at the top of the screen.

"Are you still there?" Leonard asked. I grunted. "Why is this pissing you off so much?"

"Can't you just volunteer someplace or something? Why do you have to fuck off to a monastery? Some guys like older women. Big deal."

He let a couple seconds go by. "I'm a thirty-four-year-old waiter. I've never had a real girlfriend. I'm supposed to be an artist and I barely produce. Maybe if I focused on finding the Christ in other people I could at least use my art to make somebody else's life better."

I clicked on my mail program. I hadn't done that since I'd got back from San Francisco. There were three hundred new e-mails. "Why can't things stay the same?" I asked, deleting blocks of twenty and thirty junk-mail offers for bigger boobs, dicks and mortgages at a time, until I came to one with Kiss of Death in the subject line. I hesitated, clicked and gasped: a picture of a dead girl lying at the riverside, rotting leaves and twigs around and under her head, mud and blood smeared across her slack jaw, her hands, dark roots at the back of her dirty matted yellow hair, purple bruises on her throat.

"What's the matter?" Len asked.

"I don't know," I said, gagging on fear. "Oh my god. I thought someone sent me a picture of a dead hooker and it's me. *Fuck*."

"What are you talking about?"

"I opened an e-mail from a props guy on set—oh god. Why did I ask to see these? I forgot . . ." There were four pictures. Each image was closer up until I could clearly make out the grains of mud and dirt on my fish-white skin, feel the cold on my strangled neck. A big drop of rainwater slipped off the branches overhead and wriggled into my ear again.

Under those shots were four more of my corpse on the shower floor, a pale peach curtain covering my torso and thighs, wet hair stringing over my limp hand. My neck looked as though it had been broken. "Why would I take a job like this right after she died?" I said, my voice high and faraway, like some small self begging.

"To pretend you don't give a shit. You always do stuff like that."

"I don't," I muttered.

"Whoa! Is that you? Cool." Frank leaned over my shoulder now. I recoiled. "Are those from *Kiss of Death*?"

"I gotta go, I'm late," I said into the receiver and hung up.

Frank's hand came in and scrolled up so he could see the rest of the images. "Jesus. These ones by the river are really creepy. You look *dead*. Man. We should post those on our site. There's guys totally into this shit."

I stiffened. "What?"

"E-mail them over to Brian's."

"No. These are property of the studio. We could get s-sued," I stuttered in my chair. "These are dead pictures. They're not sex. They're *dead!*"

He chuckled. "Don't get all pissed. I just thought it'd be funny. We could charge 'em up the whazoo for these. On that other page I'm building, you know. Actually we could just mail them copies for twenty bucks a pop or something. Like with your panties." He looked at me like a kid looks at someone with cake.

"Would you . . . fuck off!" I shut down my mail program and lurched out of my seat. I shook my hands in front of me, my spine wiggling away from him with a shudder. He laughed and grabbed me around the waist, making some kind of perverse ghoul howl.

"Get your mitts off."

"I was just kidding!" he yelled as I went down the hall to get dressed. "Oh, by the way, I paid your Visa bill. Happy birthday."

"What're you talking about?" I called from the bedroom, hunting for a bra.

"They called from Visa yesterday and you were over your limit so I transferred two grand from our site account onto your bill."

I pulled my jeans on. "Thanks." This was rather un-Frank. "What got you so fired-up thoughtful?"

"I didn't want my girl running around with no credit." He stood in the bedroom door now. "And I ordered you some really cool slutterwear. And I needed to charge a new camera."

Figured. "How much was the camera?"

"I've been bulking up search words that'll bring guys straight to your page. Traffic's gonna be major soon."

"How much was the camera?"

"Fifteen hundred."

"Are you out of your mind?" I looked at him aghast. "Why didn't you put that on your own card?"

"My limit's only five hundred. You know that."

I grabbed my purse. "I guess I'm paying for these acrylic nails you bought me then."

He hauled me into one of his arms and reached into his pocket. "*We* are. I almost forgot." Pulling out a wad of bills, he peeled off three hundred bucks behind my back then stuck it in my bra. "Here's a little mad money. Now, give Daddy some sugar."

"Oh brrrother," I said, my mother's letters fluttering in my head.

Expo '67; Canada's birthday; Charles de Gaulle; "If You're Going to San Francisco"; Love, Frankness, Contemplation; Haight-Ashbury; Eastern mysticism; New York; Fun City; Barbra Streisand; Free and Easy; Jackie goes to Cambodia; The Doors; Carl Sandburg; *Come on, come on, come on, come on, now touch me, babe*; Bobby Kennedy; Pope Paul; Vietnam; Berkeley; Mohammed Ali; *Hell no nobody go*; Martin Luther King; Norman Mailer; urban revolt; Detroit riots; National Guard; race warfare; anti-riot bill; Black Panthers; *it's a gas gas gas*; Rap Brown; Che Guevara; kill for peace; between a chuckle and a sneer; Six Day War; "Can't Take My Eyes Off of You"; "Come Back When You Grow Up."

Celia's digs in Atlantic City are at the Claridge Hotel, a quick hop from the 500 Club. Sinatra was in town the week before and Skinny D'Amato puts her in the suite he had.

"Sonuvabitch left it in good shape this time," Skinny tells her when he calls to see that she's settled in all right. "Didn't leave no punch holes in the wall or nothin'." He invites her to dine with him at the club but she thinks she'll order room service, give herself a chance to unwind before the show.

After hanging up, she stretches and falls back on the bed, a sense of déjà vu hitting her, though the Sands is barely recognizable anymore with that monstrosity of a tower they've added.

A knock comes. She lies still a moment, wondering if it could have been next door.

Another knock. She tiptoes over. Smiling at herself, she drops down onto her heels—too much thinking about the Sands. Okie Joe. A shudder ripples through her.

Whitchurch-Stouffville Public Library (WSPL)
905-642-7323
www.wsplibrary.ca

Customer ID: *****2295

items that you have checked out

Title: Cease to blush : a novel
ID: WS1292277
Due: Thursday January 09, 2020
Messages:
Item checkout ok. **You just saved $34.95 by
using your library. You have saved $2,688.80
this past year and $7,999.30 since you began
using the library!**

Title: Dance your troubles away
ID: WS5771125
Due: Thursday January 09, 2020
Messages:
Item checkout ok. **You just saved $34.99 by
using your library. You have saved $2,723.79
this past year and $8,034.29 since you began
using the library!**

Title: Wartime at Woolworths
ID: WS5845644
Due: Thursday January 09, 2020
Messages:
Item checkout ok. **You just saved $15.99 by
using your library. You have saved $2,739.78
this past year and $8,050.28 since you began
using the library!**

Total items: 3
Account balance: $0.00
Thursday December 19, 2019
Checked out: 3
Overdue: 0
Hold requests: 0
Ready for collection: 0

Messages:
Patron status is ok.

"Hello?"

"Hello! I'm looking for . . . Celia?"

She opens up. Staring a moment, she gasps and throws her arms around the tired-looking little man. "Teddy! Oh my god. Teddy."

Teddy the Ghost squeezes her back, his fingers tremulous. Taking hold of her arms, he sets her away from himself. "Lemme look. Madonn'! You got more beautiful! How's that possible?"

And you got old and shrunken, she thinks. *So frail.* "Well, get in here," she says, her eyes tearing as she pulls him inside.

"I think you musta grew while I was gone, honey. Like a skyscraper now!"

She titters. Just as he joins the laughter, he covers his mouth.

"What happened?" She touches the hand over his gapped smile.

"Na, I don't want you seein' that. Just a couple teeth. I'm gettin' 'em fixed soon. Haven't had time to make myself pretty again." Lips together, he smiles.

"Sit down, I'll fix you a drink." She walks to the bar. "When did you get out?"

"Few days ago." Setting himself in an armchair, he looks around the suite. "Still a nice joint, this place . . . Sinatra had a maid here once, years ago, all upset on account of her husband needing an operation. She didn't have no money. Frank got Skinny to see if she was on the level, then, *bam!* like that, he had Skinny make the arrangements. *I'll pick up the tab*, he says to him, *but don't you crack to anyone it was me.*"

Celia puts a scotch on the rocks in his hand, sits down with a flute of champagne for herself. "He can be a good man, ol' Frank."

"You gotta little water I could put in here? Can't take it straight no more."

She jumps up, brings a pitcher back and pours.

Teddy watches. "You come to be a real magnificent woman."

She reaches and squeezes his fingers.

"I used to think about you all the time. One of the guys in the joint was a beatnik kinda fella you know, always playing that folksy shit on the transistor. This one song used to come on." He croaks a bit of a tune and sings, "*When a kiss from a prison cell is carried in the breeze. That's when I wonder how sad a man can be. Oh, when will Celia come to me?*'" Voice breaking, he pulls out a handkerchief.

Her own throat tightens as he dabs.

He coughs. "Ah, don't mind me. Catchin' cold." He blows into the hanky.

"I would've come, Teddy, but Johnny said—"

"No, no, no." Shaking his head, he shoves the rag back in his pocket, straightens his jacket, takes a drink. "You stayed in good touch with Rosselli, then."

She nods. "Haven't heard from him lately. Surprised he knew where to find me—well, *pff*, he always knows where to find me."

"He was in the Sansum Clinic in Santa Barbara for a while there."

"Sick again? Why didn't he call me? I remember he was in there a year or two ago for his chest."

"He's a hypochondriac, that guy. I think he just wants a rest from this Friars Club thing. Poor bastard, if they nail him on somethin' like this . . . be a shame, him gettin' engaged and all."

Celia chokes on her champagne. "Engaged?"

"You didn't know? Sure. Nice girl too. Widow. But this thing with the Friars Club is a bum rap. Sonuvabitch though, those guys had themself a nice setup." Teddy smiles into his hands as he imagines it. "Drilled holes in the ceiling so's you could see down on the card games. The guy'd sit up there, keep the hustler wise with this little transmitter gizmo strapped to his chest. John knew the score I bet, but he don't cheat. Not his style."

Celia forces a smile. "I'm sure."

Teddy studies her. "What that? You ain't been makin' it with Rosselli."

"'Course not." She lights a cigarette.

"You smokin' now?" Plucking it from her fingers he mashes it out in the ashtray, looks at her again, puts his head in his hands. "This isn't what I wanted for you. 'Member I wanted you to go to stewardess school? You'da got yourself a good square husband and some kids by now. 'Stead, you're runnin' around the country shakin' your can, spending time with . . . You should go home to your folks."

She picks up her cigarette case, tosses it back down. "Actually, I've been considering doing something else for a while. One of my friends has been campaigning for the next election."

"*Campaigning?* Buncha puppets." He squints. "She's not hangin' around those Kennedy pricks, is she? Sons-a-bitches— the brother, he made his goddamn bed, that guy. We put millions into that sonuvabitch. You gonna fuck with people, they're gonna—" He coughs and reaches into his jacket as the hacking takes him into a fit.

She runs and pours him a glass of water. Regaining composure, he guzzles. A bit of red is on his handkerchief. "Is that blood? Jesus, Teddy."

"Ahh," he waves it off, sets the glass down. "Chest cold. S'nothin'. Gets raw inside."

"Let me call—"

"I don't need nothin'. I'm fine. I'm headin' for Vegas tomorrow, got a meet tonight . . . Listen, I don't want you workin' politics. Whatever you heard about this thing," he looks around himself, "least these people, they got some respect and honour, take care of their own. Fuckin' politicians: you buy and sell 'em and—" He starts to cough again.

Celia refills his water. "You cuss like me when I came home from the carnival." She forces a playful tone. Laughter twists through his hacking. "Let me call someone."

He cuts his hand across the air as he shakes his head, spittle flying.

Skinny raps at her dressing-room door. "How's our girl?"

"Hey! How's the house look?"

He spreads his arms, "You gotta ask?" Sits down on the vanity. "So, the Ghost's out of the bucket now, huh? Crazy old bastard."

She opens a lipstick.

"Not making much sense anymore." Skinny taps his temple. "I think those kennel rations they give him rotted a hole in the old marble bag."

She sets the lipstick down. "He was coughing a lot."

"Spoutin' all kinds of crazy shit when I seen him."

Her arms feel funny, hairs bristling. "He seemed fine. Meetings with this one and that one, heading to Vegas tomorrow . . ."

"Vegas." Skinny breathes a long look at her, says nothing for a few seconds, watches her recheck her Wayne Newton mustache. "Well, kid, you knock 'em dead."

At the end of the night, she calls the hotel. "Teddy? It's Celia. Meet me for a drink?"

"I'm waitin' for a guy to buzz me, sweetheart. Why don't you come up."

"Oh, come on. When's the last time you were in Atlantic City? He'll call back."

Teddy won't budge.

When he opens the door, she puts a finger to her lips and nods down the hall.

He follows her to the stairwell. "What's doin'?"

She glances at the walls, the ceiling. "Have you seen Skinny since you got to town?"

"No, I'm gonna see him tomorrow before I leave."

"He said he saw you."

"He talked to me on the phone."

"He said he saw you. And now you're going to Vegas . . . a lot of guys being arrested in Vegas with the skimming and all that."

Teddy looks taken aback. "Who told you that? *Skimming.*"

"For godsake, *Life* magazine is running stories on it."

He wags his finger. "That shit's blown way outta proportion. They don't wanna pay Internal Revenue money they could be payin' girls like you. If they didn't skim—"

"Fine. I don't care. But why don't you take a little vacation in Florida or something instead of running off back to work?"

He pats her arms. "I don't know the last time I had someone worryin' over me. Not since my Angela, god rest her soul."

"Where are you supposed to be for your parole? Illinois?"

"Ah!" he waved, "Slip 'em a few bucks, they don't know nothin'. Gettin' my parole moved to California anyway. For my health."

Back in New York, Annie trudges to the kitchen table with the Sunday *Times*. "Why did we start getting this goddamn thing. S'not like we read it." She flips through the sections and pulls one. "Oh right, the funnies, I almost forgot."

The phone rings. Celia jumps for it, knocking the table and spilling Annie's coffee.

"Christ in a crapshoot! Expectin' money?"

Phone to her ear, Celia says, "Oh, Johnny. Hi. Have you heard anything from Teddy? I saw him in Atlantic City and he didn't look so hot . . . why?" The receiver hits the floor as she yanks the paper out from under Annie's arms. Ripping the front section open to page three, Celia reads the headline: "*Ghost Found Dead in Beverly Hills . . . Recently paroled mafioso Teodoro (Teddy the Ghost) Gossitino was found dead in the Beverly Crest Hotel in Los Angeles, California. An apparent suicide, maids were shocked to discover Gossitino dangling by the neck at the end of a rope, which had been secured to a chandelier . . .*"

Annie picks the receiver off the floor. "Johnny? I don't think she can talk right now. She's pretty . . . uh, okay . . . he wants to talk to you." Annie holds the receiver to her ear.

"Celia," Johnny says. "Can you hear me?"

"Yes," she says dully.

"He was a very depressed man and I guess it got the best of him." Silence. "The funeral's in Jersey but I don't want you going. Teddy wouldn't want it neither. Gonna be a lot of Feds there and you shouldn't be mixed up with that. You listening?"

"Yes."

"No funeral, okay?"

"Uh-huh."

"I'm sorry, honey. He loved you very much. And you know I love you."

She hangs up.

Days later, while Annie's down in Miami, Celia picks up the phone to an English accent.

"S'at Celia? Hello, love, it's Pete . . . Uh, Pete Lawford," he clarifies.

"Oh. Hi."

"You've heard the spectacular news about Bobby jumping in the race for the Democratic ticket?"

"Sure."

"And Johnson's dropped out as of last night!"

"I heard." She listens suspiciously. In her limited experience, Lawford's accent becomes stronger when he wants something. He sounds straight out of a London travelogue now.

"Crowds are going crazy for Bob," he continues excitedly, "tearing at his shirt cuffs, at his buttons—you must've seen it on the telly. The reason I'm calling is because I'm in New York and I want to have a little impromptu party for him tonight. I hoped you might swing by. We're trying to get all Bobby's pals on board."

"Actually, I have been thinking about getting involved."

"Fabulous. Why don't you come by about ten. It'll be here at the Plaza."

Celia hangs up, her spirit nosing out of its dark hole.

She knocks at the Plaza suite at twenty past. Inside, the Stones blare "Jumpin' Jack Flash." Laughter and chit-chat. Nobody answers. She knocks again. Finally the door swings open and there stands Lawford, his grey hair cut shaggy and Beatlesesque, wearing a black turtleneck and Indian beads. A cigarette in one hand and a martini in the other, he opens his arms and slops gin down her back.

The room is loaded with women in ass-length miniskirts, teased hair and white lipstick. A few men in dark suits mingle among them. "Where's Bobby?"

"Any minute. You look spectacular, baby. You really do." His eyes loiter down the length of her. Taking her coat, he offers to fix her a drink.

"Thanks." She glances around, does a double take at one young woman she recalls from lounges in Miami. "That one," Annie once pointed out, "rents herself out to stag parties as a door prize." Another girl Celia recognizes as a pit girl from Vegas.

"Drink up and be somebody, baby!" Lawford nudges Celia's shoulder with a martini, splashing it over her arm this time. "Oh shit, sorry, hon, 'lemme get you a napkin, lemme . . ."

She shakes the gin off. "I'll just use your ladies'."

Closing the bathroom door she turns on the faucet and looks in the mirror. Suddenly agitated, she dries off and stalks back out to find Lawford.

"Pete. Are you actually expecting Bobby tonight? Or have plans changed?"

"Love, plans is plans. Of course he's coming. Bobby's my bro'."

Flint-eyed, she says, "I heard you weren't a Kennedy anymore."

A hurt look sweeps his face and vanishes. "Not technically . . ." He pokes her shoulder. Then in a slurred whisper, "S'like the mob: once a Kennedy, always a Kennedy."

She rubs at the spot where he poked and notices a young girl on the sofa, her lime-green mini so mini, you could see she was neither a fan of lingerie or a natural redhead. "Any of these fellas part of Bobby's campaign?" Celia asks. "I'd like to talk to someone about—"

"*I'm* part of Bobby's campaign. And *you* are contributing just by being here, baby. You are beautiful."

"I'd like to talk to someone about campaigning."

He takes her hand. "We thought tonight you could do your thing." He shimmies in demonstration. "Do your little dance, put a little happy in Bobby's pants. And in the meantime . . ." He ducks his martini under her hand, dunks her fingers and brings them toward his open mouth. She yanks back. "Ah come on, baby," he giggles. "See that little lady over on the couch." He points to the green miniskirt. "She's dying to dance with you. Now, *that's* a campaign contribution."

Celia stares.

"Oh come on, what's the big deal? You swing, I swing, we all swing for something . . ."

"I should've known better. Where's my coat?" She shoves past him. Lawford follows, commanding her to relax. Down the hall she finds a bedroom with a bed full of wraps and coats. Pulling hers from the heap, she turns as Lawford closes himself in with her.

"Come on, take it easy. Why don't you give Petey a private show?"

"Petey can go bugger himself."

"Why don't you like me, Celia. Celia Dare de Derrière?"

"Because you're the only thing between me and the door." She steps toward him.

He spreads his limbs wide. "You'll have to get through meeee."

Trembling with adrenaline, she slams a fist into Lawford's soft booze belly.

He jerks forward and spits up on the carpet. "Fucking cunt."

She yanks the door open, shoots through the suite and out to the elevators. Thumbing the call button, she paces back and forth and clenches her hands, turns and throws her foot into the elevator door, which opens on impact.

Three men stand facing Celia's glare, Bobby in the middle. His lips part in surprise and they move on into the hall.

"No need to rush, boys, there's whores for everyone," she says and shoves past.

"I'll catch up with you," Kennedy tells his cohorts and ducks back between the doors.

Thick quiet permeates as they move down the elevator shaft. "Were you just, ah, did my brother-in-law . . ." Bobby pauses for words. "I hate to ask what you had the misfortune of running into in that suite but I can assure you, I—"

"Bullshit. Lawford used to pimp for your brother too." She glares at the descending numbers. "I'm so stupid." Doors open, she walks straight ahead toward the front entrance.

"Please, Celia." He catches up and takes her elbow. She snaps it back but stays.

Softly, Bobby says, "I have great respect for you, ah, I don't know what my former brother-in-law said to you but I, ah, I had no idea he had even planned to invite you."

She allows him to steer her toward a quiet corner of the lobby.

He sits beside her. "I've thought of you often, but out of respect, ah, for your wishes I haven't tried to contact you. I would never do anything that might insult your integrity or . . ." She looks away. He rubs at his nose. "I did once confess to Pete that I had a terrible crush on you. Perhaps in his drug-addled mind that was code for something else."

Celia's pulse has slowed to normal but her eyes continue to sweep the room.

"Nothing would make me happier than to spend what's left of the evening talking with you, but I, ah—please don't misunderstand me—between the reporters and the Republicans . . . would you, ah, consent to joining me in my suite?"

Sitting on Bobby's sofa, she sighs. "I'm sorry I went at you like that. Just, the way Lawford was . . . and a friend died recently. I guess I'm still a little raw."

He hands her a drink then sits beside her. "Someone you were close to?"

She nods. "Sort of a surrogate father when I first left home." She takes a swallow from the drink. "He looked awful. Excuse me. I don't mean to . . ."

"You needn't ever be embarrassed in front of me. I'm embarrassed that someone connected to me treated you poorly this evening." She waves it off. "Well, it certainly wasn't the circumstance in which I hoped we'd meet again. May I ask what was going on up there?"

"Nothing in particular. A few men and a lot of girls. I had hoped I could help with your campaign, but Peter felt I could best do this with my clothes off."

The phone rings. "Hello . . . hi . . . uh-huh . . . Jesus . . . what's he . . . ? no. I think I'm going to call it a night . . . That's fine." He hangs up. "Apparently the party's thick with marijuana smoke and Pete's handing out, ah, LSD." He looks into his lap. "I'm going to have to talk with him. His association can only hurt us. I'm actually trying to steer clear of celebrity endorsement."

She studies his face. "Did you really work with Joe McCarthy?"

He gives a self-conscious smile. "My father got me that job—it was my first. I thought there was a serious internal threat to the country and Joe seemed to be the only one who was doing anything about it."

One of her hands is resting palm up in her lap and he reaches over with his, lays his hand lightly against hers, examines the contrast and adds, "Between working with Joe and bulldogging for my brother, I made a lot of enemies."

"To say nothing of the Hoffa stuff." She lets his fingers lace through hers.

"Hoffa deserved what he got. They stole millions and then you bring these fellows into court and every damn one of them takes the Fifth. And there was this constant chant, *What's wrong with taking the Fifth? It's part of the Constitution.* As if somebody were performing a major patriotic act in refusing to answer for his crimes."

A tiny smile plays over her mouth. "Did you ever think it was wrong?" she asks. "I mean, did you ever agree to bugging someone . . ."

He sighs. "There were a couple things I did to keep Hoover off my brother." He looks down at his sleeve. "This was my brother's sweater."

She touches the cashmere.

"A fellow I know once asked Johnson why he didn't fire Hoover. He said, *I'd rather have him inside the tent pissin' out then outside the tent pissin' in.*"

She laughs.

"If I win this election, I'd like to nail that demented old queer to the wall."

"You'll win."

"Or I'll prove what everybody who doesn't like me says: that I'm a selfish, ambitious little SOB who can't wait to get his hands on the White House."

"That's not true. Lots of people love you."

"I don't know. Sometimes I get the idea that there are those around who don't like me." He grins and moves his hand from hers, up her arm, and brushes her cheek with one finger. The touch sends sparks through her.

That night, the two of them fall asleep on the couch, fully clothed.

In the morning, he checks the hall for bodies and eyes. Coast clear, she ducks out.

Eighteen

~

BRILLIANT RED, INCH-LONG AND BLUNT TIPPED, MY NEW talons made it pretty much impossible to write. I wanted to file them down a little but Frank loved them. He said they were perfect for the big show. I couldn't type either so he bought me a headset to use, a mike that allowed me to answer verbally what the jerkflirt guys typed in. He'd also bought me a blonde wig and yet another sparkly G-string and bra.

"I thought you said you liked it dark." I pulled the wig on in the mirror, finger-combing straw-coloured ends over the sequins on my new screaming-pink showgirl bra.

Standing behind me, Frank shrugged. "I said it made you look like a slutty librarian. But when you think about it, the wig helps to disguise you better. I mean, the mask works but the wig would kinda kill two birds."

"The colour is shit." I pulled wisps around my face. "You're more freaked about someone recognizing me than I am."

He arranged my bangs in the mirror, wiped a smudge of eyeliner off my cheek and picked up my lip brush. "Every guy wants his girl to be a virgin in public—" he glossed more red over my bottom lip "—and a whore in bed. Besides, if you ever get another acting agent, you don't want anyone knowing you do porn." He put the brush down and pulled a tiny brown envelope from his shirt pocket. "You wanna take one now or wait till she gets here?"

"May as well wait. Can you get me another glass of wine though?"

"You don't wanna be drinking a lot before you take X, I told you that. It's bad for business if you look too out of it." He stuck the envelope back in his pocket, reached into my medicine cabinet and took out his Rogaine. Filling up the eyedropper, he held my makeup mirror behind his head. "Do you think this stuff is doing any good."

I examined the back of his head for him. "To think they can grow hair on a rat's ass . . . Here. Gimme." I took the eyedropper and squirted some on, patted it into his thinning bit. "Okay, out of my way before I grow fur on my palms," I said, rinsing in the sink. "Another glass of wine. I'm nervous, okay. Placate me."

The intercom went. I buzzed her in, and went back into the bathroom to grab my robe.

"She's he-e-ere," Frank sang from the kitchen. I heard him clap his hands, rub his palms together. Finally realizing his dream. To observe anyway.

I opened the door to Sienna's false eyelashes and swingin' sixties hairpiece, her deer eyes crinkled with glee. She wore a pleated schoolgirl skirt in black and yellow plaid. "Vivian? You're a blonde again?" she said with an uncertain face. I'd only seen her once since the night at Nevermind, a quick hello and goodbye when Frank and I stopped by their studio. She stepped into the hall.

"Frank bought it. He thinks it'd make a nice contrast with yours. I think he's just pissed that I cut my own hair off."

"Ohhh," she answered after a pause, as though I'd said something that had taken her a great deal of juggling to comprehend.

I pulled the wig off. She brightened. "That's better. Where is he?"

"He's right here, my little beauties." Frank walked merrily toward us as we came into the living room. He handed us each a glass of red. "You took it off?"

"They know Lucinda as a brunette," I reminded him.

"Plus I want us to be twins," Sienna said, two hands clutching her purse in front, swaying in little screw-turns back and forth, skirt swinging a beat behind her torso.

Frank took the envelope out of his pocket and shook it like a maraca. He dumped three tablets in his palm, one for himself, it seemed.

"Are we doing X?" Sienna asked.

"Oh yeah," he said. "Feel the love, girls."

"Frank, relax," I said and patted his hand closed. "We don't have to if you don't want," I told her. "I've just never done this before so I thought it might relax me, make me more lovey-dovey. Did you know they used to use it for couples counselling?"

"You've never been with a girl?" Sienna asked, wide-eyed. "You're, like, a virgin?" she twittered. "So you need me to be gentle?" She giggled more deeply and hugged me.

I stiffened, gulped some wine. "Let's sit down."

"Yeah, sit, sit." Frank looked from Sienna to me as if we were pie and ice cream.

"Brian told me you even outearned me last week?" She plopped down on the couch, skirt fanning out around her. "Boy, the two of us together? You know we're doing $9.99 a minute for the duo right?"

"Yeah," I nodded. The jerkflirt site had banners up advertising Lucinda and Sabrina's hot girl-on-girl action, featuring Lucinda's first lesbian experience. Available for private and private group-shows only. Groups were limited to four at a time with a fifteen-minute minimum. Our first two group-shows were already booked with regulars.

Sienna examined what appeared to be a cat scratch on her knee. She pulled off the first tiny scab of the dotted line; a prick of blood burbled up and she gasped. "Oh no, look what I did." She sucked the drop off her finger.

Looking at the tablets Frank had left on the coffee table, I asked if she wanted a bandage.

"Umm." Her swooping eyelashes fanned the scratch. She pressed her fingertip against it once more. "No. It'll be all right. Thank you." She smiled up as if I were her fairy godmother. Looking at the pills too, she reached for my hand and giddily said, "Okay, let's do the ecstasy. I only like to do it with people I feel safe around. And you're really nice."

Frank held his breath. I suddenly felt like his old work mule next to Sienna's new pony. The thing about ecstasy is that, generally speaking, it hadn't ever made me feel idealistically adoring the way it does some people, but it often gave me a more understanding self, the ability to see these jerkflirt guys as just poor schmucks who needed attention, someone to answer their questions, be compassionate. It gave me sympathy, coupled with a sort of stark realism: I was one of the highest-paid shrinks around. Sienna counted 1–2–3 and each of us popped a pill with a slug of wine.

Frank grinned as he bounced his knee and chomped his bottom lip. He seemed to be already grinding his teeth—another X effect. "Let me put some music on." He bounded to the shelf, ran his finger up and down CD spines, looking for just the right thing. God only knows what possessed him, but he grabbed one of those old crooner compilations I'd bought. Louis Prima's hoarse rasp suddenly filled the room with "That Old Black Magic" and Keely Smith smoothed in every other line clean and clear. The raspberry red of my mother's dress rustled around me.

Frank danced with himself a little then looked to Sienna. "You should see what we did with the bedroom, it's a regular Den of Iniquity . . . I draped cream-coloured satin down from the ceiling like, like, an Arabian Nights theme!"

"Cool!" Sienna squealed and I thought of my mother's friend in San Francisco. Minnie Mouse on helium. *Did I make that up?* "This music is really cool too? Whereja get it?"

"Picked it up somewhere." He offered his hand and she jumped up to join him. The two of them jived and wiggled and I watched them from forty years away. Dinah Washington slipped onstage behind them and started into "What a Difference a Day Makes" and the backs of my eyes ached. *Vivian* somersaulted into my ear from somewhere and I looked into my lap at Frank's hand as it picked up mine and brought me to my feet. "Come dance with Sienna," he said, placing my hand in hers.

Sienna's mouth formed an *eek* as though she were heading up the first steep incline of a roller coaster. She put her head on my shoulder and let me lead, me in my bathrobe and her in her canary-yellow blouse and pleated skirt. Soon Ella Fitzgerald cut in with "Something's Gotta Give" and Sienna gave a whoop and started a sort of half-jive half-waltz with me. The mood of the song perked me up but I was feeling more and more as if I were wearing someone else's skin. By the time Rosemary Clooney sang, *Kid you're good lookin' but you don't know what's cookin'*, a hot rush zipped up my arms. The X was kicking in. I clenched my teeth.

"Five minutes, babies," Frank yelled from the kitchen. "Five minutes till ring-a-ding time!" *Ring-a-ding time?* I could hear him rattling ice in the martini shaker.

"Why did you say that?" I asked and realized that my mouth hadn't actually opened. Shots of cold alternated with the heat in my arms. My spine felt as though it had been dipped in Noxema. Frank slicked back into the room with two icy crantinis and suggested we head for the bedroom, get ready to show those jerk-flirts what their mothers couldn't. I wished he hadn't said *mother.*

Cream satin and cotton draped the bed and hung from the ceiling, throw cushions lay over bed pillows heaped around sheets. Frank had laid out a bouquet of vibrators and dildos. My laptop sat on the blanket trunk at the foot of the bed. "Wow," Sienna grinned. "You guys got toys galore, hey?" She dumped her bag on the floor, started to take off her platforms then stopped. "I'm gonna leave my clothes on? and then we can, like, undress each other?"

I stood mute in my robe, my brain fritzing like shaken soda, my lungs cold and clammy. Beads of sweat had sprung up across my nose and cheeks. Neither Sienna nor Frank seemed to be reacting the same way. He picked up the remote keyboard and woke the computer. The jerkflirt site filled the screen and Harry Belafonte called, *Mama, look a Boo-boo*, from the living room.

"Two minutes, girls!" Frank clicked here and there and added, "Holy shit. The first three shows are booked solid and the first show already has three voyeurs signed on." The voyeurs could watch but had no input, no ability to make requests. Peeping today would cost them $4.49 a minute. "You girls are some kinda hot commodities," he whooped. There was altogether too much whooping going on. He reached over to the shelf and grabbed the feathery pink mask he'd bought to match my lingerie. Teasing it over the skin on my arms, his lips spread away from his teeth. I flinched. "Sensitive?" he laughed and slipped the mask over my head. Sienna reached into her bag for hers, set it over her eyes. He had my headset and another microphone set up near the bed so we could answer the men without typing.

I sat down and Sienna moved in close, took my hand and beamed at the webcam as Frank said, "Okay, we'll start with the group chat for a minute so we can try and take on any of the stragglers as voyeurs. Man, we're gonna *cash in* . . ." I gripped her hand as Frank counted down and pointed. "You're on!"

"Hi boys," Sienna said. Like some kind of shape-shifting lizard, her Sabrina voice drawled and dropped two octaves lower than her usual squeak.

Frank sniggered and, remembering the mikes, cupped a hand over his mouth. Instant messages flipped rapid-fire onto the screen. Our regulars: Lojo, SugarDaddy, Loverman, Gimme2, Diggler . . . *U girls r hot; Kiss her; Take ur tops off; Touch her pussy; Do u do anal? U r angels.* Then GuySmiley popped up, the first one to ever book me in a private. *Lucinda*, he typed. *U ok? U look sad.* The screen took on a plasmic warble, as if it were penetrable, a liquid door I could crawl through and find someone who would see the oily crows flapping in my chest and hold me. My mother's thin cancerous fingers. My black birds.

Iggy typed: *Sabrina, Lucinda looks fuckable.*

"She's definitely fuckable," Sienna groaned. She turned my chin and kissed me. My hands floated up without command and took her face. It was soft as though I could pierce it with my thumbs. I wished I could climb all the way inside her mouth, like a cat in a cubbyhole. I needed to be wrapped in someone or something. She rolled the robe off my shoulders and batted her lashes at the webcam. "We're late, boys," she drawled. "There's some big spenders waiting for a private *sssex* show. There's still room for some peeping Toms . . ." And she waved goodbye. Frank poked at the keyboard and two still photos took the place of our moving selves. A message explained: *These Models Are Currently in a Private Show.* A second screen came up and four private members' names and their comments flashed white against the black. Frank was suddenly on his feet, lighting the candle on the bookshelf and adjusting the helmet again. What was his obsession with that goddamn helmet? My eyes stuck to its raised visor. Sienna tsked and looked at me as if searching for some punchline.

You look sad.

Frank's teeth glowed at me now as if they were black lit and Sienna pushed her tongue deep in my mouth. A dark cold sliced the heat in my arms, flapping up and through my neck, pulsing and feathering in behind my eyes.

Kiss Her, they typed and my brain bubbled. *Tongue; lick; fuck; pussy; more; Baby It's Cold Outside; lips; hot; dildo; lick; cunt; Something's Gotta Give; These people are often called oblates; ChaChaCha D'amour, More obscene than all the dirty four-letter words poured into all the dirty books; suckling like a baby; I'm an old stupid woman; One-two-three, what are we fightin' for; Why Not Take All of Me? Slap her ass; tongue, lick; Are you living in a vacuum, no purpose, no challenge, just exist-ing?; harder; strap-on; bite; Tune in, turn on, drop out; finger; deeper; tongue; more more more.*

And then our fifteen minutes of fame were up. Frank had swapped screens on the laptop and a sign reading *These Models Are Currently on Break*, filled the screen. *Next Show in Ten Minutes.* "Holy fuck, was that hot! I've never been so hard in my life," he crowed, clutching at the crotch of his jeans.

Wayne Newton said *Danke shoen.*

"Are you okay?" Sienna asked me. "I never did dominant before! Was it okay?"

"It was fucking hot," Frank hollered at the top of his lungs and then he was beside me. The touch of his fingertips shocked me and I flinched. He shoved his tongue in my mouth as he yanked his shirt off and I drifted, oozing and fritzing. Pink skin, all around, all gone, everything gone. Wings flapped slowly in my ears, giggles and moans laced through feathers, mouths inside thighs, fingers wrapped, someone inside, mouths lapping, *One-two-three, what are we fightin' for, don't ask me I don't give a damn, next stop is Vietnam.* And then the oily black feathers came down all around, suffocating, a heavy black cancerous curtain, just pinpricks of light. I had to hold tight to the pinpricks. I screamed for light.

"What's wrong?" Sienna squealed, jumping back.

Light through holes in the dark, gunshots through black felt.

"What's wrong?" Frank repeated.

"No more," I said. "I don't like it. Just—no more."

Sienna sat back now, her mask sagging off to one side. None of us was clothed.

Frank's pupils were glistening black platters. "Are you freaking out? What's wrong?"

I shook my head. "I don't want to do this."

"You feeling sick?" he asked. "You guys still got two shows to do."

I shook my head hard; wings flapping as if a little girl had run through pigeons.

"Baby, you were totally into it two minutes ago. What happened?"

"No." I shook my head again. "No. You don't even know me."

He looked at his watch. "Shit. Just calm down. It's, like, two minutes till the next show. Just do this next one, okay. Come here, Sienna. Sienna's gonna look after you."

I shook my head. "Why do you keep touching my helmet?"

"Yeah, Frank." Sienna giggled. "Are you going to use this for the download site too?" Frank must have made some motion that caused Sienna to say, "No way! You're bad! Vivica! I mean, Vivian! You know Frank's taping this too, right? . . . You can't tape and not tell," she squealed. "It's in the helmet, it's in the helmet!"

Frank barked a wooden ha-ha. "Big mouth."

"You've been taping this? You've been taping us since I got home."

"He's got a camera there, right there underneath," Sienna shrilled, pointing one long nail toward the face of the helmet.

"She knows," Frank said, his erection sulking now as he worked the keyboard again. "We've got about a minute left. Just do this one, baby, and then we'll get you something to eat or whatever. You had too much to drink, that's all. Just fifteen minutes and I'll give you a massage."

My head swivelled to and fro, trying to get the songs out, get Martin Luther King out, Bobby, Annie, Johnny. I wished I had Johnny. I wished I had someone dangerous on my side. "What are you *doing*?" I said out loud, to me and anyone else who could answer the question.

"Forty-five seconds," Frank said. "Baby, it's no big deal. I taped it when we fucked a few times and I put it on another site. It's under the helmet so you wouldn't be self-conscious. Don't worry, no one can tell who we are. I figured you knew. How do you think I keep giving you all that cash?" He leaned in and straightened my mask.

"I don't care," I said to my bare knees. They looked like russet potatoes now. My mother smiled in the garden. My mother onstage smiling, tumbling, brunette to blonde, to me and her and Frank said, 5, 4, 3, 2, 1.

"We're back, you bad boys," Sienna drawled at the webcam.

I stared at the helmet's visor. Spy cams. Nanny cams. Instant messages gunned down the computer screen. Sienna glanced at me with a sort of bemused look and giggled. I realized I'd been humming. The motion in my head stopped dead and I sang, *"And it's five, six, seven, open up the Pearly Gates, there ain't no time to wonder why, whoopee, we're all gonna die."* And then I laughed. And Sienna laughed. "Why don't you ask me what I'm singing?" I suggested.

"Okay." She tried to bring my hand to her breast.

SugarDaddy typed "Feels Like I'm Fixin' to Die."

"Not you," I reprimanded the webcam. I pulled off the mask and the room tilted, slammed into focus, a straight concise grid. The crows were gone. Other bodies in the room looked as though they were in stark relief, hyper 3D. Hurt fizzled across Sienna's face. Frank's pupil-filled eyes loomed and pleaded.

"Frank, why don't you ask me why I keep watching old news videos? Why I'm reading about Kennedys and mobsters and Judy Campbell?"

Instant messages battered down the screen. *Who's Frank?; Lick please; Eat her pussy; yes yes yes; fuck 4 me!*

"Don't you want to know what's in her trunk?"

"Frank?" Sienna chirped nervously, her Sabrina self had scampered under the bed.

"Vi—Lucinda!" Frank stuttered.

"My name is Vivian," I said calmly to the video. "I'm Vivian Callwood and my mother used to be a stripper called Celia Dare. My boyfriend, Frank, doesn't know any of this, because he's been too busy secretly videotaping us fucking." A deep wide sea chuckled out of me and I felt bright and airy. "Come on, Sienna, confess! It's fun, it's better than being with a priest!"

"For chrissake!" Frank howled as he tapped at the keyboard. *These Models Are Currently on Break*, the screen read again. "You drank too much. You're tripping. You, you—shit . . . we're losing, like, fifty, sixty bucks a . . . I gotta call Brian."

"No," I said. I felt serene. Like the eye of a big fleshy vibrating storm. "You should go home. Call Brian from home. You too, Sienna. You can head home."

Ecstasy can cause a person to take things to heart and tears dribbled down Sienna's soft dewy cheeks now as I pulled on my robe. I sat down beside her again and wiped her face with the sheet. "Don't feel bad, I'm just having an epiphany," I explained gently. "How old are you anyway."

"Eighteen," she whispered. I handed her her blouse.

Frank paced, hands rubbing up and down his folded arms, shoulders huddled. "Your mum's name was *Josie* and she was a militant feminist . . . teacher . . . *bitch*," he said. He curled into himself and grabbed his shirt off the floor as his teeth ground. "Fuckin' X is too speedy, man."

"I hid her mink coat in the closet," I announced. "I believe she got it from a gangster."

His face red and contorted now, he looked like a throbbing blister. "You knew I was taping us," he gasped as he fumbled with buttons. "You just like pretending so you don't have to take responsibility." He pulled on his jeans. "I thought you'd feel self-conscious and you did too so you just let me and pretended like nothing was happening."

"Nope. I didn't," I said cheerily and went out of the room and down the hall. "I thought something was peculiar but I didn't know what," I called back. In the closet, I shoved clothes aside, the blanket I'd thrown on top, and opened the trunk. Kneeling, I pushed my face down, ran my cheek along the fur before I pulled it out and draped its stiff bulk around me.

Back in the bedroom, fat luminous tears rolled off Sienna's face onto her thighs as she bent forward and pulled on her shoes. Frank cuddled in beside her, offering a comforting arm and soft murmurs. "Frank," I said, standing at the foot of the bed, mink over bathrobe. "You would fuck my mother but you'd never *date* her. Can you see how that's fucked up?"

"I see *you're* fucked up!" he blurted, helping Sienna to her feet and past me to the door. Letting her go a moment, he stomped back, picked up the helmet and ripped the squat camera off the shelf.

"Weird," I observed. "Where does the tape go?"

1968: Tiny Tim; Eartha Kitt; Doctor Spock; *Refuse Induction!*; Jackie Kennedy & Aristotle Onassis; Julie Nixon & Dwight David Eisenhower II; secret military research; *We shall overcome, We shall not be moved*; Black Power; Yippies; Abbie Hoffman; demonstration; nightsticks and tear gas; Columbia University; *Up against the wall, Motherfucker!*; Welcome to Chicago; Tet Offensive; King—*Mine eyes have seen the glory of the coming of the Lord*; Gunned down in Memphis; Bobby Kennedy—*I had a member of my family killed but he was killed by a white man*; Year of the Monkey; Eugene McCarthy; Let us begin again; LBJ—*I will not accept the nomination of my party for another term as president*; the Ambassador Hotel; *Some men see things as they are and say why, I dream of things as they never were and say why not*; Senator Kennedy has been shot.

Annie walks out on a dinner date with red eyes and shaking hands. Coming home to the apartment, she finds Celia on the couch eating Cheezies. She stands between Celia and the television. "Micky D."

"Huh? From The 92 Micky D?"

"He's dead. They found him . . ." her voice strangles " . . . at the bottom of Lake Erie with his feet stuck in two buckets of cement and scuba gear on his back."

The telephone rings and they both jump. "It's never good when that damn thing rings," Annie says and begins to cry again.

"I know," Celia agrees. "It's like playing Russian roulette lately." She goes to the kitchen and Annie follows. "Hello? . . . Oh, it's you," she says softly. "How *are* you?"

"Not so great," Bobby answers. "Martin Luther King was shot tonight. In Memphis. I thought you'd want to know."

"Oh god. When is this going to end?"

"I said the same thing. I've got to speak in a few minutes. In a ghetto."

She gasps. "There'll be riots. This should come from, from . . ."

"From whom? I should go. I just needed to hear your voice."

"*Bobby!* They'll kill you."

He sighs, resigned. "If it's not them, it'll be someone else."

"Don't say that. Just, just let—"

"Talk to you soon."

Celia puts the phone down. "Martin Luther King was shot."

"Fuck!" Annie hurls her purse on the floor.

The receiver isn't in its cradle ten seconds before the ringing resumes.

"Don't answer it," Annie says. She grabs for the cord, threatening to yank. "No more."

"Okay." She raises her hands in surrender.

For days to follow, black America riots, a collective wail burning through the country. Nearly a hundred thousand federal troops and National Guardsmen are dispatched to contain the uprising.

Annie and Celia stay inside, ordering food when they can stomach it. Over the airwaves, King's last speech rings out: . . . *And I've seen the promised land. I may not get there with you. But I want you to know tonight that we, as a people, will get to the promised land. And I'm happy, tonight. I'm not worried about anything. I'm not fearing any man. Mine eyes have seen the glory of the coming of the Lord.* Bobby's speech in Indianapolis weaves through: *For those of you who are black and are tempted to be filled with hatred and distrust at the injustice of such an act, against all white people, I can only say that I feel in my own heart the same kind of feeling. I had a member of my family killed, but he was killed by a white man. But we have to make an effort in the United States, we have to make an effort to understand, to go beyond these rather difficult times . . .*

After King's funeral, the mourners hike six miles to Morehouse College, King's alma mater. News cameras close in on Bobby, his jacket slung over his shoulder, as he marches alongside Sammy Davis Jr. Crowds cheer at the sight of them.

Though Annie still refuses, Celia begins picking up the phone.

When he calls again, back on the campaign trail, he sounds tired and a little remote.

"I keep thinking about you," she tells him.

"Do you?"

"Of course." The long silences from him make her want to reach through the phone and grab him by the throat. "Do you think about *me*?"

His voice is soft and low. "I'll bet you look like a million bucks right now." He drifts off and when she doesn't fill in the silence he finally says, "My day is better when I talk to you."

She picks up a pen and doodles on a newspaper. "I think the worst of it is reading your wife's name. They write about her hair every other day."

"She's rarely with me—I bring along that wig she wears and everybody's happy."

Pops of suppressed laughter from the two of them give her a little relief but she wishes he'd say something substantial. "I feel like an elastic band is tightening."

"I know what you mean. If a sniper doesn't get me before this is through, I'd like to—"

"I hate it when you talk like that."

"What doesn't kill you makes you stronger."

"Cut it out."

Another long silence then suddenly he blurts, "Meet me."

"What if someone sees us? . . ."

The next evening, Celia drives from the Indianapolis airport in a rented car and checks into the small-town motel under an alias: Nancy West. She wears a dark wig. The last room in the place—all the rest are taken up by campaign workers and press.

"The Plaza it ain't," she says, dropping her bag. She takes out the bottle of wine she brought and sets it on the dresser, smoothes her skirt and looks around the sparse room.

She takes off her coat and sits on the bed. Standing up, she goes back to the wine and wonders if she should let it breathe. No corkscrew. She turns in circles and roots through her purse, picks up the phone and calls the front desk. It's about eleven-thirty when the Merlot finally gets some air.

She arranges the glasses and the bottle just so and sits back on the bed. Finding her compact she reapplies lipstick, checks her eyeliner, powders the shine from her forehead. Remembering her wig, she pulls it off and runs to the bathroom to fix her hair.

It's nearly midnight when several cars pull in to the parking lot, doors opening and slamming, feet on the balcony, laughter.

Eventually, a knock at her door. She opens to Bobby's grin. She pulls him inside. "What took you?"

"I had to change out of my shirt, it was filthy. And wash my hands before touching you. And wait till the press—Jesus, you're here." He clutches her face and inhales deeply as he kisses her. Turning the lock behind him, he steers her to the bed until the two of them fall on the spread, his hand pulling up her skirt.

"No, just—*Bobby.*"

He freezes. "What's wrong?"

"Well—can you talk to me a little? Or something."

His head drops into her shoulder. "I'm sorry. I've made love to you in my head so many times, I . . ." He sets his lips gently against her temple now. She pushes the hair off his forehead and smiles as it falls back.

"You know I'm crazy about you, don't you?" he asks.

"What am I going to do?"

He wraps his arms around her.

She kicks her shoes off.

"That's a good sign," he says.

She digs her toes into one of his heels and pries at his shoe until it's half off. He shakes it loose. Bit by bit they remove each other's clothing and cling and slide and slip, slow then fast, and slow again.

They doze in the night. A dart of light from the window illuminates his fingers, the scratches and scrapes. "What happened?"

"Shaking all those hands. They really dig in sometimes." Slipping an arm around her stomach, he pulls her closer, curves his body to the back of hers and slips inside.

In the morning, she holds his hips to her until she moans and gasps and falls back again, letting the ebb and flow of him wash over her. There is a light rap at the door.

Her eyes bug.

"Don't be so worried," he whispers.

"Bob, are you com—" A voice from outside the door. "Are you up—awake?"

"Uh, yeah, I'll be right there." He bites her chin.

"Who was *that*?"

"Kenny, I think. One of my guys."

She watches him dress, his slight frame disappearing under his baggy suit. "Where will you go today?"

"Columbus, Edinburg, Franklin . . . all the way back up to Indianapolis. Why don't you meet me there tonight. We'll be at the Marriott."

"Are you sure?" She looks at the door.

Another knock and a low-voiced "Ah, Bob, everyone's ready to go."

He scoops her up in the blankets. "Come on, you can snooze in the back seat."

"No!" she yips, giggling, and he loosens his grip.

He grabs his coat and whispers, "Who's Nancy West?"

She shrugs.

"I'll make a reservation for you," he says.

As he closes the door, she hears, "How did you know I was in there?"

"The whole place heard you in there."

She flips on the radio. Tom Jones's "Delilah" fills the room. She flips it off. Stretching her limbs, she sweeps them across the bed, before reaching for the phone.

Late in the afternoon, she drives into Franklin. There isn't a soul on the street but she hears bullhorned voices in the distance. Music and cheers. She parks when she spots the crowd a couple blocks up, checks her wig in the mirror, taps the bridge of her sunglasses and gets out.

A few men on a flatbed truck, and four or five hundred people jammed into the small street, pushing and shoving. Bobby is on the truck, arms outstretched, shaking hands. All around him they scream and weep, reaching to touch the hem of his garment. Suddenly he is yanked off and dragged into the crowd.

She starts toward them then stops when Bobby pops up like a grinning scarecrow, hands from every direction yanking and pulling, fingers in his hair, his name chanted and screamed and wailed.

Later that night she opens her door to Bobby's thin dishevelled self. Hands bleeding from new cuts and old ones reopened, his shirt sleeves are black. She takes him gingerly by the wrists. "Where are your cufflinks?"

"They steal them." He kicks the door closed. "We have to bring a bagful every day. They stole one of my shoes last week." He smiles at his dirty arms and sleeves. "I was going to change and shower but when I heard Nancy West was in the building . . . god, you're so pretty, I hate to come too close and—" he kisses her mouth "—get you dirty."

She tugs him toward the bathroom. Turning him around, she sits him down on the toilet seat, turns on the faucet then straddles his lap and undoes his belt as hot water fills the tub.

Alone the next morning, she stares at the ceiling. Ethel will join him today. Ethel and her goddamn hair. "What am I *doing*?" she bellows into the sheets and calls Annie.

"You're picking up the phone again?"

"Yeah," Annie says. "Truman came over here the other night and got me sloshed. Then we went to a bar in the Village. Truman says he doesn't know why these Kennedy boys get laid so much—he's seen the goods and they got nothin'." She giggles.

When there's no response, she says, "Marty's been looking for you. He's climbing the walls."

"He said he wouldn't book me till I came up with a new act."

"I don't know. When you coming home?"

"My flight's at one."

The moment she comes though the apartment door, Annie passes the phone.

"Where have you been, sweetheart?" Johnny. She hasn't heard from him in weeks. His voice has a quiet malignance.

"Nowhere. Just hanging around."

Annie sits up on the kitchen counter.

"Is that right? You sound so relaxed, I thought you might have taken a vacation but then you wouldn't do that without Annie, would you? Leave her all alone while you scamper off."

Her jaw pulses. "So, what's doing with you? You married yet?"

"No. Are you?"

"I heard you were engaged."

"If I were going to get married you'd have a ring on your finger."

"Jesus, you're full of shit."

A knock comes at the door. Annie hops down and goes to answer.

"You'll have to come and see me soon. When are you booked in L.A. next?"

"Marty won't book me until I get a new act together."

"Be careful, my darling."

"What's that supposed to mean?"

"Don't let your career die from distraction."

Men's voices in the living room. Annie appears in the kitchen entrance, her eyes round. "We have *visitors*. Federal Bureau of Investigation," she enunciates.

Celia's mouth drops before she whispers, "*FBI*? What the hell are they doing here?"

"Stay calm," Johnny says softly. "You have nothing to tell them. They'll go away."

She hangs up and follows Annie. Two men in dark suits wander the living room, eyes picking over furniture, knick-knacks, papers left around. They glance up. "Good afternoon, Miss Dare. How are you today?"

She nods pleasantly.

"I'm Special Agent Dodge and this is Special Agent Richards." Badges flash.

"I'm Celia—you know that. My roommate, Annie West." She clasps her hands.

"We'd like to ask you a few questions."

Celia sets herself on the sofa. The agents remain standing and look to Annie who, other than to fold her arms, doesn't budge.

"Do you know a Sam Giancana, Miss Dare?" Dodge asks.

"No."

"*No?* Sam Giancana," he repeats firmly.

"I was introduced to him once. But I wouldn't say I *know* him."

"Do you know John Rosselli?"

"I've met him."

"Everybody knows these guys," Annie says. "What's your beef?"

Celia gawks at her. Dodge stares at Celia. "Miss Dare, I believe you know John Rosselli quite well. Does he pay your rent?"

"Why would I need someone to pay my rent?"

"Does he buy you gifts?" Dodge asks.

"We both get gifts every night we're onstage," Annie snipes.

The men ignore her. "John Rosselli is your boyfriend, Miss Dare?"

"We have some friends in common; he's not my boyfriend."

"Are the two of you lovers?"

"Are the two of *you?*" Annie spits.

The men look at her, expressionless, then back at Celia. "You haven't been performing lately, Miss Dare, why is that?"

"I took a couple of months off."

"It makes one wonder how you're managing to pay your bills. Perhaps you might be doing some things you're not proud of."

Annie takes a step forward. "This girl makes six, seven grand a week when she's onstage. Why don't you go catch a rapist and leave us the hell alone."

"You could be a big help to the security of your country, Miss Dare." Dodge hands his card to her. "Your friend Mr. Rosselli is facing some serious charges. We'd like to keep him out of trouble but we need the help of people like yourself to do it."

"Oh you Boy Scouts, always helping old ladies and gangsters across the street." Annie opens the front door. The two men nod to Celia and leave.

Peering through the blinds, Annie watches them climb into an unmarked vehicle in front of the building. "Pricks. Does Bobby know you're friends with Johnny?"

"No."

Annie turns back from the window. "It's all the same rats in the same damn maze."

Once Celia unsticks her mind from the FBI, she calls Marty Sugar.

"You're booked in L.A. next week," he says. "At the Grove. Then Caesars Palace."

"You said you wouldn't book me till I had a new show."

"Well, use an old one," he says.

"Look, I've been thinking maybe I want to sing, you know, just straight legit singing."

"Celia, honey. Striptease is your whole gimmick. No one's gonna pay to see you sing if you ain't gonna show 'em your ass. No offence, sweetheart, be a realist."

"I need some time off."

"Eight for the week, they're payin'. Ten at Caesars. Don't make my head ache. Just be a good girl, collect your cheque and take a vacation later."

In Los Angeles, Johnny takes her to dinner at his favourite, La Dolce Vita. She tells him again what was said when the FBI showed up. Annie's remarks make him guffaw. "Are the two of *you?*" he repeats. "I've missed you."

"That girl dump you or something?"

"I remember the first time I saw you. You walked into the Copa Room full of piss and vinegar. You remember that? Frank and Dean were onstage. You were really something."

She releases a bored sigh.

"Don't be like this. Sons-a-bitches might deport me, you know."

She glares into her hands.

"I'm twice your age—that, I can't forget. And I've had these pricks on my tail and I never wanted you mixed up with that. Now, they want to charge me with this shit at the Friars Club. After everything. No loyalty." He gives her a steady look. "Loyalty is more important than anything."

"You think I'm not loyal?"

"They came to your home and you played it exactly right." He reaches into his pocket and sets an oblong box of royal-blue velvet between them.

Heat runs up her arms. She opens the box to a diamond-and-sapphire necklace and her breath is caught by the shimmer. He comes round, lifts the necklace and fastens it at the nape of her neck. He kisses the crown of her head. "When I beat this thing, I want you here to stay."

Later, in her suite at the hotel, he says, "I've realized how foolish it is, keeping you at arm's length. They show up at your door regardless. And we can as easily beat them together as apart." He turns her chin but she ducks from his mouth. "What's the matter?"

"You can't just disappear then change your mind and expect me to be there."

"What's the longest you've gone without hearing from me? You think I keep in touch with everybody that way?"

She moves to cross her legs. He catches her thigh as it comes across and takes the back of her neck in his other hand. She pushes half-heartedly at his shoulder.

"I'll never walk away," he tells her. "Let me take care of you."

A swampy mess of love and doom oozes in her and she opens her mouth to him.

The L.A. papers carry stories of both Bobby and Johnny. Up on charges of wilful failure to register as an illegal alien, photographs appear of Johnny arriving at court each day via limousine, dark suited and tanned, his steely hair coiffed, his eyes solemn.

Adjacent pages show Bobby, vibrant and boyish, on the campaign trail. When Ethel appears beside him, Celia closes the paper.

He calls her in Vegas.

She recoils and craves at once. "How'd you know I was here?"

"Your roommate spilled the beans. I hoped you might meet me in Portland tomorrow."

"Ethel got a toothache?"

"I—tomorrow should be a quieter day. Will you come?"

"In other words she just left."

"What's wrong with you?"

Rubbing at her forehead, she sighs. "Nothing. I can't, I'm working."

"I really want to see you. It's been—"

"I can't just drop everything because you found a moment away from your wife and your dogs and your kids and your campaign. I have a life too."

"I've got a lot on my plate, you're damn right. But I still want to see you. I thought you felt the same way."

"Someone's at my door, I have to go."

As if on cue a knock comes at her hotel suite along with Johnny's muffled voice.

"You knew I was married, we both knew I was married," Bobby says in her ear.

Another knock at the door and, "Are you awake, honey?"

"I have to go." She hangs up. "Coming." Rushing to the door, she holds her trembling hands behind her back as Johnny stands there smiling.

"What are you doing in town?" She shows her teeth, hoping it looks like a smile.

"How can I stay away? Did you hear the good news? They're extending your Vegas engagement. Due to popular demand."

She tilts her head. "Everyone seems to know what's going on but me."

Bobby calls back at the end of the week. "I'm sorry about our last conversation."

"I'm sorry too. I have a lot of guilt about you."

"You're not even Catholic."

"Still in Oregon?"

"They hate me here. It's a big teamster state. Will you meet me? Please?"

She closes her eyes. Johnny's gone back to L.A. for a court date.

After her show that night, a knock comes at her dressing room.

"Miss Dare," Agent Dodge says as he opens the door. Richards nods.

"Hello, gentlemen," she greets them as nonchalantly as she can. She removes the last pin from her wig and pulls it off.

Dodge takes an envelope from his jacket and pulls out a sheaf of black-and-white photographs. He gazes at the top one a moment then sets it on the vanity in front of her: *Johnny coming through the lobby of the Ambassador.* "That's from a week ago. You were staying at the Ambassador Hotel, were you not, Miss Dare?"

"So?"

"Are you still saying you don't know this man?"

"I never said I didn't know him. I'm acquainted with him."

He lays three more in front of her: *Celia and Johnny leaving the Ambassador; Celia and Johnny entering La Dolce Vita.*

"Oh look, here's one of you and John Ro—excuse me—Filippo Sacco—leaving Romanoff's restaurant. Seems fond of you. How do you feel about him, Miss Dare?"

She removes her earrings. "I have nothing further to add."

"Show her those two," Richards suggests. "They're my favourites." It's the first she's heard Richards speak and his voice is snaky.

Dodge sets down a picture of Celia with Annie at the peace rally in Central Park last year.

"So what. Me and fifty thousand other people."

"Lending aid and comfort to the enemy, your president would say. But this one . . ." He sets a picture down of Celia sitting on someone's shoulders, raising a joint to her lips. "Smoking an illegal substance as Americans burn their draft cards onstage."

She throws her last piece of jewelry on the vanity. "What do you want? Yes, I know John Rosselli. We've had dinner together." Pulling a tissue, she scoops a blob of cold cream. The room is quiet. "What!" she suddenly bellows. "What do you *want?*"

Leaving the pictures, they let themselves out.

She grabs the phone. "The fucking FBI were just here. In my dressing room."

"Here too," Annie says. "Two different guys. They were asking where you were from, how long I'd known you."

"They had pictures of me with Johnny. And me with a joint at that damn demonstration."

"Shit."

Johnny calls her at the hotel. He's been convicted of failing to register as an alien. The Friars Club trial will start in three weeks. In the meantime he's free on bail. "I gotta go to Boston for a couple days. My ma's sick. Don't worry. They just want to rattle you. That's the right hand—the left one does not want to see me testify. This thing'll go away, you'll see."

Two days later she is in a Portland hotel room tangled in sheets and Bobby. "If I don't win, I'm going to kidnap you," he murmurs.

She pushes her face into his neck and dozes off.

Bobby's howl comes to her in the dark. He bolts upright, panting as her voice tumbles over him. "What? What?"

"Oh Christ," he whispers, trying to catch his breath.

She rubs his back. "It was just a dream."

"No, it wasn't."

She puts her arms around him. "I get so scared."

"No point being scared," he says. "If they want to kill me, we can't stop them."

Before she leaves for the airport that afternoon, she checks in with her agent.

"Jeez, good that you called." Marty sounds peculiar. "They want you back at the Grove for two nights. So, ah, yeah, you just head back."

"Why would they want me back there?"

"Your ticket's at the airport. Don't worry. Everything's jake."

Outside the nightclub, her picture isn't up. Bobby Darin's is. She asks at the hotel desk if Darin cancelled. Not that they are aware of.

Twenty minutes after she's checked in, Johnny shows up. He closes the door and leans back against it. "Where were you the last couple days?"

She folds her arms. "Vegas. Remember, you were there too."

"Don't bullshit me, kid." He doesn't blink.

"The FBI showed up at Caesars. They had pictures."

He walks toward her. She backs until she's flat to the wall.

"I don't want you to lie to me again."

"I was in Oregon."

"With who?"

"None of your business."

He raises his hand. She flinches, her head knocking the wall. Laying his palm across her throat, he sets his fingers lightly into her flesh.

"I'm not scared of you," she says.

"I don't want you to be. I want you to care enough not to *fuck* me. I tell you I want to share my life with you and you run off and screw that little puke." He takes his hand away. "I brought you back here to save you from your goddamn self."

He grabs her by the face. "You want me to marry you? I'll marry you to-goddamn-day!"

"I'm sorry."

"You're sorry." He unzips his pants and hikes up her dress. "I love you. You're going to stop this." Pulling fabric aside, he pushes himself inside her. "Are you going to stop this?"

Nodding, she kisses him, crying. "I'm sorry."

That night on the news: *Robert F. Kennedy Loses Oregon Primary. Next stop, California.*

Nineteen

~

THE MOMENT THE DOOR TO MY APARTMENT DOOR CLOSED,
I went to the living room and shut Frank Sinatra's big yap
smack in the middle of him doing it his way. I had a sudden
urge to throw up. Or make myself throw up. Heading for the
bathroom, I put my head in the toilet, stuck my finger down
my throat and heaved. I felt better instantly; lighter.

My Frank hadn't bothered to turn the lock behind him. I
flipped it myself, which seemed suddenly useless. I called a 24-
hour service and placed an order for a guy to come and replace
it. I called Leonard while I waited for the locksmith but he didn't
answer. Last I'd heard he was heading to the monastery for a
couple days to get a feel for the place.

After the locksmith left, I winced at my reflection in the
mirror, took off the fur coat and broke out the makeup
remover. I stood under hot water for a good half hour, letting it
batter every bit of me, soaping and scrubbing.

I towelled off and stalked naked to the kitchen, grabbed a
big green garbage bag and began tossing everything I saw that
felt like a louse in my flesh. I threw in the long blonde wig and
the hot-pink bra and thong, the webcam; I snatched the
motorcycle helmet off my shelf, double-checked it for spy-
cams and trashed it. I chucked the candle, my cigarettes, the
ashtray, the dildos and vibrators; I ripped the Arabian Nights

satin from the nails in the bedroom ceiling. I chucked the ivory cushions Frank had bought, then stripped the bed and jammed it all in tight. I paced from room to room, filling another bag.

Clean lines, I said out loud, no clutter.

Ecstasy can be, as Frank put it, speedy. Drugs may or may not be the reason, but in the two years I'd lived in this apartment, this was the first time I'd not only felt an urge to clean out my fridge but had acted upon that urge. Most of the condiments had expired. I vacuumed the living room, washed my dishes, scrubbed counters and mopped my kitchen floor. I cleaned the grime from my bathroom sink and tub, wiped smudgy fingerprints from the doorjambs and light switches. It was weirdly exhilarating.

Around two in the morning, I hauled her trunk from the closet into the living room. I dragged the carcass of her coat from the bathroom floor to the trunk and tossed it on top. Taking pictures down off my wall, I grabbed a hammer from my junk drawer and nailed the mink up by its collar and sleeves to the newly cleared space. There was a small tear under the collar I hadn't noticed before and under the nailhead's single eye, it looked like a grimace. I spread her things underneath: the heart, the dress, the shoes, the photos. I laid her letters out. I set out my notebooks and biographies: *The Chic Mafioso*, *Pack of Rats*, *The Story of RFK*, *By Cover of Assassination*, Judy Campbell's *My Story* and sat in the middle, read snatches aloud, the overlaps and conflicts, truths and lies. I scrawled and ranted and drank glass after glass of water. I charted John Rosselli's whereabouts. L.A., Florida, Cuba, murderer, lover, orphan supporter. I charted Bobby's campaign trail. On my VCR, I ran footage of his speeches, watched him brush the thicket of hair off his forehead over and over. His speech in the ballroom before he was killed in the kitchen. Shot by Sirhan Sirhan. Shot by a bodyguard. There were six bullet holes. There were eleven bullet holes. One mysterious girl in a polka-dot dress. Dozens of girls in polka-dot dresses.

By six in the morning, everybody on my TV screen was dead and I was filled with a morose longing. Billy Graham's pulpit-pounding drawl echoed: *Are you living in a vacuum, no purpose, no challenge, just existing?* Some people pop a Prozac when coming down from Ecstasy to avoid the Tuesday blues. In the past there was always company for my misery.

I went into my bedroom. Several hundred dollars lay crumpled in my top drawer. Frank had given me about fifteen hundred over the last couple weeks, playing some kind of sugar-daddy pimp role. Not wanting too much cash on me, I'd been chucking it in my bra drawer. I piled the bills on my dresser top and packed an overnight bag.

In San Francisco, I rented a car at the airport and wondered if I should be driving after twenty-four hours without sleep. I grabbed a coffee, got on the highway and headed for Danaville.

Parked in Annie's cul-de-sac again, I leaned to look through the passenger window at the milkshake-pink plaster of her house. It was dessert. The home of Hansel and Gretel. I thought I could make out movement through her window. I grabbed the mini photo album, my notebook and purse then paused to stretch out one hand and observe its tremor. In the rearview mirror, dark circles pooled my eyes. "No guts, no glory," I said and turned off the ignition.

The sun was high and my skin felt as though it was sizzling with toxins. I waffled at her front steps then headed around to the back.

The flowers in her rock garden were a shrill of colour under the glare. Annie lay on her chaise lounge, the big umbrella tilted against the sun, sweaty glass of iced drink at her side, romance novel in her hand. She looked up, slight alarm in her voice, as she said, "Yes?"

I stuttered out a greeting. "Hi, Annie. It's me, Vivian, Celia Dare's daughter."

"Oh for godsake," she said with exasperation and slapped the open book on her stomach before she pulled herself up and tossed it on the ground. She sat on the side of the lounger for a moment, her head drooping, shaking her face at the grass.

"I promise I won't stay. I've just been rolling around what you told me and the letters. And what the books say and— couldn't we please talk again?"

"No."

I felt as if I'd been punched in the throat.

"What're you doing?" She squinted at me. "Oh, don't start with the waterworks." She made claws of her hands and threatened her scalp with them. "It's the *past*," she said. "What do you wanna dredge all that up for? What does she say about you asking this stuff?"

I clutched at all my armful of papers and pictures. "She's dead. She can't help me."

"I mean. Yeah." She shook her head as if that might jar things back in place. "What did she say before? I don't like talking about those times. I told you all there is." She grabbed the arm of the lounger and pushed herself up.

"Your ankle's better," I said, noticing the cane was gone.

"It was just a little sprain. I don't like canes." She turned and went through the open glass door to the kitchen. I followed but stayed outside. Looking back, she rolled her eyes dramatically and waved me in. "You wanna drink or something?"

"Just water."

"Water," she repeated and took a bothered breath.

I sat at her table, put my things down. "I just want to understand what happened at the end. Why she decided to quit. She was dating Bobby Kennedy around the time he was killed, wasn't she?"

"Yes," she stated as if answering a phone survey. She held a tall glass under the spout of her water cooler.

"And she got involved romantically with Johnny Rosselli at the same time."

She set the full glass on the counter beside her and gave another matter-of-fact affirmation.

"Did they know about each other?" She looked at me but didn't respond. "Did Johnny know?"

"Yes."

"Did Bobby know?"

Her jaw moseyed around like a field cow's. "Eventually."

"Was he angry?"

"Yes."

"And Johnny was angry." She didn't answer. "I wondered if— Did he try to get Bobby to help him with his trial?" She peered at me. "He was on trial for the Friars Club thing." I looked at the glass of water but it seemed she'd decided not to give it to me. "They subpoenaed her to testify against him, right?"

She ruminated briefly. "Yes."

"She must've been scared." Her eyebrows moved slightly. "He was on trial in L.A. at the same time Bobby came here to campaign. She must've been in California too. It must've been messy and scary and, and fucked up."

"Yes," she said, her face registering a little something. "She was booked at the Grove."

"Did Johnny ever try to get Bobby to call off the investigation? I mean, did he try to enlist Celia to get him to help?"

"They didn't like each other," she stated coolly.

"Were they pissed off at her?"

"Yes." Her face was still and then, "He was a sonuvabitch at the end."

"Bobby?"

"I'm taking you back to New York." Sitting on the edge of the bed, Johnny reaches for his slacks.

"I take it I'm not really booked at the Grove." Still under the sheets, Celia props herself on one elbow.

He pulls on his shirt. "We're taking the three o'clock flight. I'll pick you up at one-thirty."

"You're *escorting* me back to New York? This is ridiculous."

He stands to tuck his shirt. "I think so too. But that's the way it goes."

She falls back in the pillows. "Can we go across to the Derby for breakfast?"

He straightens his jacket, "I'll see you at one-thirty," and walks out the door.

She lies still a moment then grabs for the telephone. Annie picks up and says, "*Finally!* Didn't you get my messages? I left two last night."

"No. Furthermore I'd appreciate it if you'd keep your trap shut about my whereabouts. *Why* would you tell him I went to Oregon? I thought he was going to put my lights out."

"Bobby? But you—"

"*Johnny!*"

"I didn't."

"Bullshit—who else knew but you? You told someone."

"No. I didn't."

"Bobby's in town and Johnny's about to run me out of L.A., for godsake." Silence on Annie's end. "I know I have to end it—I just want to see him once more."

"Don't."

"Don't tell me don't. If it weren't for—"

"I don't want to discuss this over the phone. I gotta go out of town. I'll call you." The line goes dead.

Celia slams the receiver down, climbs out of bed and throws some clothes on.

As she heads out the door, Agents Dodge and Richards walk toward her.

"Celia," Richards says. "Just the girl we want to see."

She hesitates then plows ahead. "Since when are we on a first-name basis?"

They follow, one on either side as she jams her thumb in the elevator call button. "Your first name is actually Audrey, isn't it?" Dodge asks. "Must've been sad for you when they noosed up Teddy the Ghost and then next thing you know Micky D gets dredged from the bottom of the pond."

"Like scum." Richards nods sombrely.

The three of them step into the elevator. Celia hugs herself as they descend. "You have me confused with someone else."

"I'm sure I've got this right. Just a second." Dodge reaches inside his jacket with one hand and presses stop with the other. They lurch to a standstill.

She stares at the envelope held out to her, *Call my lawyer* echoing in her head. She snatches it from him and, slipping her fingers in, takes out a single photo: her skinny sixteen-year-old self in a cocktail uniform at The 92. Micky D's birthday. Holding a cake, she stands over a table of the Boys and their girlfriends.

"They say he was a good dancer," Richards sighs. "Light on his feet."

"Kind of ironic that he died with cement shoes on," Dodge adds. He hands her another envelope. *Celia D'arelli* is typed across the white. "Here's my concern, Audrey."

"I think she'd be more comfortable if we addressed her as Celia," Richards suggests.

As she tears the flap, trembling takes over and both envelopes float to the floor.

"Oopsy daisy." Richards bends and picks them up, tucks the first in her purse, opens the second before handing it back. "There, I got it started for you."

She pulls out a page folded in thirds.

"It's a subpoena," Dodge explains. "Micky D and your boyfriend, Teddy, got a couple just like it. Micky was turning out to be one of the good guys, you see, he was on our side. But then he was on their side. You can't play two sides. Someone always gets hurt."

She throws the page on the floor. "Call my lawyer."

Richards bends again. "You've been served. Once you've touched it . . ." Tucking the paper back into her hand, he sets the elevator into motion.

Dodge looks at her sympathetically. "You seem like a nice kid. I'm sure we can find a way out of this."

Doors open, the men leave. Doors close. Alone, she swallows. The doors reopen and two women chatter in, followed by Rosselli. His eyebrows bounce playfully at the sight of her. "Caughtcha," he says. "Come on back up, I want to talk to you about something."

Taking her hand, he leads her back to the suite, lets them in. He watches her eyes on his key. "I got us a second one. We're not going back to New York tonight . . ." She pushes past him, sits on the sofa and stuffs her hands under her legs.

"You're still upset with me?" He sighs, standing in front of her. "Look, we're going to do this thing and we'll take you back to New York tomorrow."

Finally she blurts, "Do you know who killed Micky D?"

"The guy in the lake? Of course not." He stares. "How could you ask such a thing?"

"Was he supposed to testify against someone?"

"I would have no idea about that. I didn't know the man."

"What about Teddy? Was he supposed to testify?"

"He'd just got out of *prison*."

Tugging her hands out, she hands him the subpoena. "They said Teddy and Micky got ones just like it. And now they're dead."

"Horseshit. I've been called to testify. Am I in the lake?" He scans the page. "You're a loyal girl. People know." He folds it back up. "All the more reason . . ." He reaches inside his jacket. "Kennedy's back for the convention tomorrow. I want you to give him this."

She accepts yet another envelope. "What is it?"

"He'll understand."

"Should I tell him about that?" she eyes her subpoena.

"Yes." He takes her hands and speaks softly. "Tomorrow is the last time you're going to see him. If you care about him *and* me, you'll do what I ask. And if he cares, he'll take care of this business. We'll go back to New York tomorrow night." Standing, he tugs her up with him. "This is the hard part. After this, it'll all be downhill."

She frowns. *All downhill.* Coasting to a good thing or plunging to a bad?

He suggests they go over to the Brown Derby the way she wanted. As they come through the door of the restaurant, her ears fill with a hollow din as if she's walking into a seashell. She takes in the diners' faces all split wide, and it's hard to tell at first if they're laughing or screaming.

After lunch, he walks her back to the hotel. His gaze coasts over the lobby, the fountain in the middle, water falling in torrents as he holds her shoulders. "I gotta go." His hands drop to her waist, travel firmly up her ribs, thumbs brushing her breasts.

She looks past him to the glass entrance, imagines herself on the top floor, galloping toward the windowpane, thrashing through in a tackle of shards and limbs, the screech soaring out of her mouth and ears and eyes and nostrils, howling to the pavement. And quiet.

Johnny kisses her mouth. "Be good. I'll come by tonight."

People stroll past the fountain, front desk to the bank to the café, the lounge. Floor numbers light over the elevators and she starts toward them, stops and goes to the front desk. "Do you have any messages for Celia Dare in 510?"

"Certainly, Miss Dare, I believe there are—oh, no. I'm mistaken. You must have picked them up already. You received yesterday's and this morning's?" She shakes her head. "Perhaps the other guest in your room . . ."

In her room, she dials home. No answer.

A knock at the door. She opens to a bellboy who hands her a chilled bottle of champagne, compliments of Mr. Rosselli. The moment the door closes, she pops the cork and pours a glass. Waiting for the foam to die, she slugs from the bottle and paces to the window, looks down on the gardens. She takes the bottle into the bathroom, runs a bath.

By five, the champagne is gone and the bath water refuses to warm up again. On the television: news coverage of Bobby's exhaustion in San Diego. In the clip he suddenly stops speaking and sits down at the edge of the stage, his head in his hands. The cameras catch Ethel's fright as he is led offstage. Celia's throat constricts. Bobby comes back to finish, raises two fingers in a peace sign at the crowd.

She roots in her suitcase for pills. A thick tarry sleep is what she wants now, viscous black nothing. She calls room service and orders more champagne.

In the dark, Bobby plays and runs in the hotel hall, a football flying. Kids and dogs, barking, Ethel, Ethel, Ethel, her hairspray, and hair and hair and hair, and the kids playing with a baby monkey. The monkey has Ethel's wig on its head. Ethel crawls in bed, taps her forehead to Celia's. "You're next, little girl," she says. Pills rattle and Johnny himself wraps round her, stroking her temple. The weight of him, the slide of his tongue. Then barking. Bobby's dog, Freckles, licking her hand and her knees, nosing up between her thighs. Stewart is over her, spreading her legs carefully like a surgeon would. He asks Dodge and Richards to hold her still as he prints A.u.d.r.e.y. up one leg and down the other.

When she wakes, her neck is sloppy and useless, head drooping side to side. She opens her pills again, swallows two more with a bit of flat champagne.

Sometime later, she feels the pitch of the room, the air dense against her. Opening her mouth, she tries to make a noise.

"It's okay, I'm here. I'm here," she hears.

She struggles to make words. His hand smoothes her skin and she feels him behind, above and below. "After tomorrow, everything will be fine."

When she opens her eyes again, the drapes are open. Sitting up, she suddenly feels queasy and staggers to the washroom. She kneels at the toilet, dry-heaves. She puts her finger down her throat but her stomach is empty. Standing up finally, she splashes cool water on her face and then flips on the shower.

Room service delivers lunch. Sampling everything slowly, to keep her stomach steady, she picks up the envelope that Johnny left and wonders how she will face anyone today. How she will get on a plane? After a few bites her stomach settles enough to call the front desk and ask for Robert Kennedy's room.

"All the way with RFK," someone barks in her ear, chatter and cackles in the background.

"Hello," she stammers. "Bob—is Bobby in?"

"Not for a couple hours. Wanna leave a message?"

She mines her brain. "Could you tell him Nancy West called. I'm in 510."

"Here at the hotel? You're right down the hall . . . I'll tell him." The line goes dead. Facing the wall, she imagines them on the other side, aides and campaign workers, busy busy busy. She guzzles coffee.

Later she stands in the mirror, wearing a summer dress, white with black polka dots. It buoys her a little, makes her feel like something fresh from the box. Her roots are beginning to show. She fusses at her makeup, wondering how good they are at passing on messages over there.

Then, a knock. She pushes at her hair a last time.

Door open, Bobby stands waiting, peach-pit lines of exhaustion around his eyes. A quick glance down the hall and he comes inside. "God, you're a sight for sore eyes," he says and grabs hold, kicking the door shut. They hold like that, breathing in one another a moment. His body is a mass of ticking nerves, a disembodied bug's limb that continues to flinch.

"I saw you on TV, stopping to sit, and I . . ."

"You thought they poisoned me?" He steps back. "Just exhaustion." He paces across the room and back. "I got cramps in my stomach and felt dizzy. I just had to sit a second before I fell. It's been such a—Hey, we took South Dakota!"

"You did?" she beams. "Oh! I'm so proud of you." She hugs him.

"Results just in." He nods rapidly and dives his tongue into her mouth. "I've been wanting you so much. Look!" His hand jerks from her face, dips into his pocket and presents her with a palm-sized box from his pocket. She takes the lid off and, out of the tissue, lifts a red heart, inscribed with gold.

"So *pretty*." Inlaid gold reads, *My heart is wax moulded as she pleases, but enduring as marble to retain. B.* She touches the lettering and her hand swallows the comfort of its weight. "I wish I could remember words like you, pull them from the air . . ."

"It's from *The Little Gypsy*. Thought of it after I saw you in Oregon." He pulls at her skirt. His hips push against hers in steady waves, his thighs insisting hers apart. "Oh god," he says, "you're shaking."

Doom oozes through her chest again. She closes her eyes, imagines herself sinking through the bed, the floors, down and down through dirt and beetles and grubs.

Seconds later he gasps and slides down onto the floor, rests his head on her thigh. A quick stroke with his fingers and he tugs her dress back down. She opens her eyes.

"I'm sorry," he sighs. "I've got to get back to the suite." He stands and retucks his shirt, draws up his zipper. "Polls are about to close and Ethel's going to be here any minute."

"You're leaving?"

He pulls her up off the couch and squeezes her. "Peter's having a victory party at the Factory tonight. Will you come?"

Clenching her teeth, she feels things fluttering out windows, disappearing with no explanation. "I have to go back to New York tonight." *No more*, she thinks. *I don't want to do this.* But it sticks in her throat. Seeing Johnny's envelope on the coffee table, she says, "The FBI's been questioning me."

His head swings. "About me? Shit. *Shit!* That cocksucking fairy never quits."

"About me. They've been asking about my friends and, ah, they've subpoenaed me . . . I just . . . I thought maybe you could help me."

"Help?" He looks incredulous. "What are they questioning you about?"

She hands him the envelope.

Tearing it open, he paces as he reads. "What's—" He stops, raises his head, a look of bewilderment turning to hatred. "You . . ." He shakes his head over the page and back at her. "You mercenary little bitch. Your friends think they can shake me down like this?"

"What? No, I didn't—what does it say?"

"I should've known better . . . A *stripper*." He slaps a nearby lamp off its table. "You're nothing. Just another whore." He starts for the door.

"Bobby, please. He just told me to give it to you." She runs after him. "I would never—" She tries to get him to turn around.

"Don't touch me!" Yanking his arm free, he catches her face and sends her sprawling.

"Bobby, no. *No.*"

He turns, takes a step and stops but he doesn't turn around.

A wail pours out. "*No,*" she howls, on her hands and knees. He walks out the door.

Minutes later, a key is in the lock and Johnny stands over her. "That prick." He kneels. "You see now?" He tilts her head back, examines her face. "I think he broke it . . . little puke." He lifts her off the floor. Looking around, he reaches for the radio and flips it on, volume high. "Please Release Me" takes over the room. "Probably got you bugged," he murmurs near her ear.

"I think I'm going to be sick," she says, and half crawls, half runs to the bathroom. As she throws up into the bowl, her stepfather's voice echoes in her head, *Those who don't trust generally can't be trusted.*

Johnny stands in the doorway, frowning. "Are you on the Pill?"

Celia glances to him then heaves into the toilet again.

When she's done, he helps her to the sink. "I'm going to get you out of here."

Twenty minutes later, he has her belongings jammed into the suitcase as she sits numbly on the bed. Tossing her dark wig on her lap, he whispers, "Go out the back. I'll send a cab around."

"You're not coming?"

"Plans have changed."

She stands on the edge of the parking lot out back, wig on, suitcase in hand, nose throbbing. A cab rolls up and she gets in, lays her head back for the trip.

"Did he hit her?"

Annie tucked her chin under like I was a bit nuts and ambled over with my water. "No. But he was good and damn mad. She coulda cost him the nomination, carrying on with him and a fella with Johnny's reputation."

"Did Johnny hit her?"

She sat down with her own drink across. "Why do you think anybody hit her?"

"She had a nose job and I thought maybe it got broken."

She shrugged and sipped. "It got broken but it was accidentally. I wasn't there. It wasn't all bloody or anything, it just hurt and it was a little wonky. There was a lotta hoopla and mayhem and people got shoved around that night and I think she got knocked off balance."

"The night Bobby was killed? She wasn't wearing a polka-dot dress, was she?"

Annie gave me another of her big-action eye rolls. "That polka-dot-dress thing was a whole lotta crap. Her and whose army? Every girl I knew around then had a polka-dot dress."

"But she was in the Ambassador the night he got shot."

"I told you. She was booked at the Grove, which was in the Ambassador so . . . *ipso facto*. Everyone wants to make a big conspiracy. That little Arab had the gun in his hand. And ah, Rosie Greer—who was Bobby's bodyguard, him and Rafer Whatsits—they had to wrestle it out of his hand. Musta been fifty people in that kitchen saw it for themselves. Anyway, it was a whole lot of threats from people who had their own agenda and I never got my head around it."

"What was? Whose threats?"

"Those FBI people. They were chasing after the girl like she was public enemy number one because they wanted to put Johnny away. Nothing to do with her. And it just so happened she was there at the hotel too. Me too. I stuck my nose in that ballroom but I don't like those big crazy crowds like that. And then afterwards, all the screaming and crying and carrying on—Cops holding people and confiscating their cameras to see who had pictures of what and, of course, that leads to more speculation and conspiracy and *The Girl in the Polka-Dot Dress*. Big deal, she had polka dots; that's got nothing to do with anything. She even thought she might have seen that little guy in the Embassy Room there, that Sirhan Whatsit, chatted with him. Maybe she did. Maybe she didn't. What's the difference, she didn't kill him. Wrong place at the wrong time."

"A lot of people say Sirhan Sirhan couldn't have shot him because his gun was never pointed at the back of Bobby's head."

"A lot of people are idiots."

"So Johnny must've been pissed off at her being there."

"Don't think he knew. If you're seeing more than one guy you don't go shooting off at the mouth."

I took the heart out of my purse and set it on the table.

"Huh. Look at that." She picked it up. "Yeah, this is the *gift* he gave her," she sneered. "*Moulded as she pleases* . . . he could be a real pretentious jackass sometimes. Shakespeare this and classic that. Maybe he should've tried calling in some favours instead of giving her this dopey little pissant thing and letting them chase her into the ground like . . . Some guys try to make you feel bad about what you do with your life, you know. They like the showy clothes and the nice figure and maybe they even instigate some risqué stuff with you, but then they're real sons-a-bitches about it. They want you to be a virgin when they say so. They don't like you having control of your own self. And they like sayin' how the other guy's bad, not them. Just like that stepfather of hers. She finally turned to him at the end, all that carrying on he did for her to come home and so she finally went. She didn't want to testify and they were trying to get her to wear a bug to catch Johnny and she ran away back to Scarsdale. I drove her there myself. He was the same selfish prick as ever. Her mother was passed on by then and he figured he'd take up with Celia. But she didn't want him. And what do you think the crazy bastard did?"

By the time she arrives at LAX, she's determined to talk to him one last time. He can't think what he thinks. She walks dazed into the airport. Ticket counters before her, she turns around to the pay phones. Looks away. Hauling her suitcase, she sits on a bench.

She checks her watch. The red-eye for New York won't board for two hours.

A minute later, a locker door closes on her suitcase and she tosses the key in her purse, heavy now with Bobby's red-and-gold heart, then rushes for the taxi stand.

On the second floor of the Ambassador, the ballroom is jammed with close to two thousand people. Kennedy supporters wear buttons on their dresses and lapels blaring *ALL THE WAY WITH RFK*, carry signs that read, *Bobby Is Groovy* and *We Love You, Bobby.* Hundreds of banners, balloons and posters decorate the room. California is Bobby's and the place is a torrent of jubilation.

Drink in hand, Celia stands off to the side with her head down, dreading the sight of a familiar face. "Stupid. Should have just headed down to the Factory later." She smoothes her wig and hides her face behind the glass of wine.

Close to midnight, cheers erupt as Bobby comes in. Wearing his blue pinstriped suit, he looks princely, Celia thinks. Ethel climbs up onstage with him in her orange-and-white minidress and white stockings. The papers say she's pregnant again.

In the lobby, Annie asks at the front desk for Celia Dare's room. "What do you mean she checked out?" Sighing, she looks around the lobby. "Christ, it's a morgue in here."

"Everyone's upstairs at the Kennedy celebration," the clerk grins.

"Did he win California?"

"You can probably catch his victory speech. He's in the Embassy Room."

Annie heads up the stairs.

In the ballroom, Bobby steps to the microphone and thanks everyone from Ethel to Freckles. The room cheers and blares.

"Think he might be president?" This from a young dark man beside Celia. A couple inches shorter, he runs a drunk gaze over her figure.

"Maybe," she answers, looks away.

Applause rages around the room with shouts of "Bobby Power" and "Kennedy Power."

"Can I buy you a drink?" the little guy asks.

"I'm fine." He looks Mediterranean or something, cute, eyes so dark you can't see where iris and pupil meet. They mesmerize her a moment.

Annie walks into the throng and shoves her way through, looking for her roommate.

"And despite," Bobby tells them, his voice turning serious, "the violence, the disenchantment with our society, the divisions whether it's between blacks and whites, between the poor and the more affluent, or between age groups, or over the war in Vietnam—we can start to work together again. We are a great country—"

"We should get closer," the man tells Celia. "Want to?"

Her eyes move to the flop of hair on Bobby's forehead. He brushes it aside.

"So, my thanks to all of you, and it's on to Chicago and let's win there." Bobby gives the peace sign, and grins as he leaves the platform.

We want Bobby! We want Bobby!

"Come on," her new pal says, tugging her wrist. "Maybe we can shake his hand."

She follows him through the mob. Ethel is slow coming off the stage and Rosie Greer steps in to help. Celia trots to keep up, setting her glass down along the way. Soon they're out of the ballroom and walking through a kitchen corridor. "Where are we going?" she yells over the din.

Bobby is just ahead, talking to a couple busboys. Ethel is back in the crowd somewhere.

If Celia could just tell him that it wasn't what he thought, she could let it go. A few feet away, she stops beside a security guard who concentrates on Bobby and the busboys.

She looks around the pantry: the serving trays, concrete and stainless steel. Can't talk to him here. The guy who befriended her has disappeared into the mix. She turns to go.

"Kennedy, you sonuvabitch."

Her head spins.

The boy-faced guy has a revolver in his hand now, a sickly smile on his face as his arm stretches out. Pops sound. Shrieks and scuffles.

Rosie Greer and Rafer Johnson catch him in a stranglehold, slam him down onto the steam table. He continues to fire. All around: screams, people ducking and falling.

"Bobby!" Celia scrambles toward him. The security guard's arm flies out, knocks her back as he takes out his own gun. Celia comes up off the floor, cupping her nose. She checks her fingers for blood as shots crack around her, looks up just as Bobby's hands jump to his head. He drops a few feet away, limbs spread, blood pooling.

The security guard holsters his gun. A busboy cradles Bobby's head in his hands.

Frantic cries echo off walls, a reporter turns on his tape recorder. "Senator Kennedy has been shot. Is that possible? It is possible, ladies and gentlemen. It is possible . . ."

Staggering to her feet, she rushes for the door. Somewhere in the distance she hears her name. Negotiating the stairs down the back of the hotel. A Youth for Kennedy girl is standing on the stairwell, smoking a cigarette. "He shot him," Celia whimpers as she gropes the banister.

"What? Who did you shoot?" the young woman asks, a confused look on her face.

"Senator Kennedy," Celia says, trying to keep from falling. "He shot Senator Kennedy." Sobs stab through her.

Out back she runs through the short tunnel to the parking lot.

She spins at the parked cars, the glare of lights on chrome and glass. "Celia," echoes behind her. She turns. A man's voice. Agent Richards. "Hold on, let me help you."

"Celia?" from the other direction. A woman's figure hunched against the hood of a car.

Her head swivels from Richards to the woman.

"Celia!" The woman stands, throws down her cigarette.

"Annie?" Celia rushes toward her. *"Annie!* He shot him."

"What? Who the hell is that?" She looks past Celia's shoulder to the agent rushing toward them. "Come on. This is me here, get in."

The two jump into Annie's rental, Celia staring back to her pursuer, who stops as the ignition turns. Annie throws the car into gear and Richards jogs back toward the hotel.

"What are you doing here?" Celia watches out the rear window as they speed away.

"Looking for you, stupid. I left messages and you didn't call back. Are you supposed to testify against someone?"

"What?"

"Two guys showed up asking questions. They asked about you and Johnny. How long you knew Bobby. If you'd been in Florida, here, there. I think someone's bugging us."

"Oh god. What's *happening?*"

"I ran into Lawford last week, gassed out of his tree. He said he knew a guy used to work with the PI who tapped Monroe's phone. He had four clients he was taping her for—She was bugging *herself,* for chrissake. Lawford kept saying, *The walls have ears* . . . You wanna call Johnny?"

"No! I think *he's* been doing it." She nods to herself. "I do. Him and them and . . . How did you know where to find me?"

"They said you'd checked out, so I looked in on the convention. It was such a goddamn free-for-all, I went outside to get my head together."

"I thought you had to go out of town."

"I did. I was dancing in Pittsburgh and then those jokers showed up and I fucked off." She glances in the rearview, flips on the radio.

Live audio is now broadcasting from the Ambassador. Hollow cries behind a reporter's voice. " . . . rumours of a conspiracy already circulate. I have with me here a Youth for Kennedy Committee member from Pasadena. Can you repeat for our listeners the story you just told me?"

"Well," she begins, "I was standing out back on the steps when this girl came running down saying, 'We shot him, we shot him,' and I said, 'Who did you shoot?' and she said, 'Senator Kennedy.'"

"I said, *He*," Celia yells at the dial.

"Can you describe the woman you saw?" asks the reporter.

"Caucasian, maybe twenty-four or twenty-five, slim, and she wore a white dress with black polka dots . . . dark hair, bouffant style and she had a funny nose."

Annie reaches over. Turning Celia's face, she whispers, "Nice one."

She pushes Annie's hand off. "That security guard. I think he shot him, it was him."

Annie sticks her eyes to the road. "What do you wanna do? Get that damn wig off."

Celia pulls pins from her head and stops. "There's blood on my arm. On my dress . . . I don't know if it's his or mine. Oh god." She touches her nose and winces.

"I think we should drive to Phoenix and get a flight from there."

"Why Phoenix?" Celia demands.

She shifts gears and turns onto the freeway. "We can go to Salt Lake City and camp with the Mormons if you want. I just think we should get the hell out of Dodge, that's all."

Celia licks her finger and touches the dried blood. "My mother used to say that, get out of Dodge. I think I'm pregnant." Tears start and she faces the passenger window.

"Sweet Jesus. How pregnant?"

She wipes at her eyes.

Annie watches the headlights in the road. "You think they know anything about your parents? Do they know your real name?"

"They called me Audrey. They know I worked at The 92 and about Teddy. I never told anyone my real last name. I can't. I just . . ."

~

Gravel crunches as the car rolls into the tree-lined Scarsdale driveway. Letting the screen door slam, Stewart walks across the shadow-dappled porch to the edge of the steps. He waves.

Celia waves a stiff hand back.

"Be it ever so humble," Annie says as she parks the car. "Nice digs."

A pair of Annie's pedal pushers drooping off her hips, Celia gets out.

Stewart takes her shoulders. "You're home." He tilts her chin up. Her nose is bent and there's bruising around her eyes.

"I tripped," she says.

"We'll have to have that looked at." Stepping back, he appraises her with, "You look like an orphan."

"They look better on Annie."

He turns to Annie and shakes her hand. "Nice to meet you. You girls fly into Syracuse?"

"Montreal, actually." Annie tells him.

"Well, let's get your luggage," Stewart suggests.

Celia folds arms round her purse. "I left my bag in L.A. Change of plans."

Stewart nods. "Are you hungry? You'll be joining us, won't you, Annie?"

Celia turns pleading eyes on her.

"Sure. That'd be nice. Thanks."

The smell and sight of the house rip through her, a comforting nightmare: the musk of the Persian rug, the piano keys, the record player—cocktail parties, performing for friends and neighbours. She glances up the stairs, some small part expecting her mother to descend, a look of disapproval on her face.

Dinner conversation is awkward, the three of them in the long stretch of backyard, Stewart asking about the nightclubs and theatres. "I took Audrey to the El Morocco for her sixteenth birthday," he says, shuffles in his seat and then asks what Sinatra's really like. "They say he's got mob ties. Did he introduce you to any gangsters?"

Annie shoves a hunk of steak into her mouth and chews, staring up at the brawny old apple tree.

After dinner Celia walks her out to the car. "Can't you just stay the night?"

"If we both hang around here, we won't know what's going on. Next person who asks I'll say you're on vacation." She puts her arms around Celia. "We'll get through this. I'll call you." She gets into the car. "From a phone booth."

In the kitchen, Stewart fills the sink.

Celia stands limp beside the cleared table. "Can I help with the dishes?"

"How about we do it like old times: I wash, you dry."

She picks up a plate and wipes it.

"Lots of your old clothes upstairs, but if those don't fit, I'll take you shopping tomorrow. I was thinking we should get you in to see Mort Mason. Remember him? He's in private practise now. Does facelifts and nose jobs for all the New York socialites."

"I can't go to the hospital," she blurts.

He nods calmly. "That's why I thought of Mort. He could come over and have a look. I took the liberty of calling him when you were outside."

Her eyes widen.

"Only if you want." He shoves his hands deep into the sudsy water. "I know you're in some sort of trouble . . . I'm glad you're home."

In the morning, she comes into the kitchen where Stewart is having coffee and a scone.

He grabs her a cup, pours some coffee. "Rough morning," he sighs and sets it down in front of her. He watches her take a gulp before he nudges the morning paper over. A NATION GRIEVES.

He puts a hand on her shaking shoulder then moves his chair closer and lets her fall against him.

When she can speak, she starts to babble in six directions. As her story ebbs, he asks, "So these fellows who came to see Annie in Pittsburgh—they were *not* FBI?"

"She thinks CIA."

"This story about the CIA and the mob has been floating around for a while. Did your friend Johnny ever tell you he was involved with government?"

"No."

"Maybe they're worried—they don't know what you know." She blinks. "When is Mort coming? What should I say?"

"Tell him you were playing softball."

She spends the afternoon rummaging through her closets and drawers. Blue jeans she remembers as loose fit her like a girdle now.

Stewart comes into her room with a couple of her mother's old sundresses. "These might fit. I remember you really loved this yellow flowered one on your mother—your eyes are so much like hers."

"Hello? Anybody home." A man's voice downstairs.

In the kitchen, Dr. Mason moves her head like a doll's. "Boy oh boy. Should I ask?"

A flash of Jackie comes to mind: elegant hands on bridle reins, photographs of Bobby and her together on horseback. "Riding," she says. "Guess I'm not the equestrian I thought."

He sighs. "I'd much rather do this in an operating theatre. But your father says it's a problem, the press and the tabloids— quite a superstar since I last saw you, young lady."

She raises a Jackie-esque hand to her nose.

"We could do it tonight. It's a relatively simple procedure." He sits on the edge of the table, turns her face again. "I can't guarantee your profile will be exactly the same."

"That's all right. A change won't kill me."

For the next week, she lives in dreamland, coasting on painkillers as Stewart brings cold compresses and lemonade. Summer break at the university allows him hours to concoct purées and soups. He throws her cigarettes in the garbage and pillow-props her in the chaise lounge under the apple tree, monstrous sun hat on her head. He offers to play Scrabble with her, cards, but she says she'd rather read. He does his best to give her space.

A call from Annie after three or four days chafes her. She's just quit smoking, Celia explains, "if I sound a little cranky. And the painkillers make me tired. Can we talk later?" She asks Stewart to say she is sleeping if Annie calls again.

Soon the splint is replaced with bandages.

"That's a damn nice nose, if I do say so myself," Mort exclaims. "It's delicate though, keep your head elevated now that the packing's out."

Mort leaves her outside in the shade and is quickly replaced by Stewart bearing tea and biscuits. "The bruising's really subsided, hasn't it?" In the interest of keeping her nose elevated, he dashes to pick up what she drops.

She nods and takes her book from him.

He stands staring as she reads. "Your friend called again. I think she's worried."

She keeps reading. "Okay."

"Okay," he says. "You don't need to speak with anyone."

The following night Stewart prepares an elaborate dinner. On the record player Mario Lanza sings, "Santa Lucia." Celia watches from the table and sips from her glass. "I better watch this wine-and-painkillers thing," she muses aloud. "I'll turn into Monroe."

Stewart turns. "Ever meet her along your travels?"

"Ohhh, yes."

He laughs, working hard to lighten the mood. "You met 'em all, kid!"

"You're sure full of hops tonight," she says, almost feeling sorry for him.

"It's a special night."

"Oh yeah?"

"Yeah," he says taking lamb from the oven.

As they eat, Celia tries to make half-decent conversation, or at least do better than her usual monosyllabic responses.

By dessert, Stewart has started to fidget. Taking a last forkful of peach pie, he raises his port glass and calls for a toast. "To new beginnings."

She raises her glass then blinks into it a moment before she looks at him. "Thank you. For taking me in."

His face brightens. "My god. How could I say no?" He takes a breath. "Audrey. You know my heart literally aches when I think of how things ended up. I've thought over and over how I could make things right . . ."

Her stomach rolls. "Stewart . . ." she says with a sigh, hoping to keep things from getting maudlin.

"Shh, just let me . . . it means a lot to me that you let me be the one to help. You have no idea."

She puts a hand to her forehead, hoping he'll take the hint.

"I knew when I saw you that first day home—" he reaches into his pocket "—that you had come back to me for a reason." He takes out a small box. "You can't go back. You want things to change. Let me change them." He opens it in front of her. The ring sparkles.

Both hands come to her temples. "I feel sick."

"Oh god, I'm sorry. I know it's a lot to absorb—I never should have let you drink so much. Here . . ." He stands and helps her off the chair. She tries to pull away but she's too dizzy. "Let me bring you upstairs. You'll be okay."

On *Dr. Kildare*, she thinks, they said it was good for pregnant women to have a drink each day. It calms them. She doesn't say this. She hasn't said anything about a baby.

Bunching pillows, he eases her onto her bed and tugs the cover up. He smoothes the hair from her forehead. "Should I bring you a cold compress?"

"No."

"I love you, Audrey," he says softly and backs out the door.

Cyd Charisse and Fred Astaire looked quizzically from the fading cover of *Photoplay* still tacked to the wall. A brittle magazine ad beside it reads: *Cyd Charisse Loves Lustre-Creme Shampoo*. Celia's eyes limp back to *Photoplay* in time to catch Cyd's head shake in dismay. "What did I tell you?"

"You were right," Celia whispers, falling into the dark as Fred tsks.

Soon she is dancing round and round, her skirts whirling, the room expands with the orchestra's rendition of "Santa Lucia," the ceiling rises, the floor falls, the walls slide back. Vibrant skirts in cherry red, the plums of royalty, cornflower and lemon, colours and colours as he waltzes her round the ballroom. *Those sweet rabbit teeth*, she thinks, laughing and breathless. *It's okay, I'm here*, a uniformed soldier says in her ear from behind. *After tomorrow the war will be over*. She lets her head fall back on his shoulder and he puts a small glass candle holder in her teeth. She rights her head and faces Bobby, who parts his jaws, takes the candle, flame to his throat. His skull glows.

Back in the hotel, catching a nap before her show. A girlish voice says, *It's okay, I'm here*. Celia smells her perfume, feels the weight of her on the sofa, soft hands on either side of her face, the platinum blonde, the red bow of a mouth. *You're very sweet to me*. Sets a pillowy kiss onto her mouth and runs a hand over her forehead. *We have to go before they bite us*.

"We have to go," Celia agrees. "We have to go."

"It's okay, I'm here."

She drags her eyes open and just as she sees white-white skin, the music stops. She looks at Stewart on the edge of her bed. "You were having a bad dream." He smoothes a hand over her face.

Squinting toward the ballerina clock on the opposite wall, she tries to focus on the limbs as they move round the dial, a leg on the six, and one on . . . something. A rattlesnake coils in her belly, tensing and tensing. "How long have I been . . ."

"A couple hours. I wish I could keep you from ever having a bad dream again." His eyes droop like a hungry basset's. "I love you so much." Her jaws clench. He looks into her eyes then leans and brings his mouth to hers.

The snake's tail shimmies now. Can't breathe. Suffocating. "Stop it!" She shoves him back. "You're taking bites. You're just like everybody else, swallowing!"

Startled, he sits back. "Honey, it's me. It's Stewart."

"I know who you are. You're my *father*. I'm not your girl-friend. Your wife. Ever. Stop touching me."

"What kind of game are you playing, Audrey? Or Celia, whoever the hell you are? You came to me." He throws up his hands. "You love me when? When you want something?"

"I came to you for help because you're my family."

"You think you can play with my emotions like this? Flirt and torment me?" His voice levels and he adds, "You're a sick girl," before his shadow slams from the room.

As her eyes adjust to the dark, the pink of the ballerina's limbs cluck round. Her face, normally in profile, turns to Celia now with a hideous grimace. Celia closes her eyes, wipes tears before they reach the bandage and opens her mouth for air.

It seems as if she's been awake all night until she hears Dean, Frank, and Sammy come up the stairs, Dean singing, "Ain't That a Kick in the Head." Logic burbles as she tries to remember where she is. Unable to get her eyes open, she tries to deduce.

"She's in here." Dean. *I miss Dean.* If only she could wake up; she wants to look nice.

"I guess she's still sleeping." Stewart is with them? If she could just make real noise, it would bring her into the daylight.

"Audrey . . . You've got to get up now. Come on, we're tak-ing you back to New York." The rust of early sun scrapes his face as Agent Dodge jostles her.

Spinning out of the sky, she slams back down in Scarsdale. Her bedroom. The ballerina's hand is on the eight, her pointe shoe on the three. Stewart stands at the door with Richards. "Careful of her bandage. Her nose was broken."

"Since or prior to her arrival?" Richards asks.

"Before. She had some sort of mishap the night Senator Kennedy was killed."

On her feet, with the assistance of Dodge, she stares at Stewart.

"Do you want to change your clothes or shall we head out?" Dodge asks.

She looks down at her mother's dress. "I'd like to change."

Twenty

~

BETWEEN THE LACK OF SLEEP AND THE ECSTASY HANGOVER, I was consumed by anxiety and gloom. "How long did they keep her?"

Annie's mouth formed a frowning moue. "I don't know. Few hours. They took her to some motel outside the city and put a scare into her. I was thinking of her when all that Monica Lewinsky crap was going on. Did that to her too, held her in a room, told her all kinds of this and that if she didn't testify. And everybody arguing whether she was an innocent or a tramp."

"So, what happened? She came home?"

"Yes. I thought she was still up in Scarsdale and the next thing I know, she's standing in the doorway looking like a wet rat. Scared the hell out of me. And she was making strange. You don't know who to trust sometimes, you know. But she couldn't keep a secret to save her soul. Not from me anyway. They made her wear a bug-type of thing and they parked out front."

Annie watches *Rowan and Martin's Laugh-In*. There's a storm outside, and the apartment is dreary and dark. Blue light from the television traipses over her blank face.

A key slides into the lock.

Her face jerks. She reaches under the couch and barks, "Who's there?" The door handle turns. She pulls out a baseball bat, raises it over her head as she creeps forward. "Who's there?"

"It's me," a small voice says. Celia stands in the entrance dripping wet, bedraggled bandage across her nose, Annie's pants sagging off her hips.

The bat drops. "What are you doing here?"

Celia droops. "Things didn't work out."

Grabbing the blanket off the couch, Annie drapes it round Celia's shoulders and hugs. "Jesus, what happened to you? Did you have it reset?" She rubs Celia over the blanket, steers her toward the sofa. "What happened?"

Celia is sitting on the motel bed, maybe fifty miles outside New York City. Dodge and Richards have their coats off and their sleeves rolled up as they pace, asking if she knows this one or that one, for how long and how did they meet.

"I don't know," and "Not to my knowledge," dominate her side of the conversation.

"Did you ever deliver a package or briefcase for Rosselli?"

"No."

"Did you deliver a message to Senator Kennedy from Rosselli?"

"No."

"Were you in the pantry of the Ambassador Hotel on June 4?"

"No."

"Your stepfather says you were."

"He also asked me to marry him. He's delusional."

The men exchange glances. Dodge goes into a leather satchel, pulls a polka-dot dress from the bag. "Everybody keeps talking about a girl in a polka-dot dress. Does this look familiar?"

No response.

"We can prove that you have been intimately involved with several organized-crime figures. What do you think these guys'll do when they realize you are going to testify? You think

Rosselli's going to save you? What if it leaks to the press that you had a sexual relationship with not only an assassinated presidential candidate but hoodlums like Rosselli and Teddy the Ghost and Micky D . . . ?"

Her stomach somersaults and she bends and throws up. Dodge stares down at his shoes.

"Stewart asked me to marry him."

"He *what?*"

"He's crazy," she says dully.

"Are you expecting someone?"

Celia wraps the blanket tighter. "No. Why?"

"You keep looking at your watch. Lemme see." Annie turns Celia's wrist over, examines it. "Stewart give you that?"

"Yes, I guess he did."

Annie's eyes drift to *Laugh-In*, John Wayne saying, *Well, I don't think that's funny.* "I think someone broke in here a couple days ago. My suitcase was open and stuff was—oh, I don't know. Maybe I'm losing my mind."

Celia's eyes glaze on the TV dancers as they wiggle between jokes.

"Shit, I almost forgot, Marty keeps calling. He says Dean wants to book you on his show." The phone rings. "Probably him again." She gets off the couch. "I told him you were in Jamaica . . . Hello? . . . Oh! Johnny." She eyes Celia for instruction. "How're you? . . . As a matter of fact . . ." She hands the phone. Celia takes a deep breath before saying hello.

"You're back. All suntanned?"

"No, I went to my family's instead."

"Hmm. I thought that'd be the last place you'd go."

"Should've been."

"I'm sorry. How are you doing, sweetheart?"

"I'm all right."

"You sure? Whatever happened with that subpoena?"

"They want me in court in a couple weeks."

"Well, you never know. Sometimes people change their

minds about these things. I'll be in town tomorrow. Can we have dinner?"

She nods at her watch.

"How's that sound?" he asks.

"Fine. Sorry, I had a little accident. I'm still feeling kind of wonky . . . painkillers."

"You okay?"

"Yes. Just my nose. I fell and I have a bandage on it."

"Oh no! You tell me all about it tomorrow. If you wanna have it looked at, I know the best nose-guy in Hollywood."

That night she dreams four FBI agents stand as bedposts. Nobody notices.

Johnny shows up at seven on the dot. As they step into the evening air, he merrily waves to the dark van across the street. "They been here all along or just since you got back?"

She hesitates, her pulse thumps. "That's them? How do you know?" She stares over her shoulder as he opens the passenger door.

We'll be with you the whole time. You might not see us but we'll be there.

Celia looks back to see the van coast off in the opposite direction.

Johnny glances in his rearview. As they pull out, a black car coasts in behind them. "Christ, they sure turned it up on you."

"Why do they have to look so ominous?"

"Intimidation is part theatre. Let's have some fun." He stomps the gas and peels around the corner. The car behind jumps the curb, battling to keep up.

"No! Please, Johnny." She puts her hands up.

He slows and glances at her bandage. "Okay, okay. What the hell happened anyway?"

"Oh, it was nothing. There was an announcement about Bobby at the airport and, ah, people got all upset and I got pushed and fell. Stupid."

"Why do you keep looking at your watch? Am I late?"

She shifts her look out the window. "I was just thinking it's early for dinner."

"Thought we might take a walk in Central Park. Build up an appetite."

"Central Park?" she repeats a little loudly.

"Yes!" he bellows back. "Nice this time of year, and who knows when I'll be out here next. Maybe the trial won't go so good."

She looks at his frost-blue eyes, the contrast from pupil to iris. "We'll be fine."

When they park, he comes round and opens Celia's door. "Madam . . ."

"Thank you, sir."

Slipping his arm around her, he watches the black car park on the other side of the lot. The van rolls by without stopping. "I thought we might have a conversation but this is putting a damper on it. Bad as L.A."

About to check her watch, she looks at the rhododendrons instead. Johnny speaks but her mind has slipped through a hole back into the motel room with Dodge and Richards, the watch they laid on the bedspread. A passage from Bobby's crime-fighting book came to mind. " . . . *he had been using a recording device concealed in his watch. Suddenly the face of the watch dropped off and hung dangling from wires that were attached to the recorder . . .*"

"This is different," Dodge insisted. "It's a tiny bug—the technology is far more advanced than what we had ten years ago. We can also monitor your whereabouts. If you read the senator's book then you know what these people are capable of. Why go without protection?"

Rosselli looks at her now for a response.

"Sorry. I'm having such a hard time concentrating." She opens her purse, pulls a tissue. Seeing Bobby's red heart, she snaps it shut.

"Better take it easy on those pills." He squeezes her, steers toward a busy promenade.

Fifteen or twenty yards away, a long-haired hippie strums guitar and sings Dylan songs. He winks at Celia. She flicks her eyes
away. Johnny throws a buck into the case as they pass. "I think we
should figure out this thing." He keeps an overtly breezy manner.
"I leaked to the papers last year about Cuba, just a little something so they'd know it's a bad idea putting me on the stand."

"Do we have to talk about this now?" She puts her watch
arm behind his back.

"I'm just saying, maybe it's better if you don't talk about that
stuff. But they'll ask you things. If you ever made a delivery or—"

"I didn't!" she blurts.

He laughs and nods.

A beat or two of waffling and she says, "I don't understand
this Friars Club thing. What's it got to do with you?"

He shrugs. "Guys were playing cards, games were fixed.
They figure I had a piece."

"Did you?" Her insides twist.

"Listen, I'm in a certain position—"

A coughing fit takes Celia. She waves her hands and hacks
into her tissue.

"Let's get you some water."

"I'm fine," shaking her head no. His face is quizzical.
Grazing her eyes over the park, she cradles her wrist and taps
her forefinger at the new watch. "I think I'm just hungry."

"All right. Let's go eat." He offers his arm and walks her back.
"So, how was Boston? You see your mother?"

In the car, she rummages in the glove compartment as he
talks about how ill Mamma Rosselli is, how much it hurt to see
her that way. She pulls out the owner's manual, rips the back
cover off and prints, THEY'RE LISTENING. MY WATCH.

He looks out the windshield. She writes, I'M SCARED.

"She couldn't have been more than seventy pounds." He
swipes at his nose.

In the restaurant they settle in, order drinks, casting glances
about the room. She flips the business card she took from the
maître d's podium and writes, HELP ME GO AWAY.

He nods. "You ever hear from those pricks again? Pudge and Snitchards."

She spurts a laugh. "Not since the subpoena." Slides the business card to his side.

"Gotta get you a good lawyer. Here . . ." He reaches into his jacket for a pen, takes out one of his cards and turns it over. "This guy knows his way around the G." He writes, YOU GO, YOU DISAPPEAR FOR GOOD.

She gives him a startled look. "What's his number?"

"Oh," he tsks and writes some more. "This guy's great." He passes the card over. "Remember those Boy Scouts on the way from Drucker's? 'Member the big one? Turns out he's queer as a three-dollar bill."

She keeps her hand over the card as the waiter nears. Johnny orders appetizers. Waiter gone, she says, "I wonder if that's the guy Truman told me about. He had a fling with an FBI agent once who liked it from behind. Hard."

Johnny pounds the table as he wipes a napkin over his chin. "Oh, that's rich . . ."

She uncovers the card. CHANGE NAME. NO CONTACT. "I can imagine that."

He reaches a foot across and touches hers.

Johnny has just dropped her off when there's a knock at her door.

"That was a strange conversation you had tonight, Audrey," Dodge informs her.

"What do you expect? I can't sleep I'm so self-conscious."

"You're not doing yourself any favours," Richards says. "If you extract the sort of information we need, you won't even have to show up in court. You can be far away from all this."

"What makes you think I *want* to be far away?"

Dodge interjects. "We have bank records that show you withdrew five thousand dollars from your savings yesterday."

"So?"

"So, we've frozen your accounts."

The next day Celia answers the phone to Johnny. "Hello,

lovely. It's my last night in town and I thought if you girls don't have plans, I'd love to take you to dinner."

"That sounds wonderful," she says, suddenly sick to her stomach again.

At quarter past eight, Johnny pours gin and vermouth into the martini shaker as Celia fits one of her dark wigs on in the bathroom mirror. "I'll be there in a sec," she says, adding a last swipe of Annie's screaming-red lipstick. "I'm just changing my bandage." The bandage is gone. She stares in the mirror at her altered nose, dabs concealer on any redness.

When she comes in the living room, Annie smirks at the sock-filled bust of her dress on Celia. Celia sticks her tongue out.

Wearing Celia's Peggy Lee wig restyled, and a bandage across her nose, Annie is bursting out of the stretchiest gingham dress her roommate owns.

Both Johnny and Annie come in for a closer look at Celia's nose, turn her face right and left. Annie touches thumb to forefinger in an O of approval. Johnny kisses his fingertips. He grabs the martini shaker and begins to joggle it up and down. Celia holds her watch to the clatter as Annie undoes the clasp.

"So are you going to do Dean's show?" Annie asks as she fastens the watch around her own wrist. "I think you should try and get on *Laugh-In*."

"Yeah," Celia says, trying to keep her mouth as near to Annie's wrist as she'd be to her own. "I can't believe the cracks they get away with."

"The censors don't get half the jokes," Annie says, reaching over and tucking a stray lock under Celia's wig. "Somebody was telling me they had seven pot jokes in the first show and the censors never caught *one*."

Johnny nudges her and hands over a new passport, driver's licence and birth certificate. He sighs and sets his mouth. "Better get going, we'll lose our reservation."

"I'll get my coat." Annie excuses herself and returns with her mink, Celia's sable and a brown envelope. She looks haunted. Celia takes Annie's coat and Annie holds on to Celia's.

"Jesus, how'd you get a tear there," Johnny asks, taking Annie's coat from Celia. Sitting on the couch, he takes out his wallet, pulls a razor blade and makes a slit in the lining near the collar. Annie and Celia stare as Johnny pulls several stacks of money from inside his jacket and drops them down the cut.

"So you don't forget," Annie says, pulling Celia's attention back and handing her the envelope. "It's your turn to vacuum tomorrow." Celia looks inside: first, an eight-by-ten of Annie: *To Celia, Ain't life grand when you got the guts for it. xox, Lifers, Annie.* And Frank's: *Celia, You're cruel, baby! But when you're right, you're right.* The last photo is one of her own. Also in the envelope is a small album, *You Oughtta Be in Pictures!* in pink glitter across the front. A slip of paper inside reads WRITE ME AT MY MOTHER'S and a San Anselmo address. The first photograph is a shot of Celia and Annie at the El Morocco.

Celia wipes her eyes.

"You driving tonight, John?" Annie asks.

"Uh-huh."

"Cuz I think I'm going to bring my car too. I kinda made a late-night date and he's way off in Brooklyn."

"Brooklyn," Johnny hoots. "I had higher hopes for you, kid."

Outside on the sidewalk the three of them mill for a couple moments. There is no more hugging, only long looks offset by chipper words, Annie now wearing Celia's sable, Celia wearing the cash-heavy mink, the gold of Annie's dress catching flashes of light underneath. The white bandage on Annie's nose is incandescent.

The girls fix on each other.

"Okay, we'll see you at the restaurant then, Annie?" Johnny winks at Celia. "I'll order you a drink if we get there ahead. Another martini?"

"Vodka this time." Annie says. "I'll see you there," and Celia walks off, brunette locks bouncing as she gets into Annie's black Valiant. Johnny and Annie head for his car.

Streetlight glints off Annie's new watch as Johnny dominates the conversation, something about breaking spaghetti, whether this makes a difference in taste.

He turns his engine over and moves into traffic, watching Celia in the rearview. The van heads off around the block and the black sedan slips in behind Johnny.

Back in the Valiant, Celia grips the steering wheel, coasting behind, toward the restaurant. Slowly she allows cars to cut in between herself and the black sedan. When she can no longer see them, she turns a corner.

"So was she pregnant or not?"

"*Pregnant.* Who said she was pregnant?"

I couldn't remember now whether it was me or her. "I just—well, she was with both those men and I started thinking, one of them could be my father, couldn't he?"

"Your *father?*" Her dark eyes sat on me for a good five seconds before she said, "How do you figure that? She say that?"

"No. She said my father died in Vietnam before I was born. But my birthday is in spring and that was in the summer and she didn't seem to want me to know much."

"When's your birthday?"

"March 29, 1969."

She put out her hand and started counting off, "June, July, August . . . that's a stretch, kid. Anyway, it was the sixties. Showbusiness people aren't like other people, you know, we're not virgins till marriage. We had lots of boyfriends."

I must have looked a little appalled. She said, "Sounds like she met a guy on her way up to Canada. What difference does it make? You're here and you're healthy and any way you look at it, he wouldn't be around anymore. Doesn't matter where you jump in the river, you still gotta swim."

I started to choke up again. "I just thought it would be nice to know someone who knew my father. Knew who he was or something."

"It doesn't matter," she said. "You know your mother. Some

people don't even know that. And now you know her a little better maybe. So, you can get on with things."

I drew circles in my notebook and let the air ease back into me. "Didn't occur to me you'd have a car in New York. I thought everyone took cabs."

"I liked my freedom. You must like it too, driving around like that. You got a husband or boyfriend?"

"So, the FBI, they kept bugging you?"

"Actually . . ." She stares off. "I don't think she had bandages by then. Aw, I don't know. She must've. Giancana used to throw on a toupée and a mustache and it was like he was invisible."

"What was he like? Did you like him?"

She shrugged.

"When did they figure out it was you who had the watch on?"

"I can't remember how it all went. I moved out here and got married. Had a baby. They kept coming around though. Wanted me to tell them this or that, testify. Then they didn't. Then they did. Then Johnny testified. It was in the papers. Then he was dead." She shrugged again. "I got married a couple more times. Now, I'm alone. That's how it is."

"Your daughter's in New York?"

"Yup."

"You talk to her much?"

She looked out the window a moment then at me. "Sometimes when you have a daughter you start seeing yourself in her and you—well, maybe not hate, but you wanna wring your stuff right out of her. Who wants to see all that crap in a fresh new person?"

She wouldn't give me her phone number. And she didn't see any point keeping in touch. "The past is the past and the truth changes every five minutes." Her curtain moved as I sat out front in the rental car, feeling deflated, anticlimactic, wondering what to do next.

I took out my cell and waffled, debating whether or not I

could handle a night with Marcella, or whether it was rude to call her up out of the blue just for a couch to sleep on.

She answered in a whisper. "Viv?" She had call display. "Guess what. I'm getting married."

Annie's curtain flickered again. It must have been irking her that I hadn't pulled away. "To whom?"

"The *cardiologist*," she hissed. "I'm in L.A. He's got a big conference here."

"You finally sleep with him?"

"Ah—*yeah*. I'm pregnant. I haven't got tested but I just know, you know." Suddenly her voice boomed, "Yes! And I've rededicated my life to Christ!"

"Is he there?" Sudden visions of Marcella in the baptism pool, babbling her holy head off.

"He's wonderful! Would you like to talk to him?"

"Not really. Well, that's good."

"You have to be a bridesmaid!"

"Sure. Terrific. Well, congratulations. Let me know when you've set a date."

Putting the car in drive, I found myself heading back to San Francisco International. In the boarding lounge I nodded off until a standby flight came available and my name squawked over the intercom.

Twenty-one

~

" . . . I STARTED THINKING MAYBE YOU WERE RIGHT. IT'S JUST as honourable to devote yourself to a person as it is to a vocation," Len said. "Join the human race instead of leaving it."

"I said that? God, I'm full of shit sometimes." I stirred bits of rice around in the little soy-sauce dish with my chopsticks. We were sitting across from one another in Miko Sushi finishing dinner.

"So, that's really it for Frank, then? Now what?"

I shrugged and set the sticks down. "I talked to him on the phone once. He's coming for his stuff tomorrow."

"I mean, what's next for you. You going to move?"

I watched the kimono-covered waitress pour more tea in our cups then mince away. "She just wanted to change *everything*, you know. Get rid of the crap. Change her world and her life and her—her *brain*."

Len watched me. "I know."

"She went really drastic though. I mean, talk about cutting off her nose to spite her face. Literally. Not that I blame her. I can't *imagine* getting another acting agent right now and her life was . . . The way she was going, if she didn't get out, they would've sucked the life right out of her." I swallowed some tea. "She went to such *extremes* though."

"Look who's talking."

"Yeah well, look who's talking about who's talking."

He smiled. "We're extremists."

I sighed. "Did I tell you my extras agent called me to play a reporter on the courthouse steps? Freaked me out. I'm thinking of getting some blonde stripes in front."

"Oh relax," he said, rolling his eyes. "You don't look like an anchorwoman. Reporters are more streety and cool." He looked past my shoulder and suddenly his eyes brightened. He waved.

A moment later Eunice Chelsey was beside our booth. Len stood and hugged her, kissed her full on the mouth and together they tucked back into his side of the booth.

As Len introduced her, she extended her hand to me. I reached out and shook it, noticing her long slim fingers, the chunky yet elegant rings. Taking her hand back, she smiled at Len as she tucked her hair behind her ear. I ran my glance over her straight jaw and high cheekbones, the simple earrings that dangled. Everything about her looked breezily chic, cosmopolitan, accessories and manners she'd picked up in Italy, Greece, Spain.

"Is it tomorrow that you're going over?" he asked me then turned to Eunice and explained. "Viv still has a few things at her mother's house."

"Yeah."

"What's going on with you and Sally anyway?" He turned to Eunice again. "Sally is Viv's mum's girlfriend—well, like, her wife."

Eunice nodded as though she recalled that detail.

"Going on?" I repeated.

"Yeah. Are you hanging out at all?"

"Let's not go crazy," I said. "We're . . . whatever, we can be in the same room. We're fine. I just have a few more things to get out of the basement."

"I've got an SUV," Eunice interjected. "And the seats go down. If you need to move something bigger."

"It's nothing big," I assured them and tried for a smile but my face felt stiff.

Len had lit up since she came in, the two of them had. They knew each other's secrets. Like real lovers. I looked away.

"Well." I grabbed my wallet from my purse. "I should get going." I put a twenty down on the table.

"Oh." Len looked at the money, then me, a bit startled. "Aren't you going to come to the movie?"

"Yeah . . . no. I'm really tired. I don't know what's with me lately." I slid out of the booth. "But it was great to finally meet you, Eunice."

I moved quickly out onto the Robson sidewalk and stopped. I stared up and down the street a moment, looked at the cars full of young guys cruising for girls. Their laughter careened from the open windows.

The sun seemed to hang in the sky interminably this time of year, the last of it blinding drivers with long brilliant amber rays.

I would've given anything to be cloaked in cool blue night right now.

Twenty-two

~

I STARTED TO PUT ON MAKEUP THEN WASHED IT BACK OFF. Why ruin a perfectly good clean slate? My fan was on high, the windows were open, the apartment door was open, all to get a decent cross breeze flowing. Vancouver had turned unreasonably hot in June, and half the province was in flames that summer.

My apartment was the cleanest it had ever been. My mother's things were put away. I'd pulled all nails out of the walls and ceilings including those I'd used to put up pictures. The framed prints were now on the floor, resting against walls until I decided the fate of each. Pollyfill stuffed the old holes and the new-paint smell had mostly disappeared. The kitchen whiffed of citrus from an old lemon I'd tossed down the garburator. I was making boxes out of the cardboard flats I'd bought at the housewares store.

"Hey. What're you doing?"

I jumped.

"Your door was open . . ." Frank said almost apologetically. He stood in the hall watching me with a look on his face just the bewildered side of blank. I recognized it from the reflection I'd seen in my mirror when I got home from San Francisco.

"Hey. I'm just getting rid of some books."

It had been a couple weeks since Frank stormed out with his spycam.

"It's so bare looking in here. And white." He walked past me into the kitchen.

"It's *bone*, actually."

He opened the fridge. "Man. You gone Zen on me or something? There's water and mustard in here." He came back into the living room and glanced into a box already filled with politicians, gangsters, strippers and actors. Seemed silly to separate them.

He looked as if he didn't know whether to shake my hand or French-kiss me, so he sat on the couch and bent over his laced fingers a moment. "Sally sell the house?"

"Yeah. Didn't I say that on the phone? I signed last week."

"Real sellers' market now." His chin bobbed and bobbed. "You going to buy yourself an apartment?"

"Not yet. Maybe next year."

He reached into his pocket and took out an envelope. "Ah, from the site and stuff. There's sixteen hundred here. I split it fifty-fifty between us. After Brian's cut. He took 30 percent."

"No wonder he's living so well." I fanned through Mum's copy of the Marquis de Sade a moment before I set it in a box on top of Andrea Dworkin, with a quiver of pleasure.

"Sorta cut ties, me and Brian. And you don't have to worry about that footage or anything. I got rid of it. I'm really . . . I'm sorry I . . ."

"Mmm-hmm, you told me."

"I just . . . wanted you to know for sure. He got pretty weird last night, talked about how he could sue us and shit like that. Guy's crazy . . . whatever." He leaned and picked out a Rosselli book from one of the boxes. "I want to say too, that I'm sorry I never, ah . . . I thought you wanted to work through your own stuff and you'd talk when you were ready."

"You were probably right," I said lightly.

"Maybe I even kind of exploited you, getting you to do that Internet stuff when you were going through a fragile point in your life." He tossed Johnny back.

"It was my idea. Maybe I exploited you."

He winced as though I was taxing his brain, bruising his compassion.

"There's no point blaming and all the rest now," I said. "We should make our lives the way we need them to be."

He gave me a couple rapid blinks then looked back in the box and plucked Judy Campbell out. "Was your mum really a stripper?"

"Yep. She's finally going to get her wish though." I got off my knees and went to the desk, tossed a couple of school calendars in Frank's lap. "I haven't decided which one yet."

"What made you decide to do *this*?" He fanned pages of the Tsing Tao School of Journalism at UBC.

"I don't know . . . Malcolm X, Billy Graham, Marcella."

"Who's Marcella?"

"The artist formerly known as Erin. I never got to do the school thing. Maybe I'll like it. And if I don't I'll quit."

"I guess you can afford it now." He squinted down, swallowing. "Great," he said, forcing energy into it. "Probably be good at that, journalism. You like asking questions and arguing and—" he shook Judy Campbell and tossed her "—reading. Do you think things would've been different if we'd gotten married?"

"Not particularly," I said, as though he'd asked if I regretted never having had the shingles. It seemed like eons ago now and I didn't much want to discuss the dead baby of our relationship.

"Have you got a beer?" he asked suddenly.

"There's a couple in the cupboard. I was going to chuck 'em. I'm on a booze fast for a little while."

"Excuse me?" This, he apparently found most incredible of all.

"I wasn't exactly liquor hound of the year."

"Runner-up." He looked smug. "Len go to the monastery?"

"Nope. He's in love. She's nice, I met her. Quite beautiful and . . . worldly."

"Worldly?" He laced his fingers back together. "Wow. That's sudden."

"It's a-a-all so sudden . . . end of an era."

I could feel his glance and decided I'd better meet it and let him get whatever he needed to say off his chest.

"I love you," he said in a low blurt. His lips quivered as if they couldn't get a grip on any further sound. I didn't say anything. "I would marry you if you wanted me to."

"That's very chivalrous of you."

"No, I mean, I'd like to. Is that what you . . . would . . . have liked?"

My no clanged on the floor like a cast-iron pan. He was terribly serious all of a sudden. It took some work on my part to maintain eye contact. "I need to be alone. I've never done that. Maybe if I took all my pissed-off energy and actually did something with it instead of flailing around, I'd be marriage material. I need to get a bigger self right now."

"The self I am isn't *big* enough for you?"

"The self *I* am is not big enough for me."

"Oh." He looked out the window. "I guess Sienna will be relieved. We've kind of been seeing each other."

"I see," I said. "Well, there you go." The phone interrupted.

"Hey," I answered. "Speak of the devil . . . Oh . . . Can I call you back, I've got company . . . all right." I set the receiver down. "Marcella. She's getting remarried. Wants me to be a bridesmaid." My fingertips pattered my thighs a second. I was in shorts and a T-shirt but the sweat glued everything to my skin. "I don't want to deal with her right now."

He stared into my eyes, mute.

A quick check of my watch and I said, "Your things are in those bags. Videos, clothes. You liked that Sinatra . . . I hate to give you the rush but I promised Sally I'd come sort through some stuff before the movers show up." Heading to the kitchen cupboard, I pulled out two warm bottles of beer.

I handed them to him as he nosed through his stuff. "Everything there?"

"I can just come back if something's missing."

I didn't respond. He took a long breath, stuffed the beers in and picked up his shopping bags. I went ahead to get the door.

Holding it open, I tried to think of what to say. "Well, take care. I hope great things happen for you," I told him. And I meant it.

He nodded. "You look so virginal without makeup." I forced the corners of my mouth up. He leaned and kissed my cheek before he moved into the hallway, schlepped a little ways and turned back.

It was a bit like an old Disney movie where the kid has to throw rocks, send the coyote back to the woods for his own good. I waved. "Bye."

He turned and trudged on. Once he rounded the corner, I heard the building door open and clank shut.

At my front window, I watched him load his belongings into the trunk of his old black Mustang. He slammed it shut, paused and took out a pack of smokes, lit one. He rarely smoked when sober. He looked up and down the street. Leaning against the car, his head drooped and I could vaguely see his thinning patch in the sunlight, like the soft spot on a baby's head. He took a long drag. When he exhaled, the smoke plumed in a cloud around him and seemed to cling to the hot still air.

Eventually, about halfway down the cigarette, he opened the car door.

I picked at my T-shirt, plucked a sticky bit from my chest as I watched him pull away.

People kept yammering about the heat that summer, the melting tar in the streets, the forest fires; it was all on account of global warming. But I didn't much buy that. I think these things go in cycles and we happened to be in a hot one. The earth was burning what it didn't need or want, I reasoned, like a dog shaking off fleas. We've all got to do this now and then.

Thanks and Acknowledgements

~

I WOULD LIKE TO THANK THE FOLLOWING INDIVIDUALS AND organizations for their invaluable help in creating *Cease to Blush:* Jackie Barnard and Allen Ingram at M Squared Productions for their openhanded tour of the online adult entertainment industry; generous financial support from the BC Arts Council; Hank Benson for handing me bits of his life on a fodder platter, hunting down potential resources and, of course, for his very large pompoms; generous financial support from Canada Council for the Arts; Michael Carmen at Mac Station for his selfless acts as my computer's physician; Anne Collins for her razor-sharp editorial insight coupled with a preternatural ability to divine a writer's intent; Dixie "The Marilyn Monroe of Burlesque" Evans at Exotic World in Helendale, California, for walking me through her Burlesque Hall of Fame, and leaving a lasting impression about the people those dancers were and are; Helen Heller for guidance and for smoothing my feathers when the frantics had the better of me; Roger Holden for pointing out that my title had been pinned to my bulletin board for months; Timothy Kelleher for providing a Los Angeles bed, breakfast and steady soothing belief; Nancy Kress and Aaron Daulby for graciously taking me to Pentecostal congregations and answering my likely ungracious questions; Ledig House for their idyllic sanctuary;

Dave Pelletier for employing me on his set in a way that both paid my rent and let me get some reading done; the Pedrero Family for their warmth, sustenance and software; Robert Priest and Clare O'Callaghan for helping me with the esoteric angles of jazz vocals; Marilyn Robert and Karen deVito for their notes on palliative care, the Rockefeller Center, and for knowing the importance for a four-year-old to have a Kitsilano Showboat experience; Becki Ross for her sleek self and informational generosity; and Don Winkelbaur for weaselling me inside the infamous pantry of the now-closed Ambassador Hotel in Los Angeles.

This novel could not have come together were it not for a multitude of books that came before it. Of particular help were: Judith Campbell Exner's *My Story*; Max Décharné's *Straight From the Fridge, Dad: A Dictionary of Hipster Slang*; Barbara Fuca's *Mafia Wife* as told to Robin Moore; Sam and Chuck Giancana's *Double Cross*; C. David Heymann's *RFK: A Candid Biography of Robert F. Kennedy*; Robert F. Kennedy's *The Enemy Within*; William Klaber and Philip H. Melanson's *Shadow Play: The Untold Story of the Robert F. Kennedy Assassination*; Shawn Levy's *Rat Pack Confidential*; Shirley Maclaine's *My Lucky Stars: A Hollywood Memoir*; Charles Rappleye and Ed Becker's *All American Mafioso: The Johnny Rosselli Story*; James Spada's *Peter Lawford: The Man Who Kept Secrets*; A.W. Stencell's *Girl Show*—with extra thanks for his willingness to speak with me in more detail about "the canvas world of bump and grind" and Tempest Storm's *The Lady is a Vamp*.

Video and audio reportage were also enormous aids. My thanks to the producers of *Assassinated: The Last Days of Kennedy and King*, Turner Original Productions; *The Century: America's Time*, ABC New Productions and the History Channel; *Fabulous Sixties*, produced by Document Associates in association with CTV Network Ltd.; *History of the 20th Century*, an MPI Home Video Presentation of an ABC Video Enterprises Inc. Production; *The LBJ Tapes*, Barraclough Carey Productions for

Channel Four; *The Plot to Kill Robert Kennedy*, American Films, Ltd.; *The Rat Pack*, A&E Biographies; *The Rat Pack Live at the Sands*, Capital Records (audio recording); and *Louis Prima, the Wildest*, Image Entertainment Inc.

BILLIE LIVINGSTON published her critically acclaimed first novel, *Going Down Swinging*, in 2000. Her first book of poetry, *The Chick at the Back of the Church*, was shortlisted for the Pat Lowther Award. Her award-winning short fiction has been published in Canada, the U.S., the U.K. and Australia, and her short story collection, *You Sound Tiny*, is forthcoming from Random House Canada. Born in Toronto, Livingston now lives in Vancouver.

A NOTE ABOUT THE TYPE

Cease to Blush is set in Monotype Dante, a modern font family designed by Giovanni Mardersteig in the late 1940s. Based on the classic book faces of Bembo and Centaur, Dante features an italic which harmonizes extremely well with its roman partner. The digital version of Dante was issued in 1993, in three weights and including a set of titling capitals.